SMALL KINGDOMS

SMALL KINGDOMS

Anastasia Hobbet

THE PERMANENT PRESS
Sag Harbor, NY 11963

This novel is a work of fiction. Any references to historical events, to real people living or dead, or to real locales, are intended only to give the fiction a setting in historic reality. Other names, characters, places, and incidents are either the product of the author's imagination or are used fictitiously, and their resemblances, if any, to real-life counterparts are entirely coincidental.

"My Sister" by Muhammad Al-Ghuzzi, from *Modern Arabic Poetry*, edited by Salma Khadra Jayyusi, copyright © 1991, Columbia University Press. Reprinted with permission of the publisher.

For information, address:
    The Permanent Press
    4170 Noyac Road
    Sag Harbor, NY 11963
    www.thepermanentpress.com

Library of Congress Cataloging-in-Publication Data

Hobbet, Anastasia—
    Small kingdoms / Anastasia Hobbet.
        p. cm.
    ISBN-13: 978-1-57962-191-9 (alk. paper)
    ISBN-10: 1-57962-191-0 (alk. paper)
        1. Kuwait—Fiction. I. Title.

PS3558.O33638S63 2010
813'.54—dc22   2009031326

Printed in the United States of America.

To Randall

And to Ma

And to those who never came home

ACKNOWLEDGMENTS

To my friends in Kuwait, who relished discussions about the inner workings of this complex society, and especially to those Kuwaitis and South Asians who allowed me into their confidence, I offer my thanks. Without their generosity and trust, I could not have approached the difficult task of portraying their cultures from the inside. If there are misrepresentations in my story, the responsibility lies with me and the imperfect perception of my heart.

These dedicated readers and friends, Karen Dorrough, Linda Foust, Laird Harrison, Randall Hobbet, Antony Johae, Janice Johnson, Kumkum Kabir, Cinda MacKinnon, and Terry Shames, analyzed early drafts and gave me just what I needed: all the news, good and bad. Karen Dorrough took a draft and made it into a real book by hand. She printed and bound it herself in soft, rich leather using eighteenth-century techniques, then gave it to me for Christmas. I'll never forget unwrapping that heavy little package, the last one under the tree.

Thanks and gratitude to Judith and Martin Shepard of The Permanent Press for their dedication to the novel as a lively contemporary art form, and for the quality they bring to their work.

To my husband Randall I give the golden crown of loving forbearance. Once, as I was wrestling with the manuscript, I raged to him that the whole thing was falling apart. "No, it's not," he said. "It's falling together."

Do not ask how, before cock-crow, my sister had departed
Making her way through arcane cities
Deep within us she lives
As the tree hides in the kernel.

—MUHAMMAD AL-GHUZZI

A Mysterious Balance

A CRASH on the ground floor, metallic and heavy, brought Mufeeda upright from her prayers. She listened, kneeling, her graceful hands in the air, as she waited for what must come next: the wail of her two-year-old daughter, Fauzia, who had recently abandoned mere walking in exchange for exuberant, headlong runs. The family had grown used to frequent collisions, followed by melodramatic tears.

One second, two, three.

The silence exonerated Fauzia. This meant something worse, probably that the cook Emmanuella had dropped another pot. The sound of the impact ran through Mufeeda's mind again, a dismal clang like a bell underwater. Yes, a pot hitting the kitchen floor, a big pot, which could only mean the biryani. Dinner was all over the floor again.

Leaping to her feet, Mufeeda mended the tail end of her prayers with apologies—God is merciful—and flung the door open, trying to take that mercy to heart: she'd need it for Emmanuella. In the last weeks, the girl had dropped not only several pots and pans, but she'd also broken a Murano vase, a cut-glass Baccarat tumbler, and a ceramic water-pipe belonging to Mufeeda's mother-in-law, Umm Saleh. Before this last accident, when Emmanuella had stumbled and shattered the pipe against the marble floor of the hallway, Saleh's mother had shown no regard for the thing. Nor had anyone, for it was ugly as a dwarf. But by the time Saleh arrived home from the hospital late that night, Umm Saleh had proclaimed it a precious memento, the most valuable object in the house.

9

Mufeeda paused on the landing, hearing what she expected and dreaded below: the growing rumble that foretold Umm Saleh's imminent explosion from her room. She would have heard the dull boom of the pot too. Fortunately, none of Mufeeda's daughters was present to witness Umm Saleh's temper this time around. Mariam, the eldest at eleven, showed a strong tendency toward fits of capricious anger herself, a trait she had not learned from her mother.

Umm Saleh's door burst open on the floor below and she lumbered across the threshold, hollering for all three of Mufeeda's daughters, "Mariam! It's the Iraqis!" robe flapping, a slipper in either hand, her fat feet thumping the marble tiles. "Where is our little Fauzia? They've come again to kill us all! Sara, where are you? Oh, we will die!"

If there was an advantage to having such a mother-in-law, who could remember to call everyone's name but Mufeeda's at the onset of another Iraqi invasion, it was that Mufeeda could always look calm in comparison to her mother-in-law in any emergency, especially a false one. The thought of Saddam still in power and brooding over the 'lost province' of Kuwait never left anyone's mind; but the last significant crisis since the war, when he sent his troops south again to mass along Kuwait's border, was almost two years past, though no one would guess it by Umm Saleh's bellowings.

Mufeeda descended to the second floor, chastening herself yet again for her ungenerous thoughts. Umm Saleh deserved sympathy: her younger son, Jassim, had disappeared during the war. It was only since then that she had become so short-tempered, and no mother could blame her for that. Umm Saleh still maintained hope that Jassim was alive, but Mufeeda couldn't share it. Jassim had been the more fiery of the two brothers, and the less prudent. He wouldn't have fallen silent in prison, under guard by the Iraqis he hated so passionately. Given the rumors they heard of prison conditions up north, it seemed to Mufeeda a worse fate to be still alive there after six years of so-called peace. More than six hundred Kuwaitis had disappeared in this same way, overnight, without a word, into Saddam's ghastly realm.

"There is no God except God The Magnificent, The Forbearing," she murmured to herself, and on the second-floor landing, she said calmly into her mother-in-law's panic, "Umm Saleh, it is a pot. Emmanuella has likely dropped a pot, that's all."

But this, it seemed, was even worse news than invading Iraqis. "A pot? She has dropped a pot again? This girl is impossible. How can she drop pots?"

They parted, Mufeeda down the stairway, Umm Saleh, ranting, into the elevator. As the lift doors slid shut, muffling Umm Saleh's voice, Mufeeda broke into a run, throwing all dignity aside, careless of the two housemaids who stood amazed in the dining room as she passed.

She stopped at the sill of the kitchen door. A ragged mountain of basmati rice steamed like a spent volcano on the kitchen floor, surrounded by chunks of lamb and bone and vegetables, a landscape of disaster. The upended pot had rolled under the sinks, and the cook was nowhere to be seen.

Mufeeda whispered, switching into English, "Emmanuella! Where are you?" Emmanuella's grip on Arabic was no better than her grip on pots. "Emmanuella!"

The pantry door, open an inch, emitted a whimpering cry. "Oh, ma'am, I'm here."

"Stay, then. My mother-in-law comes."

There was no need for this warning. The neighbors could probably hear Umm Saleh's muttering descent to the ground floor. Mufeeda stepped outside the kitchen again and shut the door softly behind her as the elevator gaped open in the hallway.

"The girl's hopeless. We've been idiots to keep her. She destroys everything she touches. We'll send her back to Goa. Tonight."

She moved as if to plow Mufeeda from her path but Mufeeda smiled down with serene immobility on her mother-in-law's balding head. "I'm sorry the noise disturbed you, Umm Saleh. I'll see to the cleanup immediately."

11

"Cleanup? What about the dinner? What will my son eat? Your stupid girl has ruined everything and you'll have to begin again. What will Saleh say? He expects his house to be well-run, with efficiency and cleanliness, in peace and health, and we're reduced to scraping our food from a filthy floor! What will he say to this?"

Mufeeda knew what Saleh's response would be. He'd agree with everything his mother said, would rant a little himself in order to condole with her, and in the privacy of their bedroom, tell Mufeeda gently to bear the tantrums as well as she could. "It's Jassim, of course. We must always remember that," he'd tell her, reminding her also that the fluctuations in a diabetic's blood glucose could cause abrupt shifts of mood. He remembered his mother from his boyhood as sweet and kind, "like you," he'd tell Mufeeda, stroking the long curve of her chin and kissing her with such tenderness that all the strains of the day dipped into insignificance. If Saleh could show such benevolence then surely she should be capable of it also. Then again, he was at the hospital ten to fourteen hours a day. She allowed herself to wonder if his indulgence would survive a week's test on the battlefield itself.

"Get out of my way!"

"Umm Saleh, please calm down. Remember your blood pressure." She put a hand out to escort Umm Saleh back down the hall, but the elder woman snatched her arm away as if Mufeeda had threatened to cut it off.

"What will worry Saleh more than spilled food," Mufeeda murmured, bowing her head, "is that I'd allow household problems to trouble your mind. It won't happen again, *inshallah*."

"Ha."

"I shouldn't have been upstairs at such a critical time. Saleh and I have been married almost twelve years, thanks be to God, and yet I still have so much to learn from you about how to care for him. And for our home. I hope you'll be patient with me."

A slight delay in the delivery of Umm Saleh's next retort gave Mufeeda hope that the tide had turned.

12

"How do you intend to serve dinner tonight if it's scattered all over the floor?"

Mufeeda said with quiet confidence, "With your guidance all will be well, *inshallah*."

This appeal to her mother-in-law's vanity thinned her anger to crankiness. "This girl has broken even my prayers. I must go and begin again."

Emmanuella had remained cowering behind the door. It would take all the rest of Mufeeda's patience to persuade her that she was safe.

"Come, Emmanuella," she said, trying to draw the girl forward with a firm hand on her wrist. But Emmanuella cried out as if Mufeeda had twisted it. Then tears. With both arms clamped tight across her belly, she wept.

"She'll send me back to Goa!"

"Emmanuella, do not make this noise. My husband is your sponsor. It's he who has paid for your visa and holds your passport, not his mother. Remember this. We'll prepare for dinner instead of biryani a chopped salad. And there's lentil soup and pakoras in the freezer, yes?" They were left over from a large batch that Emmanuella had made a week before.

"Yes, ma'am," the girl said miserably.

Mufeeda didn't know what to make of Emmanuella's recent clumsiness. She'd shown so much promise in the kitchen. Umm Saleh, typically, had taken an immediate dislike to her; she disliked every servant Mufeeda hired and said so loudly from the first day of employment. Usually, with training, the new employee gained Umm Saleh's tolerance if not her approval. But just at the time when Emmanuella had achieved some degree of confidence, the accidents began. Umm Saleh took this as confirmation of her original appraisal of the girl as a fool, the corollary being that Mufeeda had been a fool to hire her.

Mufeeda directed Emmanuella to bring the pakoras from the freezer and bent to the task of scooping the biryani into the dust

13

bin with a serving spoon, tasting its delicate complexity in the very steam.

Was the girl losing interest in her work? She'd arrived more than a year ago from Goa, from a Catholic family so poor that it had been willing to falsify her age on her visa so that she could come to the Gulf and send money home. She arrived a short while before her seventeenth birthday and looked younger, a spindly, underfed child. Mariam at only ten had been her equal in size, and had seen advantages in this that Mufeeda didn't like. "You're not to order Emmanuella around, Mariam. You're to do things for yourself." But she'd caught Emmanuella scurrying around several times at Mariam's behest. "Make me a sandwich and chips. Hurry up! Don't you dare tell my mother, either."

Mariam's English was perfect and her manner perfectly arrogant. It had been at Saleh's insistence that the girls attend the American School in the city. He thought the curriculum excellent. "They'll learn to speak English eloquently. That's a great advantage in this world."

Mufeeda was not so certain. All three girls now spoke English better than Arabic, even tiny Fauzia, and Mariam resented studying Arabic at all. Her calligraphy was disgraceful. "It's an art to write our language, Mariam. You must learn it. You can scratch away in English if you must, but in Arabic you must make your letters beautifully."

Mariam looked like her grandmother when she frowned. "Father doesn't make his letters beautifully."

"He's an adult. And a doctor," Mufeeda told her grimly. "When you're an adult—and a doctor—you may write any way you wish. Now go and copy this again."

Emmanuella was at her side. "Ma'am, please stop and I will mop the floor now."

"Have you found the pakoras?"

"Yes, ma'am."

For all her youth, Emmanuella had a natural gift as a cook. Though hired as a housemaid she'd helped in the kitchen during

Ramadan last year, allowing Mufeeda to observe her talent and ease with food. Emmanuella had probably spent her childhood helping her mother cook for all her younger siblings. Even so she was a quick study, and after Ramadan, Mufeeda had brought her into the kitchen often, soon curtailing her other household duties altogether. Her quick promotion had made an enemy for the girl in Succoreen, the senior housemaid, but Succoreen had always had her jealousies and this one would pass away in time. Emmanuella's skills had earned her the post. After being shown just once how to prepare Mufeeda's family recipes, she'd cooked them on her own without hesitation and soon improved them in some mysterious way that she would not admit to or didn't consciously recognize. It was, perhaps, her bold use of spices, all freshly ground, but Mufeeda couldn't discover the mysterious balance herself.

Mufeeda washed her hands at the deep double-sink. "How many pakoras are there, Emmanuella?"

"Ma'am, two dozen. It is not enough. I'll make more in two minutes. I'll make another dish."

"Certainly it's enough. We must all eat less, especially when it comes to your pakoras."

"But Sir will not have enough!"

"My husband is getting fat thanks to your cooking. He'll eat three pakoras and be quite happy. I'll tell him so myself."

"Oh, ma'am! He'll be very hungry."

Mufeeda suppressed a smile at the girl's genuine horror. "Continue your work, Emmanuella. I'll call one of the housemaids to mop the floor."

It was true that Saleh was getting fat. Mufeeda herself had lost her slenderness to childbearing. In her mother's time, this plumpness had been considered a sign of health and prosperity, with no recognition of the toll it took: in her mother, diabetes and an early, painful death. She would not leave her own girls alone so early in their lives if she could possibly help it—not in these times, when there was so much uneasiness in the world, especially for girls.

15

A TRIFLING CLEANUP

LEFT ALONE in the kitchen, Emmanuella ran to close the door. Squatting before the waste basket, she checked its contents. Just as she'd hoped, there had been a clean plastic bag in the bin when Ma'am Mufeeda discarded the biryani. Emmanuella would be able to salvage most of it.

But she couldn't be caught at this forbidden task. Closing her eyes, she listened intently for footsteps in the hallway. Hearing nothing but the tick of the kitchen clock, she pulled a freezer bag from a drawer and quickly shoveled most of the biryani into it. The door swung open just as she finished. Expecting Carmen— for Carmen was the housemaid Ma'am would normally send to mop the floor—Emmanuella turned, ready with a smile for the gentle Filipina. But it was Succoreen who stood in the doorway, hands on hips in her customary attitude of eager accusation. It wearied Emmanuella to look at her. Squat and pimpled, Succoreen always wore a scowl.

"What are you about, Emmanuella? You're not to touch the bins!"

Succoreen had been in the household nearly twenty years and wanted all the household staff to acknowledge her as the head servant, though she'd been given no such authority by Sir or Ma'am. That Ma'am had dispatched Succoreen instead of Carmen, who had been in the household only five years, to do this trifling cleanup, proved the point; but Emmanuella didn't press it. As a cook she enjoyed a natural superiority over any maid, which gave her the grace of restraint.

"You're slow in coming, Succoreen," she said, standing up. "How am I to cook with such a confusion?" She hid the steaming

16

bag close to her body in a fold of her apron. It burned, but this couldn't matter. Succoreen mustn't see it.

"You cannot step around the bin?" Succoreen cast a cold eye across the enormous kitchen. "This room isn't big enough for you? How will you manage when they send you back to Goa?"

As Succoreen intended, this unnerved Emmanuella, but she would not show it. "Leave me be. Go about your work. Ma'am sent you to clean the floor."

Succoreen's purplish face ripened further. "You dare to speak to me in this way?"

Emmanuella eased the bag onto the counter, hiding it behind an open bag of flour, the skin of her belly afire. She longed to open a button of her housedress to check for injury but couldn't risk it. Succoreen would miss nothing, even as she banged her mop and sloshed her cleaning water far and wide in her determination to provoke Emmanuella.

With enforced calm Emmanuella laid the few, damp pakoras on a metal tray and turned on the smallest of the four ovens. Its digital controls stared at her in unblinking orange. Like all men, Sir had a good appetite. If he went to bed hungry tonight, he'd blame Emmanuella and begin to listen more closely to his mother's demands that she be sent back to India. As the eldest child of a fatherless family, she bore heavy responsibility for the welfare of her brothers and sisters. If she lost this job, she'd have forsaken them, and there were no jobs at home, nothing to greet her there but the shame of failure. Though she earned a small salary in Kuwait, her remittance was a great boon to her family, like Christmas coming every month.

Succoreen spoke again, this time in the singsong voice of a badgering child, "Rosaline heard the Grandmother say that you'll go back tomorrow."

Though her terror rose up like sudden nausea, Emmanuella began trimming parsley with a quick pinch of the stems. "God will be angry with Rosaline for listening at the door."

Succoreen laughed heartily in her vulgar way. Everyone knew that no barrier, let alone a door, could keep the Grandmother's opinions secret.

"Better if God is angry than the Grandmother," she said. Her voice then softened just perceptibly. "Every day it's another pot, Emmanuella. Why do you do this?"

Emmanuella let a stem of parsley drop. It was all the pinching and washing and chopping, all the endless work. Her hands felt weak and painful; her whole body ached with weariness, but she wouldn't complain. She prayed. She asked God to help her endure what it was necessary to endure. After all, she was more fortunate than others she knew, others close by. She glanced at the window over the counter which overlooked a darkening view of a narrow alleyway and the blank windows of the villa next door. She began to pray softly, ardently, *Hail Mary full of grace* as she brought a chef's knife down across a towering pile of parsley.

Through the Burning Air

Theo arrived near dusk on a late-summer evening after almost thirty hours en route. Despite his exhaustion, he began to feel wakeful when the pilot announced that they were over Jordan. A more natural flight path to Kuwait would have taken them south from London directly over the fertile valleys of the Tigris and the Euphrates; but the Gulf war six years ago had left Saddam Hussein in power, and so commercial airliners kept Iraq carefully quarantined, skywriting its ominous borders at 30,000 feet.

He trained his eye on the barren land below, thinking of the concentration of human history here, in such a small corner of the globe—and yet how clean and innocent the desert looked from the air. After a lifetime spent in the urban landscapes of California, he liked this easy legibility of form, the broad and simple sweep of it, and played with the notion that his life here could reflect the same spacious characteristics. He wasn't a political person, and he'd be here only a year or two, not long enough to put down roots or complicate his life with significant connections. His old friend Rajesh, who had trudged through medical school with him, had tried to talk him out of coming here for even this short span of time.

"Theo, you can still change your mind." They sat drinking a beer together. Theo had just finished packing: two bags, both small. "It's hellishly hot there, all alcohol is forbidden, even cold beer in July. That alone tells you how difficult the Arabs are, and they're easier on white heathens like you than on Indian polytheists like me. But even so, you won't find them easy. And what about the future? There's no more calamitous place on earth than the Middle East."

"Your father's lived there for years," Theo reminded him.

"Ha!" Rajesh's laugh sent him sprawling back in his arm-chair. "My father. Exactly. He's one of the calamities."

Theo smiled. An old topic. "A son's obliged to feel ambivalent about his father."

"Then it's the only obligation he'd say I've met. Have I ever told you what he said when I decided on pathology instead of following precisely in his footsteps?"

He had, several times, but Theo didn't say so.

"He said, 'Poof.' That's it, as though he'd just taken an x-ray of me from head to toe and saw that I was hopeless. Because of me he won't take kindly to you either. What kind of person can you be to count me as a friend?"

Rajesh leaned forward to toast with Theo. "Then to make things worse, there's Rachel." His wife was a New Yorker, and Jewish. "You know, Theo, my father doesn't wish to be loved. Nevertheless, tell him that his son——." Their glasses clinked. Rajesh's usual ebullience died away. "Please tell him that I honor him."

"Brilliant! You're ready, then?"

Theo angled the receiver away from his ear. Jane Scarborough had a voice like a bull's. "Ready," he said, picking up one of the hotel pens.

"Good. Go out to the Gulf Road. You can't miss it. You'll be in the bathwater if you do."

"Gulf Road," he echoed, writing it down.

"Mind, turn toward the Towers. Bloody ugly things, like monstrous golf balls set on bloody awful tees. That's north, or rather close to north. I know you men think in literal terms about directions. Take a left turning there. You do know your left from your right?"

"I think I've mastered that."

"Right, then. Follow that 'round. It will curve 'round the end of the peninsula there. Look for a building on your left with a large flag painted on the side. You do know the flag here?"

"Uh . . ."

"Stripes. Red, white, and green topped by a black triangle. Horizontal. The natives became wildly nationalistic after the war. You'd think they won it for themselves."

"Can you give me an address?"

"Address?" She turned from the phone, bellowing to an audience of colleagues, "This Yank wants an address!"

Theo heard roars of laughter in the background.

"Quite a new one, are we? Fresh from the native shores?"

The concierge at the Marriott had insisted that this British woman was the best English-speaking real estate agent in the country. What could the others be like?

"Go on," he said.

"When you see that building, go past it. Just beyond but not too far beyond, perhaps it's half a kilometer—if you see the Grand Mosque you've gone too far—you'll see a U-turn. Take that and come back. Now, this is critical: look for a sign that says, 'Al Babtain, Agent for Pro-Amateur Photo-Equips and Sewing Machines.' Got that? You'll make that turning and proceed straight until you hit the curb."

"Hit the curb?"

"The natives think it's a ramp, but we won't disillusion them at this point. Drive over it and into the car park. We're at the far side behind the mosque."

Theo squinted at the scrawl of his notes. "The Grand Mosque?"

"Oh good Lord, no. You're not listening. If you see the Grand Mosque you've gone too far."

Navigating his way to their rendezvous point, Theo saw that driving in Kuwait was going to be a challenge even for someone who had spent four years on the freeways of Los Angeles. The modus operandi was a free-for-all, and at furious speeds. What few addresses he could see—5, 12, 2, 517—looked as if they'd been called in a bingo game. How he found his way to the flat expanse of pitted sand Jane Scarborough called a car park, he'd never know. Luck. He hoped it would hold.

21

"Brilliant!" she boomed at him as he got out of his car. The water of the Gulf shimmered far off, a sheet of blue aluminum so hot it hurt the eyes.

"Theodore Girard, is it? You're very tall," she said, holding out a hand the size of his own. "Call me Jane. You follow directions well. I like that in a man."

Gray-headed, broad-shouldered, she had the face of a bullying halfback enduring a rough season. Despite the trembling heat she wore a wool suit coat and knee-length skirt. Lodged under one arm was a clipboard fluttering with computer printouts. "Well, we're off."

He left his rental car in the parking lot and folded himself with difficulty into her battered but spotless Subaru, its windshield filigreed with cracks emanating delicately from a half-dozen impact zones. She hit the ignition and the little car leapt to life as if she'd given it a swift kick.

Joining the fray on the Gulf Road she swerved around a big white four-door American car that was drifting into her lane and came within a foot of an overloaded truck in the other lane.

"Bloody idiots!"

Gunning the engine she shot out ahead, throwing a ferocious look at the driver of the car, a man dressed in a linen gown and headdress, the costume of the native male, it seemed to Theo. Talking on a cell phone, the man ignored Jane and his driving equally.

"Let me tell you something you must know as a newcomer," Jane said, hauling the wheel to cross three lanes at once. She shot off the arterial onto a side street. "Yield is not a concept the Arabs comprehend."

Directly ahead, traffic blocked both lanes. Jane seemed not to see it. Theo gripped his knees as if this could save him. At full speed she barreled between the lines of traffic, making a middle lane on the spot.

"Hold on," she said, screeching to a halt at the hemline of a pedestrian's *gellibiya*. On their right was an ancient truck loaded with sweating laborers in ragged turbans; to the left, a gleaming SUV driven by a woman cloaked in black and wearing enormous sunglasses over her face-scarf. No one so much as glanced at them, not even the man Jane had almost creamed.

"So you're a doctor, are you?" She gave Theo a piercing look of scrutiny, sweeping from his pale blond head to his big feet splayed on the floorboard. "Not many American doctors here, you know. They'll suspect you, wonder why you'd come here when you can make millions in America. You're from San Francisco, are you?"

"The Bay area. Oakland."

"Only crank doctors come here, you know. That's what people here think. Doctors forbidden to practice medicine in their own countries. You're not a crank, are you?"

Her cell phone bleated. Grappling with it, she tooled around a scrawny water vendor on a bicycle at the curb as the light turned green, and roared into the phone, "Hallo!"

A sign in Arabic and English whooshed by on Theo's side: "SPEEDING QUICK WAY TO PRISON OR DEATH."

Brake lights flared in the road ahead. "Bloody hell," Jane said to the caller and Theo alike, turning to peer at the traffic rushing toward her back bumper. "It's like running with the bulls at Pamplona."

He'd expected to see some scars of the war. But there was nothing that spoke of the violence, not even a tank posed as a public memorial. Expansive new areas of clay-choked sand had been opened for private development, "since that rout," Jane told him. It was as if growth had been the country's vengeful response to Saddam. Spanking new three-story cement mansions sat on lots only meters bigger than their outer walls; all the freeways had been rebuilt; and the Cornice along the Gulf had been redesigned in its entirety, stripped bare of its immediate history as a battleground of the war. And everywhere, litter. It blew with the

23

sand and grit of the city, tracing the fence-lines and thorough-fares, and cluttering the flat, dismal beaches. Children, standing on car seats, always unbelted, threw paper cups and candy wrappers from car windows like confetti, opening their little fists into the hot wind. The cold-white buildings lining the highways looked like part of the litter too, great cement goliaths built of marble from God knew where, though no dust storm would ever blow them away.

One apartment near the hospital seemed the best of all those Jane showed him. It was new and clean, and only two blocks from a market street where he could buy groceries. He walked through the stark rooms, hands in pockets, as Jane wandered separately, losing herself in admiration of the ten-inch thick walls. Her Wagnerian voice bounded off the cement, echoing until she seemed to be in all the rooms at once, declaiming.

"You won't see construction like this in California! The Arabs may not be able to do much but they can build a solid wall, God bless them!"

It was much larger than he needed, but 'nice' and 'small' didn't come together in one apartment here. All the decent apartments were new but huge. He wondered how he'd ever make the place feel homey. Its half-dozen blank, square rooms would challenge his determination to accumulate as little as possible.

"Look at the depth of those window wells!" Jane bellowed from somewhere down the long hall. "Remember this, Mr. Girard: If Saddam finds one of those spare Scuds somewhere and tosses it this way, just duck behind an inside wall."

CONTRACT SIGNED, move-in date pending, Jane took Theo home with her for dinner. Her husband wanted to meet him, she said. Theo couldn't have said in advance exactly what he expected of Jane's husband other than iron fortitude, but he would never have guessed his name as Hamid. But Hamid he was, a broad, bluff, smiling Arab dressed in a crisp *dishdasha*, speaking in a clipped

British accent. Jane deserted them at the door, going directly upstairs to change. Theo hoped that he'd covered his initial shock when Hamid offered his hand in the entryway, "Welcome! Come in, come in," and led him into the living room.

A young Filipina appeared soundlessly, bearing an engraved silver tray. On it, a large bottle of single malt Scotch and three heavy glasses.

"Ah," Hamid said, beaming. He directed the girl to a table adjoining two couches where she should set the tray, and sat down well within its reach. "Please," he said to Theo, indicating the opposite couch.

Theo sank deep into the down-filled cushions. Couches lined every wall, muscle-bound with embroidered silk. There were no armchairs. Heavily carved side tables anchored the couches, and on them stood ponderous golden lamps with fringes of braided gold rope. Gilded porcelain urns three feet tall loomed in the corners, filled with silk flowers lit by halogen spotlights in the molded ceiling fourteen feet above Theo's head.

"So what do you think of our little country, then?" Hamid said. "Have you been treated well?"

"Very well," Theo said. "Jane's been a great help."

"Oh, yes," Hamid said with proud affection. "Jane is . . . inimitable." He poured generously into the glasses. Handing Theo one, he raised his own in a toast. "Let me welcome you to Kuwait, Theo."

"Thank you. I'm glad to be here."

"I believe Jane said that you'll be working at Al-Ghais Hospital. Really? It's an ironic name for the place, believe me. *Al-Ghais* means diver, you know, the man who brings up the pearls. And it's a beastly place. It was far better before the war, when all the Palestinian doctors and administrators were still in charge there. But the government ran most of them out, you know, after Yasser Arafat threw in with Saddam. And now . . ." Hamid shrugged elaborately. "None of the other public hospitals is any better, I'm afraid, and it's mostly small private hospitals otherwise, clinics really, a sad state of affairs. Personally, if I develop a toothache, I go directly to London. I could help shift you into the private sector if you'd like. Only say the word."

A reckless generosity. It amused Theo. "I haven't reported to my first job yet," he said. "The father of a friend from medical school is on staff there, that's my connection. He heads Internal Medicine."

This failed to impress Hamid. "He's a Kuwaiti?"

"An Indian," Theo said, feeling compelled after a moment to add, "Trained in the U.S."

"Ah. A Hindu then." Hamid's wide, expressive face grew grave. Leaning forward with a deep intake of breath, he contemplated the opposite wall for a long moment, adjusting his testicles thoughtfully through his gown.

"Let me tell you something if I may, Theo. I have nothing against Hindus. As you see, I'm not a religious man," he said, lifting his glass high as evidence. Pious Muslims did not drink alcohol. "But you won't make quick advancement here by association with Indians. They have no power. They come here because they make very little money in India and they don't compete as well with Caucasians in the U.S. or Europe. This isn't because they aren't excellent doctors but because they're black, and however liberal you believe yourselves to be in America, white people want white doctors and so do Europeans."

Theo took a sip of the fiery Scotch. Its woody soul was burnished with gold. "Perhaps that used to be true, but there have been a lot of successful Indian physicians in the U.S. for a long time now."

"Oh, of course. May your young friend be among them. But I know your country well, and I can tell you that the white patients of those successful Indian doctors, when they tell others about their medical care, rarely fail to explain—just as you have—'He's from India. But of course he was trained in the West.'" He took a long swallow of the Scotch, eyeing Theo all the while. "Meaning of course that he's more white than he looks and more worthy than his Hindu name would imply."

26

He registered Theo's skepticism with a nod. "Kuwait is far worse. The class-consciousness here will shock you. If you're not Kuwaiti born and bred, you're no one; and if you're so unfortunate as to be a South Asian housemaid or laborer, you're worthless, invisible, and in constant danger. Look at me. I'm an Arab. I've lived here for twenty years. But I'm not a Kuwaiti citizen because I'm Palestinian. The reason they didn't run me out during the war is because I'm a good businessman—and I'm married to Jane. Only Jordan has offered citizenship to Palestinians. No other Arab nation has done this, though the Israelis drove us from our homes in 1948. The Kuwaitis put up with us because we're well-educated and willing to work hard. We make lots of money for them. But they don't like us and they don't trust us. They think we're vulgar and inferior. So we live in our neighborhoods, and they live in theirs."

He lifted his glass once again, his fond gaze traveling over Theo's head to the marble staircase beyond. "Ah, here is my Jane."

THOUGH SHE and Hamid had no children, Jane showed all the military strengths of a seasoned mother. In the space of a day, she set Theo up for housekeeping as if he were her only son heading off to college. She chauffeured him to furniture stores and carpet souks, advising him at top volume about his basic requirements and bargaining ruthlessly with the luckless merchants, who gave Theo withering glances of contempt for his submission to this blaring woman, or so he supposed. Deliveries were arranged on the spot at no extra charge and extras thrown in to get her out the door: a pole lamp with many stork-billed shades, a dusty basket of fake ivy, a pouting plaster cupid. A couch followed them to his apartment in the back of an open-bed truck.

Promising to come back that evening with a supply of kitchen ware she had packed away at home, Jane left him to his leisure in the company of the new couch, marooned against a far wall. Doubtfully, he posted the pole lamp next to it, dumped the ivy in

27

the sink to be washed, and stored the cupid away in the back of one of his empty kitchen cabinets.

How was it that a little furniture made the place look emptier?

Wandering to the window he looked out over the flat roofs of the smaller apartment buildings and residential houses in the neighborhood, all of them sprouting multiple satellite dishes aimed at overlapping quadrants of the sky. On a single roof nearby he counted seven. In the dying day they looked almost lovely, tilted toward heaven like the giant, solemn faces of Easter Island.

No breeze stirred in the street below. Not a soul was visible, and from this vantage point the nearby arterial road disappeared. Theo's eye caught the glint of low sun on metal for blocks, a maze of parked cars on all the adjoining streets. And then a brush of movement in the garden below: the single, stiff branch of a date palm springing up and down in the still air. His eye searched for the cause. A line of the dust-green date palms stood against an enclosing wall, covered with a thick bark like the scales of armored dinosaurs. Atop the wall sat a scrawny calico cat nearly hidden in a narrow band of shade, looking out over the motionless street.

Restlessness rose up in him like a sudden claustrophobic fog. The yawning emptiness of the Muslim weekend, Thursday and Friday, still stood between him and the beginning of his employment. He had to get out, he didn't care where, and it was too hot to go walking. He grabbed his keys and took the elevator down to the deserted lobby.

Heading northeast out of the city, he followed one of the two paved roads available. He chose the road closer to the Gulf, the one the Iraqi Army had taken in a desperate convoy in those brutal final days of the war, ending their journey in a mile and a half of shredded metal and flesh on Mutla'a Ridge when the Allies swept down from the sky like avenging spirits. He remembered the place from aerial photos after what some had called a massacre, a long, twisted spine of smoking metal. It looked utterly ordinary now, but for the occasional lone and shabby camel pacing with weary dignity along the barbed wire fencing bounding the road. In the distance the hot bath of the Gulf merged with the white sky, a wavering mirage where the horizon must lie, lost.

From the ridge's highest point he still felt blind to any beauty of the land. It took an airplane for that, apparently. He pulled the car to the narrow shoulder of the road. The bare scrub of the desert stretched out to all horizons, a waste of endless baking space. What was he doing here? His reasons now seemed hazy to him and possibly naïve. The grand gesture, for what? His desire to live in a culture wholly different from his own could have been met easily at home by moving back to LA, or to West Oakland. But no, he'd come to the opposite side of the world, isolating himself from his family and friends, and the sensuous plenitude of northern California. The nearest wine country, he figured, was in Iran, a country deeply distrusted by the Arabs; and it didn't grant visas to Americans anyway. Kuwait was a desert island, isolated by unwelcoming neighbors and the empty salt sea of the Gulf.

Turning back toward the city he saw a bright white speck in the distance moving rapidly at an angle toward the road. Distorted by the heat rising from the desert, it looked at first like an enormous bird, then like a glider; then, closer, like a brilliant white ghost standing upright as it swept forward through the burning air.

Theo slowed, eyes glued to the wavering apparition. Through the dust he saw it change course slightly, moving more directly toward him. Could he have somehow crossed the border into Iraq without realizing it? It seemed crazy to think it—but could this be some odd, low-flying border patrol vehicle swooping down to arrest him? He should bolt, he thought. Step on the gas and go.

The image resolved—and into something no less odd: a man in a white *dishdasha* standing at full height, driving a dirt-brown jeep one-handed at breakneck speed across the trackless land beyond the road. Waving an arm, the man turned directly into Theo's path. Theo braked as the jeep raced toward the road and lurched over a low berm, landing in front of Theo's bumper like one of the world's first attempts at flying machines. A dry deluge of dust and grit and scabby earth rained down on the rented car. Just able to see through the scrim of the windshield Theo made out gleaming teeth in a wide smile, a wave from a broad hand. The man's lips moved.

Theo lowered his window, one hand on the gearshift, aiming for Reverse. The jeep rumbled and shimmied and snorted.

"Hello there! Are you British?" The accent was pure BBC. Even at a yell it sounded cultured.

"American!"

"Ah, an American. How very fortunate I am to meet you. You're most welcome here." The man threw an arm toward the pale brown western horizon, empty and razor-straight. "You must come and have tea with my family. We're camping just a mile or so from here. But tell me first, if you will: My young son has opened a gate he should not have opened. Have you seen a herd of goats?"

ADD 'INSHALLAH'

Dear Dad,

How are you? We're all fine.

Kit shut her eyes, willing another sentence into being. Even a modest word with two syllables, something that began to suggest her surroundings and hinted at the distance she and the children had traveled in the last week, rather than this stupid thing, a near-duplicate of every letter she'd written from the third grade on, mostly thank-you notes in the wake of birthdays. She didn't know how to write a letter except as a promise to spend the money wisely or put it in the bank.

She confronted the empty page, filled with distaste for the thick, blue stationery with its rich, textured surface that promised so much—what had she been thinking when she bought it?—interesting descriptions, perceptive insights, intimate asides. She would never come up with any of them, she knew, even once she got over the jet lag.

The trip was long but okay.

The truth—that both kids got sick just before touch-down in Amsterdam, and that Kit spent the eight-hour layover there mopping up and consoling and getting just enough warm soup into them to begin the cycle all over again—was one only her mother would have been interested in knowing. Had she ever talked directly to her father before without her mother as a buffer or a secondary audience? She couldn't recall a time other than the simple one-sentence communications of daily living. *I'm home. Pass the gravy, please. Goodnight, Dad.*

She wouldn't cry. She wouldn't turn her loneliness for her mother into self-pity. If she missed her mother, how must her father feel? He had to bear the emptiness of the house, the emptiness of the kitchen.

Tears rose to Kit's eyes. Ignoring them, she set the pen to paper, urging her inner voice to take over. Did she have one? At the very least she should comfort her father about her safety here. She'd seen no evidence of the war and no one seemed to think there was much of a security risk, though it had alarmed her to realize that Iraq was only fifty or sixty miles away. Jack had said, dismissively, that Saddam Hussein still coveted the idea of Kuwait as the nineteenth province of Iraq.

I can't believe we're really here.

She'd imagined being her father's eyes in this new place, his witness to this other world. No one in her family had ever lived anywhere but in or near Stillwater, at least until Kit went to college, and that hadn't been far from home either. She'd somehow expected that the distance itself would transform her. You couldn't go so far and not be changed by the experience. But here she sat half a world from home, as tongue-tied and conventional as ever.

It's very hot and flat, flatter even than western Oklahoma.

She bit the end of her pen, fighting a fierce urge to crumple the sheet into the trash and escape into some other activity—anything else. But what? There was nothing else to do. She and Jack and the kids had to stay at the company's guest house, a big and glossy hotel-like villa, until the plumbing could be fixed in their own . . . villa. She wasn't supposed to call their house a house, according to Jack, and in his new job managing all of the company's construction projects in Kuwait, he wasn't to be contradicted. Houses were called villas here, he said, a word that in Kit's mind evoked grand terra cotta mansions tucked into sunny Italian hillsides. She tried to imagine herself, after growing up in the outskirts of a red-dirt Oklahoma town, saying 'our villa' aloud without self-mockery. She gave it a try, "our villa," and winced at the sagging paunch of her Midwestern vowels, which made it sound like a joke anyway.

Maybe a cup of tea. Problem was, she couldn't simply go downstairs and make herself one. Residents of the company's guest house weren't allowed in the kitchen. They were too exalted for that. So requesting a cup of tea triggered a big, bustling production: a quart of tea in a silver pot on a tray with a polished creamer, sugar bowl, a spoon so tiny it looked like a baby's, and a selection of cookies and cakes, presented to her like the crown jewels. "Ma'am? Your tea." "Oh, thank you! How nice!" when all she wanted to do was dunk a tea bag in hot water and be done with it. The staff took care of everything else too, every detail, every meal, every plate, every crumb, every whim. They even took the children away for a couple of hours in the morning so that she could do whatever she wished. And what was that? Not writing letters.

Jack had even instructed her to leave the beds unmade in the morning. "It's their job. You don't do their jobs here or they'll think it's a criticism." But it was an order she had great difficulty following. You got up in the morning, you made your bed: Mom's rule. Like brushing your hair or your teeth. It mortified her to stand by, hands hanging at her sides, an obviously useless human being, as the upstairs maid slipped in—"Good morning, ma'am," whispered respectfully—and buffed the room to such perfection that even a single hair in the sink later in the day seemed a shameful thing. The children could touch no surface without leaving prints in long, swiping arcs. Had they been so greasy at home? She found herself polishing the marks away with the sleeve of her blouse.

The nearly blank page reproached her from the desktop. She faced it once again.

We haven't moved into our house yet. A couple of our toilets don't work because the Iraqis ran seawater through the city's pipes during the war and corrosion's a big problem, Jack says. We have two other bathrooms—four total—but somehow that's not enough for four people, so we're here instead.

But how could bathrooms be the first subject of discussion in her new life? It was not a good place to start. But it was too much work to begin again. She forged on.

Our house is huge. I've already lost the kids once. (Unfortunately I found them again.) It's really two houses in one, two apartments, one on each floor, only there's no separation between them. They live in extended families here, so each house has two or three generations living in it.

Why didn't Americans do things this way? The thought twisted at her heart. It was something only her mother would have appreciated, the fantasy of everyone living happily together in one big house. To her father, a house was mostly just the place he was penned until it was time to go back outside again.

Jack likes his job but says the natives have a lot to learn. He says some of the local engineers don't know a double-cast support beam from a two by four. Neither do I. In fact I made that up. I can't remember what he said.

Her dad probably wouldn't appreciate those little jokes about terminology any more than Jack did. He'd never joked much about business: selling agricultural equipment was too hard a life for laughs. And he definitely knew the name of everything.

But her thoughts seemed to form with her mother in mind or not at all. Her father wouldn't care that she and Jack had already met one of their neighbors, a woman named Mufeeda, who lived down the street. What an odd name. But then her own must have seemed rather strange to Mufeeda. "Keet?" she'd said, looking troubled. She was probably sitting in her own house right now thinking, Who would name a child Keet? It's the squawk of a bird.

Their contact had been brief. Jack had left Kit sitting in the car at the curb while he rushed back into the villa to pick up his measuring tape. Curious about the state of the garden beds outside the wall—they looked as if they'd never been cultivated—Kit got out and inspected them. Sand, mostly, and layers of spiky, desiccated weeds.

A big white car rolled by. Kit saw, briefly, the ivory oval of a woman's face in the back seat. Instinctively she smiled and waved—a neighbor!—then remembered that Jack had warned her against just this kind of thing here. Respectable women didn't wave on the streets.

34

At the corner, the car stopped dead. Gears shifted. The car rolled backward. It occurred to Kit that it might not have been a woman in the back seat. Perhaps it was a man's face she'd seen—some men here used chauffeurs too, and the windows were heavily tinted. Maybe she'd just waved gaily and provocatively to a Kuwaiti man from the curb.

The car rumbled to a smooth halt directly in front of her. Where was Jack when you needed him? She hauled open the door of her own car, ready to jump in and lock it, honk the horn, get Jack out of the damned villa—when Mufeeda stepped from the limousine, smiling.

"You are the American," she said. "Welcome."

Her ordinariness, despite the limousine, was what had struck Kit. She spoke English almost perfectly, with a soft, rolling accent; and other than the scarf wrapped around her face and neck—very tightly, like a mummy—she was dressed much like Kit, in a modest skirt and jacket. Her husband was a doctor at one of the big hospitals. She invited Kit over for tea just as any neighbor back home would, although she hadn't said when; and as Kit had thought about it since, the idea of actually going had begun to make her anxious. There was a British underpinning to tea here, tea as a formal event of some sort.

She covered the topic of Mufeeda for her father in a couple of quick sentences, going into more detail about what the tea might entail: too many forks.

Jack says they eat with their fingers here but he doesn't know everything (and he doesn't know that either). ☺

She had more momentum now. It felt good to just let the words flow from her pen.

Everybody has a lot of servants, and they do everything for you. Every morning just after dawn, two of the guest house maids go out and wash our car, and the street is full of other servants washing the neighbors' cars. It's dusty here all the time, of course, and when it does rain, it's only in the winter.

That was a thought for her father alone: a rainy winter. How would he get through winter at home without her mother?—that

35

lonely time of year when the days were so short and business slow. She could see him on a Saturday afternoon, reading his newspaper under a lamp in the living room, as Kit's mother went about her household chores, chatting with him now and again, then saying, *Walt, I'm off to the grocery now*, as if, indoors, he turned into a foreigner and had to be told the important things in very simple English. He'd nod, looking up to see her at the door in her coat, fiddling with her pocketbook. *Okay, Annie.*

A tap on the door, barely discernible.

"Come in?"

It was the steward or the butler, she didn't know what to call him, with the morning newspaper in one hand, folded as cleanly as a dinner napkin. He was one of the Indians, a man so dapper in his dress slacks and white shirt, so handsome with his amber eyes and shining hair, that she found his obsequiousness deeply embarrassing. In Stillwater, a boy as handsome as Jairam could swagger and pose and do nothing worthwhile, and everyone would still say, "What a fine boy!"

Jairam bowed, holding the paper out to her. "I'm sorry to disturb you, madam—"

"Not at all!"

"—the paper did not come 'til now—"

"Oh! Thank you. How nice of you." She hated the forced joyfulness in her voice.

"—and you take it with your breakfast."

Only because it usually lay on the table, angled for reading while she ate. She'd never been much of a newspaper reader before.

"Thank you so much, Jairam."

He bowed, smiling. His moustache was a line so thin it looked as if he'd plucked it. "Thank you, madam. Can I do anything else for you, madam?"

"Oh no!" An edge of horror. She hoped he hadn't heard it. Still he hesitated. Did he expect a tip? Jack had said never to tip the staff, that they were salaried employees of the company, with jobs others like them would kill to have, jobs with a Western company that paid more and treated them better. But here Jairam stood, having kindly done her a favor.

Perhaps kindness had nothing to do with it, though. Perhaps he'd simply kept the paper so that he could manipulate her into giving him a tip. And if she gave him one, setting a precedent, the paper would be mysteriously late every day. Even as she rejected this idea, she gave the door a nudge. A heavy plank on brass hinges, it swung inexorably shut, thudding into place like a great gate in a palace, giving her a last impression of Jairam's dark, bowed head.

She stood frozen in place, holding her breath, imagining his sense of insult. Or would he be insulted? She had no idea. But she knew what Jack would say: You make too much of everything, Kittie. If he'd been here, he'd have taken the paper, thanked Jairam without a fuss and merely closed the door. Here was something she should learn from him, if only she could.

She took the paper back to the desk and sat again, opening it over her letter. It was an English-language daily made up of articles translated from Arabic by an Arab staff. Jack considered the paper a joke but she found it fascinating. This wild rush of articles, the least newsworthy of them crowned with brilliant blue headlines an inch tall, indicated what the Arab editor thought would interest Western readers. He didn't seem to think much of their intelligence. Fashion in Europe and America took up more space than the daily news, with half-page color photos of scantily-clad models striding down long runways like gunslingers. Not what she had expected to see in the newspapers here, where many women covered themselves from head to toe. Nor had she expected the ads for skin bleaches—'Fair and Lovely, the Fairness Cream, gentle and safe! Super Bleaching Cream!'—and 'lady secretaries'; and pearl diving exhibitions, and weather forecasts that referred to 120 degrees as 'warm,' and the daily one-line Arabic lesson that had no obvious connection to the lesson the day before. She liked the optimism of this, the implication that you might actually learn Arabic by memorizing one random

37

phrase a day. Yesterday's sentence had been particularly random: "This is a big word." Today's lesson read, "'Araka marra okhra.' I will see you again. (Add 'inshallah')"

She murmured the words aloud, wondering at the instruction to 'add inshallah.' It meant 'God willing,' this much she knew. But was it compulsory to add it to statements like this? Would Arabic speakers find you rude if you didn't?

Another ad caught her eye:

Oh, her dad would get a kick out of that one.

She opened the main desk drawer and found it empty, then the top drawer on the side and—oh, for God's sake, it had been unlocked all this time—a pair of bright, sharp scissors along with tape, paperclips, labels, a calculator, a selection of pencils, pens, and even a small packet of colored highlighters. It was a wonder her son Kevin hadn't discovered this dangerous little pile and carved up the desk, if not himself.

She clipped the Arabic lesson and the shoe ad, then put the scissors in the locking middle drawer where they should have been in the first place.

Folding the letter she realized that she hadn't quite finished it, and sat for long moments wondering how to bring it to a close. Her father would open the envelope, she knew, after he was in bed. He still slept on the right side as he always had and kept her mother's pillow beside his own. He'd glance at the clippings, putting them aside until after he read the letter.

Don't worry about us, Dad. We're safe. Araka marra okhra. I miss you. And Mom too, so much. It's six months on Thursday exactly. I want to believe in ghosts just for her, so that I can expect a visit.

Love,

Your Kittie

An Admirable Action, If True

NINE O'CLOCK. Fatma's party would have begun by now. Mufeeda had to finish getting ready. But still she sat unmoving, studying her own dark eyes in her mirror. Why this hesitation?

Her gaze in the mirror slipped to the reflection of the bedroom at her back. It looked far away, like a lost world in a peaceful past, a place of soft light and deep yellow satins, eminently desirable but beyond reach tonight. If only she could stay home. The house was wonderfully quiet. She had sent Emmanuella and the housemaids to their rooms after dinner. Saleh had gone to a medical *diwaniya* and would be out late; his mother had retired to watch television in her room; the two younger girls were in bed; and Mariam was staying with a friend from the American School. What a perfect evening it would be to sit and read.

Her Quran lay open on the seat cushion of her armchair, the pages glowing so brightly that they might have been the source of the room's tender light. If only she'd studied more dutifully. So much time had slipped by in her years of motherhood. Almost half her life might be gone already, and yet what half of anything had she mastered? Not the Quran, and that should have come first. Only since the war had this become clear to her. She wasn't the only one who had let slip the obligations of her religion. The war, it seemed to her, had been sent from God as a reminder of this to her and all her countrymen, a destruction brought upon them to bring them back to the Book. She'd not been alone in her belief. While the oil fires burned, many people had turned again to God. While the city lay empty under that black sky, they'd asked humbly for forgiveness. While the Iraqis pillaged and desecrated the city, raped its women, kidnapped its young men or shot them in cold blood before the eyes of their families—at that time many people had turned desperately to God with solemn pledges: If you will only save us . . .

A troubling thought. She pushed it from her mind. Her own pledge, taken since the war, was that she wouldn't allow herself to dwell on any obligations but her own; and specifically she would not judge Saleh for failing to keep the pledge he had made during that time. Yet so frequently her thoughts traveled to that very point before she could catch them, inflicting the usual wounds. Old ones now. Saleh had failed.

Again she faced the mirror. If she couldn't force herself into a happy attendance at Fatma's party then she had to settle for a perfunctory one. Either way, she had to make her preparations now. She had no good reason to dread this party: fifty other women might be there, and the coolness between her and her oldest friend wouldn't be noticed. Intimacy couldn't be expected at such a big gathering.

But that wasn't the core of the matter. She and Fatma had gone to primary school together, studied together at Kuwait University, had each married within a single year and shared one another's pregnancies like sisters. What the other women at the party might notice mattered less than what she'd be forced to witness again for herself: that she found little to admire in Fatma now. Her husband had married a second wife, and done it secretly. Fatma's anger had turned sour and ruthless. Understandable enough. But in her anger she attacked others' happiness. She had told Mufeeda bitterly that Saleh was capable of the same duplicity, and that she was naïve to think otherwise.

A true friend would forgive Fatma, would feel some compassion for her, instead of this . . . what? Mufeeda couldn't quite name it. It had the taste of disapproval but this was not the only flavor present, and she feared examining the matter too closely. She couldn't have expected that the circumstances would leave Fatma unchanged. They were too upsetting. Yousef had given no hint to Fatma of his restlessness, let alone his decision to marry again. Every woman in their circle had heard reports of second wives hidden shamefully away in apartment buildings in the city, but no one had ever had a personal connection with such a humiliating situation and thought it a practice of the lower classes. Vague rumors that made a little too much sense in the face of Yousef's frequent absences had pushed Fatma to confront him, and he'd admitted the marriage rather casually. He told her that the woman was Syrian, a widow mistreated by her late husband's family, not wealthy, and therefore willing to settle for the position of second wife in order to gain the security of marriage.

"The security of marriage." Fatma laughed harshly as she told this to Mufeeda. "He'd have me believe that all his motivations are noble. This, a man who cares nothing for his religion, knows none of its content except that it allows him four wives. How revered and holy he is."

That the new wife was beautiful and just nineteen years old were not details that Yousef had decided to offer in that first interview. This news had reached Fatma by rumor too. The Quran required that a man treat all his wives equally. "He'll build her a villa to make a show," Fatma told Mufeeda. "But I will not be made equal to a second wife." What action she'd take wasn't clear. In other segments of society, at its heights and at its depths, among religious people and the secular, divorce wasn't uncommon; but among Mufeeda's friends and in her family history, it was rare.

Could the weaknesses in her own marriage, in Saleh, in her, drive them toward divorce? How important was it that Saleh didn't seem to pray, didn't go to mosque? Could it be right, as he'd told her, that his religion was an intensely private thing, not to be judged by external appearances? Or did he care only to cloak his lack of faith from her questioning gaze?

Closing her eyes, she ordered these thoughts from her mind. Doubts were corrosive. Saleh was a good man, a man with a fine and generous heart. She loved him and admired him for his dedication to his profession, for the respect he engendered among his colleagues. He was one of the best, and not just in Kuwait. Anywhere.

Far from comforting her, these thoughts filled her instead with a fear of having invited ill fortune. Saleh called such stuff superstitious nonsense but still she felt the weight of fate's unblinking eye. Complacency would be punished as readily as doubt.

Her mood lightened a little as she slipped on the jacket of her suit, a creamy linen that softened her complexion. Examining herself in the long mirror she thought she looked very well for her age. She was now, after all, solidly in her mid-thirties. Saleh never wanted to hear such equivocations from her. She smiled, imagining him in the room, countering what he considered her excessive modesty. "Mufeeda, you look more than well." He'd come to her, touch her chin or brush her hair from her cheek. "You're very beautiful."

Beautiful. The thought of the word on his lips stirred her. Such a bold conclusion about herself had never been allowed to her as a child, the youngest daughter of four, and even now she couldn't manage it, though she did believe that Saleh sincerely thought her beautiful. Her father had always joked in his stern way that he'd wanted to name her 'redundant' when she was born, and settled on Mufeeda—'useful'—only because it would inspire her to a better destiny. Useful. Had she lived up to it? The memory humbled her—as it should, she thought.

Wrapping her scarf around her head and neck, she buzzed the *mulhaq* on the intercom to let Rafiq know she was on her way down—"Is the car ready?" "Yes, madam"—and picked up her high heels as she left the bedroom. She could run down the staircase faster in her stocking feet and spare herself two stories of discomfort as well.

In the corridor she bent to step into her shoes and caught sight of a flick of movement beyond. One of the children out of bed? She marched forward soundlessly, still carrying her shoes, and found not one of her daughters but Emmanuella on the

42

stairs, rushing upward, hugging close to the banister like a thief.
Seeing her, the girl stifled a scream.

"Emmanuella!"

The girl cowered, choking back tears with a fist at her lips.
"Oh, ma'am!"

"Why are you downstairs? I sent you upstairs long before."

Suspicion awoke in Mufeeda's mind. "Are you visiting the
men in the *mulhaq*?" But Emmanuella answered with a horror
that could only be honest. "Oh, no, ma'am!"

"Then why?"

"I thought—"

"Speak."

"Ma'am," her voice dropped to a whisper, "I thought I put
the lamb improperly for tomorrow. It has blood, and I wrapped a
cloth with it."

A reasonable answer and an admirable action, if true. "Then
why do you cry?"

Hesitation. She wouldn't look at Mufeeda. "I thought Succoreen will come. She will be angry."

Was she implying that Succoreen visited the men? This
seemed unlikely. Though timid, Emmanuella was not craven,
and had never informed on another servant. The idea was preposterous anyway: Succoreen was forty-five and fat as a buddha.

Mufeeda didn't inquire further. She'd learned as a child in
her father's house that one didn't interrogate the servants about
such things. Under pressure, they'd say anything, even Emmanuella, to implicate all others and keep their own names clean.

"Succoreen should not come here, no more than you."

"Yes, ma'am."

"Do not come here again in this way, even if you have duties.
It will wait."

"Yes, ma'am. Thank you, ma'am." Emmanuella darted up
the stairs.

CROSSING THE THRESHOLD

ON THE top floor, just inside the door to her room, Emmanuella stopped to compose herself. How could she have forgotten to take the letter downstairs? What a mistake it had been to run back up here to get it—and find herself face to face with Ma'am. But all was well, thank God, and so the risk was worth it. The employers of the maid next door had forbidden her to receive mail, and so a letter from the girl's mother was as important to her as food.

From the bottom of a shallow drawer where Emmanuella kept her few pieces of underwear, she drew a thin envelope with her own name and address on the front, written in a spidery hand she'd become familiar with only in these last weeks, since she offered to receive the other maid's mail for her and deliver it in person. She'd written to the girl's mother herself, giving the address, avoiding the reason why this change had become necessary, for the girl said it would worry her mother too much. The mother must be ill to write so poorly, like an old woman.

Emmanuella dropped the envelope into the wide pocket of her housedress and slipped out the door of her room once more to the landing where the female servants each had a tiny room just below the roof of the villa. Ma'am had gone. Listening, she heard the usual sounds of the late evening: the Grandmother's blaring television resonating in the dense wall of the villa; Rosaline snoring softly, though her light still showed beneath the door—she'd fallen asleep reading her Bible; and Gloria singing softly to herself the long, sad songs from her Filipino childhood. Carmen's room was dark. Like the little girls of the family, she fell asleep fast and slept soundly. All was well. Emmanuella ran swiftly down the stairs.

The swinging door of the kitchen whooshed shut behind her. Relatively safe. The soft sloshing rhythm of the dishwasher eased her; how calm it sounded. She laid a palm on the metal of its face, savoring the gentle warmth on her tired fingers. Not long ago she'd only heard of such a contraption. Dishwashers existed in Goa too but not in the homes of anyone she knew. And in those more innocent days she'd wondered why anyone would spend money on such a machine when sinks and running water served as well. But now she knew that machines of all kinds were integral to wealth. There were a dozen in this kitchen alone.

From the back of a lower refrigerator shelf she drew out the bag of lamb kabobs and rice. At the counter she raised the blind just enough to reveal the villa next door, its shaded kitchen windows with their heavy bars. No movement. At first she hadn't believed the girl when she insisted that she was the only servant in the villa; but the gossip of Mufeeda's staff confirmed it: no one, not the other housemaids nor the men in the *mulhaq* had ever seen another soul. No children, no parents, no gardener, no housemaids. The young wife there even drove her own car. When she left the house, which she often did for days at a time, the man was alone with the housemaid. Gloria had told Emmanuella what this meant. *Alone with a girl like that, he will always take her. For their honor they do it, to show they are men.*

Emmanuella paused at the door, saying a silent prayer, and turned the knob. The hot air of the evening sent a tingle up her arms. She often went six days at a time without crossing the threshold, until recently. Darting across the short, tiled space to the wrought-iron fence between the two villas, she looked over her shoulder at her own. She was most vulnerable here, visible as she was from the windows of the upper floors. Or if one of the men from the *mulhaq* were to step out for a cigarette, he'd see her.

Resolute against her fear, she moved to one of the tall posts of the fence and placed the bag on the ground against its far side, wedging the letter beneath. She gave the bag a final pat, as if it were the head of a small and beloved child. *Please God, let her come quickly, before the stray cats.*

An Assistant Only

The room was nearly bare, the walls gray-green and fading. Dead plants furred with dust stood on the peeling windowsill, and the air smelled faintly of cardamom and an unflushed toilet somewhere. Against one wall stood a line of chairs, and at the far side of the room across a sea of speckled tile sat Rajesh's father at an aircraft carrier of a desk, its metal decks cleared for battle. Lean, rigid, with folded hands and pursed lips, the old man moved not a muscle. The overhead lights flashed in the half-lenses of his black-framed glasses.

"Out. My clinic will open at ten o'clock."

Theo stepped from the hospital corridor and closed the door to the silent hallway. "I'm Theo Girard, Dr. Chowdhury," he said.

The glassy eyes stared.

"Your new associate."

"Speak up!"

Rajesh had said that his father was a little deaf. "I'm Theo Girard, your new associate."

Offense sparked in the eyes. "Assistant. You're an assistant only."

Well, it was something. Theo put out a hand. "I'm very glad to meet you."

Rajesh's father moved then as if galvanized by a quarter in a slot: pushing his spectacles to the far tip of his bony nose, he folded one arm atop the other as if he were about to levitate and looked Theo over, up and down.

"You don't look like a physician."

Theo let his hand drop. He wasn't surprised to hear it. Starting with Jane Scarborough he'd heard much the same from

46

almost everyone he'd met, including the administrators in his morning's quick round of introductions, men and women from all over the Middle East and South Asia, none of them taller than his chin. He was beginning to think he'd be treated with outright condescension here, albeit mostly benign, as if he were merely a lanky, overgrown boy who should know better than to pretend to any knowledge of the world, particularly this one.

Rajesh's father adjusted his glasses again. "And why are you so tall?"

Minus the black disapproval of his gaze, Theo might have construed this as a humorous question about his family heritage asked in the same blunt style he'd noted among newly-arrived Indians in the U.S.: Where do you live? What is your salary? It was better to ignore it.

"I saw Rajesh a week ago," he said. "He sends his . . ." Respects? Such an old-fashioned word. When was the last time he'd used it? ". . . warmest affection," he said.

Rajesh's father settled back in his chair. "You will sit here," he said, extending one finger to his right with an elegant rotation of the wrist. A straight-backed wooden chair squatted beside the desk like a naughty child sent to the principal's office. "For now, you will take notes as I speak with my patients. This is your purpose." He flourished a gleaming watch on the same wrist by shooting the arm forth from its white cuffed sleeve. "The clinic opens in twelve minutes. In the meantime, you may tell me why you are here."

Rajesh had warned him of his father's resemblance to a prosecuting attorney. Theo gave Dr. Chowdhury the same reasons he'd given his acquaintances at home for his decision to come here, the outward and obvious ones: opportunities to travel, to live in a society widely disparate from his own, to treat people who'd had little access to Western medicine.

Dr. Chowdhury said nothing and waited, utterly immobile, for something else.

The deeper reasons Theo couldn't articulate clearly, even to himself. They were the same as the reasons he'd traveled to

Guatemala, to Costa Rica and Brazil: He needed to get away from California, at least for a good stretch of time, and the less like home his destination the better. Home didn't exist anymore, outside of his imagination. Nor had it ever, he knew. Not in the way that he longed for it.

"The pay is more than I could expect at home," Theo told Dr. Chowdhury, thinking that an admission of his typically mercenary American soul might satisfy the old man.

There seemed to be considerable variety in Dr. Chowdhury's silences. This one shifted to sly disbelief. Finally he spoke, so bleakly he might have been implying Theo's involvement in a dark conspiracy.

"My son of course has written to me about you."

"That was very kind of him."

What Dr. Chowdhury distrusted in him Theo couldn't fathom. He'd hired Theo and Theo stood before him, ready for work. If Rajesh had told his father of Theo's inheritance, the mention of salary might have backfired. But it seemed unlikely Rajesh would have violated Theo's privacy by mentioning his father's death, let alone his estate. It wasn't a fortune, only a bare competence. Poets didn't make millions, not even a well-respected one like Theo's father. Yet Rajesh might have found it impossible to refrain from dropping the name, considering it a kindness to Theo, a way to ease the initial encounter. Bengalis marinated in poetry from birth—poetry written in English, in Bengali, and in a convergence of the two languages so richly braided that they experienced it as a single tongue.

"One wonders," Dr. Chowdhury said, tapping a pen slowly on the empty desk top, "why one might choose to accept this position rather than another—if indeed there were another position for one to accept."

So Jane had been right: Everyone would wonder if Theo was a crank with a medical past worth running from, even the physician who had hired him.

"You have my CV, I think," Theo said.

"Who would send out a bad one?"

48

Theo gave the end of his nose a scratch, blocking an exasperated smile. "I don't have the imagination to falsify mine."

Dr. Chowdhury considered this, dramatic with gravity. "I choose to believe you. But of course all will come out in your work. I'm known as an excellent diagnostician. Ask anyone. I can judge a man by his work in an instant."

Before Theo could weigh this threat, a din of voices and running feet erupted in the hallway. A tiny young Arab woman dressed in white slid sideways into the clinic and leaned hard against the door to force it closed on a crowd teeming at her heels. She had to be a nurse, Theo thought, though her uniform reminded him of a nun's habit.

"Good morning, Professor," she said, her reverent voice just audible over the clamor of the throng. The only window to the corridor had been covered with a sheet of rough cardboard limiting the view behind her to the slits along the edges, a narrow kaleidoscope of dark motion and an occasional staring eye.

"Good morning, Sister."

Dr. Chowdhury faced the door with the look of a determined commander at the head of outnumbered troops.

"Sister," he said. "Remind our patients that they believe themselves to be part of the civilized world." He made a sweeping gesture with both arms as if the room contained another collection of silent, highly cultivated peers and not just Theo folded into his assistant's chair and the child-like nurse at the door. "Tell them no one may enter until all are silent."

She opened the door two inches, bracing it with a diminutive white-shod foot, and broadcast a warning Theo couldn't even hear. Nevertheless, the hall plunged into silence. Closing the door again, she waited, hands folded, her eyes expressionless and downcast. She had an almost perfectly oval face.

Her eyes flicked to Theo and caught him staring. She looked away before he could, instantly, her dark face blanker. Theo fumbled with the battered notebook Dr. Chowdhury had thrust at him, embarrassed that he'd watched her so openly and for so long when he knew not to stare at a Muslim woman.

Dr. Chowdhury didn't introduce them. "Let the melee begin, Sister."

A mass of people stumbled across the threshold as if a vacuum seal had broken when she opened the door. She rejected them, "*La, la!*" and called out five names from a clipboard. The lucky few grappled their way into the room along with a plump and disheveled woman in a lab coat who hurried head-down and with clumsy speed to a small table on the opposite side of the room.

Dr. Chowdhury's voice resonated like a preacher's. "You're late once again, Dr. Asrar."

He was addressing the woman in the lab coat. No one had mentioned a third internist to Theo. All the prohibitions fled from his mind again. He stared. The woman seemed not to have heard Dr. Chowdhury. She wore no head scarf, and beneath the grayish coat, a white blouse and dark skirt. She looked less like a doctor than Theo.

With urgent whispers the tiny nurse swept the patients, two of them limping, toward the chairs along the wall where they settled into mute hunches, glancing warily at Dr. Chowdhury. A murmur rose and vibrated in the hall.

Dr. Asrar pulled a stethoscope from a drawer. "My daughter is ill again, Professor." Her voice was conversational, low, dignified, her accent in English distinguished, as the accents of all the Arabs Theo had met seemed to be, by a precision of pronunciation and delicately rolled r's.

"Do you address me?"

She faced him, raising the volume of her voice while keeping its peaceful timbre the same. "My daughter is ill again, Professor."

"Yes, yes, yes. She's always ill. You must take her to a doctor other than yourself."

Feeling like an eavesdropper, Theo rose from his chair, unkinking to a height that seemed ridiculous even to him, but Dr. Chowdhury was fully up to ignoring this too. Opening a broad, screeching metal drawer in his desk, he took out several ballpoint pens and inspected the ink supply of the barrels with fascinated intensity.

Theo bowed his head briefly toward the women. "Good morning." Their astonishment showed in fleeting, electric glances that allowed him a flash of their unguarded faces. Dark, luminous eyes. Neither said a word. "I want to introduce myself. My name is Theo—"

The drawer screamed shut.

"Yes, yes, ladies, this is our new assistant physician from America." A pen had been selected. Dr. Chowdhury now busied himself with a two-foot stack of dog-eared files and fine adjustments to his spectacles. "He's here to teach us all a thing or two. This is Sister Wafa and 'doctor' Asrar."

Dr. Asrar betrayed no recognition of this sarcasm. Theo reached out a hand to her, remembering as he did so that this too was forbidden between unmarried men and women. Gracefully, she avoided a response by seeming not to see his hand.

"Doctor . . . ?" she said.

"Theo. Just Theo is fine."

Dr. Chowdhury slapped a folder closed and peered toward the patients along the wall as if preparing to gun them down. "They will honor you with the title you have earned," he thundered to the patients. They cringed. None looked likely to speak English. "Unless of course you haven't earned it." He turned his basilisk eyes back to Theo. "Now, if you are finished with your introductions, may we attend to our business?"

FROM TEN o'clock to three in the afternoon, the flow of patients came in at flood stage, a jostling, odorous mix of *Beduin* from the poorest segments of Kuwaiti society, men, women, and children; and imported laborers and household workers from South Asia, North Africa, and the Middle East, ranging from late teens to mid-thirties. All ragged, natives and non-natives alike, many illiterate, badly nourished and frightened. Every nation in the region Theo could think of was represented: India, Pakistan, Bangladesh, Sri Lanka, the Philippines, Iraq, Iran, Jordan, Syria, Egypt, Morocco, Sudan, Somalia. Dr. Chowdhury ordered them

51

before him while the rest waited humbly in their chairs, and questioned them in a peremptory stew of English, Hindi, Urdu, and Arabic, translating occasional phrases for Theo preceded by, "Write this down!"

A tea boy, a silent, slender, black-skinned young man padded into the clinic and, bowing, offered thimblefuls of hot tea on a small salver to the staff. Others like him, men who appeared to be the hospital's general flunkies, came and went regularly, serving as pickup and delivery men, of files, laboratory orders and results, messages from the administrative office, occasional summonses for Sister Wafa or Dr. Asrar. All wore what looked to Theo like a monkey suit: high-water trousers and a short button-up jacket. They seemed not to know how absurd they looked. Or, Theo surmised, they had chosen dignity over humiliation.

Dr. Chowdhury bulldozed through every interview, dispatching patients after brief, growling cross-examinations, "Speak up!" and briefer physical exams, to the radiology department, to the lab, to the pharmacy, to other specialists, and sometimes off with Dr. Asrar for an injection in the next room. His pace was slowed only by his occasional failure to decipher one of the many dialects of Arabic spoken by his patients.

"Sister! Tell me what this patient is saying. I cannot hear a word of this Moroccan nonsense."

Wafa, preparing an injection, a naked syringe in one hand, a vial of golden fluid in the other, said, "He says he does not want women to hear."

"Yes, yes, then explain to him that you are all deaf."

Wafa bowed her head, hiding a smile. "Blood comes in his water. He has pains there."

Dr. Chowdhury ordered the patient to the lab. As the man was shunted out the door, Wafa handed him a tiny plastic cup with no lid and no label, and said three or four words to him. However compact her Arabic, this telegraphic speech couldn't have included hints on how to accomplish the necessary semi-sterile specimen, or how the patient might catch anything but spray in a cup identical to a Nyquil jigger.

"Next!"

A spare and trembling young Indian man offered himself to Dr. Chowdhury for a machine-gun interview in Hindi. Theo felt rather than saw Sister Wafa step behind him. He heard her soft voice over his shoulder.

"I am sorry, Doctor, I do not speak Hindi but I will try. He says he has pains when he moves, and when he is still, he has bigger, more pains, and fever. His heart runs fast in the night."

Theo turned to thank her, astonished at both her facility with language and her modest assessment of it, but she had already stepped away, her face averted.

The man was between eighteen and twenty-two or so, Theo guessed. Malnutrition had kept him small. He was thin to the point of fragility, the bones of his face sharp, his hands delicate, nervous, his eyes those of a cornered dog. He'd brought an envelope of x-ray films and a sheaf of pink, tissue-thin lab reports for Dr. Chowdhury's perusal. He handed both across the desk, peeling the pink sheets from his sweating fingertips. Dr. Chowdhury gave the lab results a single glance. The chest x-ray he held briefly up to the light of the window and laid aside dismissively. He offered neither to Theo nor left them within his reach.

"Normal, everything is normal." Dr. Chowdhury spoke in English though Theo felt certain from the panic in the man's face that he didn't understand a word. "You are not ill. I told you this when you came last week. Yet I have done all the tests, x-rays, blood, urine, and all is normal, normal, normal. You must not bother me again."

He turned abruptly to Theo. "You are not writing. You must mark all of this down. Write! I will repeat everything in Hindi now."

He went on and on at the patient, his voice growing screechy; then, switching to Arabic, apparently for the benefit of the *Beduin* patients, he gave a longer oration, making broad, angry gestures toward the young Indian, who sat miserably before him. He hadn't touched the patient; nor had Sister Wafa or Dr. Asrar. He went unweighed, the basics of his blood pressure and temperature unknown.

"Mr. Assistant Physician, why do you wait? You must document my thought processes."

If only Theo could have guessed them. "I apologize. I don't speak either Hindi or Arabic. I took down what few basics I could after your broadcast in English."

Dr. Chowdhury sat rigidly upright, took in a steadying breath. "You Americans amaze me. How can you speak one language only and consider yourselves educated? You must learn Arabic. Hindi is less necessary, as I am here to translate and Sister Wafa speaks some Hindi as well, though it's execrable. Sister! Give him the name of the woman who is the linguist, the Arabic tutor. Now, about this case: you will write this down. This man has acute anxiety due to a sexual neurosis."

Theo's pen froze on the page.

"You require further explanation? How obtuse you are. But I'll give it to you. I'm not unreasonable. He has left his young wife behind in Rajasthan for two years and has remained faithful to her. He's to be congratulated. If the Kuwaiti government," he waved violently in the direction of the roof, the hospital, the country, "allowed these workers a decent salary—these people who do what the Kuwaitis are too proud and lazy to do—they could bring their families here and I'd see none of these poor men. He's religious, he's dedicated to his family, but he's suffering because of the cruel parsimony of this country's citizens. He longs for his wife. Can you blame him? 'Who, being loved, is poor?' It's all he has. But what of his salary here, you ask? Twenty-five dinar per month. Perhaps eighty American dollars. For this he lives in a cement room like a beast with twenty other men, working twelve hours a day, six and seven days a week. They prepare their own food on gas rings on the floor. One toilet, no AC. Twenty such men, all missing their wives. Is it any wonder he's nervous at night?" He turned wild-eyed to the *Beduin*. "Write it down!"

54

THE CONQUERING HORDE

Once a month, Jack had told her, the entire company—husbands, wives, children—gathered at the company guest house for dinner. It was not to begin until seven, but Jack, always overly prompt, rushed Kit and the children downstairs at six-thirty, well before any of the others arrived, and then insisted the kids sit like dolls on the raft-like sofas. Kit found it hard to act as much of an example: she felt squirmy too. The ice-cold marble rooms had been transformed. She gazed in awe around her, remembering to keep her mouth closed, but just. The half-dozen chandeliers, never illuminated for the residents, glowed like constellations, joined by brilliant halogens spanning the ceiling and spaced along every wall. Every floor and table lamp had been switched on and reflected its own yellow light in the heavy mirrors and gleaming windows, doubling every view.

At seven o'clock the other guests began arriving like a con-quering horde, spilling over with children at the edges, dominated by chattering women dressed to kill in swishing silks and gold jewelry, leading their silent husbands. Kit rose and took a deep breath, embarrassed by her cotton skirt belted at the waist, her dull, flat shoes, and straight-as-an-arrow hair, hanging lifelessly to her shoulders. She smiled, holding on tight to her children's hands for comfort. Jack stood grinning beside her in his typical pose, his arms folded high across his chest, looking like an Egyptian mummy propped against a wall.

The crowd logjammed just past the broad foyer with women greeting one another in swooping voices as if it had been years. Following Jack into the fray Kit lifted Kevin to her hip where he buried his face in her neck. Carla tugged at her skirt, wanting up too. "Ask Daddy," Kit said. But Jack was oblivious, beaming at everyone, shooting out a hand to the men. Kit brought Carla's head close to her hip with an encompassing hand, patting. Strange indeed: the women bussed one another on the cheeks, left and right, instead of the usual little hug. Perfume swirled in a gassy cloud. One man began introducing Kit and Jack to his wife. "Honey, you don't know Jack," and a male voice from somewhere behind him said, "Hey, Jack doesn't know jack!" and everyone nearby howled. Jack laughed too, throwing his head back in a way Kit had never seen before. His usual laugh was a slow and deliberate huh-huh-huh, as if to carefully ration out his amusement. She'd only rarely seen him among his colleagues before, she realized. Still, what kind of joke was that?

She fought against feeling intimidated by the women, reminding herself that her first impressions were often wrong. They looked cold and hard and unfriendly, and she could see the speculation in their glances, the decisions to engage or ignore, the smiles pushed up as if against sore muscles. Some looked almost ferocious. *Welcome to Kuwait!* But Kit was no more sincere. *Hello! Happy to meet you! Yes, we're so happy to be here!* All the while defending her children against their plucking fingers. *And who are you, little guy?* Kevin broke into tears. Carla was kidnapped by a woman who shot Kit a conspiratorial smile, as if this would be just what Kit wanted. *You look like you're just about my Deborah's age!* and whisked Carla away to a back room where the children were apparently to be imprisoned for the evening. A housemaid came to take Kevin from her. Kit shot Jack a desperate look, but he gave her a quick shake of the head: Don't make a fuss. So she let Kevin go. He wailed, going beet-red. Women swarmed around her, their noise now tuned to quick comfort. *He'll be just fine! They have all sorts of toys back there. Free baby-sitting! It's one of the perks.*

The meal itself came as both a relief and a disappointment. At last there was a diversion from the face-to-face torment of first meetings, something to do besides manufacture small talk; but this 'special' dinner, which she'd hoped might be exotic, was only bigger not better, with heaps of Western-style food set in fancy warming dishes: chicken *parmigiana*, grilled steaks, fried fish, mashed potatoes and gravy, scalloped potatoes, green beans in a swamp of buttery juice, mushy broccoli, baskets of bread and dinner rolls. A separate table set off to the side bore cheesecakes, pies, puddings, cookies, and fruit. She'd never seen such a lavish ordinary meal before.

The staff members serving it interested her more, Jairam among them. She'd seen them setting up the tables in the afternoon, striding through the guest house with self-confidence and purpose. Now they stood meekly behind the buffet table serving the guests, their faces stamped with servile politeness. Jairam stood duty dishing up mashed potatoes and gravy *One or two, ma'am? More gravy, sir? Thank you, ma'am,* as if their choices were of critical concern to him. She nodded in confusion, unable to look him in the eye when her turn came, feeling as though she'd caught him out in something shameful.

"Indians," Jack said to her, giving her a nudge, "lots of them here." He boomed forth proudly at them in his rudimentary Arabic as his plate grew conical with food—*Min fudluk! Shukran!* But didn't they speak Hindi in India? Kit saw Jairam's eyes shift uneasily, saw him glance expressionlessly at Jack and the raucous, overdressed crowd before bowing his head to his work.

AFTER DINNER the crowd divided as if by order into male and female groups, the men drawing up a broad circle of over-stuffed chairs together in one end of the living room, the women dragging the dining room chairs into tight clusters at the other, reminding Kit of old movies she'd seen of European society where the men expected to be left alone with their cigars. Jack didn't give her as much as a glance, so she sat in an empty wing chair feeling abandoned and cast a smile around bravely, wishing she could be back with the kids. A nearby group waved her in and as she tried to edge the heavy chair forward, one of them rose to help her. "Come on over. We'll gossip about the men." They weren't so bad after all. Of course.

Safely in the group she was relieved that they forgot her so quickly, the ebb and flow of their talk sweeping her into a semi-relaxation, the talk of women everywhere, with a few exotic names sprinkled in, of diets and chocolate and trips, and children, children, children. *A pedicure this time . . . sat at my feet . . . too much, can you believe it? . . . went to Istanbul on the way home . . . she said to me, and I said, Well sweetie-pie . . . nothing, absolutely nothing . . . just past the McDonald's on the Gulf . . . same teacher as last year . . . got an A for doing nothing . . . so cute! . . . saw this necklace I had to . . . in Oman last time, and then in Dubai . . . beach hotel on Phuket . . . forever reminding him to pick up his underwear . . .*

PATIENT OR SPECIMEN

To: Dr. Thoedor Girard
Subject: Welcome to Hospital!

Good afternoon Doctor!
 Welcome to Hospital Family! Door Key to Room 127 please find. I hope to be connecting with you, but the circumstance usually change by time to time, anyhow may office already changed from (Room 7- 75) in Sturgeon Building to the partition area (Room 7 - DDF) in the EX - Dead Record Building as mansion above, so time will come to meet. If any request or order regard your paperwork, please send your memo singed to keep your order in queue, otherwise we apologize to ignore it.

Kind regards,
(Officers of Security Dept.)

A HEAVY brass key marked '127' arrived with the memo, delivered by a tea boy, allowing Theo to guess Security's intent in its communication: At Theo's insistence, and almost two weeks into his new employment as Dr. Chowdhury's scribe, he'd been assigned an office. He hoped it wasn't in the Sturgeon Building, since he wasn't a sturgeon but an internist.

The messenger, a meager Sri Lankan, explained through Wafa that he was to guide Theo to his new office. Why became clear: it was a hike. Theo followed doggedly in the messenger's wake into the cacophony of the hospital's main lobby, jammed from wall to wall with wheelchairs, gurneys, patients and staff, a Last Judgment vision of boiling humanity that Theo hadn't yet accommodated. It didn't help that his beacon-like height topped with pale fire blond hair turned every face gaping in his direction.

Beyond the lobby, the route was long and circuitous, taking them past the 'ladie's blood-drawing room,' the 'mens blood-drawing room,' and the 'patients dispensing pharmacy' where women in black *abayas* contested elbow-to-elbow at the counter, and three beleaguered pharmacists sorted ragged sheaves of documents, shouting names into the pandemonium. A wheeled cart set in the busy lab doorway held a full harvest of open urine samples set atop damp pink sheets, and in the women's waiting room Theo glimpsed a vision from an ancient nunnery: wooden benches filled with quiet, black-shrouded women, their hands folded serenely in their laps. Via a series of passageways and battered metal doors, he and his guide passed into the obstetrics and gynecology department, and Theo began to think that the tea boy would do well as a taxi driver in New York.

A final turn took them down a short hall where his guide stopped at a scarred and windowless metal door marked 'Room 127' spaced closely between two others: 'Supplies Cabinet' and, mysteriously, 'Patients and Specimens.' Theo fitted the key to the lock, smiling at the absurdity of it, and saw a wall of boxes before him, forty or fifty of them, bunged up with age and frequent migration. No desk, no phone, no window. He gave one box a soft kick—immovable, as if filled with cement, and squatted to decipher a few of the faded labels scrawled in Arabic and quasi-English in pencil, ink pen, marker: 'Kidny,' 'Heart,' 'Womans.'

Women boxed whole. He wouldn't doubt it.

Turning back to the guide he found the hallway empty. He'd been abandoned. He sank onto a pile of boxes, his big feet on the threshold, and gazed down the barren little hall, gearing himself up for the return trip. Meanwhile, at least he knew where he was: in his cozy office a quarter mile from his department where he was employed as an underling of a maharaja.

The private sector, Hamid had said.

Tempting. But too soon. Surely even this frozen bureaucracy could see its way to clear out a small roomful of boxes. And Al-Ghais was no worse in most ways than any public hospital anywhere, streaming with people at every hour and sunk in surrender to its own mediocrity. The original building, with the riotous lobby at its heart, was a cement-block fortress thrown together sometime in the sixties, he judged, and the subsequent builders— you couldn't call them architects—had seen no reason to change the style of the additions. The old building still housed admitting, the pharmacy, the main labs, and offices for members of the administration who lacked the connections—*wasta* in Arabic, a word common in everyday parlance here, even in English—to get out. The hospital as a whole was now a flat-roofed, five-storied maze spread across twenty acres, framed in a mammoth gravel parking lot, its metastatic vigor restrained only by the bulwark of three freeways and the teeming, dilapidated neighborhood to the south. Inside, ugliness had sunk its thick and tumorous roots into every brick and tile, every procedure and administrative detail.

It could be far worse, Theo reminded himself. Other than the open urine specimens, he'd seen no other truly egregious procedures, no reuse of needles for instance, and the drugs at the pharmacy were well-regulated and from respectable pharmaceutical houses of the Western world. It was a better place than it looked.

A shaft of afternoon sun came down the hall from the main corridor, shifting with the shadows of the passing crowd. He looked at his watch, feeling the drag of a long afternoon, yet it was only three-thirty.

"Good morning, sir!"

His guide reappeared in the corridor, smiling triumphantly: he'd brought help. Behind him trooped a band of Sri Lankan colleagues, men so underfed all their lives that Theo, standing to greet them, towered over them like Goliath as he looked down on all their dark heads. A hospital administrator showed up too, one of the several Theo had met during his first day on the job, a tall and grave man, dignified and remote, dressed faultlessly in

61

a bleached-white *dishdasha*. He explained to Theo that these miniature men, not Theo, were to move the heavy boxes in Theo's
office. He stood by to make sure he was obeyed, a tall white pillar
of grim authority, as the Sri Lankans began to shift the stacks into
the hallway. Though the records could have no connection with
Theo's work, the administrator directed him to look inside each
box and decide which would go and which would stay. Theo's
insistence that everything had to go made no impression on him:
the job of opening each must be accomplished. The administrator then turned to the Sri Lankans, gave them a lecture in
scalding Arabic, and left.

The workers grew instantly light-hearted, casting smiles and
nods at Theo, offering their few words of English to him with shy
pride. *Good morning, sir! You come Sri Lanka, sir, please.* Patting their
hearts. *Beautiful country, sir.*

Having no dolly, they improvised with a sagging, old-fashioned
typist's chair they'd snagged somewhere, piling boxes on the
torn seat three or four high and pushing it away down the hall,
clustering around to keep the boxes steady as they flashed more
smiles over their shoulders at Theo. The tiny wheels screamed
for mercy.

Theo readied the next load while they were gone, taking a
cursory glance in each box and finding an unsorted mass of old
patients' records from long years past, none of them obviously
connected even with obstetrics or gynecology despite the occasional 'Womans' label. If these were dead records, and he hoped
they were, what was in the ex-dead record building? And was
there a permanently-dead record building?

The workers ended their work day by shoving an enormous,
upended metal desk across the threshold for Theo, gouging fresh
striations in the scarred linoleum. Eyeing the hallway warily
for oncoming administrators, they lowered it to its uneven feet
and showed him, whispering fervently in their own tongue and
miming in translation, what a poor desk had been dumped on
him, a thing of pure horror. Gray paint gave way to rusted metal

at the corners; one drawer had no handle and another required a mighty tug to open. Under Theo's direction, they joggled it into place, then stood around tsking at it with deep disapproval, offended to their souls on Theo's behalf.

"I'll need a chair," he told them, miming a comfortable, springy cushion and armrests. Full of confident assurances, they consulted among themselves and presented him proudly with their hand truck, the arthritic secretarial chair.

"Thank you," said Theo, and they bowed their way backward into the hall.

He sat on his desk top, gazing down the narrow hallway with its long vista of scuffed linoleum lit by the late sun. A phone would take a few days. Regarding a computer, no one would give him a commitment beyond the universal, "No problem!" which meant anything but. His laptop and cell phone would have to do, along with a packet of yellow legal pads he'd purchased himself.

"Hello there."

An Arab man had stepped into the hallway from a door half-way down the hall. "You're the new one, the American, aren't you?"

A black-cloaked woman, perhaps pregnant, perhaps not, floated past him over the threshold and turned toward the main hallway followed by a brisk Filipina nurse four-and-a-half feet tall writing on a clipboard. The man, a broad-shouldered and handsome Arab in his late thirties strode toward Theo, smiling, and clasped his hand.

"I'm Saleh. Welcome to my grand domain."

"Theo Girard."

"I know what you're thinking about your 'office,'" Saleh said. "Mine's not much bigger. When my nutritionist and one of my patients join me for a talk we have to take turns breathing."

"So . . . you're the ob/gyn department head?"

"An exalted description. I'm burdened with the responsibility, yes, but there's no credit attached to the position. Administrators award only blame, you know."

.

63

"I'll feel right at home then."

"I can see you haven't been here long."

"You must have spent a lot of time in the States. You sound like an American," Theo said, wondering if he'd made another faux pas.

But Saleh seemed pleased. "UCSF. And you?"

"UCLA. I grew up in the Bay Area, though. Berkeley. My dad taught at Cal."

"Then," Saleh offered his hand again. "We're already brothers."

BOMBS UNACCOUNTED

Having abandoned their children to their housemaids, a group of company women breezed into the guest house as if it were a country club. They lounged on the couches with elegant self-assurance, ordered the maids around with magisterial ease *Diet Pepsi, and give me some ice this time!* and demanded that Kit allow herself to be scooped up into their midst for a guided tour of the city featuring the neighborhoods and stores she'd need to know in order to perform her duties as her family's primary hunter-gatherer. She hated this prospect but couldn't decline gracefully. Everyone knew that she had nothing to do and nowhere to go until she'd moved into her house and mastered driving. There were no secrets here, and no immediate social circle other than the company itself.

Compressed into a car with five chattering women *Hey, ladies, when's lunch?* she was chauffeured around the maze of the city, dizzy with the turns and traffic-circles *This one's called the Circle of Death* blinded by the screeching speed of the freeways and jumbled sameness of the buildings alongside. Only sometimes did a landmark rise into view: the towers at the waterfront, the few taller buildings of downtown *Okay, now here's where you want to zip right onto the First Ring Road* but the peninsula of the city made the perspectives tricky, and she never knew where she was.

Over lunch at a French restaurant as intimidating as anything she could imagine in France itself—starched tablecloths, lustrous wood beams, engraved menus without a word of English—Kit struggled to get the women's faces and names straight, trying not to worry yet about the welter of kids' and husbands' names, or the fact that a couple of the women seemed resentful of her because of Jack's position *Hey, maybe the boss' wife should treat us.* She liked one woman named Tessa, a spirited, springy-haired blonde in her thirties who seemed to hear these comments with dismay and made a point of giving Kit a little wink, as if to say, Forgive them, they're idiots. Yet even the idiots among them had done much more than Kit, and with what seemed like effortless assurance. They all drove on these madcap freeways, went shopping on their own, managed to find doctors and pharmacies and arrange for maintenance of their homes, enrolled their kids in school, planned all their family's international vacations, interviewed and hired maids, and sat around in expensive restaurants with all the easy confidence of the leisured upper class. As much as anything she dreaded the idea of hiring a maid, and yet even Jack expected her to take advantage of the opportunity. "Maids are really cheap here, Kit. Like two-fifty a month for full-time live-in."

The company women were carving two pieces of chocolate cake into surgical slivers when a scream of jet engines ripped the air, rattling the windows like thunder. Kit ducked instinctively, a hand over her head, opening her eyes in time to see dark streaks—a trio of fighter jets—grazing the nearby horizon. Not even the smooth equanimity of the company women withstood the shock of it. Someone shouted, "They're headed toward Iraq!" electrifying the whole crowd, and the waiters rushed to the windows en masse, peering out into the now-empty sky. Kit saw several cloaked Arab women jump to their feet to leave, their faces hidden in their robes.

Most of the company women grabbed for their cell phones. Tessa calmly put a hand on Kit's arm. "Listen. No sirens."

She looked intently into Kit's eyes as she focused beyond the hubbub of the restaurant. Her face cleared slowly. "Listen, girls," she said into the clamor. "No sirens."

Across the restaurant the frenzy subsided as suddenly as it had begun.

"It's a drill," Tessa said, giving them all a clownish grin. "The pilots are male. What do you think? They're buzzing their girlfriends' villas."

Relief infected the women with a thin gaiety that soon gave way to uneasy talk of the Gulf war and the constant threat of another. The last war had never really ended, they told Kit. *They still shoot it out up there, you know.* They instructed her to go up onto her roof some night at a certain time, any night, and see the changing of the guard in the no-fly zone at the border: two American fighters flying south and two flying north. *You can't call that peace.*

The waiters returned with coffee refills and benignant smiles, as if nothing had happened. The women drank cup after cup, talking earnestly in low voices, their heads bent over the table, as serious as Kit had ever seen them. *Saddam's an absolute lunatic. Why Bush didn't march up there and get him when he could I'll never understand. . . . Raped a lot of the women and God knows what they did to all those Kuwaitis who never came back. . . . Not a chance they survived. Her neighbor's son was shot right on their doorstep for being a spy, so the Iraqis said . . . the company's evacuation plan . . . oh, right, as if I'm going to wait for the company to tell me when to leave.*

Kit saw the glances at her: Jack was essentially 'the company' in Kuwait. The bill came and the women pulled calculators from the depths of their purses. *He got out, but she got trapped here and ended up hiding in the American Embassy for months, drinking the pool water and eating god-knows-what. . . .* Exact divisions of the bill were made, tip included. *Dinar* piled up on the table. Kit added her own contribution and a little more. . . . *But there are still all sorts of bombs unaccounted for, a bunch of those Scud missiles . . .* Tessa noticed and gave her a wink and a smile. *Oh, but it's really short-range, though . . . Short-range, oh right, but just how far do you think we are from Iraq, something like fifty big, whopping kilometers?*

SOME SORT OF PARADISE

THE HOUSEMAID from the villa next door was outside again, this time in the furnace of midday. Emmanuella watched her sweep a roll of dust and sand slowly toward the street across the terrazzo enclosure in the piercing glare of the sun. How desperate she must be to come out onto the white tiles in her thin-soled shoes. The girl glanced furtively at the kitchen window through the tall wrought-iron fence, and when their eyes met, she lifted her brown fingers to her lips, cupping them there hungrily. Dark moons marked her hollow face in the harsh light.

"Oh, God!" Emmanuella whispered.

Behind her the tea kettle piped. Stay, she told the girl with a gesture. Wait. The girl's shoulders dropped and she turned away, edging toward the slender blue shade of the *mulhaq*.

Emmanuella had begun to think of her by her name, Santana. A beautiful name. No doubt Santana heard it rarely. Her sir and ma'am would call her 'girl' or 'you' or nothing at all.

Pulling the heavy kettle from the stove, Emmanuella heard the kitchen door swing open.

"Is it not ready yet, Emmanuella? The Grandmother is waiting!"

Emmanuella steadied the kettle, lifting it with both hands, surprised by this angry tone from Gloria, who had the mildest temper of any servant in the house.

"Don't rush me!" she said, fearing every moment the scalding cascade of water entrusted to her unreliable grip.

Emmanuella had always credited Gloria's good temper to the fact that she was Filipina rather than Indian like herself. Filipinos

68

seemed to be a calmer people, while the Indian staff were restless and short-tempered beneath the smiles they presented to their masters.

The boiling water splashed onto the fine brown Sri Lankan leaves in the bottom of the teapot, the Grandmother's favorite blend, and a column of sweet aroma rose with the steam. What more could she do for Santana? Her courage still wavered every time she thought of Mufeeda catching her on the stairs, and in her fear she'd allowed herself to do less. What a coward she was.

Gloria sighed, drawing Emmanuella's attention again. She had sunk onto one of the bar stools and unfolded a handwritten letter in her generous lap. Her eyes gazed past it to the floor.

From her son, Emmanuella guessed. Of Gloria's several children, only this son wrote regularly, as a child should, thanking her for sending her monthly wire transfers amounting to nearly all her salary. His last letter had broken dark news, though: Gloria's youngest daughter had been set upon by thieves in the family house and badly beaten. The son hadn't said what else they might have done.

Emmanuella laid her hot pad on the table. "What's the news, Gloria?"

Gloria took a ragged breath. "He says she's in hospital still. They cracked her head. My son says . . ." She crumpled the letter tight against her belly. "He says she will not be right."

"You must go to her." Emmanuella clapped the lid onto the teapot.

"I have no money."

How weary she sounded, how defeated. Emmanuella's impatience rose in a storm. "There's always money. Money is nothing."

Gloria looked Emmanuella over as if a stranger stood before her, a ridiculous one. "Nothing? I have nothing, you have nothing. That's what is nothing."

"Ma'am will give it to you."

"Ma'am? Ha! Who will ask her?"

"Tell her. She will give. But you must tell her." Emmanuella's doubts ran fast on the heels of her words. The rules were different under this god they called Allah.

"You've cracked your head too, Emmanuella. Do you know how far is Manila from here? India's near, but my country . . ." She faltered at the thought.

Emmanuella settled the teapot onto the tray. "Tell her how the men attacked your daughter. She has daughters too."

The intercom squawked, making them both jump. Gloria clutched at the collar of her housedress—afternoon tea was her responsibility. She looked with keen accusation at Emmanuella.

"You speak," she said. "I'm late because of you."

Emmanuella hesitated, summoning strength. She hadn't anticipated punishment from Gloria. But it wasn't undeserved. She stepped to the intercom.

"Ma'am, this is Emmanuella. I haven't made the tea quickly. Gloria comes now."

None of the staff knew how much English the Grandmother spoke. She answered in Arabic, louder than before. The words fell like fists on Emmanuella's head, deep, angry words she couldn't understand. God protect her from ever learning this language for fear its meanings matched its sound. She closed her ears to it, murmuring a prayer, and verified again with a glance the supplies on the tray: sugar, cream, biscuits, cake. On the edge of her vision she saw Santana sweeping and sweeping outside in the heat. It was still hours until dark, when she could help the girl.

Gloria hadn't budged. "You must carry it up to her," she said.

Emmanuella lifted the heavy tray. The Grandmother showed no discrimination between the members of the staff when she was angry. It was only fair that Emmanuella should bear the impact of whatever else was to come.

But as she pushed the door open with a toe, holding the tray steady in her treacherous fingers, Gloria touched her shoulder.

"Give it to me, Emmanuella. You are kind to me and I talk to you like Succoreen." She lifted the tray. "I'll do this."

Emmanuella stood alone in the kitchen, weak with relief, massaging one hand with the other, holding back tears. The door swung quietly on its hinges and came to a halt. She wouldn't cry: she was a woman now, fully grown. Tears belonged to childhood, and once they started she feared losing control. In the unaccustomed silence she could hear her own breathing, much faster than the muted ticking of the big clock over the sink. Now she must think about Santana.

The girl had withdrawn again to the *mulhaq*'s pale bar of shade, her broom at work in slow motion on the eternal dust at her feet. Emmanuella took the few steps to the windows. The girl stepped forward as well, to the bars of the spiked black fence, her face solemn, her dark eyes brilliant and eager with hope. Emmanuella stared. How much alike they looked: both small and quick, with the same long black hair pulled back into a heavy braid, the same white housedress of cheap cotton, hanging from thin shoulders. But these were unimportant similarities, a sameness on the surface that the Grandmother would never see beyond. This young woman was beautiful, her skin the color of golden sand, and smooth as milk. At home, in Goa, the boys would always trouble her. The boys had never troubled Emmanuella, nor would they. Not ever.

What were their separate fates? Her own she felt she knew. If she avoided being sent back to Goa in disgrace, the whole of her working life would be spent in this burning place. Her mother, in her letters, was already suggesting that she marry, and she'd soon find her a potential husband via connections at home. The boy would be sent here to work and to marry Emmanuella, or a boy would be found among those already in the country. Everyone at home had a son or a daughter, niece, nephew, goddaughter, friend, toiling somewhere in the Gulf, and the wedding network included them as if they were still in Goa.

Emmanuella and this boy—she could picture no face, imagine no form or flesh—would marry and live apart, perhaps for years, he in some other villa, as a chauffeur or a houseboy, until they

71

could manage to find employment together, if they could ever do so. If he was talented, he might find a lowly profession that would allow them a meager place of their own, and they might raise a family. Keeping that vision alive in her mind took more energy than she could manage. The grimmer one took its place as a likelier forecast of the future. He'd live somewhere in a communal apartment for men, and she'd stay for decades in a huge, marble box like this one, doing the endless work of her life until she was old and cruel like Succoreen.

She tried to imagine the boy, her future husband. It astonished her to realize that he existed somewhere even at this moment, whoever he was, alive and breathing, young and tender—blissfully ignorant of this future as her husband. Once they were wed, they'd meet on Sundays at church and for a few weeks of leave every two years. Even in Goa, on those rare, precious trips, they wouldn't be left to themselves. Their friends and family, even neighbors they barely knew, would expect lavish gifts, as if the young couple had come back rich from some sort of paradise. *Where are our presents? Our lychees, cloves, cinnamon? Where's our chocolate?*

She saw an image in the glass, a haggard thing staring at her: narrow, round-shouldered and absolutely still; the eyes deep-set and staring, a skull's.

Her own face. She took a startled step backward, banishing the illusion. God had called up this skeleton, shocking her from her reverie in which she mourned a future as a wife and a mother. Shameful. She could have shared Santana's fate.

She must act. As penance. She mimed to the girl: I'll bring you food.

The girl lifted a hand to shade her eyes from the blinding sky. Now? In daylight?

Yes, yes. Now.

Emmanuella whirled toward the refrigerator, that great box of benevolence, that keeper of plenty. She pulled the wide door open, spilling a river of cold at her feet, her mind scanning back to her bleak image in the glass. Mongrel dog. Plucked chicken. She reached for a block of cheese, a sausage half-gone. This image, perhaps, had been a message from God. If so, she'd reacted to it unworthily, with vanity rather than grace, scorning her own face, which had also been God's gift.

She took a whole round of flatbread. Four bananas lay in the fruit bowl. She took one. Another. Four breakfast bars, a packet of tiny, powdered doughnuts, and a clean trash bag from the box in the drawer. All went into the bag and the bag went into the front pocket of her housedress. She patted the pocket as flat as it would go and glared up at the ceiling, defiant. The Grandmother loomed up there, biding her time until she was able to catch Emmanuella outright in another blameworthy act that would justify shipping her back to Goa empty-handed. Such as this.

Dread turned her limbs heavy, but she wouldn't let cowardice defeat her. God had sent her an image in the glass.

Clutching the gaping pocket against her belly, she opened the kitchen door onto the terrace between the houses, letting in a blast of heat, and stepped outside. The girl backed away from the fence, sweeping madly toward the barred first-floor windows of her villa. Emmanuella turned from her, eyeing the *mulhaq*, inventorying the men who lived there, ticking off their probable whereabouts. Rafiq had driven Ma'am to the Sultan Center in Salmiya for groceries, and the lazy gardener Brazio would be fast asleep, lying in a wrinkled heap on his cot. That left Frederick, the Grandmother's driver, and he was likely to be in the *mulhaq* at this time of day as well, though probably not asleep. He'd be smoking or reading the paper without much interest. Gallant, slippery Frederick, who had passed up his home-leave to the Philippines twice in a row though he had a wife and three children in Manila. For Emmanuella this was enough to earn her distrust, but rumors were that he loaned money and charged high rates, even to other Filipinos, a shocking disloyalty. Here, each nationality banded together in a strong community; they had no one else to depend upon, no influence, few laws to protect them, almost no money, and embassies that did little but promote them as cheap labor. Yet Frederick identified with no one, shared allegiance with no one. He never attended church either, though he wore a filigreed gold cross at his throat. It was this hypocrisy that needled Emmanuella the most. She wanted nothing to do with him.

To Santana she spoke softly in Konkani. "I don't have much."

The girl's words rushed together in her panic. "Anything. I'll starve here. They'll let me starve. He lives upstairs now, and she downstairs only. They scream at me but never talk to each other. He tells me his wife must give me food, not he. She says it's his job. He won't divorce her because she wants divorce and he'll give her only what she doesn't want. What will I do?"

Emmanuella angled slowly toward the street where the dumpsters awaited their daily pickup. The *mulhaq* didn't have windows at the street end. She'd make the transfer there. She thought the girl might grab at her through the fence.

"Sir says he'll lock me in the house. He says I can't be trusted."

Emmanuella passed the bag quickly to her through the open railings of the fence. The girl snatched it, seizing Emmanuella's hand as well, and holding it so tightly that Emmanuella winced in pain.

"He closed my AC. He says a donkey doesn't need cool air. He says I cost too much money, I eat too much. For breakfast they give one cup of tea and a roll. For lunch, a cup of rice. For dinner, they both forget."

"They don't forget."

"He prays and prays, more than five times a day."

"Then he knows he's evil," said Emmanuella.

Santana thrust an elbow out. "Look. The wife burned me with the iron, the hot iron." A blistering triangle on her upper arm mirrored the iron faithfully, a portrait in branded flesh. "She pulled it from the wall and ran for me, roaring, because I didn't finish a blouse properly."

A darker undertow of apprehension hit Emmanuella. Was the man raping her? It would explain the wife's brutality. She'd be jealous of such a beautiful housemaid and aware of every look her husband cast in Santana's direction. If he took Santana to his bed, the wife would feel no bars to vengeance.

"Santana, does he . . . touch you?"

The girl's eye's sharpened. She said nothing, but her bitter silence gave Emmanuella all the answer she required.

"God help us," Emmanuella murmured.

The girl answered with scorn. "God."

They were taking too long, talking too much. Someone would notice.

"They say I must become a Muslim," Santana said. "If I become a Muslim they'll give me money for leave to visit my family."

"You can't listen to this. They have to send you home to see your family. It's the law, their own law."

A tear welled. "My mother is sick. If I become a Muslim they'll let me go to her."

"How can you believe them when they starve you?"

"They say he's the same as our God, the same God."

"They say." She wanted to scream at the girl. "Where's your food? How do they care for you? Think what this man does. This is what speaks."

A faint squeak of dry metal from the door of the *mulhaq*. Both girls heard it. Emmanuella's hand flew to her lips. Her eyes met the girl's briefly as Santana scrambled backwards, dropping her broom.

Frederick had slipped through the door. He stood before them, shading his eyes against the sun. Sly, quick-eyed Frederick, with his slow, suggestive smile.

Pushing his black hair from his eyes he bent to give them a mocking bow. "Ladies. How nice to see you."

THE GRAIN OF THE WOOD

Theo turned into a sandlot to park. This was the right building as far as he could tell, although it lacked an address. Through the eddies of dust on his windshield he saw a decaying cement block-house in a warren of buildings just like it, an expanse of mean existence that looked as though it had been lightly shelled during the war and forgotten. Trash lined every windward wall. A single *sidr* tree, lean and staggering, rose up out of the earth to offer a pittance of shade, its leaves jaundiced with dust.

As he got out of his car, the guard for the building, armed with a push broom and dressed in a tattered gray *salwar kurta*, met him warily at the low wall of crumbling tile that surrounded the property, his dark moustache curled down in a scowl. The broom couldn't have been put to much use lately.

An obligatory greeting. *"Salaam al leikum."*

Theo closed the door and let his hands drop to his sides. *"Al leikum salaam."*

"You come Arabic lesson with lady?"

"Yes."

The man's unfriendly scrutiny deepened. A lined face, a flat-footed stoop. In the U.S., he'd be fifty. Here, given his experiences in the clinic, Theo judged him thirty-five.

"Go." He flapped a hand at Theo's car so there'd be no confusion about where. "You go now."

An order or a suggestion? Theo tapped the face of his watch. "I have an appointment."

The man advanced slowly on stiffened knees as though Theo might be a land mine. Except for his black and wary eyes, he looked made of dust. *"Shu ismak?"*

Theo knew this much. "Theo. I'm glad to meet you."

The man blinked at this alien lisp of a name. "Theo?"

"Yes. Theo."

This flummoxed the man for a moment. Then, seeming to decide that this was a matter requiring sympathy, he held out a hand. "Abdullah my name." He pronounced it slowly for Theo's edification. "Ub-dull-luh. I from Cairo. You go this lady, learn Arabic?" He indicated the crumbling house with a tilt of the head. "This lady, sir. She no good teach Arabic." He made a poisonous face. "She Palestine."

"Abdullaaah!" A woman's voice, powerful as a trumpet.

Abdullah drew back, cringing, his push-broom head-up before him like a useless umbrella, as a torrent of Arabic fell on their heads from a window of the building.

"She!" he said to Theo under the barrage, which broke now into English.

A young woman with long, black hair leaned far out over a sill on the second floor. "Ignore this stupid man," she called to Theo. "He wants you to tip him. You're Mr. Girard? I am Hanaan, your teacher. Come up."

Theo gaped. On the phone she'd sounded dry, brisk, aloof, leading him to expect a Kuwaiti schoolmarm swathed head-to-toe in black.

Abdullah gave Theo a warning flick of the eyes. In the corner apartment on Hanaan's floor, an older, beak-nosed woman in a scarf was throwing open a window to investigate the noise. Spying Hanaan, she screeched out an indictment, jabbing a finger at every phrase. Hanaan joined the fight with eager acrimony, flinging back what sounded to Theo like insults of the blackest hue. The old woman leaned over the sill to pitch her voice with more energy, throwing out an acid bath of abuse—*You and your little dog too!*—then abruptly withdrew and whammed her window shut.

Hanaan recovered in an instant. This was old hat, apparently. She smiled down upon Theo's head, a font of benevolence, her black hair flowing.

"Come up, come up," she said, her voice now melodious. "We must begin."

Theo made his way slowly up the uneven steps to the second floor, surmising as he went. The old woman had given Hanaan hell for taking male students into her apartment while otherwise alone, little doubt about that. Given her youth and obvious beauty, it surprised him too. Even in his old laissez-faire apartment building back home she'd earn some huffy indignation from the neighbors if she hallooed men in the street from an open window. Here, knowing what little he knew about the culture, it seemed downright dangerous.

Sunk in thought and a newborn doubt about his instructor upstairs, he ran headlong into an overhang at the landing. It came only to his shoulder, an architectural absurdity that nearly cleaved his skull.

When Hanaan opened her door she found him bleeding, hand to brow. "What's happened to you?" Her eyes shot over his shoulder, "It's this Abdullah. He's hurt you!" and tried to charge past him in pursuit.

"No. I ran into a chunk of concrete, the underside of the stairs going up to the next floor. Your builder apparently didn't plan for anyone more than five and a half feet tall."

Expecting some degree of solicitude he got instead a cool and measured gaze from Hanaan. Without a word she waved him into her flat, closed the door behind him, and disappeared down a short, tiled hallway into the darkness beyond. Trailed at a cautious distance by two well-upholstered cats, she came back with cotton swabs and a bottle of antiseptic, which she plunked into his hands.

"You speak of plans," she said, settling her arms across her chest. "Many glorious things in the Arab world have been built with no planning. Muslims allow God to design their lives, not human beings. You Americans want everything according to plan, a plan you make. But the plan is God's."

Theo felt a droplet of blood oozing between his thumb and forefinger. "I'm sorry. You'll have to show me to the bathroom. I can't see what I'm doing."

Perceiving then the awkward task she'd thrust on him of holding the bottle, pushing his hair aside, and daubing the wound all at once, she took the cotton swab from him brusquely, "I'll do this," and tended it herself with a gentleness her tone didn't predict. She went on with her lecture.

"The great seagoing *dhows* of our history carried thirty pearl-divers." It might have been a thousand such was her pride. She sloshed more antiseptic onto a fresh swab and turned him toward the wan light of the small living room, giving Theo an impression of cement walls and battered furniture under a low ceiling. "We built these boats hour by hour, with great love."

She was standing so close as she pressed the swab to his brow that he could see glints of light in her dark eyes, and the deep soul of the pupil, wide with concentration. "The master shipbuilder—we call him *al Ustad*, the professor, the master—let the grain of the wood inspire him. Compare the beauty of such a ship to those gray American monsters like sharks in the Gulf. I wonder, what is there of God in them?"

With this, she looked down from the wound on his forehead and into his eyes, a moment that embarrassed them both. She stepped away, her hand at the delicate cup of her throat. Even now she wasn't wearing a scarf. Her dark hair fell shining across her shoulders, and she wore a dress rather than an *abaya*, simple and modest, but not black, and not entirely shapeless. Through the constrained grace of her movements he saw a slender voluptuousness.

He nodded. "From now on I'll think of this building as a great *dhow*," he said, which won him a fleeting smile.

"Your neighbor," he said, thinking she would launch an immediate explanation. But she shrugged, waiting for more.

"She's . . . noisy."

"Nosey is the correct word," Hanaan said, dismissing the topic. "I call her the old goat."

They sat at a battered folding table set up near the window, loaded with newspapers and books in Arabic, French, and English. Her fit of pique had dissipated without a trace. She asked about his work, how long he'd stay in the country. He didn't know. He'd go back to practice in the U.S. but he didn't know when or where. He surprised himself by telling her that he'd felt rootless for a long time, and more so since his father died.

"I'm sorry your father is dead," she told him quietly. "I love my father very much. He's worked very hard for his children, all his life. You see, we are withouts."

He waited for this to make sense to him.

"A without," she said. "A *bidoon*. A stateless person. That is what we're called."

"*Beduin*, you mean?"

"No, no. *Beduin* is the plural of *Bedu*, the desert people, a tribal people. *Bidoon* means 'without.' You'll learn this in your lessons: coffee without sugar: *qahwa bidoon sukkar.*"

He'd assumed that she was a native, but her family was Palestinian, she'd said, not Kuwaiti, and everyone who lived here knew the difference. She'd been born in Kuwait, but this didn't make her a citizen. Her father, an immigrant in the sixties, and a proud man of mixed Palestinian and Syrian blood, had arrived after oil changed the fortunes of the region and the Kuwaitis had closed all doors to naturalization, securing the largesse for the lucky few. Accorded almost none of the rights and benefits of sanctioned citizens, denied even the state-supported health care given to workers from non-Islamic countries, a *bidoon* was an official nobody.

"We're very low class here," she said. "They think of us as stray animals, especially since the war. No one wants to own us."

"Someone else mentioned this to me, something about the Palestinians," Theo said, trying to recall it. "The husband of my real estate agent, Jane Scarborough."

"Jane and Hamid? But I know them! Jane sends me clients from time to time. Hamid is a distant cousin of my father's."

Another cat, this one long-haired and elegant, a Persian— how many cats were there?—leaped onto the table and with great purposefulness sat down directly in front of Theo, tail flicking, its snub-nose giving it an expression of mild, persistent disgust. Theo didn't touch it.

"Have you thought of leaving?"

She looked as if she'd gone blank on the meaning of the word.

"Going someplace else. To another country."

"But this is my home. My family is here." There was stiff offense in her voice again. "Or do you mean that all of us should go?"

What a volatile woman. "I meant for a job. Like me coming here."

"But I have a job. I will teach you Arabic."

"I meant at a university, for instance. Dr. Chowdhury called you a linguist. You have to be well-qualified or he wouldn't have recommended you. He's not easily impressed."

"Ah." She shrugged off this compliment but her tone gentled. "I did teach at the university here. Until the war. But I wouldn't work for an Iraqi and so I stopped my job then. After the war, I couldn't get it back. It's my Palestinian blood, you see. That fool Arafat supported Saddam. All *bidoons*, since the war, have even more troubles than before. The Kuwaitis don't trust us."

She rose from her chair and strode restlessly away from the little table. "The university isn't a good place anyway. Not anymore. My department is run by the Egyptians. It's like in Italy. You know this thing they call the Mafia, *la cosa nostra?* It's the same with Egyptians there. Egyptians for Egyptians, and everyone else is in danger. They can't even speak their own language. Like Abdullah outside." She shut her eyes against the thought of him. "That's why I was rude to you, because I'm angry with him."

This was probably as close as she ever came to an apology. He didn't need one.

"Anger works in this way," she said, "to go in every direction, you cannot control it. If you could hear him speak Arabic! It hurts the brain to listen.—Why are you smiling so?"

"He said the same about you."

"Me? He said the same about me!"

A Sepia Ghost

Ms. Ford, Mariam's teacher at the American School, telephoned in the afternoon, a woman whose pronunciation in English was so odd that Mufeeda could barely follow her. What nationality could she be? Mariam often mimicked her at home, batting her eyelashes, "Now ah want ch'all to git out ch'all's books. Quick, quick." How vividly alien Mariam became in such moments.

But Ms. Ford didn't sound deserving of such mockery on the phone. Her voice was calm, firm, deliberate, and her overall message clear enough. Mariam was showing increasing rebelliousness in class lately. Ms. Ford recited what sounded like a checklist to clarify Mariam's misdeeds for Mufeeda: loud, inattentive, disruptive, and ". . . even sometimes rather lewd."

Lood? Even if Ms. Ford had not said 'loud' in the same sentence, the hard, minor note of this other word told Mufeeda that the problem went beyond noisiness.

A parent-teacher conference must take place immediately, Ms. Ford said, and with both parents in attendance, if for no other reason than to impress Mariam with the seriousness of the situation.

Mufeeda went directly to Saleh's study after the call, working to calm herself. Mariam knew better than to misbehave in the classroom. Babies were expected to make noise, as were very young children, and boys of any age couldn't be prevented. But girls of eleven had their wits about them and were required to keep their voices to themselves.

Closing the door she drew from Saleh's crowded bookshelves a fat dictionary of American English and opened it on his large and polished desk without sitting down. Lood. Lud. Lude. Leud. Lued. Nothing that made any sense, and she could imagine no other spellings, no other likely assortment of those maddening English vowels. Arabic was so much more sensible, and infinitely more lovely. What was the point, beyond the merely pedantic, of writing out every vowel when they meant virtually nothing? They made English spelling into a fully random code, one she couldn't crack.

She stared, unseeing, at the bright windows of the study. Could Ms. Ford have said loob? It was a word all right: The clay or slimes washed from tin ore. She tried all the variations of the vowels. Nothing.

Saleh would know the meaning of this horrible word, of course, but she couldn't make herself pick up the phone to call him. Though she must, she knew. She couldn't schedule a time for the conference without allowing him to check his schedule.

Where would he place the blame for this? Surely it belonged with Mufeeda herself, who had produced a daughter unable to control herself in public. If Saleh didn't come immediately to this conclusion, his mother could be relied upon to supply it.

She closed the book and paced across Saleh's study, automatically checking the surfaces for dust with a fingertip. The servants had a sixth sense and grew instantly negligent if Mufeeda relaxed her oversight—except for Emmanuella, who had always kept to her own strict standards. Until recently.

She brushed the thought aside. Too many worries.

Perhaps it had been loot. T's and d's in English often confused her ear. She flopped the heavy book open again and made her way through the pages. Loot. Goods taken by force. Plunder.

Stealing? She tried to remember: What had Ms. Ford said exactly? She's even rather a loot? She's loot? She searched Saleh's shelves for an English-Arabic dictionary but found none. He wouldn't need one, of course.

She made herself sit down in Saleh's soft and tufted leather chair, though doing so felt vaguely uncomfortable, as if her body were designed only to pace and fret. Again she opened the heavy American tome, and made her way to P.

Plunder. To rob. To take by force. Mariam was a thief.

By God, she remembered this word now. The Western press had used it in talking about what the Iraqis stole from Kuwait, nearly everything, including the contents of its glorious national museum. Loot.

A thief for a daughter. What had happened to her intentions to raise her daughters well?—to become thoughtful, gentle, reflective, intelligent women, assets to themselves and to the families that chose to accept them as daughters-in-law? Instead, the American School was raising her daughters—and they were turning into Americans.

She thought of the satellite dishes bolted to the roof of the villa, one of the constant sources of contagion Saleh invited into the home. Television, Mariam's radio blaring American music, this wide world web thing, and the stupid, stupid cellular contraption. Mariam talked endlessly to her American School friends, almost always in English. Mufeeda had seen some of her little schoolgirl notes to her friends, including the Kuwaitis. All in English too. *Only kids who don't know English write in Arabic, Mother.* Mufeeda reminded her that this was an Arabic-speaking nation and got a shrug in response. No wonder the girl could barely form her Arabic letters.

Mufeeda closed the dictionary, firmly. How quickly she justified her own failures. Blame Saleh, blame the West. Blame anyone but herself, the mother of the child. If her children overdosed on evil it was clearly her responsibility to make the home a powerful antidote.

It had been only three months since Mariam's periods had started. Saleh might well say that the hormonal shifts of pubescence were implicated in this episode. But she couldn't agree. Her own periods had begun at virtually the same age and she had never once made a disturbance in her classroom. But Mariam was not anything like the child Mufeeda had been. She'd needed no explanations from Mufeeda when her periods began. The fine

84

mark of womanhood held no mysteries for Mariam. The girls at school kept careful track of such things, as if it were a race; and as for the biological information they had access to— Mufeeda couldn't speculate about its extent without embarrassment. Mariam had forged her deepest bonds with these shallow girls at school, most of whom were daughters of American workers resident in the country for a few years at most. What circle of intimates would Mariam have at Mufeeda's age? To what inner, trusting circle of female hearts would she belong? To an American one, of course, if American women were capable of such things.

Mufeeda sprang to her feet again, unable to sit still. Mariam would go off to university in America and they'd never see her again. She'd marry there too—and how would she ever meet a fine Muslim boy in America? Who could say she'd even look for a Muslim boy? She'd have grown up in a suburb of America, for that's what Kuwait was becoming since the war. Why not live and marry where she most belonged? The two younger girls would follow the same trajectory. This was Saleh's 'excellent education.' He'd always harped on it, never saying outright that Mufeeda hadn't achieved one at the University of Kuwait, but his disdain for the place was clear enough. Of course he'd send his daughters to America. This wasn't news. He'd said so. He'd gone there himself. She couldn't pretend that she hadn't known this. But now Mariam's departure seemed close, imminent, and she would never want to come home.

Mufeeda stopped herself, a finger at her lips as though she had spoken these accusing words aloud to Saleh. She knew what he would say. *But I came home, Mufeeda. Here I am, before you, home.*

Yes, you came home, Saleh. But you're not the same man who left.

A dangerous course, to compare Saleh to his younger self, devout and uncomplicated. She'd let her mind wander wildly from the issue, the call from Ms. Ford, and the need to respond. This problem wasn't so serious. Mariam was still a child, impatient, impudent, sometimes rude, but still malleable, correctible.

85

Her impulsiveness had deep roots, and it was the reason behind this thievery. Nevertheless, it was minor. Mariam had grabbed someone's sweet at lunch, or picked up some cheap token. A necklace, a ring. The whole of her father's family was impulsive. Her grandmother, trip-wired for instant detonation by the most minor of incidents. And then there was Jassim, racing off wild-eyed at the peak of his young manhood to be squashed like an insect by Saddam.

The thought of this true calamity brought back her perspective: No one's life was at stake in Mariam's fifth-grade classroom. She picked up the phone. A child had misbehaved, the teacher had alerted the mother. As yet there was no great cause for alarm.

She rang Saleh's clinic. Though his schedule was often altered by the erratic and more important calendars of his pregnant patients, he could usually get away in the afternoon if given enough warning.

A woman answered and surprised Mufeeda by identifying herself as his assistant doctor. Saleh was sometimes assigned an assistant or two, or a student in training, but never before had it been a woman. How cool she sounded. An elegant Lebanese accent. The Doctor was not in the clinic right now, she told Mufeeda. He'd be gone for an hour or two.

"Where is he?" Mufeeda demanded. The woman said she didn't know. "But then how do you know he'll be gone an hour or two?"

An elastic moment of silence opened between them before Mufeeda hung up and mortification hit. What a fool she'd been to call at a moment when she was already upset. Why had she sounded so stern and suspicious—and why had she hung up? What paranoia. Ridiculous. Saleh could easily have told the woman he'd be gone for an hour or two without revealing his destination. The woman would guess immediately who Mufeeda was—the doctor's brainless wife, of course—and that Saleh had not told her about his new assistant. Mufeeda could imagine her little smirk as she explored the reasons why Saleh might have kept such information from his wife.

She was up, out the door, and down the hallway, walking as if she were late for an urgent appointment in her own house. How absurd she was, and what a disaster the day had become. Gloria had come crying to her in the morning, asking to be sent home to Manila; and Emmanuella had gone silent as a stone, hunching at the counters in the kitchen as if expecting a blow. What was the matter with the girl? She'd lied that night on the stairs: there had been no raw lamb in the refrigerator; Mufeeda had checked. A disturbing string of events had come upon her, she realized—starting with Fatma and her worthless husband.

She took the stairs two at a time, heedless of any maid who might witness her undignified pace. Why hadn't Saleh mentioned this woman he worked with? How long had she been his assistant? How long would she remain?

In her room, she closed the door and rested against it, breathing hard from her ascent. Before her was the satin-quilted bed she shared with Saleh. Could it be right—could it be truly appropriate—for a man and a woman, whatever their professional training, to discuss the human body together, to examine the female body in the way that gynecologists must?

She couldn't phone his office again. Impossible. But she could leave a message on his cell phone. He didn't answer it unless he was away from the hospital, but he'd pick up the message, she knew.

"Saleh, you must call Mariam's teacher." She left the number, calmly. "I'm sorry: I can't understand her English, so you must call. She wants to meet with us. Mariam is a loot or she looted, or something terrible like this. Perhaps you'll tell me when you come home tonight."

IT WAS almost eleven when he arrived, though he'd called earlier to tell her that two of his patients were in labor and that he'd talked to Ms. Ford. "I'll tell you later." Lightly, as though nothing serious had been communicated to him.

Reading her Quran in bed two stories above, Mufeeda felt the abrupt change in air pressure as he opened and closed the narrow side door that led to the carports. Another dust storm had risen in the evening, bringing darkness down early in the form of a sepia ghost sweeping in from the west. Now it shifted in rapid fluctuations as if it wanted in, throwing muscles of grit against the bulk of the house.

She got out of bed and wrapped herself in the long terry robe Saleh had bought for her in London, a soft fall of fabric in brilliant white, and touched her dark hair before the mirror, clearing it from her brow. The pinched and watchful expression she saw there couldn't be brushed away. She tried to blame it on Mariam, but knew that even if Saleh told her that all was well, the watchfulness would remain. In truth, she thought mostly of the assistant physician.

God would judge her harshly for these suspicions. Against her will, she'd nursed them these last hours, fragile little things of a few syllables, into a vivid parallel life for Saleh. She'd never before questioned his devotion, nor had he done anything to warrant it now. She'd been telling herself this firmly all evening. The sin was hers, a failing of her own trust, brought on by Fatma's disintegrating marriage. Saleh deserved only her most complete and unquestioning love, which—she looked intensely into her own eyes in the mirror—banishing all doubts from her mind, she would give him. She had read the verse tonight:

Whoever works righteousness, man or woman, and has Faith, verily, to him will We give a life that is good and pure, and We will bestow on such their reward according to the best of their actions.

To the best of their actions. Mufeeda whispered the words aloud. And what of their thoughts?—for one could behave faultlessly and still have a head full of forbidden imaginings. Her mother had taught her well on this point. The control of one's thoughts was the most important of actions—conscious, deliberate, a constant struggle that must be won. She knew how it was to be effected: with prayer, constant and sincere, and deep repentance for the thoughts that had gone astray.

Saleh didn't come up immediately. He'd be in the kitchen making himself a snack. He'd have missed dinner to deliver the babies. She almost always joined him to sit at the counter snacking on leftovers, talking over the events of the day, hearing about the birth that kept him late. He'd never quite succumbed to seeing deliveries as routine. "How beautiful this child was, Mufeeda, a new light in the world." He'd said it a hundred times. However delayed he was, she struggled to stay awake in order to sit beside him in these late hours, when they could be alone and the house was silent. But tonight she hesitated to go. The kitchen was lit by banks of bright fluorescents, and she looked her age in harsh light, another thing she'd never worried about before.

She thought again of the assistant. *He'll be back in an hour or two.* The tone of it. Assertive. Condescending.

She sank onto the edge of her armchair and drew her Quran into her lap, listening, a pale hand on the soft vellum of its pages. She should go to him. He'd be wondering why she didn't come. But why had he kept this secret? His silence on so notable a topic was surely suspect.

Where are your thoughts, Mufeeda?

Her mother's voice, a whisper of love and gentle insistence. Always there. She returned to her Quran, unsure where she'd left off, and reread a verse from earlier in the evening.

If Allah so willed, He could make you all one People: But He leaves straying whom He pleases: but ye shall certainly be called to account for all your actions.

How much the book spoke to her. Had Saleh strayed? She cautioned herself: Satan could speak through the medium of these words too. Where are your thoughts, Mufeeda? Straying.

Saleh came in quietly, catching her with a hand at her heart. The low light of the room hollowed his eyes, revealing his exhaustion. Perhaps it sculpted her own features in the same way, throwing the lines of her face into relief. She was older than any doctor in training.

"I've disturbed you."

"No." She lay her hand on the pages again.

"Keep reading. Read aloud to me. You read so beautifully."

But she closed the book, gently. "May I later?"

"Of course." He slumped into the softness of the bed, rubbing at his eyes with a knuckle like a small boy. "There wasn't much to eat in the kitchen."

"Not much to eat? I left you a dish from dinner. Emmanuella made *dosa* with potatoes and onions." It was one of his favorites.

"Where did you put it?"

He often played blind in the kitchen to preserve his role as a stranger there. "Covered with cling wrap in the refrigerator."

Amusement came into his eyes. "Ah. That large silver box against the wall?"

"Yes. You have to open the doors to see inside."

He worked to untie a shoe. Glancing at her, the amusement sank away. "About Mariam, Mufeeda. I know you're worried about this."

And he wasn't? "Of course," she said; and realizing how grim she sounded, she added more lightly, "You always see into my heart. You know me too well, I think."

He sounded the same as always: wry and gently romantic. "I'll never know you too well."

Her heart opened. There was nothing in his demeanor to concern her. "Am I so mysterious?"

"Unfathomable."

His expression shifted gently to concern. She laid her Quran on the table and folded her hands before her.

"There's been a small misunderstanding. I spoke with the teacher. The woman's English is unbelievable, you were right. She used a word that, in English, means something quite different from the word you heard."

Mufeeda felt the pull of both anxiety and relief. "I misunderstood her, then."

"With the greatest reason. Who was to know what this woman was saying?"

"Tell me."

90

"Mariam——." He hesitated, uncertain how to phrase it. She'd seen this in Saleh many times, a pursuit of words defused of all explosive potential. With his mother, she admired this; when he edited so deeply with her she grew suspicious. "Mariam has become somewhat interested in boys," he said.

"Oh, Saleh——"

He raised a hand, conceding to her; the facts would follow. "She allowed an American boy to kiss her."

"What!"

"On the cheek, Mufeeda."

"But this is terrible. My God, I thought she'd stolen something. A pencil, a schoolgirl's note."

"A boy stole a kiss."

"She gave it to him. There's no looting involved."

Saleh turned his head to hide a smile, she was sure of it; but when he looked at her again she couldn't be certain.

"It is a grave thing," he said. "But she's very young and can be corrected. I'll talk to her myself."

She didn't believe he thought the offense a grave one. Yet how couldn't he? Did this American teacher have a more reliable sense of propriety than Saleh?

"Now," Saleh said. "Let's move on to other things."

Though his briskness offended her, she sought to hide it.

"There's something else," he said, watching her.

Yes, there was. Why hadn't he told her of his new assistant?

"What is it?" Saleh prompted, gentle once more.

But she couldn't ask the question of him. "It's a small matter, a household matter," she said. "Gloria has asked for money to return home for a time."

He let the shoe fall to the thick carpet. "Gloria, again. You said no."

Mufeeda hesitated. "I told her nothing final."

The sock came off. "Nothing final. You said yes, then."

"It's serious this time, Saleh. Her daughter was attacked by a gang of men. They broke into Gloria's house in Manila."

Saleh raised an eyebrow. It was a dramatic story. Servants never told any other kind.

"Saleh, they did something terrible to her daughter, and it seems they fractured her skull in doing it."

A sigh. "You believe her, then."

"Yes. I talked with her a long while. She cried and cried."

He rubbed his face. "She turns tears on with a switch. She cries every time I say a word to her."

Mufeeda risked needling him now. "That's because you say so few and only when you're displeased."

"Then I'll be displeased more often so that she gets used to it."

Said with his usual self-mockery. Her fears about the assistant flew from her. She sat beside him on the bed.

"You will not. You're not capable of such displeasure."

He ran a finger along the moon of her cheek. "Not with you."

"Please, then, Saleh. Send her home. For one month. That way she'll be back quickly and we won't be shorthanded for Ramadan."

His hand dropped. "She's taking advantage of you, Mufeeda. I've lost track of her dire emergencies."

He thought her overly dramatic, but she wouldn't relent. "She has daughters, Saleh. Like our daughters. I think of that."

"But this is how they succeed in manipulating you. You're wax in the sun."

She took his hand in her own, head down, and said nothing for a moment. She had to move carefully here.

"If I'm changed by a feeling of tenderness, is this a bad thing?" She looked up at him. "My heart is touched for her, Saleh."

He closed his eyes as a smile grew. He was defeated.

"Of course, Mufeeda. Of course she'll go. And I'll pay for it all. But no more charity cases. We'll earn a reputation with the servants and we'll have a three-act tragedy every day."

On the narrow balcony outside their bedroom something scooted and rolled in the grinding wind. A pot of mums, she realized. She'd forgotten to water it.

"How many times has Gloria's mother died?" Saleh asked.

"Twice," she said, laughing, but her mind remained focused on the sound. Saleh hadn't heard it; men never heard such small sounds as mothers did, attuned as they were to the quietest murmurings of their children from afar.

"What a remarkable family Gloria's is," Saleh was saying. "A boon to medical research. It's no wonder they celebrate resurrection."

A Burglar

Kɪᴛ's ɴᴇᴡ life began to settle into a routine, and some of her early shyness left her. Up early, a quick breakfast with Jack, then another breakfast, much less quick, with the kids. She did the dishes, made the beds, started the inevitable load of laundry. Just like life in America—until sometime after eight when the door-bell started to ring. There was nothing bell-like about this door-bell and nothing comfortingly familiar about the street peddlers who showed up several times a day to ring it. The kids got rapidly used to the game-show buzz of the bell, but it could still make Kit slosh her coffee. It was a perfect acoustic portrait of edginess, she thought, elbowing its way through every floor and wall of the echoing house.

She wasn't jumping as far as she used to at least. This was progress, however small, an item worthy of note since she hadn't made much in any other realm. She hadn't even managed to stake much of a claim in the house. The few sticks of furniture they'd brought from home were scattered across the two main stories like mile markers in an otherwise empty landscape. The downstairs living room—there was another slightly smaller one upstairs—was a Grand Canyon moved indoors. The children liked to scream into the void to hear the echoes. Tessa had told her that the houses were big here because you couldn't spend much time outdoors. Kit found herself admiring Tessa. She and her husband and three children had spent two tours overseas and still wanted more. "So think of one of your living rooms as a backyard and let the kids have it for their own." Excellent advice. A corral for all the noise and mess. Kit had enforced it immediately. The upstairs living room became the children's, the downstairs would be hers.

Kit had also asked Tessa for advice on the street vendors. Kit dreaded their visits, didn't know what to do or how to handle these poor, miserable men dressed in sweat-soaked rags and turbans. They pushed heavy medieval carts from door to door every day. She wanted nothing they sold, not the strange Indian soft drinks or the greasy snack foods that burned your digestive tract from end to end, nor even the couple of American soft drinks they hauled around. She could buy those at the Sultan Center, a clean and glossy American-style supermarket not far from home, ensuring that she'd never have to buy anything from these men.

Tessa's advice was simple enough: Say no. *'La'* in Arabic. "You don't need to go to the door. Say it once, say it firmly, and go off the air."

Easy for Tessa to say. She had a strong, vibrant voice, and she could invest that single, musical syllable with great authority: you could tell it meant no. Kit's *'la'* sounded more like 'maybe' even to her own ears, and it only convinced the peddlers that they should ring the bell two or three times more. She couldn't win. If she refused in her shyness even to talk to them via the intercom, they buzzed the door for minutes at a time, refusing to believe she wasn't home—everyone else had a maid to answer the door, after all; and if she answered, they poured Arabic deafeningly into her ear, *"Bebseesefenab!"* leaving her so befuddled that one day early on she'd yelled back, "But I don't speak English!" and slammed the receiver down.

She knew what Jack would say to all this if she told him: "Hire a maid, Kit."

She wouldn't tell him. Her timidity embarrassed her. Her fear of the men embarrassed her. Sometimes, she watched them from the upstairs living room after they'd finally turned from her gate. You had to be desperate to live such a life—wheeling carts from door to door all year long in a climate like this. The windows were mirrored against the sun, offering her invisibility and a view of their grimy, mustached faces, empty of all but the bleak necessity of pulling the cart from this house to the next.

SHE FOUND herself studying the villa as she went about her daily duties. In some ways the house was quite ordinary. Shrunken down by half it would have fit in an American suburb, a house hazily inspired by plantations, with Greek columns and a blinding white exterior. Carpeting covered the floors in both living rooms; the walls were painted a bland bone-white; windows and doors were of the usual size and operated normally. But the house also had notable eccentricities. Both kitchens had a large dishwasher, an enormous double-doored Cadillac of a refrigerator, and a tiny, built-in washer-dryer combination machine that Kit could never have imagined—meant especially for dishtowels. She could hear her mother's laughter at the news of it—if only she were still within reach of a letter. *An itty-bitty little tub only for my dishrags! Oh, Kittie, how interesting!*

But then, after all this over-the-top extravagance, the cabinetry in the kitchens was fashioned from sheets of thin, ugly gray metal screwed together so poorly that the sharp edges would cut you like a razor blade. The stoves each had six burners and two ovens, but they were fuelled by gas canisters like the ones used for barbeques back home. They had to be lit, every burner and oven, with a match. Even odder, both refrigerators had built-in locks. The landlord had left keys tied to each of the handles.

The wiring was capricious. The downstairs refrigerator had confused itself with the storage closet under the stairs, so that when you turned the closet light off, the refrigerator read this as a cue and retired as well. Jack, whose engineer's brain was constructed without a single crossed wire, had needed several demonstrations to believe that the closet and the refrigerator could have anything to do with one another outside of Kit's imagination. Maybe a person could be too well trained, Kit thought, watching him frown his elaborate, whole-face frown that really

96

meant business, and take over the switch from her like it was the control panel in a nuclear power plant. He flipped it half a dozen times, the refrigerator alternately sighing and rousing; and Kit thought how odd they'd look to any neighbor—if any neighbor could see them through the six-foot wall around the house—as they stood in the closet together in the dark and the light, looking grave. *What do you think, Mostafa, is it some kind of religious ceremony?*

Jack arranged for an electrician to come the next day, a sky-scraper of a black man who announced he was Sudanese. He couldn't understand Kit's complaint. Jack, of course, was at one of his construction sites at the time. Standing kindly aside so that Kit could see how it was done, the man turned the closet light on with delicate fingertips and cocked his head thoughtfully toward the instant hum in the kitchen. "Leave light open, madam. No problem." And he was gone.

The most intriguing parts of the house by far were those not meant for the family. The third floor, built for a staff of housekeepers, was more Spartan than Kit's old dorm room at Southwest-Central Methodist, and it was hard to top the Methodists in a precise identification of the bare necessities. It was divided into four cells with unpainted cement block walls. Each had one insignificant window, and this was blocked by a rusted air-conditioning unit, though the rest of the house was cooled by two enormous compressors parked up on the roof like a couple of SUVs. Which meant, Kit realized, that the designers of this house had considered air-conditioning for the servants as optional. The rooms had no built-in vents.

The men of the household staff were apparently exiled alto-gether. Built into the marble wall alongside the house were their quarters, a long narrow, one-story cement-block structure that looked for all the world like an Oklahoma single-wide turned to stone. The landlord had told Jack that it was called a *mulhaq*, an old word that meant carriage house or stable. It had four barren rooms under a low ceiling. They opened into the narrow, oven-like passage between the *mulhaq* and the villa. Two of the rooms were bare; one was fitted out with a battered laundry sink on spindly legs; and the fourth was a god-awful bathroom. Every window was barred.

Kit pulled another load of laundry from the mouth of the machine. At least the washer and dryer here were exactly what she was used to. Some of the company families had been supplied with European-style front-load washers, which the wives cordially despised and complained about endlessly. *I ask you, how can anyone expect to get clothes clean without an agitator?*

As she hefted an armload of clean bedding, Kit caught a flash of movement in the garden below. A man stood inside the enclosure, right next to the house. She went utterly still. One week in the house and already there was a burglar outside. She saw him from the back, a lean, dark figure standing just below the window, looking up into the palms—inside the walled grounds of the house—inside the locked gate.

Breathing into the bedclothes, trying to remember Jack's number at the office, knowing he wouldn't be able to do a damn thing about it, Kit remembered—

It's the gardener, you idiot.

Jack had told her that the landlord would supply a gardener to take care of the date palms, and that he'd have a key to the gate. He was a Paki, Jack said.

"A packy?"

Her questions often made Jack impatient. "Pakistan. He's from Pakistan." '

"Does he speak English?"

"How should I know?"

Was it necessary to go meet this guy, or could she just say *'la'* firmly into the intercom if he rang the bell? She didn't know the first thing about date palms, didn't like dates, never had. How could she give him orders, even if he did speak English? She had none to give, and he already knew what to do, presumably, how to take care of the dates, harvest them—and eat them, she hoped. All two hundred pounds' worth.

She had edged close to the window, the bedclothes in her arms, when the man turned around and caught sight of her. Startled, he bounced backward and instantly cut the eye contact.

"Okay, stupid," she told herself aloud. "You have to go down there now or he'll think you're a lunatic."

The kids were both in Carla's bedroom, quiet for once. Kevin sat rapt amidst the pieces of a giant wooden puzzle of a zoo, examining the striped head of a bulbous zebra. Carla lay curled on her bed with the half-dozen Barbie dolls they'd unpacked that morning. All were getting new hairdos after their long and befrazzling trip.

"Carlie. I'm going outside for a minute."

The dolls flew. "Me too!"

"No." Said like her own mother had said no, clipped and final, flat as a smack on the cheek.

Carla put on a pout, lips pushed far forward so her mother couldn't miss it.

"I'll be right back," Kit said, wearied by this exaggeration. "I'll just be in the garden downstairs and I want you to stay here with Kevin."

She made herself march straight downstairs and out the front door. She left the door wide open. Merely a precaution.

The near-noon sun hit her hard in the face, but the air was not as hot as she'd expected. Even in the short time they'd been here the daytime temperatures had begun to fall. Jack had said that by October the kids would be able to play outdoors even in midday.

"Hello?"

The date palms stood in a military row against the enclosure wall at the side of the house. He was gone. The gate was still closed. Had she scared him so much he'd shinnied right over the wall? Or was he lying in wait? Fear arced through her. She took a step backward toward the door.

Then she saw him—saw his head, a mop of dark hair. And a brown face. He was peeking at her from the back of the house half a block away, every bit as leery as she. He'd have had to sprint there to get away from her as she came through the door.

"Hello?"

"Mom?"

"Uh, my name's Kit Ferguson," she called to him. "Are you the gardener?"

He stepped out immediately from behind the house, smiling now as if she were an old friend. "Yes, mom! Hello, mom!"

She walked toward him. He meant ma'am, but he said 'mom' with such warmth that her caution melted.

He strode to meet her, smiling from ear to prominent ear. He couldn't be much younger than she. He stopped well short of her, grinning with such cheerfulness that she found herself smiling too.

"Hello, mom," he said softly, bowing his head.

He didn't offer to shake hands. His own were linked behind his back. He wore loose cotton clothes so old they had yellowed: a long, collarless, open-necked shirt, baggy, featureless trousers, and plastic sandals of the cheapest kind.

"I'm so glad you speak English."

"Only leetle, mom."

"You speak very well." His bowed head went lower. "The landlord sent you? Mr. Khalid?" She wanted to make sure.

His expression dimmed. "Yes, mom. Khalid."

"You work for Mr. Khalid?" She pronounced it as he had, with a soft k.

His slender shoulders drooped. "Yes, mom."

"He said you'd take care of our dates."

She could see him rerunning this sentence in his head.

"The dates," she said, pointing to the trees.

"Ah! Yes, mom."

He regarded the trees with solemn thoughtfulness, stroking his stubbly chin. With a wave he included all five. "Before, too many fruit. Too, too many."

Any number was too many as far as Kit was concerned. But she studied the trees with as much concern as she could muster.

She'd registered them only vaguely before, as huge, spiky plants that were better than no trees at all.

The gardener said, as if in confidence to her. "Khalid, he take many, many fruit." He shot a glance at her to judge the effect of this news. His own disapproval ran deep. "He take before you come." He scooped armfuls of air and mimed taking them toward the gate. "Big, big, many fruit, he take before. All *Barhi* fruit he take, only good fruit. Three hundred kilo." He nodded at the single tree still heavily laden, "This fruit no good. Not *Barhi*."

She assumed a philosophical expression hoping it might disguise her relief that the landlord had taken most of the dates, God bless him.

"I'm Kit," she said. "And your name?"

The smile flared back full-force. "Azhar. My name Azhar."

She tried to filigree the 'r' as he had. "Azhar."

He nodded, bowing his head low again, a hand at his heart, as if it were an honor to be addressed by name. "Yes, mom."

Later, from the upstairs window, she watched him work as he assiduously hand-watered the trees and strode around pulling weeds from the base of their rough trunks. He buzzed the gate as he prepared to leave, and for the first time she didn't mind answering.

"I go, mom."

"Azhar, how often will you come?"

"Eh?"

"You come tomorrow?"

"*Inshallah*, mom. Goodbye, mom!"

Kit smiled. Such exuberance: Goodbye mom! She went down to make sure he'd latched the gate—he had—and felt herself drawn again to the *mulhaq*. Barred windows. Amazing: a miniature prison on the property. She stood inside looking out, aware of the low ceiling, the cement walls. The place was like a kennel. You couldn't even see the date palms from here. Square metal rods barred the cement-block window frame giving a view of the blank, grit-scoured white of the enclosure wall beyond.

Did Azhar live in a place like this?

101

Such a Boy

Frederick was not one to waste a financial opportunity. Seeing Emmanuella alone in the kitchen, he rapped on the window, smug and condescending. She opened it the merest crack and he conveyed his threat in a few words: he would keep silent about her visits with the housemaid next door for the price of Emmanuella's monthly salary. It was a simple proposal: handouts to Santana must be balanced by handouts to Frederick.

She wouldn't look into his evil face. "No. My family will go hungry."

"Oh yes? How did they eat before you came here?"

"You will go away and leave me in peace," she said with a haughtiness she didn't believe herself.

"Will I?"

She closed the window in his face. She'd have to avoid him carefully from now on, a difficult task. As second driver, his daily schedule depended on the whims of the Grandmother, and lately she'd gone out less and less, leaving Frederick on his own. He would sometimes help Brazio with the gardening, but only so long as it pleased him. Every other task he avoided with a skill the other servants both admired and resented. As the Grandmother's servant, he was beyond reprimand by anyone but her.

Emmanuella had expected this extortion. Only the extent of it surprised her, and she didn't believe he was serious. He knew how small her salary was and that she sent almost all of it home to her family in monthly remissions like everyone else. Even Frederick couldn't be so bad that he'd demand more than a small percentage. Like others in this household the life here had made him hard. But in his heart he was still a Christian. None was beyond redemption.

  Her thoughts turned back to her mother's letter, which had arrived yesterday. She'd done little since but pore over it in her mind. The news electrified her: A church acquaintance in Goa had paid a call to Emmanuella's mother to suggest that her son, John, introduce himself to Emmanuella with the possible design of marriage. The boy worked in an office in Kuwait City and had told his mother by letter that he often saw Emmanuella at the Holy Family Cathedral on the Gulf on Sundays, and remembered seeing her at church back home.

  She could hardly entertain this thought, that a young man from home had gazed upon her at church and made such plans. And without her knowledge. Time and time again. She clamped a hand over her mouth to keep her laughter in. What kind of boy could he be?

  Emmanuella's mother didn't say that he'd been struck by love at this vision, for of course such nonsense couldn't be believed. The fact that the families knew of one another, went to the same church at home, and both had children of marriageable age in Kuwait, formed the practical basis of the proposal from the boy's mother.

  Emmanuella's mother obviously approved. She'd enclosed a photograph of the boy, one he'd no doubt sent to his mother from Kuwait. It showed a lean, round-shouldered, bucktoothed boy in a white shirt, broad tie, and too-short pants posed with pride in front of some kind of office machinery. Emmanuella couldn't identify the machine but it looked vaguely like a larger version of the copy machine Sir had in his library. Whatever the machine's purpose, she clearly recognized the boy's: to impress those at home with his newfound wealth and importance, though his salary would be, like hers, a pittance. She'd seen such boys in Goa before she came here, home on leave from their menial jobs in the Middle East, pretending to great significance in mysterious occupations far away, a pretense everyone on leave helped

103

to promote, for who could bear to tell their families the truth when the job had to be done regardless of the cost it exacted?

That cost could be kept quiet while the salaries traveled home reliably by wire, becoming rice, curry, fabric, soap, shoes, dresses, pants; and for Emmanuella's mother, a tiny, indescribably beautiful washing machine kept like a shrine in the main room of the family house, dusted daily and decorated with a bit of silk piecework Emmanuella's mother had made as a young woman. Emmanuella's mother had sent a photograph of that too, showing herself and Emmanuella's sisters and little brother grouped around it, smiling into a neighbor's new camera—another gift from another child abroad. How happy they looked. Emmanuella held the photograph close, examining all their faces. Her little brother had grown, but as usual he stood as close to their mother as he could get, with his hand in one of her pockets. He'd done this to Emmanuella too. Tears spilled to her chin. He looked almost fat now, so well was he fed. She'd done this for them.

At home, Emmanuella too would be silent about her job, like this John, whose face she thought was not a bad one. The responsibilities of men made them grave, or so such a boy would imagine. His innocence touched her, his willingness to marry because he knew his mother wished it, his determination to lift the hearts of his family at home with this photograph, assuring them of his success and well-being, granting to his mother the great pleasure of bragging about her son to her friends, who would exclaim over the boy's new clothes and excellent shoes—and determine that their sons too should go to the Middle East.

HALF AND HALF

Azhar planted a garden as the weather cooled. A remarkable young man, Azhar, Kit thought, glancing out at him as he watered his precious, healthy charges in the enclosure below. "Arab, he plant here," he'd told her, indicating the shady ground at the foot of the date palms. "Many, many year. Long, long time. Father and grandfather and his grandfather and his grandfather and his grandfather," he said, sweeping a hand out to represent the deep past, beyond imagining. "Many, many good food."

It had become her practice to take him a plastic glass and a gallon pitcher filled with ice water when he came. She readied it in the upstairs kitchen, adding lots of ice. Sometimes she set a few cookies on a napkin as well, or some brownies or a piece of cake, all of which he invariably told her, "Taste ferry good, mom." Today she had day-old snicker doodles.

She'd liked watching him prepare for planting. Even the direct sun hadn't kept her away as he prepared the beds with peat moss and gently turned the sandy soil over and over with a trowel, blending and breaking up the weedy clods. He brought seeds harvested from the landlord's garden in the last growing season, a pinch or two twisted neatly up in bits of newspaper. Though he knew none of the English names he said they were all "beautiful flower"; and when she brought out a gardening guide, he sat down in delight and quickly matched his seeds with the photographs of marigolds, cosmos, nasturtiums, hollyhocks, purple lantana, and gazania, all good choices for a warm winter growing season, she knew, but she had thought he meant a kitchen garden.

She flipped the book to vegetables, "What about these? Will any of these grow here?" and he pored over the photographs, coming to one of a brilliant three-quarter-pound potentate of a beefsteak tomato sitting grandly on a scale. "You like this, mom?"

"You bet I do."

He laid a hand over his heart. "I give this flower to you."

It was too good to be true. "What about the others?"

He looked through the pages more slowly. Cauliflower would grow in Kuwait. And chili peppers. And mint, and basil.

"I love basil. It grows here?"

"Yes, mom," he said, reaching out with his arms as far as they'd go. "Big tree."

The marigolds shot up out of the ground literally overnight, appearing as a cool, green haze over the warm soil in the morning. Kit crouched to brush a fingertip lightly over the delicate sprouts. The rest of the garden, though barren, looked lovely to her eyes, freshly tilled, neatly seeded. She breathed in its perfume, faint but recognizably of soil primed to nurture new life. Azhar had told her that his family in Pakistan grew rice. He came from a tiny village "near mountains," he said, as though this would fix the geography precisely in her mind. He generously assumed that she knew as much about Pakistan as he knew about the United States. "You like this Meester Cleenton, mom?" he asked with grim disapproval. He spoke sadly of Pakistan, "Come now many men for Taliban," and its history of military coups: "Many, many soldier, guns. Bomb." He also knew that the U.S. had once been an English colony, a fact that annoyed him. "This England," he said, "he own everybody."

He'd gone to school through grade eight, he told her, reflecting that his wife—by which Kit came to understand he meant fiancée, a girl of his village whom he'd marry once he had the funds to build a house—was in sixth grade now. Thinking that Pakistan must have a different system of grade-numbering she asked him her age. He gave this some thought. "I think, twelve." His parents had both died when he was young, six or seven, he wasn't sure, nor did he know how they had died; and he had one brother with a young son and daughter. There had been three older children in his brother's family, but all had died at five or less of what sounded to Kit like polio. Azhar mimed a limp. "No walk, no talk. No eat."

He kept his few gardening supplies—a trowel, a shovel, a badly rusted pruner, a few flats for seedlings—in the *mulhaq* along with other odd items he'd found in his walks back and forth between the landlord's house and Kit's. After learning some of his history Kit found this collection poignant: the head of a hammer, a large stainless steel serving spoon, three pink acrylic drinking glasses, and a single plastic sandal for a small child.

The garden flourished under his care. He came nearly every day to water and weed and place a new cutting or seedling into the soil here and there. Rosemary. Vinca. Pansies, which would grow only until about March, he said. "March, too much hot," a bit of information that dismayed Kit. That meant the cool season here lasted barely five months.

This time he'd brought some sort of a sling with him, a long rope with a hook at the end, and a curved knife. He pointed to the single unharvested date palm. "Fruit ready. I bring for you."

The kids trailed her into the enclosure. "Oh, good. How nice." She made herself smile. Every Christmas her mother had made a date-filled fruit cake that only Kit's dad would touch. The dates in their little box had always reminded Kit of fat roaches packed like sardines.

Sorting through his mysterious date-harvesting gear, Azhar greeted the children with a solemn nod that transformed slowly into a brilliant smile. Like a showman he raised his head to gauge the tree, kicked off his plastic sandals, hooked the sling around his waist, looped the rope over his head, and shinnied straight up the palm as if it were lying flat on the ground.

The children looked up, mouths agape.

Kit too. "Azhar, be careful!"

He lifted a hand from the trunk to wave at them all. "No problem, mom."

As he crawled around in the branches, she realized that the netting he'd put in the palms to keep the local birds away from the dates—he called them bulbuls—were actually nylon bags enclosing each bunch of dates. There seemed to be a lot of them.

Perching in the tree like a dark and leggy heron, he sliced each bunch off with a quick slip of his knife, ran the hook through the mouth of the bag, and lowered it hand over hand to the ground.

"Now, mom, you come."

The bag spilled partly open on the ground, revealing a thick, yellow-green wand like a stick of celery a yard long, loaded with dates.

Kevin was already in a squat, ready to take a sample. Kit lifted him into her arms. These dates would never pass her children's lips if she could help it. They were filthy, covered with dust from all the summer dust storms, and God only knew what bugs they attracted.

"Mom, hook now," Azhar called, making a short, sweeping motion upward with one hand. "Give hook."

She bent to release it and he hauled it back up into the tree. "How many are there?"

Azhar sat back on his haunches, the sling around his hips, gazing toward the crown, counting. "Sefen, eight."

"Eight?"

"Nine. One small. Leetle fruit, mom." He said it apologetically.

"This is plenty." She meant this one bag. Another plopped at her feet, heavier still. "Azhar, this is a lot of dates."

"Thank you, mom," he said, smiling so broadly that even in his silhouette against the bright sky she could see the whiteness of his teeth.

Down came all the bags in a circle under the tree, and down came Azhar too. He stood proudly, hands on hips, surveying his harvest.

"Mom," he said, raising a finger as if he might launch into a grave oration. Eat *nusf-nusf.* Ferry good." And he picked his way to a certain bag.

Huh?

Kevin wriggled down her hip. What a muscular little guy he was. It was like hanging on to a baby seal. She let him go. Carla still clung to her hand. Azhar pulled open one of the biggest bags and rapidly plucked a handful of dates. He opened his palm before her like a magician producing a rabbit from a hat, grinning with excitement.

"Look, mom."

The dates were cream-colored—or half cream-colored. At the stem end they were the normal brown of every date. The upper half, not quite ripe yet, was a rich, yellowing ivory.

"We say *nusf-nusf,* this fruit. Ferry good."

If only she could avoid disappointing him. "What's it mean?" she said.

He frowned, squinted an eye. "In English . . . half?" He pointed to the divide between the colors. "This date, brown half, white half. *Nusf-nusf.*"

"Half and half," Kit said. They were half-ripe.

"Yes, mom!"

His pleasure was contagious. She had to try one. What nonsense not to. In fact, whatever it cost her, she'd eat one of these dates. As she reached to choose one from his palm, though, he closed it.

"I clean, mom, you eat."

From the wall behind the palms, he drew out a long hose he used for irrigation. Turning it on full-flow, he directed it at the bags.

"Water hot, mom," he said, pointing to the sun. "One minute."

Kit lunged for Kevin, who gave forth a happy scream of greeting to the water, and pulled off his shoes before he shot across the terrazzo to the hose.

"Me too, Mommy," Carla said, shedding her shoes as well as her shyness.

"Okay," Kit said, wondering if it wouldn't feel good to go barefoot herself, "but try not to get too muddy." Fat chance: the

109

terrazzo was already awash with mud the exact color of orange pekoe tea.

Hunching like a gold-panner at streamside, Azhar locked the hose between his knees and washed the dates as carefully as they could be washed by filthy hands in brackish water. Only the house had a supply of fresh. Kit determined not to care. You couldn't come all this way and expect the standards of home.

She chose a date from Azhar's palm.

"This, mom," he said with a quick motion toward his lips.

She understood: no nibbling. Pop the whole thing in at once.

She expected a hempy mass, ghastly sweet. But a caramel melted on her tongue, creamy, touched with pineapple and edged with the delicate crunch of a perfect pear.

"Oh my God."

Azhar laughed. "Pakistani say '*wallah!*'"

The children grabbed. She didn't stop them. She chose another for herself. "*Wallah!*"

REVELATIONS

Theo hadn't been so much invited to Jane's party as summoned. She called him at the hospital, her Brunhildian voice tempered not at all for the telephone. "It's my one big do of the year, Theodore. You're not to miss it."

But he might, and without trying: the main entrance to her neighborhood from the Gulf Road had been sealed off by a random police roadblock. He'd been to her house only once and knew no other route through the maze of the old city.

He waited in a long line of cars aglow in the red of rotating police lights, an increasing hazard since the fresh grumblings from Saddam about weapons inspectors and 'reuniting' Kuwait with Iraq. A trio of severe young Kuwaiti policemen dressed in knife-crisp khaki uniforms was making quick work of the searches, but the traffic was heavy and impatient. Horns blared in every direction. As Theo approached the checkpoint, an officer with a gun holstered at his belt thrust a hand toward the open window and barked out, "Revelations, sir."

There was probably a standard set of statements that you were to make at roadblocks and no one had thought to warn Theo: his name and address, nationality, destination.

Impatient, the officer leaned in, his face lean and sharp as a falcon's. "Revelations, sir. Now, please. Revelations." He mimed holding and peering at a tiny card.

Comprehending at last, Theo pulled his wallet from his back pocket. His ear had done its best to correct for the accent and failed. *Driver's license, sir, driver's license.*

He made his way from the Third Ring Road into Jane's neighborhood via an educated guess. Seeing a glow in the sky a few blocks away he headed toward it. It was Jane's house all right, though transformed for the party into a stage-set of a mansion floodlit from every side. It cast a cold glow skyward like an earthbound moon. He turned down the single-lane street parked two cars deep by partygoers, and gazed up at the smooth white planes of the building, a fortress with a handful of decorative cornices stuck here and there to soften its three-story edges.

A valet stepped to the curb to meet him, a young Indian dressed in elegant black slacks, white shirt, and a tailored tapestry vest. The real estate business must be very profitable. "Good evening, sir." Another South Asian man greeted him on the sidewalk, directing him not to the pyramidal front staircase but to an open gate at the side of the house. Music reached his ears, the hum and jangle of voices and laughter. Beyond the gate the sidewalk broadened into a brilliantly illuminated piazza enclosed by the high walls of the villa and a blooming cactus garden dominated by a cascade of crimson bougainvillea. A scattering of people, some in evening clothes, wandered the garden, drinks in hand. Theo saw short dresses, the long curves of a close fit, the multicolor flash of diamonds in the lunar-white desert air.

The garden descended to the lower level of the house on wide-terraced steps and a set of glass doors flung open to the night. Inside he found a cavernous, darkened room thumping with the music of a band Theo couldn't yet see. A few couples danced on a polished dance floor set into acres of carpet; but the bulk of the crowd, threaded through with waiters bearing trays of delicate, bite-sized art, clumped near the bar, a twenty-foot carved wooden expanse backed with mirrors and uniformed bartenders, who were pouring generously from half-gallon jugs of booze and magnums of wine.

Theo set his bearings for the bar. His height served him handsomely: a drink came to him over the heads of others, a fine concoction replete with gin while showing an elegant reserve on the notion of tonic, and finished with a crisp section of lime. He could have tossed it back in a single gulp.

Raising his glass to the bartender he turned his eye to the crowd on the dance floor and the generous sprinkling there— among the jeans and khakis, saris, dashikis, tuxes and turbans— of skin-tight party dresses on gorgeous young women, many of them obviously Arab. He'd seen nothing like this on the streets of Kuwait. The band too was Arab, five men on drums and guitars producing a decent enough Beatles medley that Theo neverthe- less hoped was not the height of its repertoire. *All my loveeng, I weel send to youuu . . .*

A familiar *halloo* reached him through the din of the place. Jane came barging toward him through the crowd, "There you are!" her voice blaring over the music, dressed as she'd been every time he'd seen her, in a tweedy skirt and jacket and boxy black shoes that made her look like a constable.

"How's the flat, then, Theodore?" she said, cranking his hand as if he were a rusted engine that might still roar to life. "And that miserable excuse for a hospital? Have you taken to task yet any of those fools in the administration? An ironical name if I've ever heard one."

A tall and graceful Indian man in a cobalt blue silk shirt stepped up lightly to shake Jane's hand, nodding with warm cor- diality to Theo.

"Theodore, this is Sunder," Jane bellowed, "an old friend from decades back. Sunder," she leaned closer lest he couldn't make out her words. "This is Theodore. He's new here."

Sunder offered a slender hand and a look of shared, amused suffering to Theo. His thick, iron-gray hair was immaculately cut.

"Theodore. I'm very pleased to meet you." His voice rolled forth in polished British tones.

"I was just telling Theodore what a mess they've made of their institutions here. I know you agree, Sunder. I wouldn't have my nails trimmed here if one of the locals had to do it, let alone medical procedures. Thank heavens they import civilized races to do most of their work for them. They're tribal you know, down to the last and faintest impulses in their feeble little brains. You

113

can't be an insider here, Theo, no matter how hard you try. You can't buy it or earn it, or come to it through marriage; you can only be born to it. And if you're born to it, you can't lose it, no matter how disreputable you become. You can lie, thieve, rape, and murder, and your tribe will still protect you. What kind of basis for a wider society is that?"

Sunder's hooded eyes glinted mirth Theo's way. "Why, it sounds just like England."

Jane howled in delight. "You miserable ex-colonials. Independence has only made you cheeky." She put a hand on Theo's shoulder, pointing with a glance toward a broad staircase on the far side of the giant room.

"The food's upstairs. Go up anytime you feel peckish."

"Thanks. Where's Hamid?"

"Oh, somewhere, somewhere. Ham and I make our own ways at our parties, you know." She barked out a laugh and aimed herself at another newly arrived guest.

"Wonderful girl, Janie," Sunder said, watching her go. "I've known her absolutely *forever*. Now," he said, peering intently at Theo's glass, "I see that we must refresh your drink."

He took genial charge of Theo, guiding him from the bar to a less chaotic corner where they could look out over the enormous room. With a good cheer enhanced to glowing by a tall martini, he told Theo that after a thirty-year career in international banking, much of it in the Middle East, he knew a lot of people at the party, "most of them infinitely boring, let me tell you," and could identify all those he didn't know by type. It was like watching birds, he said. "One looks at the plumage, the feet, observes the flight pattern, where they roost."

Leaning sagely against a fluted marble column, the silvery martini in hand, he pointed out a dozen unfortunate specimens with fluid ease: self-important executives, diffident engineers of every stripe and nationality, mostly male; clutches of homely high school teachers from all over the Western world, mostly female.

"Indian salesman, that one. The obsequious grin is an excellent field mark. Travel agent over there, Lebanese, I'd say.

He goes to five parties a week so he's bored out of his dim wits but must still try to look charming. What an ordeal for him. An ambassador behind him, glossy shoes, fussing with his tie, hoping he appears preoccupied by some grave political crisis when he's really thinking of his mistress. Over there, a trade official," he said, squinting. "American army officers in the middle. They're almost too easy: crew cuts, bulky pectorals, and they move in flocks. A bird of prey look about them, don't you think?" He shot Theo a roguish smile, and tilted down the last of his martini. "Maths or physics professor to the right. The dingy clothing seems a matter of pride. And," he said, his delighted eye finding Jane again as she trumpeted her way from group to group, "to identify the estate agent named Jane, you need simply listen for the call."

The gin had hit bottom, easing Theo into a sense of warm expansiveness. Sunder's amiable logorrhea had its effect too, an almost magical sense that he'd engaged in a round of witty repartee, though he'd said almost nothing.

"Now you," Sunder said, bringing his focus around to Theo. "You're more difficult. One doesn't see birds close up usually, you know. One gathers the shape and pattern from afar. If I could put you at a distance, I'd have it." He narrowed an eye. "I might have said an athlete of some kind due to your height. But you look much too intelligent for that, in fact—"

Over Sunder's blue silk shoulder, Theo saw Hanaan walk out of the crowd. She stood alone, hesitant but calm, glancing into the milling throng as though she weren't a part of it. He hadn't expected to see her at such a place, hadn't thought of it. She wore a black dress a little on the solemn side, but she'd pulled her hair back into a gleaming roll, and Theo saw the sparkle of earrings.

Sunder turned to look. "How very lovely. Do you know her?"

"I do," Theo said, caught off guard by his shock of pleasure. "Will you excuse me?"

Sunder thumped Theo's shoulder emphatically. "Of course, dear boy. With all my heart."

As Theo stepped away from the bar Hanaan's eyes swept toward him, but she looked away again, uncertain or embarrassed, which he couldn't tell.

"*Salam al leikum*, Hanaan."

Her dark eyes filled with relief. "Oh, Theo, it is you. *Al leikum salam.*"

"Once I open my mouth I'm a dead giveaway," he said, feeling childish for his disappointment that she hadn't recognized him. "You haven't schooled the bad accent out of me yet."

They'd had four lessons together and she'd proved herself a vigorous taskmaster, working him relentlessly to accomplish a level of excellence he didn't fully aspire to. *Again, after me! Alif, ba, ta, tha . . .*

"No," she said, studying his face earnestly. "No, I know you from your look. But a woman here can't stare at a man, you know. I'd see you anywhere with this fair head, and you're tall. You'd be easy to see even in America, I think."

He liked this tilted idiom. As if she liked to look.

"Many Arabs say all Westerners look alike," she said. "Pale and sickly. Is it the same for Westerners? One Arab is like any other?"

"Of course. You're all terrorists, so you're interchangeable. It keeps things simple."

She smiled. "I've been told this also."

A large group surged through the door, already well-oiled from another party elsewhere. Shouts like war hoops went out to others they recognized and the band retaliated by maxing out their sound system. *Karma karma karma karma karma chameleon . . .* Where had Jane found these guys?

"So," he said, remembering the half-consumed gin and tonic he'd abandoned along with Sunder. He felt certain Hanaan never drank. "Tell me about this party. It's the first I've been to here."

"What do you mean?"

He had a lot of questions. Was it normal to have a nightclub in your basement? Was a party like this tolerated without controversy here? What was implied about the people who came? Who

116

were they? But he was more curious about Hanaan herself and her connection with Jane.

He hadn't yet posed a question when she said stiffly, "You want to ask about me, why I am here."

Her boldness in saying so was more surprising than her perception.

"Of course you do," she said, as if he'd contended against her. "Every Western man when he first comes here thinks all the women will be shut up in a house or wrapped like a package, and so he doesn't know what he thinks when he meets someone like me. Is she good or is she very bad?" She grew animated. "I am not a slave to my religion, you know. I don't respect all the culture Islam has made. God didn't say that women must wear black sheets and shut their mouths. Men say this. I obey God's laws as I see them. God didn't give me a brain so that men could tell me what to think and say of Him. I'll think and speak for myself."

Her energy drained away. She smiled. "I've given you a lecture."

A waiter glided in offering a tray of white wine. Theo reached on instinct, hesitated. Hanaan made the catch for him, swooping a glass from the tray.

"You don't mind?"

"Of course not. What a poor question, Theo."

He sipped. The wine was lovely and golden, a soft kiss of sweetness coming last on the tongue.

He determined to step lightly. "Is this a normal kind of party for Kuwait?"

She shrugged elaborately, as if bored by the question. "What's normal for Kuwait?" But as her eyes roamed the crowd Theo saw a hint of pride grow there. "Hamid is Palestinian, you see. He and my father are distantly related, as I told you. Palestinians won't lead the double lives that many Kuwaitis lead, pretending to be devout by day and falling into debauchery by night."

He edited most of the amusement from his voice. "Debauchery?" The party looked happy enough, but not more than was warranted by the appearance of an open bar. He wondered, absurdly, if she was implying that later hours brought other opportunities.

Again, Hanaan seemed to read his thoughts. "Jane and Hamid are the best of people in the world. They are not hypocrites. If they want a party, they will give a party, in public, the same party they'd give anywhere in the world."

"So . . ." he glanced at the bar, ". . . alcohol's only illegal on paper in Kuwait."

Her look told him deeply of his innocence. "What's illegal depends on who you are. It can't be so different in America."

They were interrupted by two former colleagues of Hanaan's from the university, middle-aged men dressed as their species should be according to Sunder, in blocky creased shirts, worn slacks and shapeless jackets made of stuff as indestructible as upholstery fabric. Their nationalities were nebulous but their desire to exclude Theo was not. They wanted Hanaan to themselves. Theo let himself drift into the crowd. Hanaan glanced at him as he went, an unreadable expression, or almost. He might have seen a flash of regret, a promise of 'see you later,' but knew his imagination may have supplied it. It would be easy to misread those dark and luminous eyes.

Too much alcohol too fast, he thought. It was unhinging him from the neutrality he felt around her during their tutorials when she drove him like a wedge straight into the hardwood of conversational Arabic. A mind hammered like that did not readily compute anything except the ticking away of the punitive tutorial hour.

He wandered, nursing the last of his wine, seeking a dance with one of the gorgeous women he'd spied when he came in, a novel idea shared by every other man in the room. He couldn't get within shouting distance. He danced a few rounds with the more sociable among the high school teachers instead. Sunder had unerringly tagged them from a distance. Not all were plain but they did share a latent sadness, he thought, listening to the summaries of their whys and wherefores as they made their way across the dance floor—and chronic sorrow would blur the beauty of a face over time. Once past the obligatory, "Adventure, what else?" their reasons for being here were all the same. The 'what else' was escape—from a bitter divorce, a lost job, a fractured family, intransigent debt. His own words to Dr. Chowdhury came back to him, all that blah-blah about opportunities for travel and new cultural experiences when his reason too was escape.

Again he cut himself loose and wandered, his eyes seeking Hanaan. He'd been looking for her as he'd danced too, he realized. Now he found her easily, picked her from a crush of others as if he'd memorized every nuance of her body, the fall of her shoulders, the curve of her hip. She stood on the far side of the room talking with two young men—Arabs, he thought—both of them animated, almost theatrically so. The men especially, laughing too easily and too much, leaning in too close to Hanaan. He thought of bulldozing a path through the crowd like Jane to run them off.

He snagged another glass of wine. He was drinking because he could, that was all. That's how Prohibition had worked, or failed to: booze was banned so people drank to excess every chance they got. His mood sloped downward fast with every swallow, even as he relished the smooth tang of the wine. Falling in with a group of talkers, he bottomed out listening to more stories—a young American woman divorced by her Kuwaiti husband and kept from her children; a nurse from Aberdeen who couldn't afford to go home; a cynical Gulf war veteran who never wanted to—stories told gently but compulsively under the influence of alcohol, as if the facts could be gotten rid of like the story: told and so ended, finished, filed, complete.

He listened well, in part because he found such ease with words remarkable. Even tipsy he couldn't talk about himself like this, had never figured out how to pull one sentence after another from himself about himself. There seemed so little to say. Rajesh had badgered him endlessly, *Talk, man! What kind of doctor can you be if you listen?* But from childhood he'd learned a careful silence, a quiet awareness, and a readiness for whatever might happen between his volatile parents. Even so, whatever had happened, over and over, he'd failed to understand it, and it was only when he read his father's notebooks after his death, the volumes of unfinished poems and scraps of prose aimed at Theo's mother, that he began to penetrate the silences of those years.

> *How spare that look you gave me. No,*
> *not 'gave' for there's no give.*
> *And again you're gone. Another take*
> *of leave*

His sister Julia had somehow come through the same history with more talent for talking, and yet it hadn't netted her any advantage in romance. They both had a sketchy record with the opposite sex, numerous lovers but no permanence. The breakups were usually their own doing, with little residue of regret. "We're loners, Theo, you and I," she had told him. The memory dismayed him, a predictable, metabolic side-effect of . . . four drinks. He put the glass of wine aside. Enough.

Julia confused the two things, loneliness and being a loner. A loner preferred to be alone. He did not. A mild panic rose up in him at the thought of it, spending his life as he lived now, on the fringes, solo. But how did you nurture an attraction into commitment, and how did you seal a commitment with trust? It required a skill he didn't have, a skill other people learned as children from their parents by everyday example, by acts so common and unmarked that they existed not as events but as a nourishing atmosphere. To learn that skill as an adult seemed immensely difficult, a reworking to the bones. He could as soon unbreathe the air of his childhood.

He fingered his cell phone, thinking of Julia, her throaty laugh, the calm that lay between them. But she'd hear his melancholy and worry about him, wonder if he was drinking too much, if he wished he hadn't gone so far from home. It seemed too much to reveal, even to her, a pathetic urge for comfort that would pass with the night. In the morning he'd write her an email. They'd written to one another frequently ever since the summer their father died, and he owed her one.

A momentous summer, that one. Theo had just finished his internship, Julia a Master's in Biology; their careers beckoned; their father was gone. In the weeks after his death their mother had thrown a party for them, ostensibly to celebrate their academic achievements.

Theo remembered watching her from the porch as she circulated on the lawn below, a summer party, laughter and voices drifting up on the cool, eucalyptus-scented air. On the lawn Julia caught his eye and threw a glance toward the second floor of the house. He nodded and they met in the hallway outside their father's study, always a favorite refuge. But neither had seen it since his death. Opening the door they found it stripped of everything that had made it his—furniture and books, art, wallpaper, every length of shelving—and repainted in a color so pale, a mere intimation of green, that you might have thought it was the light cast through the pines that produced the tint. But the trees were gone too. Not just felled but axed from the damp and sawdust-covered ground. Their mother had always hated the trees. *I need more light.*

Julia sank to the floor and cried.

She'd grown into a beauty in their years of college and graduate school—dark red hair in long, untidy curls. Home for occasional holidays over those years, she'd begun to attract their father's plodding graduate students, whom she ignored along with the anguished sonnets they produced. She tossed their verse onto the hearth. *Let them burn.* Theo grew tall and blond. They didn't look like siblings.

Down on the lawn, their mother would have realized their absence, they knew. While smiling a thousand watts at her guests she would strain to spot Theo's yellow head above the crowd, knowing that wherever Theo was, Julia would be with him. She'd come stalking after them before long, so they had to be quick with their goodbyes. Julia was leaving for a summer of field work in Panama in the morning.

"You have to write me. Every day." She banged gently on his chest with a palm. "Say you will."

"So I can get long letters about bugs? No thanks."

"You're making excuses."

"I'll try."

"Are all men equivocators?"

He endeavored to sound certain for all of mankind. "I will do it," and crossed his heart.

This wasn't enough for Julia. She held out a pinkie, a life-long ritual between them, and made him link it with his own.

"Now I believe you," she said.

At last he spotted Hanaan alone again. She was standing with one arm around a column, watching the packed dance floor with what looked like weary detachment. She didn't see him coming.

"Tired?"

"Oh, Theo," she said. "I'm glad it's you. Yes, I'm worn out. I'm not good at such parties. I try, but I'm not good. I'm in training, you see."

The band ended a set to the uproarious applause of the guests. Theo joined in, happy to see them go. "Training?"

"Yes." She watched the band members lay their instruments carefully aside. "I need to improve my English. There's a certain kind of English that I can't speak. I don't know it at all. This . . ." she gestured vaguely toward the crowd, "small talk, intimate talk. Not of the school room."

"Doesn't training sort of take the fun out of a party?"

She looked down, thinking, and he became aware of the graceful line of her neck from ear to shoulder where her dress crossed and shadowed the exposed skin beneath, black on cream.

"Yes, of course. But lessons are rarely pleasant. You don't enjoy your Arabic lessons either."

She said this innocently, confident he'd agree. Seeing his smile, she looked away, embarrassed.

"Hallo, everyone!" Jane stood at the top of the stairs, waving a solid arm. "No one can leave until all of this food is gone! Come up! Come up!"

A gradual migration began. Theo didn't move. "You were telling me about your training."

But she was curt with him now. "Yes, but that isn't what you want to know. You're surprised to see me here at all. I've known Jane for a long time. She sends students to me. Hamid is part of my family. Why shouldn't I come?"

Taken aback, he said nothing.

"You're thinking I shouldn't be here. But it's part of my rebellion to be here."

He tried to be amused by this, that she'd presume to tell him what he was thinking. That she did know only increased his sense of invasion, for it seemed to be a hostile one.

"Is there somewhere to sit?"

Staring off into the emptying room she seemed determined to ignore him. "At the back," she said abruptly, setting off as if she were an usher leading him to his seat.

She took him to a far-off corner, carpeted and furnished with a modular cluster of a dozen or so upholstered ottomans three feet across. Four other guests had found their way there. Another couple, young Europeans, lounged in quiet conversation on a single ottoman at the edge of the carpet, and a pair of erect British ladies dressed much like Jane sat side by side in companionable silence, staring straight ahead and draining their drinks as if dedicated to making a thorough job of it. Empty glasses cluttered a nearby table.

They sat. Theo shifted forward, elbows on knees, to keep Hanaan's face in view. "Tell me about your rebellion."

She wouldn't look at him. So serious. "No. You'll laugh."

"You judge me very harshly."

She ventured a glance. "You judge also. If I were in America you wouldn't wonder about my behavior. My life seems odd to you. Exotic, perhaps. Because it's odd. I'm odd."

"And you don't find me odd?"

The idea astonished her. "Not at all."

"Not exotic in the least?"

She became suspicious of him. "You're pulling at my leg."

"How come I don't get to be exotic?"

A smile grew but she tucked her head. "Americans aren't exotic. How can they be? Everyone knows America outside and inside. You're all over the television and movies." She looked at him directly now, bold again with her opinion. "The whole world has grown up looking at Americans. We're tired of you now."

"I'm really sorry to hear that," he said.

She gave a soft intake of breath but held his gaze. Had he sounded so sincere? He wondered what it would be like to kiss her in this semi-darkness, to breathe her in, feel his lips on the curve of her neck.

"No," she said looking away, "I'm the one who's sorry. I launch yet another lecture, to teach you something."

Always back to lessons.

"It's all right," he said. "I'm getting used to it."

She hesitated uneasily, fidgeting with her fingertips. "You don't understand. It's part of what I'm trying to learn. In my rebellion. Not to lecture." She made a soft tsk of frustration. "I don't know how to talk to a man, Theo. You've observed this by now. Unless you're my student and we're studying nouns and verbs, unless we have a formal subject, I am no good. This is difficult for most women here. We're wives or sisters or mothers or colleagues with men. But we aren't friends. I know how to teach, how to lecture, but not how to be a friend. In America men and women are friends."

"That's not so common as you think."

Sincere amazement dawned. "Really?"

It seemed the band was coming back already. Someone rolled out a drum fanfare and the crowd, flowing back down the staircase loaded down with plates and glasses, gave out a yell. An end to their relative peace. But then the voice of an *oud* rose up in sinuous clarity above the clamor and silenced it. He looked at Hanaan, whose eyes were on him now, smug.

"Now you will hear some *good* music."

They went to watch. The band members were the same but they'd packed their guitars away, replacing them with the *oud* and a zither. Promptly, as if someone had flipped a switch, they launched into the energetic, almost formless melodies of their own music, eyes closed, smiling through their moustaches.

The crowd rushed the dance floor, and an Arab man the size of a parade float and dressed in the only *dishdasha* at the party descended in stately anticipation from the upper floor, his arms out and moving to the music, long sleeves hanging. The guests parted to allow his passage, applauding him as he eased with surprising grace onto the dance floor.

"That's Ham, isn't it?" Theo said.

"Of course. Who else could it be? But Theo, you must call him Hamid. Only Jane may say Ham. He'll be offended with you. Arabs will think you're making fun with pork."

He laughed, more than grateful for the warning. "I don't see Jane."

"Oh, he won't dance with Jane."

Several of the young Arab women Theo had sought out earlier soon surrounded Hamid, bare and slender arms dancing above their heads, their torsos in gentle sway. He had them all to himself. Someone tossed a white scarf to one woman whose long hair cascaded down her back. She took it laughing, and without altering the deep insinuations of her dance, folded it lengthwise as if to fit it to her head. But she slung it low over her hips instead, bright white against the tight black butt of her

125

skirt, and tied it there like a bow as she undulated to the pulsing rhythm of the music. Confounded by this fine and unexpected pleasure, Theo joined in as the spectators clapped and hollered their approval. A spate of ululations broke out in shrill bursts like verbal gunfire across the crowd.

"Hanaan, do you dance?"

"No!"

What outsized horror. He could only smile at it. The houris on the dance floor were in the minority. There were plenty of women shuffling modestly around with their partners.

"Oh, come on," he said, offering her his hand. "Part of your training. It's my turn to teach you something."

"No. I can't."

"Friendship training," he said, sure she'd relent.

She turned from him to watch the dancers.

Theo watched too, puzzled by Hanaan, puzzled by the music, which had slowed and swirled lazily now in haunting echoes, impossible to identify as happy or sad. It mingled the emotions into a joyous sadness, a mournful joy.

"I didn't mean to offend you," he said, irritated.

He spotted Sunder across the dance floor, still attached at the lips to a martini, watching the dancers avidly.

"It's so easy for you," Hanaan said, slicing her words. "All this. Talking, dancing, saying whatever you like. It means nothing to you."

Her tone mystified him as much as the music. He couldn't read it. Was she angry, resentful, amazed?

Jane had stepped onto the perimeter of the floor, her bulky figure whirling in a slow circle, her thick arms held above her head like stalks.

Hanaan had drawn closer, or perhaps he had. He didn't remember taking a step and yet she was only inches away. The scent of her warm skin came to him and he imagined touching her cheek, following the line of her throat with a fingertip to the delicate seashell scoop at the base of her neck.

She looked up at him, her eyes black and gentle and sad once again. "You speak of friendship. Can you be my friend?"

Exasperation eddied in him. What did she mean? "I am your friend, Hanaan."

She let him take her hand, opening her palm into his. She looked him straight in the eye.

"But that's not what I want," she said. "Theo, I have been watching you all evening. It's not what you want either."

MUFEEDA'S GATE

THE TIME had been set: Mufeeda expected her for tea this afternoon. Kit felt the hour approach with dread and yet she wanted badly for it to arrive so that it could pass, a paradox that made her despair, again, for her foolish timidity.

"Dear Dad," she said aloud to herself in the mirror as she combed her hair. How flat and lifeless it looked. "Yes, you're right, Saddam is acting restless again and he has a bunch of missiles he could aim toward us tomorrow. But what really worries me is a tea party at my neighbor's house today."

She smiled at her reflection.

How to keep Carla and Kevin out of trouble while she and Mufeeda visited was at the core of her unease, and the fact that Mufeeda hadn't actually mentioned the children when she'd telephoned. With neighbor women back home this invitation was unspoken. What else were you going to do with kids this age except include them? No one got a sitter just so she could drop next door for a cup of coffee. But here everyone had maids, something she still hadn't attended to, though Jack had begun to needle her about it. She'd gathered from the newspaper that many local families used their maids as nannies, letting these young and untrained women virtually raise their children. Mufeeda certainly had a full household staff. Kit had seen servants in the street in front of the house, dark-skinned women in housecoats washing cars in the early morning and occasionally a couple of lean young men at the curb, catching a smoke. Drivers, she guessed. One time, as she and Jack and the kids were coming home from somewhere, she'd seen one of the men open the back door of an enormous car for a bulky, black-robed figure that Kit assumed must be either Mufeeda's mother or mother-in-law. He'd bowed as the woman climbed in, closed the door with a flourish, then ducked behind the wheel and drove his cargo away somewhere.

Cargo: what a thought, Kit! The woman was someone's mother. Still, she'd looked so huge, a big black ship at full sail. Only a vague moon of a face showed and it looked sour and harsh. The woman hadn't glanced their way though she would surely have seen them out of the corner of her eye. But perhaps her vision was poor. If you had a face like that it was just as well to have bad eyes.

Kittie!

Carla and Kevin looked as clean and neat as she could make them. But of course Kevin could reduce an hour of preparation to hot and sweaty dishevelment in one fit of temper, complete with a loaded diaper. Had her brothers shown their mother such rapid and vengeful transformations when they were toddlers? As the youngest of the family she had no memory of it and couldn't imagine them as pink and shining babies, only as the rough and smelly adolescents they still seemed to be, tramping around in muddy boots. She should expect no improvement in Kevin any time soon.

Carla had chosen her own clothes for the outing, and with calm deliberation: a striped blue and white smock with two big pockets on the skirt in which she jammed a Barbie each, both naked.

"Carlie, where are their clothes?"

"It's hot outside."

"But we won't be outside except just to walk across the street. Then they'll be cold in the air-conditioning."

A slow blink of infinite forbearance from Carla. "Mommy, they're just dolls."

Where did she pick up this attitude? She wasn't even in school yet. "Then they can't get hot, can they? If they're going to

129

go visiting to our neighbor's house, they have to have clothes on, Carlie, just like you and me. You wouldn't go over there without clothes and neither should they, even though they're dolls."

"But all their dresses are wrinkled!"

"Then leave them at home."

"No! You iron some clothes for them."

"No," said Kit, and smiled a big, mechanical smile to seal the discussion shut. "Now get going."

Was it a good thing that some of her most gratifying moments as a parent were short, decisive interactions like this one where she pulled rank on her children? She'd hated being on the receiving end when she was a child, all those seemingly negotiable items rendered dead in single syllables: no, no, no. Sometimes she wondered if she had obeyed those prohibitions too well.

MUFEEDA'S GATE stood even taller than their own and was made not of solid metal but of wrought iron curled in complicated swirls focusing in the middle on a dancing circlet of Arabic letters in gold. The family crest? Beyond lay a gleaming marble walkway to a set of wide marble steps leading to a broad marble porch framed by a spectacular carved wooden doorway ten feet across. Four floors of darkly tinted windows looked down on Kit with a forbidding gaze. She wanted to turn and flee. There were four buttons on the intercom set into the exterior wall. Which one buzzed the door? Kevin strained at her knee to do the job with his fat little fist. He'd pound every one.

She touched the lowest button tentatively and a voice blared out, startling them all. "Good afternoon, madam! One moment, please!"

One of the doors swung open and a young housemaid emerged smiling, dressed in a belted black dress and plain, white apron.

"Come in, please!" She caressed the children's heads, drawing them through the gate and beaming a smile at Kit. Her voice dropped to an urgent whisper. "You are American?"

Kit nodded, confused.

The whisper turned fervent. "I love America. I go to America some day. My cousin is in New York."

"Welcome!" Mufeeda was at the door. "Carmen," her voice grew firm, "bring them in," and then musical once more: "You have brought the children."

Carla had ducked behind Kit, still holding her hand in a tight clamp. Kevin rampaged ahead, drawn to the gaping interior of this new adventure as if by a tractor beam. Kit grabbed for him and missed; but Carmen, laughing, took hold of his hand as he surged headlong in her direction.

"I'm sorry," Kit said, trying to read Mufeeda's face. "I didn't know for certain about the kids. I don't have a maid or anything, and Jack . . . my husband, he isn't . . ."

"They're most welcome! You're all most welcome. Come in."

Mufeeda shut the door behind them dropping the wide foyer into a shining gloom of marble floors and walls, and took Kit's hands in hers. She wore a black scarf wrapped with what looked like punishing tightness around her head and neck, but her smile cancelled its severity, giving her face a gentle light as she looked into Kit's.

"I'm very happy you've come to me. You and your beautiful children."

Her own youngest, the only one not in school, was presented by another maid as if she were a little princess, all dressed in pink frills, her glossy black hair curled and pulled back from her round face. Mufeeda made the introductions in English, even to this tiny daughter. "Fauzia, go. Say good afternoon." The little girl toddled a few steps in Kit's direction, her wide brown eyes settling uneasily on Carla, then Kevin. They stayed on Kevin, and a deep frown took slow shape. A quick judge of character, Kit thought. Kevin stared at her, open-mouthed, a vivid preview of what he'd look like spotting a pretty girl at sixteen.

The maid who'd brought the little girl took her away again, and Carmen hijacked Carla and Kevin too. Neither of the kids made a peep. They were adjusting to life here much faster than their mom.

"And now, please come," Mufeeda said.

She led Kit down a broad hallway and through a succession of hushed rooms filled to popping with furniture in embroidered satins. Through an open door she caught sight of a dining room table like a runway lined with chairs, and behind it a buffet eight feet long that looked every inch a military hero reincarnated as furniture, all chesty with braided carvings and gold encrustations. A tall rectangle of light beyond looked like it must lead to the kitchen.

Mufeeda opened a heavy door and stood aside, welcoming Kit yet again, and Kit passed into a room that looked like a photograph clipped from a designer's dream book of an English country-garden room: blue-flowered carpet, lovely small armchairs and delicate tea tables, vases of fresh flowers, paintings of lords and ladies hanging on the walls, a silver tea service, china so thin Kit knew light would pass right through it.

"Please," Mufeeda said, gracefully sweeping a hand toward a chair. "Sit and have tea." With this, she made a quick motion at her chin and pulled her scarf from her head.

Kit felt as if she'd just seen a magic trick: Mufeeda, the humble, round-faced housewife vanished into thin air, replaced by a younger brunette with a patrician look and an elegant close-cropped haircut. She looked as if she could be from anywhere in the Western world, another beautiful young woman who spoke English with a soft, indefinable accent. Mufeeda smiled mischievously at Kit's stare.

"When there are no men I take off this head cover. We call it hijab. Unless my hair is very ugly, and then I must keep it on."

Kit checked out the silverware as Mufeeda served the tea with formality and grace. Spoon, dessert fork, butter knife, delicate but fully identifiable.

"I know the man who owns your house," Mufeeda said with the same disapproval Kit had noted in Azhar. "He lived there for a time." She leaned forward, full of concern. "Tell me, did he

132

make it nice for you? This man, he keeps every *fil*. He doesn't know how beautifully Americans live, I think."

A laugh broke from Kit. "Not all Americans. I grew up in an old, falling-apart, Oklahoma farmhouse." She meant to evoke small, dark rooms with thin walls and creaking floors. But Mufeeda put a hand to her heart.

"Oh, I know it is a lovely, lovely place."

Kit asked about the older woman she'd seen in the street.

"It is my mother-in-law," Mufeeda said. "She isn't well today or she would enjoy to be with us."

"She lives here with you?"

"Oh yes. This is our way."

"How wonderful to have whole families living together," Kit said. What she would have given to have had her mother with her in those last precious months of her life.

"Yes," Mufeeda said. But something in the steady-state smile she wore made Kit think again of that sour old face.

"We Americans mostly live so far apart from our families, you know," she said. "Like Jack and me being here, with our families way back home."

Mufeeda refilled her teacup. "You are very fond of your mother-in-law then?"

Kit hadn't thought of living with Jack's mother, a pinched, accusing woman who could find something itchy to say about everyone but herself. "You mean you're . . . required . . . to live with your husband's family?"

Mufeeda's amusement turned tender. She nodded her head.

"Oh," said Kit.

Mufeeda laughed delightedly. "Many times I think, oh, to have the American way is perfect, everyone alone."

JACK WANTED to hear all about it. "Well?" he said, opening a bottle of beer at the upstairs kitchen counter. One of the guys at work had given him a couple of samples of his first-run home brew.

133

Kit didn't know where to start. "Well, she's very nice. She met us at the door, and a maid brought her youngest daughter down to meet us—and she's so cute, Jack—she already speaks English and she's barely two. Carlie fell completely in love with her and didn't say a word when the maids took them away. Then Mufeeda took me to this beautiful tea room with those flowered chairs like you see in movies in front of bay windows with a little basket of tatting on a cushion, and a little lace tablecloth and all, only . . ."

"Only what?"

She didn't know how to continue even if she limited things to 'only.' Only how barren their own villa looked by comparison; and how plain she felt compared to Mufeeda, how rough and inexperienced, an Oklahoma hick, which was a surprise since she'd somehow come to think, without meaning to, that the people here would prove to be a little backward. Jack's stories from work had influenced her, his jokes about how taxi drivers had so recently given up their camels that they still said, 'Hut, hut!' when they wanted to accelerate. Or how the Iraqis, when they raided the country, stole remote controls and left the televisions behind because they didn't know the two were associated. Or how so many people here were illiterate and married their daughters off at twelve. She'd almost expected them to live in mud-brick houses. Yet Mufeeda had graduated from college with a degree in psychology. She'd worked a few years in human resources for a British company before quitting to take care of her family, accomplishments she mentioned casually, and only under questioning from Kit, as if they mattered not at all. She and her husband had apartments in Paris and London; she spoke French and German as well as English and Arabic.

"Only what, Kit?" Jack was gamely pouring the beer into a large glass. It had no head.

Something else occurred to her. "You know, I went to the bathroom while I was there, Jack, and above the sink there was this thick glass shelf with a couple of huge bottles of perfume in those crystal decanters like you see whisky in. But it was perfume."

"The men wear it here," Jack said with a snort. "There's a Kuwaiti bigwig on the mall site who trails a thick fog of Shalimar, for God's sake. For my whole life, my mom splashed Shalimar on before church."

"It must be a cologne that smells something like Shalimar."

"Listen, I know the smell of Shalimar like bacon frying. Everybody wears smelly stuff here. Even the money smells like perfume."

Kit had thought she was imagining her perfumed wallet. "I know!"

"What's wrong with deodorant, huh?"

"Oh, and she took off her head scarf once we were alone, Jack. She's really pretty without it." Kit put a hand to her lips. "But maybe I really shouldn't tell you that."

"What? What difference could it make?"

"Well, if they wear scarves so men can't see them, isn't it kind of disrespectful to tell you what she looks like without it?"

"Oh, geez, Kit." But he wouldn't press it. "Hey, did she serve you that nasty cardamom coffee?"

That he knew the word cardamom shocked her. "You've had some?"

"Oh, they give it to us at meetings when the ministerial people are prowling around. They serve it with these useless little spoons about the size of your thumbnail." Jack's engineering mind was easily outraged by poor design. "They drink it like a bunch of women, with their pinkies out. It tastes just like Vick's." He went back to examining the beer. "I wouldn't touch it again if you paid me."

"But you're going to drink that beer?"

He took a sip that turned painful as he swallowed.

She was smiling. "Just pour it down the drain, Jack."

"Oh no. We have enough trouble with our plumbing. First the Iraqis, then . . ." he said it with the voice of doom ". . . Dave's beer."

She laughed, warming to him. He could be funny, even touchingly tender sometimes.

He lifted the bottle. "Want some?"

She didn't even like good beer, but it was time to celebrate. "Okay. Just a sip."

He poured out a measure for her and mopped both glasses with a paper towel. "Cheers, Kittie. Here's to our new life."

"Cheers," she said, and took a sip so small she brought in only the pond-water smell of the stuff.

"Hey," Jack said, "what's that pile of garbage out in the *mulhaq*? A sandal and a hammer-head and some spoons. All stashed in a corner."

Kit wasn't sure why, but she was reluctant to tell him. "They're Azhar's. He finds things and saves them. Stuff people throw away."

Jack's face went slack. "That's what he told you, that he found them?"

"Oh, come on. Who'd steal one sandal?"

"Why hide it in our *mulhaq*?"

Kit knew the answer to that one. "Because he doesn't have any privacy at Khalid's. He lives in one room with a bunch of other men. They'd probably steal it."

Though this made sense, Jack wasn't going to admit it.

"I'm just saying to watch him, Kit. You're a soft touch and you need to keep a decent distance from these people. They'll take advantage of you every time."

FINGERTIPS

FREDERICK CAUGHT her on the one day she felt certain she was safe, when she knew in advance that the Grandmother would go to a ladies' party. She'd even checked to make sure the Grandmother's car was gone. She checked again before she stepped from the kitchen into the passageway between the villa and the *mulhaq*, fingering the paltry offering she'd managed to accumulate: a few ounces of cashews, an apple, some flatbread, a small hunk of creamy cheese. The carport stood empty. Sir had left early in the morning for the hospital, and Ma'am at ten.

Three strides from the step she heard a dry metallic chirp. She halted, her eyes on the gritty pavement, listening for the swing of the *mulhaq* door. Nothing. If she proceeded and made it safely to the street she'd have to pass the *mulhaq* again to return to the house. Perhaps she'd mistaken the noise, imagined it in her wariness.

Yes, the Grandmother's car was gone. She straightened her shoulders—no reason to wait—and took two long strides before she heard a screech of metal, glimpsed Frederick in the door of the *mulhaq*. She saw his hand flash out, so fast she couldn't avoid it. He gripped her elbow, yanking hard. Fighting for balance she stumbled toward him as he pulled her through the door of the *mulhaq*. He kicked it shut behind them.

He didn't let her fall. His grip held her up; a rough hand between her shoulder blades steadied her. The dimness of the room after the brilliant sun left her blinded, but his dark face loomed with the golden cross below. A moustache. And she could smell him. Stale cologne, greasy hair oil, pungent skin.

"Where's my money?" he said, pulling at his belt. It took one hand. He held her arm tight with the other, twisting it behind her back. The belt hit the floor. "In your little parcel?"

There was no question of screaming. He'd been an employee here for six years, she for less than two. She was forbidden outside. He'd tell them that she came to him and they'd believe him.

His hand felt for her belly and breasts, found the plastic bag in the pocket of her housedress. Greedy for knowledge of every sort, he pulled at it too hard and the contents flew, distracting him. Emmanuella crouched and spun, butting her head against him at the open zipper, and for a moment he lost his footing. She pulled her arm from his grip and scuttled to the door where he caught her again. The metal of the door burned at her back. He pressed a knee between her legs.

"Cheese? Apples? You're going on holiday?" One hand groped under her dress. She kicked, unable to do him harm, tried to bite him. He splayed a hand on her chin, banging her head against the metal door. "I mean business with you. I can hurt you. I could kill you, by God."

Terrified, she stopped struggling. He found her vagina with his fingers and plunged them hard. But this wasn't enough. He tore at her underpants, freed his penis in a single movement. It sprang at her, touching her thigh. She gave a single scream before he clamped a hand over her mouth, slamming her head hard against the metal door. "Shut up," he said, his lips close to her ear.

Outside, the roar of a truck engine rounding the corner, coming into the neighborhood. Emmanuella knew it instantly: the garbage collectors, no help to her. But doubt harried Frederick's concentration and she struck again, heaving at his slender weight to shift it. With one step back he gave her room to kick. Aiming at the horrible penis, she scored a knee. He swung at her but hit the metal door instead, scraping his damp and grimy fingertips along its rust-scarred surface.

"Ai!"

They faced each other, she flat against the door, he like a cat ready to spring. The door couldn't be locked from the inside. Behind her back Emmanuella found the lever.

"Let me go."

He flicked his head, swinging his sweaty hair from his eyes. "Give me the money."

She edged slowly to the side to clear the door. "If you will let me go."

His smile curled. He folded the wizened penis back into his pants. "I don't want you anyway, you ugly bitch, you little skinny, ugly black bitch."

Blood dripped from his hand to the cement floor, a delicate spatter at his bare feet. As he looked down in wonder, Emmanuella dragged the door open and ran into the sun.

CASUALTY

"CHICKEN," THEO announced on Hanaan's threshold, a bag of groceries in his arms. "Chicken?" she said, and he corrected himself solemnly: "*Dajaj.*"

"Don't worry," she said. "I won't test you tonight."

She let him in and shut the door. They kissed softly over the bag of groceries. "You've earned a holiday from studies," she said. But she turned him bodily toward the kitchen before he could kiss her again, gave him a gentle push. "The kitchen waits for you."

Her self-control amazed him. Though he now stayed with her after his tutorials whenever he could, she kept the evolution of their intimacy slow; and during their studies she was as she'd always been, a strict guardian of the Arabic language, determined to inflict comprehension on her student.

Cats swamped him, having detected the chicken. He waded to the small counter through a chorusing mob.

"See how attractive you are," Hanaan said. "They all come running to you."

She'd agreed to let him fix dinner for her only after some hesitation, though it wasn't due to any concern about the neighbors, she insisted: she didn't care what they said. Meaning, Theo thought, that no evening visit of his would go unremarked.

"Let's just eat out then," he'd said. "It's easier."

"Theo, people will gossip no matter what. They live for this. I won't change my ways for them. It only gives them power."

He suspected that something other than mere gossip lay behind her original reluctance to invite him over for dinner.

140

What, he didn't know; and gossip of the kind his presence would provoke probably wasn't 'mere' in this culture. Hanaan regarded Abdullah as a spy available at the cost of a tip to anyone. Perhaps including Hanaan's own family, though she hadn't said this.

"Good thing you won't test me," he said, pulling open kitchen drawers. He'd decided to stir-fry the chicken, improvising as he went. "I haven't learned the word for 'spatula.'"

He was supposed to have mastered basic household nouns, but the contents of the drawers in the flat were among the few things they hadn't labeled in Arabic with tiny yellow sticky notes during their lessons—table, chair, shelf, floor, wall, window, counter, sink—until her flat looked like a roost for yellow butterflies.

"Second drawer. In the front," she said.

His brain always felt bruised after their lessons, and yet he wasn't progressing rapidly. Only once had she declared herself wholly satisfied with his pronunciation: when she taught him the critical difference between saying 'no' the way he heard it commonly pronounced, a harsh *'leh-leh-leh'* and Hanaan's way, *"Lah.* This is all you need. Simple, lovely. People will now like you for saying no."

In general, his American English had made him lazy, she insisted. "Move your lips! Use your whole face, your hands! Arabic requires the whole body!"

He had seen that it did. Discussing the most trivial details at the hospital planning sessions: Did the new cardiology clinic require new routing signs in the halls or should the old ones be relocated? The administrators gesticulated wildly, leaning into one another's faces. It looked like genuine choler to Theo, but at the end of the meetings they kissed one another on the cheeks.

"They don't seem to smile much when they talk," he'd commented to Hanaan about this episode, and she raised her hands to heaven. "And you Americans smile too much! Even when you say something ugly, you smile, as if this will make it less ugly."

"How charming you can be," he said.

"See? You don't mean this at all, and yet you're smiling."

Cats convened in a solid block at his ankles as Theo sliced the raw chicken. Hanaan herded them toward the door in light and melodious tones of Arabic, but they came back like a flood tide on her heels. Losing her temper she whirled at them and thundered in English: "Go!"

They scattered, claws out and clattering on the bare floor, tails bristling. She turned sweetly back to Theo: "English always terrifies them."

He watched her watch her cats as he cooked, wondering at the tenderness in her face. They weren't a handsome lot, but her dedication to them was complete, even beyond the point of rationality, he thought. She'd go hungry herself to feed them and pay their endless veterinary bills. Her family didn't help her financially, that was clear, though whether this was their choice or hers Theo didn't yet know. She'd begun rescuing cats after the war. Many of the people who had fled the fighting had merely dumped their pets into the streets rather than take them along. There were far fewer dogs, and they died soon; but the toughest of the cats survived, becoming feral within months. The city was full of them, a scrawny and diseased population, gleaning their lean subsidies from the open garbage dumpsters along the curbs and in the alleyways of the city. There was no welfare agency for pets in the country, and only two veterinary clinics, both ill-equipped and under-staffed.

"Even in good times people here don't care for their animals," she had told him. "They keep them but only if it remains convenient. If they leave on holiday," she whipped an arm toward the door, "out they go! If they make a mess, out! If they have kittens, out! They don't care for anyone but themselves."

When Theo asked how she'd spent the war, how she'd survived it, she lapsed into an uncharacteristic silence before answering.

"I helped where I could. This was not much. The animals all suffered terribly. We couldn't move around without great caution but it helped that I'm of Palestinian blood. Because that idiot Arafat loved Saddam, the Iraqis thought I was their ally. For some time I helped find food for the animals at the zoological park."

"Kuwait has a zoo?"

"You cannot call it that now."

"They all died anyway, I suppose."

"We saved only a few. The Iraqis ate some of them. They consumed our country. This is how I think of it."

Her cats gradually recovered from their single-syllable battering in English and were back at the threshold where they sat in mouthy hopefulness, gazing in. They looked much alike: tigers and calicoes, small-boned and short-haired, with enormous ears.

"They all look like they're from the same litter," Theo said.

She regarded the cats with fierce pleasure. "They're survivors. Their colors are light and so they're not visible in the sand. Their hair is short so they're cool. They're small, so they don't eat much. And with big ears they hunt every bird, every mouse, every gecko in the night. They're efficient. I like this."

She swept one up in her arms, Solomon, the lanky orange male. He relaxed into bonelessness, purring.

"When I first took Solomon from the street he was so sick and sad that I called him the Solemn One. But now he's happy again, and so I'm happy. He's the light of my eyes."

AFTER DINNER, she went to make tea, as always insisting that Theo stay out of the kitchen as she prepared it.

"Just what's so secret about the tea?" he called from the table.

"No, you misunderstand." She came to the door of the tiny kitchen, somewhat sheepish, a tin of tea in her hands. "It's not like that. I want to concentrate so it will be wonderful. If you're there I'll see only you."

He stayed where he was, at the small table next to the window that served as both her dining room table and desk, where they had faced each other that first day they met and he'd begun learning his alphabet. He didn't much like being in this room alone: it pressed on him like a cell. Hanaan had bought most of her belongings secondhand, or collected them as castoffs from other members of her extended family: a battered couch, a pair of blond laminated side tables of a sort Theo remembered ungenerously from his childhood. Hanaan had tried to relieve the stark ugliness of the place with charcoal sketches of her cats, lively portraits in which even he could recognize each one; and in a corner was a collection of old Arabic coffee pots with their long beaks, set among a jumble of baskets. Another small basket on the table before him was filled with plump dates. She always had them. It had shocked her when he said he didn't prefer dates. "Prefer? What do you mean? What else can you prefer?" She'd taken it upon herself to change this. "Come, try one. Only in the Gulf is the date so delicious. It is one of our few perfections." She had popped one delicately into his mouth.

They sat on the sag-bottomed couch with their tea, fending off all cats except Solomon, who was allowed to push himself between them like a living bundling board.

"Your mother," Hanaan said, continuing their gradual exploration of one another's history, "she went away for the winters. But why?"

He hesitated. "Not for the whole winter. Winters are rainy in California. She likes the sun."

He knew this answer wouldn't pass muster, and it didn't, though he saw her struggling not to pass judgment.

"This is a reason to leave her children? She likes the sun?"

"It was more than that." He didn't want to tell her these things. "She and my father didn't get along. He was a lot older and a bit of a loner. She needed more . . . interaction."

Hanaan was grave. "And so she took lovers. This is what you mean."

"I don't *know* so."

"But you *think* so, forcefully."

"Yes."

144

"You're smiling."

"Because you think forcefully too, about everything."

"You joke with me."

He curled a finger into the warm palm of her hand. "It's history, that's all. It's in the distant past."

"I don't believe you. Something like this can't be put in the past." She brought his finger to her lips and kissed it softly. "See how you try to forget it?"

His train of thought wavered. He let the finger trail to the curve of her neck.

"You mean," she said, "that you can't change it. But that is different from forgetting." Gently she took his hand away.

He had a snapshot in his wallet taken more than a decade before of him and Julia side-by-side on the front steps of the family house in Berkeley, smiling into the camera and the low western sun. Hanaan pored over it, asking question after question about Julia, her studies, their parents, the house.

"You don't look alike." She had leaned so close that her shoulder pressed into his over the sleeping cat.

"No," he said. It had been years since he'd dug the photo from the depths of his wallet. His hair, much longer then, glowed almost white in the sun. Julia's rose up in a dark halo all around her head. "We were just kids here."

Hanaan was searching his face with a look so comprehending that he found it hard not to smile. "She isn't your sister in full blood, is she?"

He examined the photo again, cursorily, because it seemed that she wished him to. How tender they both looked. "I don't know."

He'd dismissed the question long ago as insoluble and thus unimportant. But now, seeing those earnest faces only emerging from childhood, he remembered his father's reticent eyes upon them when they were young; and his kindness, always steady, but as mild and distant as his gaze. He could think of no poem that mentioned either child, a fact that had never occurred to him before.

"And Julia," Hanaan said, as if testing the sound of it. "It's not like Theo and Theodore. It needs no other form. Your name, Theodore," she said, pronouncing it with every syllable distinct, the vowels pure and fine, rolling the r so that the name sounded beautiful to him as it never had before. "It's a difficult name."

"It's meant to be. There was a family tradition on my father's side to name the kids after saints. It was supposed to compel us to saintly behavior."

"You make fun with it," she said flatly. "A family tradition."

"I'm not making fun of it," he said, though of course she was right. It had been the easy way to shrug off the sense of loss that had come upon him. His devoutly atheistic father, presented with two children by his unsaintly wife, had chosen to follow this absurd Catholic tradition. Was it a poignant, last-ditch effort to exert his influence, or his cynical idea of a good joke? Theo couldn't tell, didn't know. His father's heart escaped him.

"It is Greek, did you know? Theo means 'god.'"

"Yes. 'Gift of god,'" he said with mock pomposity. "But I'm not religious, Hanaan. Not at all."

He didn't know how she'd react to this news; he hadn't spoken of his beliefs before. She laughed, wholeheartedly. "Not religious? That's worse than being Christian!"

But she didn't want to hear more. She passed a hand briefly over Theo's lips, to seal them. "Listen to me: religion should be private, always. From tonight, even with us, no religion. Otherwise, it's dangerous."

"Okay," he said, amused by her solemnity. A woman of such moods. "How do we avoid it exactly?" He cocked a thumb at the window, at the religion-drunk world of Kuwait beyond.

"Pay it no mind."

"Really? I've mostly found the world to work the other way around. You ignore high blood pressure, you have a stroke. You ignore a lump in your abdomen, you die of cancer. You—"

Another tap on his lips. "You doctors. You have no imagination beyond disease. So I will make it medical. Religion is a

146

poison dust. It settles deep around you. Let it lie, so that you may breathe."

Their talk shifted to her family and her mood altered again, edging toward uneasiness. She had four younger siblings, two sisters, two brothers. The youngest boy was still in boarding school abroad, and the other brother, just slightly younger than she, had dropped out of university temporarily. "He'll go back. He must."

Because her father couldn't qualify for citizenship, the family had access to none of the freebies of a cradle-to-grave welfare state: education, health care, interest-free loans, bonuses with the birth of every child.

"Every *fil*, he earned it," she said. "Not like these others who live in riches from the day they're born merely because they're sons of so-called 'first-class citizens,' these men with *wasta*. These are the people, these *citizens*," she spat out the word, "who fled to Riyadh and Cairo and London when the Iraqis came."

She clattered her empty teacup onto the tray at their side. "My father told all his children that ignorance is not for us. Neither of my sisters wanted to go to university but they went and now they're glad." Her voice lost its volume. "I don't mean to say they're happy."

"They're still at home?"

"Yes." She hesitated, gave him a bitter glance. "They speak three languages, read everything they can touch, and discuss the things he discusses—politics and business and international events. But they still play the parts of loving daughters who do his bidding, and they'll marry the men he chooses."

"But not you," he said. His earlier, obscure concern about her family reawakened and sharpened. How would they respond to him, an American who was not only non-Muslim but irreligious? Her father did not sound like a man who would walk through the deep dust of religion without a few swirls of his robe.

Her eyes skirted his. "I'm the eldest, Theo. He educated me and made me able to work, and so I'll work. Because I work I earn money. Because I earn money I may pay my own way. He

147

doesn't like me for this, but I've accepted the freedom he gave me, this is all. My sisters haven't done this. He didn't foresee that I would, and that's the trouble between us. He says I despise him with my behavior." The thought pained her. "But I don't despise him. It would be easier on my heart to hate him. But I love him."

Theo tried to draw her closer. "Can we please move this cat?"

Smiling, brushing away a tear, she lugged Solomon onto her lap. "There," and settled unresisting against Theo's side. They kissed.

"Do you see?" she whispered. "I must do my own thinking. What's the purpose of my mind if he fills it with his own thoughts?"

She kissed him back, a kiss of potent sadness that ended in a smile. Was it the sadness or the smile that mattered? He couldn't tell; it was like the music of the *oud*, both grieving and playful. He lay a hand on her cheek, finding the soft edge of her ear, intending to kiss her again and correct the ambiguities. But she drew away and took his hand instead.

THEO MERGED onto the crowded ring road headed west from Salmiya, in the direction of the hospital. He couldn't face returning to his empty flat. Hanaan would never become his lover. Things would never go that way; her rebellion didn't run so deep. Nor had he expected it, he told himself—a reminder that did nothing to banish the thought of her skin beneath his fingertips.

He accelerated, joining the traffic blurring by him on both sides. Even at 100 kph, there was a maniac in a sports car dancing on his tail, impatient for a chance to pass. The guy shot around him at 120, fishtailing for effect, a local teenaged boy with a couple of cohorts aboard. Hospital fodder for the near future. Theo edged it up to 115—safer to go with the flow—and crossed the main artery of the Fahaheel to see the hospital before him like an outworn mother ship come to earth at last. Here, at least, he could stay busy. Saleh had seen to that. With the infinite good nature of a thoroughly patient man, he had talked Theo into participating in an institution-wide review of the hospital's departments. "They'll listen to you. You're young, well-trained—and an American."

Theo had found this amusing. "You're trying to appeal to my ego?"

"Ah," Saleh said gravely, lifting his head. "I apologize. I'd forgotten for a moment how modest Americans are."

The radiology department was his assignment. He was to perform 'unannounced inspections' after providing the administration with detailed written plans for each visit. It would take a few evening hours to plan this sleight of hand.

Pulling into the reserved parking area for doctors near the emergency entrance of the hospital, he backed into a space. By some miracle the area wasn't yet blockaded by visitors' cars. City-wide, a man wearing a *dishdasha*—the long gown that indicated a native male—could park his car wherever he pleased, even in front of the ambulance entrance of a major hospital, even as an ambulance approached with siren screaming.

Switching the engine off, Theo leaned his elbows on the steering wheel, remembering with a pang of guilt that Julia had sent him an email in the morning. His recent telegraphic emails to her had gradually offended her with their brevity. *Can you maybe spend more than five minutes writing to me, hm? Come on, Theo, a few details of your existence, please.*

A few details of his existence. That's all he had to tell. A barren apartment. A chaste affair with a Muslim woman. A job as a flunky doctor.

He gazed at the fluorescent sign above the emergency room doors, half-hypnotized by its epileptic zaps. 'Casualty,' it read, in blinks and fits, the name a relic from the days of the British Protectorate, and an apt description of the whole hospital.

Throwing his car door open he crunched over the gravel toward the main entrance. The courtly guard who worked the

149

night shift rushed to open the big electric doors for him. He ushered Theo inside with the warm congeniality of a proprietor.

"Good evening, Dr. Theo. You work late tonight."

"Not as late as you do, Rajiv."

Though he'd worked this same job at the same salary for fifteen years, Rajiv seemed immune to melancholy. He worked twelve-hour shifts six nights a week.

"Yes," he said, smiling, "but one day, I will go home to Sri Lanka and do nothing at all."

Theo nodded, knowing better than to ask when. The answer would always be 'one day.'

The teeming atmosphere of the Casualty waiting room bore down on Theo as it always did, like a headache threatening to bloom. His eye appraised the crowd as he passed through with his long stride: a dozen women in *abayas* crouched against the wall talking, slope-shouldered and secretive; perhaps twenty men. The women's cloaks looked almost appropriate here in this dismal place, like black shrouds of mourning. Several men paced the room, fingering their prayer beads, ghostly in their *dishdashas*; and a handful of small children played on the grimy floor, some among them left to the care of a dark and silent housemaid standing in the corner as overseer. Her watchful black eyes met Theo's for an instant before she turned her head away as if to cancel the contact.

He made his way toward his office through the claustrophobic air of the long corridors, the low ceiling only inches above his head, thinking of the gleaming hospitals in the States. However illusory their cleanliness, their efficiency and rationality, he missed them. There, at least, some control seemed a possibility.

He knew Hanaan would see this place as she saw her equally ugly apartment building, this series of peeling metal doors, these restrooms like deep grottos dripping in the darkness, this stairway leading down into the bowels of the hospital, its breath smelling of musty paper and unwashed cement floors. Yet it was still a momentous achievement that a hospital had been built in response to the need for one. Forty years ago a mere infection, a scratch, a bout of tonsillitis, might bring a death sentence. This building stood, in all its repellent beauty, as a defense against such brutal suffering.

Theo unlocked his office and sat at his desk in the dark, feeling the weight of the place around him, suffocating, as if he were buried here. He needed to tell Julia about Hanaan. All he'd said so far was that he was 'seeing' an Arab woman, as if Hanaan were a specter or a mirage shimmering on the horizon. He knew how Julia would react to the news of a celibate relationship: with astounded skepticism. *No sex! So you have to wait for your wedding night, Theo?*

Did he mean to marry her? No. But he realized that he'd listened to Hanaan talk about marriage several times without thinking beyond the abstract about his own intentions; and yet he knew about the proscriptions in this culture. She had talked about how her father would choose husbands for her sisters, still the norm in the Middle East; and for Hanaan as well if she would let him. She'd talked about arranged marriage during their tutorials as part of an ongoing study of Arab culture, criticized its blindness to love, its unfairness to women, its ease of escape for men.

"A man may have four wives, and to divorce a woman all he need do is repudiate her. But a wife needs his permission to divorce. He may beat her, abuse her, wall her up in her own home, and still she must get his *permission!*" Yet even as he agreed that this was repugnant, she came to the defense of arranged marriage. "It's very sentimental to marry for love, Theo. Most cultures do not and never have. Marriage is for politics and money, for comfort and offspring. Most people in the world look at the West and say it's childish to think love will live more than a few weeks."

He hadn't pursued this. He preferred not to think beyond a few weeks if that's all the time she gave for love.

A note from Saleh lay on top of the stacks on his desk. He'd taken Theo into his home like a long-lost member of his family, and here was another invitation: "By Mufeeda's proclamation, you're to have dinner with me tomorrow evening. She's going to

151

a ladies' party and wants you to keep me company. She considers you an improving influence. Ah, the divine and eternal optimism of women!"

He set to work, roughing out on paper his ideas for the review of the radiology department until a phone began to ring behind a closed door down the darkened corridor. It pealed ten times, twenty. Theo lifted his head, listening. A lonely sound that renewed his pensiveness. Saleh's office, perhaps. Maybe Mufeeda was calling, hoping to catch him there after a late birth. But the office had been locked tight.

He rubbed at an ache behind his eyes, thinking of the differences between Hanaan and a woman like Mufeeda. *The eternal optimism of women.* Mufeeda did look like an optimist, a woman for whom a cheerful *inshallah* acceptance of fate was the only honorable way to face the world, a spiritual and social requirement. He'd met her just a handful of times, always briefly. It wasn't the usual thing, apparently, that she join Saleh with his friends, even in her own house. She looked the part of an ever-serene madonna, her face framed in a tight silk scarf: a quiet graciousness, a perpetual half-smile, an accepting nature that Saleh could take virtually for granted. Had their marriage been arranged? How starkly opposite from Hanaan who was also religious; but she prided herself on her clear-eyed view of the world, and this didn't quite take her into the territory of optimism. Could he be in love with such a woman?

He tried to picture where Hanaan might be at this moment. She was a night owl too. She'd be settled over a book at the little table where they studied together, a glass of herbal tea at her fingertips, readying her lessons for tomorrow. Head down, her hair falling forward to the soft skin of her arms. He yearned to touch that hair, to push it back gently, revealing her face.

How odd it seemed to him to feel this way when wariness and circumspection had been his prevailing responses to the women he dated, the only ones, sometimes, that he'd been able to identify beyond his body's desires—until Hanaan. He and Julia

152

had debated about their current lovers for years, each urging the other toward a commitment neither had ever made. *We're both of us loners, Theo.*

Eleven o'clock. Time to go, despite the insomnia he expected tonight. He'd write that email to Julia.

He locked his office and threaded his way back to Casualty. A whirl of red lights at the main entrance reflected down the long hallway approach. A couple of policemen, a small corpse on a gurney sheeted from head to toe, a doctor, a gaping circle of rubberneckers from the waiting room. Theo would have passed by but for the look on Rajiv's face. Drawn, near crying, he struggled to keep his countenance, his eyes locked on Theo's as Theo came toward the doors.

A low voice. He didn't want to embarrass the man. "What's up, Rajiv?"

Rajiv's eyes rolled toward the policemen, epauletted toothpick-thin young men with unreadable faces. One pulled the sheet back from the head of the corpse. A woman, a girl, beaten viciously. Long dark hair matted with dirt or blood lay against a crushed cheek. An eye was gone. One of the policemen gestured to someone at the periphery and a man came forward with a large camera.

"A girl from my country, Dr. Theo," Rajiv whispered. He nodded toward the front curb. "They left her there."

A housemaid, then. The photographer framed the girl's bruised and bloody face. A flash. Another.

"You mean her employer didn't stay?"

"They dropped her and went off."

Theo couldn't believe it. "They left her here to die alone?"

Rajiv pressed a finger to his lips. "Sir, they will hear!" He recovered himself with effort. "They dropped her. There, at the door. They opened the car, they pushed her out, they drove away."

Theo still didn't understand.

Rajiv hung his head. "She was dead before, Dr. Theo. They brought her dead."

IFTAR

THE CHRISTMAS decorations had never made it to Kuwait. Kit stood aghast in the storage closet under the stairs, unwilling to believe it; but she'd looked everywhere, in every armoire in the house. Nothing. The boxes—she'd marked them all so carefully back home in giant black letters, 'Xmas'—had somehow missed the boat. The family had a tree only by an odd stroke of luck, a lofty ten-foot artificial Douglas fir Jack had nabbed in October from one of his underlings here who'd sold most of his belongings before returning to the States. Jack had come home one evening like a big-game hunter with a huge, boxed beast, all smiles. "We can give that old dusty six-footer to someone else!" Neither he nor Kit had thought to actually go in search of the smaller tree at the time, though the thought had run through Kit's mind: I wonder where we put the Christmas decorations?

There was no replacing them. The stores in Kuwait that catered at all to Christians had put their best holiday guesses on the shelves already and the pickings weren't good: cheesy 'Merry Christmas!' banners made of paper, flimsy cartoon greeting cards infected with glittery dander, and tall stacks of boxed mini-lights that blared out carols as they blinked in green, yellow, red, and blue.

It wouldn't have mattered if they were going home for the holidays. But they weren't, despite Jack's earlier promise. Kit sat down solidly in a kitchen chair and gave herself a pep talk. It wasn't the end of the world. Jack's work came first—that was part of the deal when they accepted this assignment, and she couldn't let him see the depth of her disappointment. He'd given his promise before he knew the lay of the land here, and now it seemed impolitic to leave. It wasn't Christmas for the Kuwaitis, after all. She should feel proud of him: he wanted to stay on the job.

Well, she'd have to improvise—a big challenge to a non-artistic person; but you didn't grow up as the child of Walt and Annie Pollard and not learn to make do. Her parents didn't allow griping; you just did the best you could. 'Complaining never fixed anything' could have been the family motto emblazoned over the door like the Arabic swirls on Mufeeda's gate. Improvisation had abounded at home, conversation had not. *Got that alternator fixed, Walt? Well, it'll do. Good—more roast?* A cut from a hard-rumped old cow transformed via vigorous pummeling and six hours of simmering with sweet onions and salt. *Sure is good, Annie-girl.* Communication enough.

She could cook up that cow too, by God. Grabbing the kids fresh from their naps she sallied forth to do battle. Any woman who had braved the mall and Santa's Landing for six years running should find this challenge a piece of cake.

She made her way to Ace Hardware, navigating across the city completely on her own for the first time, without either Jack or a band of company women to help; into that industrial waste-land of one-lane, oil-soaked, potholed streets packed nose-to-nose with bony Third World laborers wearing tattered gowns or trousers and long, ragged shirts and plastic sandals, and what looked exactly like dirty red-checked kitchen towels wrapped around their heads. Even in early December, with no trees or greenery for miles around, the whole place wavered with heat distortion as though on the verge of meltdown. And amidst all this—it never ceased to amaze her—smack between two flat-roofed, rust-worn corrugated buildings, banged and shredded as if they'd been in one of the head-on collisions on the ring roads, sat a bristling clean, stark white Ace store with eye-popping red lettering over the door and a neat curb stenciled 'For Ace Customer's Only.' Truly it looked just like home, right down to the apostrophe.

Inside, if you didn't dwell on details such as Christmas, the illusion continued. The air was arctic; a freezer of Dove Bars stood near the line of cash registers that marched off into the distance. There were Hoover vacuum cleaners and Air Wick Solids room deodorants and Eveready batteries and Raid insecticide and Bell canning supplies. Canning supplies? It boggled the mind. There were even lawnmowers, porch swings and tiki torches staged on carpets of fake grass, though Kit had yet to see either grass or porches in Kuwait.

She gathered colored construction paper, colored markers and a plastic box of gold stars, some gel pens, a pack of envelopes. Wandering the aisles with Kevin confined to the cart and Carla trailing close behind she felt a sense of accomplishment and power. Once she'd been to Ace on her own, she could go anywhere—without Jack.

There were other things they needed besides Christmas supplies. She pulled a big jug of Liquid Plumr from the shelf and swung it into the cart, resisting an impulse to pat its familiar red twist-top affectionately. A definite necessity. The last plumber Jack called in had told them that the toilets were all fixed, "only put nothing in toilet." She questioned an Indian clerk about graphite, explaining that Jack's weight machine squeaked, and persisted doggedly with the inquiry through two other baffled Indian clerks, a young Kuwaiti manager who invited her to tea, which she refused, and a fourth clerk who finally grasped the meaning of her words as she mimed lifting weights, exclaiming, "Ah, madam! Gym giving voice!"

Delighted to have comprehended her exotic English, he led her to the correct aisle and insisted on picking up the tiny tube himself and placing it tenderly in her cart. "Thank you, madam!"

Checking out, she bought two Dove Bars, feeling that she and the kids all needed a reward. She shared hers with Kevin as they sat in a porch swing next to the gleaming dome of a Weber grill under a tasseled umbrella. Through the thick plate glass they could see their car nosed up to the curb and a stream of bedraggled workers in the street beyond wheeling their carts slowly in the sunshine.

"REALLY PRETTY, Kit," Jack said in the sparkling darkness of the upstairs. "I knew you could do it." He didn't ask and so she didn't tell him how she'd managed to find non-singing lights through Video Rosie, a black marketeer down in Fahaheel, or how she'd come up with the idea of stringing wrapped chocolates on ribbons as ornaments. After a long pause in which she knew he was struggling to decide if he'd said enough nice things, he switched on the light and sat down with his paper. *Sure tastes good, Annie-girl.* Enough for Mom but only because it came from Dad. Kit had to wait for the cookie-exchange she was hosting to get more. She could depend on the ladies, at least, to do a little gushing.

Dear Dad,

I'm so sorry we can't be there for Christmas. I'm really disappointed too, but I know Jack's right that he wouldn't relax if he came home. He'd worry about work. We have to make the best of things.

Kit sat staring at her own brave words. The best wasn't very good. She toyed with the seductive vision of packing up and leaving for the States with the kids minus Jack. Tantalizing. How long would it take for him to realize they were gone? He might sit in his chair with a newspaper for most of an evening before he realized he was alone. She smiled at the thought of his quizzical look, those blue eyes popped up over the top of the Sports section. *Where is everybody?* But it was a wild fantasy. She didn't have the nerve, and she'd shock everyone in her family and his.

Kit and Jack. Jack and Kit. They'd become a single unit to their families in the years since the kids were born, a fact she'd still noted with pride only months ago. Now it filled her with a sense of compression and vague jeopardy, like a foreboding of illness. The traits she'd admired in Jack back home—his keen focus on his work, his efficiency and self-confidence—had translated into a kind of blindness here. He operated as if he were still at home, like a scrupulous piece of machinery made for a particular task, though everything around him had changed.

I'm actually glad to be here for Ramadan, though I wonder if I'll survive it. The Kuwaitis have a tradition of taking food to their neighbors at sundown, when their daily fast ends. Every night for 30 days! It's called Iftar. So each evening right after prayer call our doorbell starts buzzing.

She hadn't known what she was in for that first night. When the doorbell buzzed at dusk she happened to be downstairs, so she went to the gate without bothering to holler a query through the intercom. Two of Mufeeda's maids stood before her, grinning happily, though they were burdened like waitresses serving a banquet. They held six dishes between them, in their hands and precariously balanced on their forearms: a whole leg of lamb on a bed of rice, a couple of bowls of breaded vegetables, an enormous bowl of *tabouleh*, and two desserts. Mufeeda sent almost as much food the next night, and other neighbors sent offerings too: fish and chicken and platter after platter of lamb. It was like thirty days straight of Thanksgiving.

I can't imagine doing so much cooking—or eating—but then all the Kuwaitis have household staffs. Mufeeda asked me how I get along without a maid. I need to hire one, I know. It just seems so weird. Me with a maid. I joked with her that she should give me one of hers. She has about a half-dozen, I think.

Thanks to Mufeeda, she now knew a little something about the holy month, enough to feel embarrassed by her total ignorance before, right down to the name itself. Because Islam's lunar calendar shifted Ramadan forward by ten days every year, Mufeeda recalled the most memorable Ramadans of her childhood partly by a cherished image of the season: a flood at Ramadan when she was a little girl, and a spring Ramadan when the desert was filled with flowers. Her father had taken the family camping for the feast days. Mufeeda remembered him

158

trapping birds and roasting them for the kids on slender sticks over a hastily built fire.

Imagine having your Christmas memories tied up with fireworks or going bass fishing at Grand Lake. Christmases all tend to blur in my memory. I wish so much now that I could remember every one exactly.

Kit sifted through her stack of newspaper clippings for a couple to include with the letter. It had become more difficult lately to find good ones. She had one headline she liked: "Turk Minister Stable After Suicide." But not much else. The longer she lived here the less amusing she found the news, and now Saddam—besides harassing the weapons inspectors in Iraq—was mouthing off about reclaiming Kuwait, as if the Gulf war had never been fought.

She rarely mentioned Saddam to her father and then only obliquely. There was no way to casually mention the memo Jack had brought home recently reporting that a Marine Expeditionary Unit would be giving seminars at the embassy on 'regional terrorism and anti-terrorism awareness,' and 'nuclear, biological and chemical agents.' Or the notice he'd emailed to the house from the office about a test broadcast on the radio 'to facilitate communication with American citizens if a crisis develops.' Jack had discounted it all. "Kuwait is among the best-defended places in the world right now. Don't worry." She had determined not to. Nor would she worry her dad.

She had plenty of clippings. One was an ad, a potential nominee: "Abayas N Things! Hijabs, abayas, dishdashas, salwar kameez, burkas, hijab pins!" But much in her stack these days was like an article she'd found only this morning. She studied it again. "Wife-beating Aggravates Problems: Spouses Should Display Patience." Three months ago she'd have sent this to her father, snorting at the absurdity of it. Did men here really have to be told the disadvantages of beating their wives? But such articles troubled her now and she'd stopped sending them to him. The ad, on review, seemed just like any other anywhere with a few odd nouns; she put it aside. Everything else in her stack related to the recent murders of three housemaids in quick succession. She'd collected every article about them she'd seen, shocked at how detailed and gruesome the reports were, while lacking what even she, a lifelong non-reader, knew to be the basics of reporting.

She fanned the series out on her desktop in date order. A passport photo of the first murdered woman had been printed in color on the top of the front page, identifying her in the caption by her full name. She'd been stabbed to death and her body dumped in the desert. A Kuwaiti soldier had confessed to the crime, and both he and a friend had been arrested; yet there were no photos of either man and they were identified by their first names only. The woman was the lover of the soldier, the article stated, though it made no mention of the source for this information.

An update two days later was headlined: "Murdered Maid on Fake Passport," and openly implied that the woman might deserve death for such a crime. "Earlier reports indicate that she demanded marriage from the Kuwaiti soldier. It was initially reported the girl was pregnant but later sources said she may not have been pregnant."

Was it her imagination, Kit wondered, or was there more outrage in the article about the fake passport and the demand for marriage than the murder itself?

The second maid had been killed and dumped from a get-away car at the curb of a local hospital. In order to identify her, the police had taken a ghastly color photograph of her bloody, purplish face and run it on the front pages of the local newspapers. Kit moved the article aside, unable to bear the sight. No follow-up story told who had spoken up to identify the woman, but soon enough her full name was in the press while the accused killers, a Kuwaiti couple who had employed her, went unidentified. They hadn't confessed to the crime. In fact, they'd insisted to the reporter that, ". . . they have no idea how she came to be lying dead . . ."

The third murder had been heralded by "Hair Clenched in Fist of Dead Maid." Yet another unidentified employer had come upon a dead body in her own house and said she had no idea what happened to the maid, a thirty seven-year-old Indian woman, again identified in full. The employer reported to the police that she found the housemaid "lying in a pool of blood, with deep injuries to her head inflicted by a hard object. . . . The housemaid fiercely resisted her killer, as her hand was tightly clenched with hair in it."

An update a few days later, a tiny article Kit had almost missed, bore the insignificant headline: "Sponsor admits to beating maid," which sounded more like a slap on the face than a murder. The Kuwaiti woman had confessed to beating her housemaid on the head with "a long wooden handled rubber cleaning wiper after an argument between them . . ." She ". . . used to fight with the housemaid for not performing housework and would hit her but not to the extent of inflicting harm . . ."

Kit pushed all the articles away, thinking of the mass of maids at Mufeeda's, and the one maid's urgent words to Kit on her first visit about going to 'America.' She couldn't believe that Mufeeda or her husband were capable of violence. Certainly not Mufeeda. And her husband was a gynecologist, for God's sake.

Well, just one clipping for Dad this time. The Turk minister could make the trip to Stillwater.

"You will come for dinner tonight?" Mufeeda asked by phone. "It's our *Iftar* meal, when we break our fast. You will join us, yes?"

The blessing of such an invitation was that it left little time to grow nervous. Kit set to work on a rich potatoes au gratin, a big double recipe—she couldn't go empty-handed after the nightly banquets from Mufeeda—and gave Jack notice by phone; he was rarely home before the *Iftar* prayer call at sundown. He agreed to leave early, not so insensible of the honor as she'd expected. He even put on a fresh shirt and tie and presented himself for inspection just as the *Iftar* calls to prayer floated out over the neighborhood. "Very nice," she told him, handing him the casserole and ignoring his little-boy desire for a compliment, her childish vengeance, she knew, for his blindness to her own little appeals for attention. He looked so crestfallen that she patted him on the arm. "You look very handsome, Jack."

Her casserole had turned out beautifully, toasted gold on the top and bubbling with cream, nothing to be ashamed of.

She had hold of the children and kept them under stern control as they made their way across the street, which helped keep her calm.

"I wonder if they're going to pray while we're there," she said to Jack. "I mean down on their carpets and everything. Mufeeda said to come right after prayer call."

Jack grunted. "I doubt it. They haven't had anything to eat or drink since dawn. Probably they'll eat now and pray later. How religious are they?"

"I can't tell exactly. More than we are. Or at least Mufeeda's pretty religious. I don't know about her husband. I wonder if they do ceremonies over the table like the Jews do, with candles and verses?" She knew that much only from *Fiddler on the Roof.* She'd never before joined a non-Christian family for a religious celebration, she realized, though she'd once gone to a Catholic mass with a grade school friend, an experience her parents considered slightly dangerous.

Jack didn't answer, which meant he knew no more than she did about Ramadan traditions but didn't want to admit it. She allowed herself to needle him a little as they climbed the steps to Mufeeda's door. "Hasn't anyone at work ever talked to you about Ramadan, someone who's been here a couple of years?"

"They eat, Kittie."

As usual, he was right. It was a very big dinner—and everyone was hungry. Kit tried to imagine capturing the sight for her dad in a letter: the crowd of adults and kids around the enormous table, the colorful chaos of dishes laid out before them, and the surprising informality of it all. She'd expected near-silence and solemnity, but the atmosphere was festive, the sort of dinner that in the States might call for a bottle of champagne, though there was no alcohol here. Mufeeda linked arms with Kit and pulled out a chair for her; Saleh shook hands with Jack and clapped him on the shoulder, then introduced cousins and nieces and nephews in a mind-numbing blur of Arabic names. The grandmother wasn't present, Kit noted. She'd never yet set eyes on this woman close-up. Carlie and Kevin were swept away once again by a maid and taken upstairs along with Mufeeda's youngest. Other maids circulated in a blur, bringing new courses in from the kitchen and replacing dinner plates with clean ones the moment anyone paused for a rest, lavishing attention on the older children allowed at the table—Mufeeda's daughter Mariam and some of her cousins. When a tall Caucasian friend of Saleh's arrived a few minutes later with a beautiful Arab woman, Saleh stood up at the head of the table and without ceremony said in English, "Hey! All you kids move down. Make room for Theo and Hanaan." The children at the foot of the table stood up dutifully like soldiers in a mess hall and shifted to the left.

Saleh introduced the newcomers around, though Theo obviously knew Mufeeda and Mariam already, well enough to tease Mariam about sitting with the adults. "So you graduated, huh?"

No mistaking that 'huh.' He was an American, though his looks recalled to Kit the Dutch she'd seen in Amsterdam en route to Kuwait, who all seemed to be blond and seven feet tall. He had a lanky, affable way about him, an unassuming warmth, an easy smile. He nodded at Kit as if he already knew her. His girlfriend in contrast was small and graceful, with grave, intelligent eyes. She was dressed as plainly as Kit herself in a skirt and blouse, but she was not plain, Kit realized with a pang of self-consciousness. Hanaan's long dark hair caught the brilliant light of the chandeliers as it fell across her shoulders, turning her subtly opulent. No wonder she'd caught Theo's eye.

Saleh's two young cousins sat on either side of Kit, a brother and sister in their twenties who looked and sounded, disappointingly, like American kids of the same age. Kit felt doddery in

163

the very act of noting this. They sat slouchy and nonchalant at the table, affecting that slightly glazed look obligatory at family gatherings, though their glances at Saleh and Mufeeda betrayed respect. Too cool to show it outright, of course. Saleh was extolling their achievements with generous affection. They'd both gone to college in the States, and Basma, the girl, was earning another degree in business at Kuwait University in preparation for opening a coffee bar downtown. "She's the next Starbucks," Saleh said. Basma's brother, in a Yankees cap and jeans, was a picture of Kit's brothers right down to the hunch and the elbows on the table. Kit had to work against the impulse to knock his hands out from under his chin, her mother's way of dealing with such behavior. She thought he ogled Hanaan a little too openly for propriety's sake too.

"This guy actually has a pretty good job already," Saleh said, nodding at the brother. "Hakim, tell Theo what you do."

Hakim shrugged, too elaborately. "I run a Kuwaiti company that owns fast-food restaurants in Kuwait and Israel."

Kit thought she'd heard him wrong. 'Palestine' was the required name for Israel in Kuwait, and she'd heard no one defy the rule before. The Israelis were the enemy.

Theo was surprised too. "Kuwaitis own businesses in Israel?"

Hakim assured him blandly that it was true. "They aren't openly Kuwaiti-owned, of course," he said, pouring a Coke down his throat. "If anyone asks, they're Israeli." He cracked a chunk of ice between his molars. "But they're not."

As Theo urged more information from Hakim, Mufeeda handed platter after platter to Kit, describing each dish for her, though Kit could clearly register only the main nouns: lamb, fish, shrimp, chicken, which all rested in glory atop thick beds of glistening rice and a delicately seductive atmosphere of cloves, cinnamon, cardamom, lemon, and curry. More platters followed of meat and vegetable pastries laid out like origami, piquant chopped salads, rich bowls of hummus and flatbreads straight from the oven. Kit gamely piled samples onto her plate until it

164

could hold no more, and urged Jack with a look to do the same. But it was too late. He'd already insured himself against obeying her by filling most of his plate with her potatoes au gratin.

Oh well. He was a meat and potatoes man; she knew that. And the meat and potatoes had to be meat and potatoes he recognized. Beginning to relax, Kit sat back in cautious enjoyment. There was so much going on that she felt no pressure to say anything to anyone, a relief when all she wanted to do was observe—and eat. Conversation rose to a low roar in a mix of languages. The kids at the foot of the table spoke Arabic and English indiscriminately. Kit caught phrases about a new teacher, something about an ice rink and equestrian classes. Hanaan and Basma were trading what looked like polite introductory information in Arabic. Mufeeda had shifted into French with a niece who boarded at a girls' school in Switzerland. Catching Kit's eye, Mufeeda smiled apologetically. "I am testing her verbs."

The men had turned to the topic of Saddam's latest threats, inevitably, Kit thought, wishing they'd thought the better of it. She didn't want to think about Saddam. Did he really belong at a Ramadan dinner?

"He hasn't rebuilt his army," Theo said, "he's bluffing," and Hakim cut in, as if backing him up against Saleh: "All he can do is talk. He won't attack."

Saleh's voice came like a slap. "Oh no? He didn't stop with talk six years ago."

Silence flew down the table, giving Kit the impression that everyone ducked a little. Saleh glanced at Mufeeda, his mildness returning so quickly that his face no longer looked capable of the flash of anger Kit had seen. He spiked up a forkful of dark meat from his plate and cast a smile at them all.

Had she imagined that moment? Theo went on blithely with the theme of war as if it hadn't taken place.

"Mufeeda," he said, dishing up something that looked like a thick chicken stew. "Saleh told me that you escaped to Saudi Arabia during the war. You must have worried about him a lot, having to leave him behind when the whole country was infested with Iraqis."

Mufeeda's reaction was discomfort or offense, Kit couldn't tell which. Glancing at Saleh, she deflected the comment entirely with a smile and a shake of the head. "But it was in God's hands, of course."

Kit knew nothing about any escape. Mufeeda had said very little about the war at all, and it struck her that Saleh had breached Mufeeda's privacy by telling Theo this bit of family history. Kit saw that Hanaan's eyes were on Mufeeda too, gently speculative.

Saleh was frowning comically at Hakim, who had leapt in with cocksure remarks about 'America's commercial imperialism' in the wake of the war. "American companies are crowding out the local ones now. Don't get me wrong. I'm as ready to make money on franchises as the next guy, but what's the cost to our culture in the long run? America's here to stay."

"Our culture," said Saleh with gentle mockery. "Here you sit, American-educated with an American accent, a foreigner in your own land worrying about our culture. Where is your *dishdasha* if you're so concerned?"

Basma knocked the bill of her brother's cap upward, revealing a dark mat of hair. "Hey!" Hakim said, snugging it back down.

"You can't see his tight jeans if he wears a *dishdasha*," said his sister.

Saleh shook his head, laughing. "Hopeless. Both of you."

He wasn't wearing a *dishdasha* either, Kit noted. He had on black slacks and a pale yellow shirt.

Baleful in the shadow of the bill cap, Hakim said, "Our government handed over the opportunities to America on a silver platter after the war."

"After the war? But the war has never ended." Hanaan. It was the first time she'd spoken up. "It isn't a matter of a new attack. There are still planes in the air every day, Iraqis dying for

166

this madman Saddam whom Kuwaitis adored until the very day he attacked, and whom the Americans wouldn't bother to kill."

Her voice was so calm and melodious that Kit wondered if she'd misunderstood the implications; but the surprise and hesitation among the other adults convinced her she hadn't. The cousins exchanged a mordant glance, expanding it to Saleh, who ignored them. Theo was waiting for more. Mufeeda's dark eyes went to the children, Kit noted.

The hesitation gave Jack an opening. "Well, of course there were a lot of variables that had to be considered at that juncture, the invasion of a sovereign nation, for instance, no small matter."

He rumbled on about troop strength and the supply problems of convoys and potential house-to-house fighting in Baghdad, and Kit saw the cousins make a modest attempt to cloak their impatience. They and Hanaan eyed each other, waiting only for Jack's drone to signal a pause, not realizing that Jack made no full stops once he got rolling. He could draw out a single sentence for hours.

It broke loose all at once. Hanaan sang out to the cousins, brushing Jack aside. "I know you don't like what I say but it's true. Kuwaitis queued up to pay their respects to that man before the war."

Hakim could hardly stay in his chair. "Oh, come on. And I thought you looked like a reasonable woman. Are you talking about the support in the press for Saddam? The press doesn't represent the people of Kuwait."

"Not just the press," Hanaan said. "But yes, they kissed his hand. They published poems to Saddam. Do you remember? The great Arab conqueror, who smiled to us and then sent in his tanks."

Hakim appealed to the whole table for justice. "Newspaper editors! You're speaking of newspaper editors, one in particular. He's given us all a black eye."

In the energy of their contention they reverted to noisy Arabic, and Kit lost any sense of whether the mood was mostly friendly or unfriendly or an unstable mixture of both. Saleh's attempts to intervene and reroute the conversation failed, but he managed to look entertained rather than defeated. Noticing Kit's silence as the communal roar of rhetoric and laughter rose up around the table, he said to her with gentle irony, "How peaceful it is with all the family at home."

Kit tried to relax again. There was no room even for edgewise words, and so nothing to do but listen. She found herself watching Theo and Hanaan. How handsome he was. She liked his quiet attention to the conversation—did he speak Arabic?—and the way his eyes kept coming back to Hanaan, who interested Kit even more. She'd seen no other Arab woman like her, and few American women either. Though she was a first-time guest in the house, she acted as if she were part of the family, accustomed to saying whatever she wished. More than that, she expressed all her opinions with the easy assurance of a man.

Addressing all the adults, Hanaan returned to English. "You'd think we would learn something deep and humble from a war. But what have we done in these years? We complain about everything. We've already forgotten how desperate we felt then. We shut off our minds with money. It's a glorious narcotic, and we want more and more."

"You know what the Americans say," Hakim said mockingly, raising his water glass. "Eat, drink, and be merry.' Now if only this were a beer."

Eyeing Hanaan, his sister raised her chin. "You talk as if our fate's in our own hands. You forget that Allah has given us our good fortune."

"I don't believe that," said Hanaan, her dark eyes steady on the younger woman. "That's what we say when we can't be bothered to change." She turned to Hakim. "You're right. Eat, drink, and be merry. The Iraqis captured our country in six hours. Six *hours*. It will be taken again forever one day, probably by Iran."

The conversation hung in midair for a moment, marked by the tinkle of silverware from the children's end of the table. Then

Hakim gave a hoot of dismissive laughter and the conversation erupted anew. It seemed to Kit that all the adults were talking at once and listening to no one. She could hear only Hanaan's voice clearly, and found herself following the rich and polished flow of it as it intermingled with the others. In the cacophony, it caught the ear like music.

"All the promises to God we made when Saddam invaded and the Americans hadn't yet come—can you remember them? What's become of those? If only God would save us we'd be humble and follow him again. We'd treat one another well. We'll remake all our ways, dear God. Oh, they were fine words. How fortunate we are that the Americans came and saved us from everything, even from our vows to God."

Only later, thinking about the dinner, did Kit realize how silent Mufeeda and Saleh had been at this moment. She saw them in her mind's eye, their faces frozen into pinched smiles, gazing vaguely at their loud and gesticulating guests.

Two Polished Black Shoes

The priest, far off and faceless in the jaundiced glare of the cathedral's stained-glass windows, mumbled on and on in his thick-tongued monotone. Emmanuella bent her head in exhaustion rather than prayer. Her luck had faltered again. Though a mass was said every hour and in several languages on Christmas day, the one mass she could attend was in English rather than Konkani, and was being celebrated by the one priest in the diocese who didn't speak English well. Surely someone whose purpose it was to link thousands of poor Catholics from more than a dozen nations should speak their common language better than they.

She tried to cast her weariness and frustration away from her. It was Christmas, and she might meet John today, a cause for hope, however feeble. Outside, after mass, he might step forward and introduce himself.

She put this unnerving thought deliberately from her mind, forcing her focus back to the pale priest, who was mumbling even the verses at the very heart of Christmas. *And there were in the same country shepherds abiding in the field, keeping watch over their flocks by night.* She looked around resentfully at the deadening crush of the congregation. South Asians filled every pew, every aisle, every doorway. So much jostling and coughing and creaking of wood, a dozen dropped missals, a murmur of prayer like rain coming in the distance—they'd exhaust God with their endless pleas.

Emmanuella fought her dismay by reading the words softly aloud like everyone else, trying to hear them as the poetry they were—*and lo, the angel of the Lord came upon them*—telling of that great moment when fear was transformed into joy.

But she couldn't make the leap herself. Her thoughts went to Ramadan. It would be upon them in days, wiping out any memory of Christmas.

Did Christmas really happen here?

Her doubt mortified her. Christmas happened everywhere, even here, even in this place where young maids were starved and attacked and dumped dead and nameless at hospital curbsides.

The black, misshapen face of the dead maid flashed into her mind so powerfully that she shut her eyes against it. Carmen had brought the front page to her room one night, shaking with rage. *Look! Look what these animals do!* She comforted herself with thoughts of her own relative good luck. She had little to complain of compared to others like herself. She thanked God with all her heart that she couldn't be pregnant. Frederick hadn't gotten so far. God had not let him cross her path again, a telling sign. Her watchfulness had doubled. She looked every time to see that he got in the car himself, that he drove away himself, that he didn't plead illness at the last moment.

Ramadan would protect her further. For an entire month Frederick would be too busy to monitor her closely. The Grandmother would stir herself much more during Ramadan, and Ma'am Mufeeda might also need him from time to time. Another blessing: there would be too much food in the house for Santana's share to be missed, the great benefit of Ramadan in her mind. Santana would eat as well as anyone in the household during these holy days.

With the thought of food came nausea. Her stomach had troubled her constantly these last days, and her hands and feet too. However well she slept, she felt exhausted, as if to the marrow of her bones. If that garbage truck had not rounded the corner, she would think now that she was pregnant.

Had that poor girl been pregnant? She couldn't keep the dead maid's face from her mind. She'd been a member of this church, had sat perhaps in this very pew, saying her prayers as desperately as anyone else under this same high roof. Had she and Emmanuella ever greeted one another after the service, exchanged a smile? She hoped so.

It was rumored that someone among the congregation had known the girl's identity and gone to the Bishop, and that he'd called the police to give the girl a name. Her heart rose up at the thought of him. He wouldn't be afraid to speak to the authorities. *This woman is not unknown.* Why wasn't the Bishop saying this mass? His sonorous voice was easily understood, and his face, though graven with sadness, was one she could have looked upon with love and gratitude at Christmas. He would have given the police their due. *Let judgment run down as waters, and righteousness as a mighty stream.*

She tried to take strength from that thought, to help see her through Ramadan. It was said by the older housemaids that the beginning of the holy month was marked, not by the calls from the mosques, but by the weeping of maids; and last year, her first, she'd collapsed in tears at the end of the first week. Sir and Ma'am met the letter of their fasting law exactly, eating a generous meal as soon as the sun went down and then another small one just before dawn to last them until nightfall. The household staff kept all its normal daytime hours and duties, and was also expected to handle the meals at dawn and all the extra laundry, ironing, and cleaning that came with the evening banquets and the many guests. This year, since Gloria had failed to return from the Philippines, the staff would be short. Ma'am had told them only that Gloria's daughter needed her 'more than we need her, so I have told her to stay.' Two or three hours of sleep a night would be as much as any of them could expect.

The service ended with "Silent Night," and the congregation moved toward the brick courtyard where the cool weather of the winter afternoon had turned darker. Attendees for the next mass wove their way through the crowd in the opposite direction. Emmanuella gave an older woman her arm and walked with her until the woman patted her cheek and turned for the bus stop. "God bless you."

"God bless you too, auntie. Merry Christmas!"

Now she stood alone. She stared straight ahead, wondering if John was nearby, equally anxious. Why she had ever thought to agree to this madness she couldn't imagine. Nothing would come of this; but even if something could, what possible benefit could marriage offer two people doomed to work as servants for their whole working lives? How could parents' expectations overpower that reality even from two thousand miles away?

"Emmanuella, are you asleep? It's raining!"

Carmen yanked at her, pulling her beneath a walkway already crowded with others. Rain spat down in pinpricks of orange dust on their skin. The deluge came in a rush, whooshing the cold gritty air up and out, lifting skirts and long braids and spirits equally. Carmen was making eyes at Emmanuella, wriggling her eyebrows in a ridiculous fashion.

"There's a boy."

Emmanuella wouldn't listen.

Carmen sang in her ear. "Manwellllllla! Over there. Look!" She shot a finger toward Emmanuella's left as if this could somehow be a discreet gesture not comprehended instantly by everyone within sight.

"We must go, Carmen. Ma'am will be looking for us."

"He asked me to speak with you. He's waiting!"

Emmanuella felt the rain might boil on her skin if she stepped into it. "Let him wait."

"You *do* see him!"

How could she not? He stood like a man afflicted from head to toe by paralysis. How skinny could a boy be? If you turned him sideways he would vanish altogether but for his nose. She wished devoutly for his disappearance.

"He's coming!" Carmen's grip on Emmanuella's wrist tightened until she winced in pain. Without looking up, Emmanuella could feel Carmen grinning horribly at the boy. She kept her eyes on two polished black shoes as big as hearses parked in the dampening dust. Black-stockinged bony ankles rose above them, exposed by gray, cuffed pants. He was still growing.

"Good afternoon, Emmanuella."

Carmen answered for her at a near-shout. "Good afternoon!" Emmanuella elbowed her firmly in her well-padded ribs. "Carmen, close your mouth."

"If you'll open yours!"

Emmanuella would not. She locked her stare on the black shoes. They shifted uncomfortably.

"I'll eat ice cream," Carmen said as if by sudden inspiration, though she had ice cream every Sunday. The rain had stopped as suddenly as it began. Still, she failed to move.

The boy fumbled in a deep pocket of his trousers and came forth with a handful of change. Without a word he offered it to Carmen, and Carmen—amazingly—reached out to take it. Emmanuella slapped her hand away.

"You'll take money for your politeness? You'll be paid for your manners?"

Carmen's face bloomed bright with anger. "What a botheration you are, Emmanuella!"

"I? *I'm* a botheration?"

"Here, please," said the boy, gently forcing the change into Carmen's hand. "Please do me the honor. It's a gift. For Christmas."

The boy's calm insistence offered no alternatives. Carmen cast a look of vindication at Emmanuella, and slipped into the dispersing crowd.

Emmanuella gave the boy a piercing once-over. "What a fool you are. Now she'll always want money." Remarkably, he stood smiling at her as though she were a handsome sight and not a spiteful one. "And you write to me that you're smart."

"It's worth the money, to have you quietly here."

"Quiet? I'm never quiet. Ask Carmen."

"But you've sent her away. May I buy you an ice cream too?"

Did he mock her? She stole another look at him. No. Earnestness shone from him. She saw it clearly, the finest feature of his otherwise homely face.

"Please, don't fall silent," he said. "There are many years ahead for that. Now's the time for us to talk."

How much the same they were: his response to fear was to be bold.

"Come, please," he said. "Let's walk, and we'll tell one another about home."

SANCTUARY

MEMORANDUM

To: *All Resident Americans*
From: *Building Warden*

   *The U.S. Embassy reports that it is monitoring the situation
with Iraq closely. In view of current tensions, it has asked all wardens to reiterate to all American citizens its standing advice to keep:*
     A two-weeks' supply of food and water on hand;
     A two-weeks' supply of necessary medications on hand;
     Copies of all official documents such as passports;
     Car in good running condition;
     Gas tanks at least half full;
     Flashlights, candles, radio and batteries on hand;
     *Traditional dress on hand (*abaya *and scarf for women);*
     U.S. cash and credit cards on hand.
     In addition:
          Pack early in case of emergency;
          Know back streets;
     Do not contribute to the spread of rumors.

THEO ZAPPED the email into oblivion and shut his laptop. He'd
received a paper version of the same document in his mailbox at
the apartment yesterday and sent it sailing into the garbage shaft
on the way out the door, a fact that its author, the little American martinet on the first floor, must have sensed via the ether; it
was his job to get the embassy reports out to the handful of U.S.

citizens in the building whether they wanted them or not. Theo needed little advice from the embassy. Hanaan would never leave, whatever crisis Saddam might eventually manufacture, and Theo would not consider leaving her behind. Case closed.

She was waiting for him outside her building when he drove up, an empty cat carrier at her feet. Beyond her, Theo saw Abdullah hunkering down in the doorway of his little room and gave him a wave, getting a grin and a mighty semaphore in response.

"Don't encourage him," Hanaan said as he loaded the carrier into the back seat. "He thinks you want to be his friend."

They got into the car. "I do."

She lay a sheaf of papers in her lap and sorted through them intently. "That's naïve. You give him money. I've watched you from my window."

"He makes twenty-five dinar a month, eighty bucks."

"This is his salary. When he tells you this number he doesn't include his tips."

"How much can he get? There are six apartments total in the building and you won't tip him."

She had found the sheet she wanted. "Go to the Gulf Road. I'll give you instructions from there."

She said nothing about having pulled him away from the hospital. She was in her all-business mode today, and he'd learned in their tutorials how durable it could be. Throw in a needy cat and it became impenetrable.

He turned onto the Gulf Road heading north and spotted a tall, buzz-cut, sunburned Caucasian man jogging along the waterfront wearing shorts and shoes and nothing else. As buff as he was he could only be a soldier—and he looked American. It was an obvious faux pas: few young men here showed off their legs and torsos, however fine their physiques.

Hanaan, intent on identifying the correct turn, missed the sight entirely. Just as well. Theo had received sufficient lecturing from helpful individuals here about the frequent blunders Americans made in their blithe indifference to cultural distinctions here. *Theo, my friend, let me tell you something.* A common theme even with Saleh who always excepted present company, a nicety others didn't always observe, including the young woman at his side.

"Theo, not so fast. We turn soon."

Soldiers were an infrequent sight in public. They lay low; Theo had seen little evidence that the U.S. stood ready at any moment to launch cruise missiles toward Iraq from the deck of a ship out there in the Gulf somewhere. The opalescent horizon lay empty and illusory, as close or as boundless as you allowed yourself to imagine it. Only on CNN did the violent possibilities come to life, but he'd learned to see those vivid images as no more worthy of trust than the guesses his eyes made as they searched the horizon for an edge; where did it lie?

Kuwaitis seemed relatively calm in the face of this crisis, one of a handful since Liberation in 1991. It was Saleh's theory that a dangerous complacency had settled over the citizenry, protected as it was by a U.S. Army base dug into the northern desert and a moving shield of fighter planes and ships of war.

The Third Worlders were another story, many of whom could feel no confidence in the protection of their employers in times of trouble. Theo had heard a raft of stories in recent days from nervous tea boys and guards at the hospital who had been marooned here during the war. The risk of another war had them in anguish, and they pleaded for Theo's advice as if he could read the future. Should they give up their precious jobs to run for the safety of home? Surely this tall, rich American would know. "I'm sorry," he told them, facing their disappointment as humbly as he could, wishing that he had their religious faith, at least, and could say to them sincerely, God bless you.

Even away from the hospital he was solicited by South Asians for information. *Sir, you embassy, what he say?* He'd found this an irony, that they trusted the U.S. Embassy's information when most Americans found it evasive and thin; but he'd learned since that the South Asian embassies gave out almost no information or support to their citizens, worried in part that frank assessments of the danger would offend the Kuwaiti government and threaten the easy flow of 'guest workers' between the nations.

Hanaan flapped a hand. "Here! This turning!"

Theo swung west along one of the city's ring roads to a wealthy neighborhood of blocky villas set squarely inside high white walls of marble. Hanaan's brother Samir normally drove her on these errands of mercy for felines, always against his will; but this time he'd made excuses: he was going on a trip.

"So where's your brother off to?" Theo said.

Perched on the edge of her seat, she peered at the landmarks of the neighborhood. "I'm not certain. Out of the country."

An unusually vague answer from Hanaan. Theo had caught sight of the supercilious Samir from her apartment once, preening himself in the side-view mirror of his ten-year-old Toyota. He was one of what Saleh, fingering his chin as if he had whiskers, called 'the bearded ones'—a religious fundamentalist; but Hanaan had rolled her eyes when Theo asked about her brother's newfound devotions. "They're not real, they're the fashion."

She wasn't wearing her seat belt. Few Arabs here wore them, despite a seat belt law; and few even put their children in restraints. Hanaan's explanation for this lapse was that if God intended you to die in a car crash you shouldn't try to prevent His will, a thought impervious to logic. But they'd had that discussion: "Why steer the car, then? If God intended you to go somewhere in particular, like off the side of the road—" She laughed, enjoying his absurdity, but seat belt-free she stayed.

"It's a typical case," she was saying, squinting at a street sign. "The wife is angry for some reason, so her husband brings her a Persian kitten to make her happy. This is how well he knows her. She doesn't like cats, has never liked cats, is allergic to cats, so he brings her a cat. She sneezes. She is more angry than ever. But the eldest boy falls in love with the cat, so they keep it until it's too old to be easily taken elsewhere. Then, of course, the son wearies of the cat and it falls ill because no one has given it immunizations or care of any kind."

179

"And so they call you," Theo said.

"This turning! Turn now, now!" she said, rapping hard on the passenger-side window as if he needed an audio cue to know left from right.

Her mood always shifted to martial the moment she picked up a message about a cat in need of rescue. He'd seen the transformation. Always busy with her students or with him, she usually turned the ringer of her phone off altogether; she wouldn't be intruded upon. Ready to review messages, she sat before her machine with a notebook and took down the essentials.

"As long as we abuse even helpless animals," she had told him, "we are capable of doing any kind of terrible thing to other human beings."

They threaded through a maze of side streets, empty of all but a double line of gleaming cars in the harsh light of the waning afternoon. Looking up at a stark white edifice bare of a single tree or bush, she said, "We're here," and cranked the car door open before he'd come to a halt.

"So what do I do?" he said. But she was already marching up the crumbling sidewalk to the fort-like mansion, the car door flung open behind her.

He was to bring the unwieldy crate from behind, he supposed; but he stayed where he was, a sense of anxiety creeping over him as she drilled the doorbell on the double gate with a forefinger. That Hanaan had no scruples about the effect on him of her mood shifts and flashes of temper was a fact he'd recognized and accepted early—she had a tempestuous nature—but it made her an unpredictable force at a stranger's threshold. He'd realized this fully after the *Iftar* dinner with Saleh and Mufeeda when Saleh commented dryly to him on her 'independence of mind.' Theo had thought it an absorbing exchange that night, if a little testy. "She offended you, I think. I'm sorry," and Saleh laughed. "No, not I, but I think Mufeeda couldn't hear it all happily. Nor what my cousins said. They'll meet anyone blow for blow. But it's a dinner party. What's a dinner party for if not talk?"

Still, Theo saw some further reservation in Saleh, a thread of rumination in him ever since. It seemed unlikely that Hanaan's outspoken ways could be responsible for this, but the possibility recurred to him. Also, she was a stateless person, a *bidoon*. Could even Saleh feel a prejudice against her?

The deeply scrolled and gilded front doors of the villa swung open and a family spilled out. The father, bulky and mustachioed, registered surprise upon seeing Hanaan, then pleasure. A teen-aged boy, some small girls. The mother, in black *abaya*, her scarf drawn severely around her too-fat face, sounded off so clearly that even Theo got some of the words. *Cat. Bad. Take the cat. Son.* Something about smell, a bad one judging by the mass of drab and motionless fur that lay in the boy's arms with its tail hanging dead. The woman's dark eyes flitted from her husband to Hanaan and Hanaan's simple dress, her thick and flowing hair, and then to the boy, haughty and handsome, feather-lean in his long, white *dishdasha*. He cradled the cat with some measure of tenderness, though, Theo thought. The two young girls stood in the doorway, shy and pink, near a slender housemaid on the steps.

Hanaan was listening, sober, her temper under good governance. It was the wife who looked edgy. The husband smiled too much, and in Hanaan's direction—definitely the wrong direction from the wife's point of view—and though Hanaan remained impassive, the wife's temper snapped. She remonstrated with Hanaan, spilling out words too fast for Theo to catch; but her anger needed no translation. Turning, the wife snatched at the cat, though the boy tried to avoid her, and Theo saw the shift in Hanaan. Protesting, she told the woman that the cat was sick. That word—*mareed*—Theo heard. Aiming a glare at the mother she reached for the cat—but the mother jerked the boy away by the shoulder and ordered Hanaan to go, shooing her rudely toward the car.

Theo took in a long breath. Staring calmly at the wife, Hanaan began to talk. Theo could pick up nothing, an ominous sign. Noisiness, even of an irritated sort, generally indicated fair weather in Hanaan. Silence could take any turn. She was directing herself now to the boy, talking to him—perhaps about how to take care of the cat, what shots it needed. But no: the mother was objecting again, flashing a hand at Hanaan as though she might strike her, pulling her son back again by the shoulder, away from Hanaan. Hanaan never wavered. She talked to the boy, earnestly, quietly, a long stream of words until, abruptly, head down, he turned and held out the cat. She lifted it from his arms. The mother's screech rebounded off the marble walls. She grabbed at the cat but Hanaan had swung toward the street, her face filled with grim triumph, and was on her way back to the car. The mother, fuming on the steps, broke free of her husband's restraining hand.

The sidewalk was a long one. Theo had a moment to think. Leaping from the car, he came to see why Samir complained about this job—getaway driver for a cat burglar. As he snapped the crate open, Hanaan lifted the motionless cat up and in, and he saw a matted expanse of blond fur, the flat back of the head, shaggy ears. It didn't look alive. "Go," Hanaan said, sliding onto the seat as the mother closed in from behind. "Go!"

They slammed the doors. Theo floored it, and they screeched around the corner, hitting a pair of speed bumps near the mosque. Something dragged and banged below: Theo's muffler or bumper. A skin-prickling grind of metal. No wonder Samir drove a ten-year-old heap.

"Did you see her looks?" Hanaan laughed, drunk with victory.

"Hanaan, you stole their cat."

"What! They abandoned this cat inside their house. I've rescued it. The boy gave it to me."

"His mother chased you down the sidewalk."

"I had no choice. One minute she wants me to take the cat, the next minute she says I can't take it, the vet will euthanize it for her, she tells me. What can you say to such a woman?"

Traffic converged at screeching speeds as he turned onto the arterial road. "Well, you obviously found a lot to say to everybody.

And then you stole the cat. We'll probably have the police down on us," he said, glancing in his rearview mirror.

"The police," she said. "They won't call the police. People like that don't call the police about a cat. It's not worth their effort." He felt the weight of her critical glance. "I don't understand you, Theo. If I left that cat, the woman would have killed it, and what would the boy learn from that? A cat is disposable, that's what he'd learn, that it's okay to dispose of a cat if you don't want it. No one cares. Even his mother says it's okay. She teaches him to think only of his own desires. Other creatures aren't important. And when he's grown and comes to dislike his cat or his maid or even his wife, what will he do? He'll grow up to be like these people who kill their housemaids. You saw one of these girls. I can't let him learn this."

She twisted, turning herself around so that she could kneel in her seat.

"Hey!" He reached out to stop her, his hand brushing her hip. Disconcerted, he swerved in his lane. "Hanaan, I'm about to go on to the ring road. Sit down."

"I am checking on the cat."

"Can you let it wait?"

Traffic roared by on all sides, funneling into the two choked lanes of the access road. An ephemeral third lane was forming ahead, slicing between the other two. Cars rumbled by on the gravel of the shoulder, raising banks of rolling dust. The door to the crate squeaked open. Hanaan spoke to the cat, her low voice a soft song of comfort.

"When I took him from the son I knew he was thin and dehydrated. And unneutered," she said. "Only God knows what else."

She leaned farther into the back seat, her comely rump at Theo's eye level. He heard a muted, piteous meow.

On their left, a car load of young boys whizzed by in a Jaguar, grit flying, all eyes leaping into focus on the curving horizon of Hanaan.

"Hanaan . . ."

"But he will live," she said, plopping back into the seat, her face pink with exertion, her dark-water hair flowing across her shoulders.

The Jag slowed, came abreast. A flash of windows descending, boys hollering, leaning out the windows, waving their arms.

"Can you put on your seat belt?"

She regarded him insolently. "I'd neuter these boys as well."

In this mood she could mean it. But she was smiling, her eyes lit with brilliance. He dragged his eyes away.

"I thought I'd make you speak," she said, disappointed. "You're too quiet, Theo."

But there was no voicing his thoughts.

"You're angry."

Still he stayed silent, wary of the alien mix in his heart of anger, lust, admiration, disapproval, impatience, longing—and a febrile territoriality around those stupid boys. He saw her posture stiffen.

"You feel I take advantage of you, asking you to drive me."

He didn't believe she'd just realized this. He changed lanes, maneuvering for her exit. "I left the hospital to do this. I could end up in jail."

"You keep saying this. I could wish for such a thing, that the police will care enough about a cat to put you in jail."

The driver behind leaned on his horn in complaint at Theo's slower speed—only ten kph over the posted limit—and rushed Theo's bumper, filling the whole rearview mirror. Theo saw a raised fist.

"Learn to drive, Hanaan. Borrow your brother's car."

"In this crazy country? Look at these wild drivers. And you know I can't afford a car."

"Take a taxi then."

"How can you say this? You know the taxi drivers can't be trusted with a woman."

"If it's so dangerous to drive, why aren't you wearing your seat belt?"

He expected an explosion. Instead, her shoulders drooped.

"Of course, you're right. I'm a selfish person. And thoughtless also." She buckled up and sat quietly, her hands folded in her lap.

The boys in the Jag muscled their way ahead and braked to a near-halt on Theo's front bumper. The two in the back seat appealed to Hanaan, mouthing unheard praises to her beauty, their hands over their heads, over their hearts, invoking God's help. One pressed a slip of paper against the glass—his cell phone number, unreadable at this distance, then produced a phone and held it to his ear, waiting with extravagant expectation for her call. Intermittently, they cast dark, melodramatic glances Theo's way.

"You observe the young men of this country?" Hanaan said. "A promising generation, isn't it?"

"You might as well be in California."

"Exactly."

Theo passed them but the boys followed doggedly into the market street near Hanaan's apartment. Theo halted at a stop sign no one else ever paid attention to and opened the door.

"Theo, what are you doing!"

"You think I'm going to lead them straight to your apartment? You'll have a bunch of stray males meowing below your windows."

He unfolded himself slowly, wishing he were as bulky and menacing as he felt, letting them get the full effect of his height, at least. At six-four he towered over most Arabs and these were mere boys, scrawny, pimply, with desperate little smudges shadowing their upper lips; it might be enough.

The Jag's elegant motor revved out a growling challenge. In reply, Theo assumed a mask of patient boredom. Hollering taunts from the windows, the boys finally gave up and the car purred away, pulsing with a sudden onslaught of Middle Eastern rock.

"Well, thank you, Mister Hero!" Hanaan declaimed as he got back into the car. "I am safe from some children."

He put the car in gear.

"You make them important this way. Don't you know this?"

Yes. Humiliation swept through him. Was he trying to impress Hanaan? Standing there in the street like a thug, threatening a bunch of pockmarked twenty-year-olds. How ludicrous. Hanaan had long since passed beyond impressions; she had absolute opinions on every topic, even those she hadn't thought about yet.

"I'm sorry," he said, turning into the dusty lot. "My judgment isn't always what it could be." He parked under the *sidr* tree and let the engine die. For the first time ever he felt impatient to leave her, to get away. "Especially lately."

He felt her glance, as soft now as her words had been harsh. To his surprise she didn't challenge him on the ambiguity of these words.

"You looked very brave with them."

He glanced at her. Amusement crept across her face.

"A hero." Her laugh broke loose, melodious and full-throated, joyous. "My knight in white armor!"

He joined in, happy to laugh at himself for the reward of her laughter.

He carried the cat into her flat for her and they lapsed into the necessary language of the task at hand. He set the crate on the table and prepared a bag of glucose solution for subcutaneous injection. She drew the cat from the crate and laid it on a large, folded towel for a more thorough examination. It lay like a rag doll, its breathing barely visible. She examined it carefully, with gentle, thorough competence. The cat would need two hundred milliliters of fluid, at least, she said. He was very thin. Worms, probably, almost for sure. Eyes clear, though.

Her own cats, hearing their arrival, had set up a mournful chorus from the prison of her bedroom. It grew raucous. Theo recognized the bass viol impatience of her favorite, Solomon, the lanky orange tabby she had rescued as a kitten.

The new cat didn't so much as flinch as she inserted the needle and started the fluid flow. All his other problems were less worrisome than dehydration, she said. Would she isolate him? he asked. Oh, yes. She had a spot in the bathroom ready. The cat might have anything: fleas, leukemia, viral pneumonia, which was endemic in Kuwait. She wouldn't expose the other cats.

Theo crouched at the cat's head to convince himself that it was farther from death than it looked. The face was snub-nosed, matted, broken-whiskered, the nostrils crusted, the inner surface of the ears black with mites. Intelligent gold-leaf eyes opened slantwise to regard him calmly in return. Hanaan had told him that her rescued cats always knew when they'd reached safety. He rubbed one of the grimy, tufted ears between thumb and forefinger. The eyes closed again and, though not a muscle moved, the rumble of a purr started up. Sanctuary, at last.

BULLDOZERS

THERE, SHE heard it: the car pulling into the drive. Mariam was home finally, thank God.

Mufeeda opened the refrigerator door and bent to look inside, her nose almost touching the containers stacked four deep with Ramadan leftovers, and took a deep breath of the cold air. When her daughter stepped through that door, she must see her mother calm. In ten days *Eid al Fitar* would begin and Mufeeda had yet to feel the peace and humility of the holy month. She could blame no one but herself for allowing the trivialities of the household to roil her mind—Gloria's continued absence, her irritations with her shorthanded staff, the stream of *Iftar* visitors.

A car door slammed.

But the other things were not trivial. That horrible girlfriend of Theo's had upset her terribly. In a few thoughtless, reckless words of much stupidity, brazen *bidoon* that she was, Hanaan had struck deep into Mufeeda's private life. And now Mariam, again Mariam. Late an hour from school without a call. She'd be like Hanaan one day, all noise and show.

The side door from the carport opened and closed. Feeling the silent presence of her daughter behind her—thanks be to God that she was home safely—Mufeeda chose a wedge of cheese with unhurried deliberation, a container of sliced melon. The little ones needed an afternoon snack.

"Rafiq had to change a tire," Mariam said in the lifeless voice she'd recently adopted. She wasn't yet twelve.

Mufeeda popped open a container of *kushari*. It was half-empty, a surprise. "You turned off your phone. Why?"

"The teachers make us! You know that. Then I forgot to turn it on, that's all." She banged through the kitchen door, her backpack slung like a shield on one arm.

Grimly, Mufeeda proceeded with preparation of the little ones' snack, laying out on plates the miniscule amounts her youngest required to keep their small lives in good order. Why did we so soon outgrow these simple needs?

Mariam's continuing misbehavior was bad enough for one day's news, and yet there had been much worse: a wildfire rumor that the Iraqis were digging mass graves with bulldozers—and filling them with Kuwait's missing. It was said that a Kuwaiti man recently returned from Iraq had come forward to testify. The rumors were detailed with the stench of rotting flesh and the roar of diesel engines, words that injured like a bitter truth, and yet shifted, when tested, like a lie. How could a Kuwaiti have witnessed such a thing and escaped? And how could he have identified the dead as Kuwaiti?

Mufeeda pushed the plates across the counter, repelled by the sharp smell of the cheese, and turned to the house telephone.

"Frederick, tell Rafiq to come at once."

It took Rafiq long, foot-dragging moments to present himself outside the kitchen door. Stepping inside he halted on the mat, squaring his toes with the edges. She had intended to frighten him, but this had already been accomplished.

"Madam." Eyes down, fat hands clutched together at his belt. His white shirt, too large for him despite the big belly, had gone yellow with age.

A weak man, not a bad one. How old was he now? Fifty? Fifty-five? He'd come to the family from India as a young man when Mufeeda herself was a girl, and had driven the women of the family thousands of miles through the decades, in car after car.

She spoke to him kindly. "Rafiq, you must say more than 'madam.'"

He concentrated on what that might safely be. "Yes, madam." Further struggles. "We are late, madam."

189

"Yes, more than one hour."

The words almost choked him. "The tire . . . it is becoming . . . I was hitting glass."

"This is what my daughter has told you to say."

His head fell lower.

"Rafiq, today is the second time she comes late. Why? You are the driver. She's a child."

Not to him, she saw. To him Mariam had become a tyrant, to be crossed only at the risk of his employment. His large family in Mumbai depended solely on him—or perhaps it was Calcutta—including three children at university. He'd never dared to say so, but she knew he was determined that none of them would follow him into this career.

"She says to you that her grandmother will send you away. This is true?"

He shrank further into his big shirt.

How pitiful a man to be terrified by the threats of a child. "You drove her again to Salmiya. For meeting with her friends."

He closed his eyes. "Yes, madam. She is a very strong girl."

"And her friends, Rafiq? Who are they?"

He recognized with horror that her concerns went beyond Mariam's tardiness. "Madam, I keep my eyes on her! Every minute I watch her. She is safe with me, madam. Never, never, there are no boys."

Devout in his religion, he could be trusted to speak the truth. "I want the names of all the children. Every name, Rafiq."

Eagerly he focused himself on names other than his own. He gave them with the grave concentration of a formal witness in no way guilty himself.

"This is all, every one?"

He stood like a shabby soldier before her, hoping for dismissal. "Yes, madam. All."

Though she hated to lose him as a driver, she couldn't let him go unpunished. A couple of weeks would do. He must understand that by giving in to Mariam's childish threat he had met with Mufeeda's mature power, risking his employment all the same.

"I cannot allow you to drive, Rafiq. Brazio will drive now."

"But madam, he is the *gardener!*" Tears of humiliation glittered in his eyes. He pressed a knuckle hard on his upper lip to stall them.

"I know his position in my household. He drives also." She raised a palm as he took a ragged breath to protest again.

"You may go now, Rafiq."

TAKING THE snacks upstairs for the younger girls, Mufeeda glimpsed Mariam closeted cozily with Umm Saleh on Umm Saleh's big bed. She paused in the hallway, pretending not to have noticed their break in conversation at her approach.

"Mariam, you walked away from me when you knew I had more to say. You will go to your own room now and study quietly until you are called."

The girl, her shoulder buried in her grandmother's bulk, stared blankly ahead with stubborn impassivity.

"Immediately," said Mufeeda, and Umm Saleh gave Mariam an almost imperceptible nod, her challenging eyes on Mufeeda's face.

The girl hauled herself from the bed and slouched down the hall without a word.

In the little ones' room Sara banged on her miniature piano, producing a racket that had not prevented tiny Fauzia from falling asleep. Fauzia lay on her belly, spread-eagled amongst a wasteland of dolls on the rumpled coverlet, an image that seared Mufeeda's eyes. *Bulldozers*. Quickly she set the tray on the bedside table and rolled her limp daughter onto her side, working against her urge to shake her roughly awake. Mufeeda lay her face against the warmth of her daughter's. She was breathing, of course, thanks be to God.

Mufeeda tidied the dolls too, setting them upright against the pillow, but she didn't like these poses either. How corpse-like they all looked, staring blindly ahead.

"Sara! Shhh!" she said, desperate to stop the clanging. Sara stared at her in bruised surprise, unused to harshness from her mother.

"How pretty that was, Sara," Mufeeda amended. "Come now. I've brought you a snack."

Bulldozers as instruments of burial were not new. It was well-known that during the Iran-Iraq war they were used at the front where so many thousands of young men lay slaughtered, and also in Saddam's extermination of the Kurds in the far north. Now the Iraqis had brought the monsters forth again, this time to clean up murdered Kuwaiti prisoners. She reminded herself that she'd heard of this at a ladies' tea party, where rumor always thrived. The women had been morbidly sarcastic about the bull-dozers, to take away their awful power. *One day we will bulldoze him.*

Fauzia's eyes fluttered open. With a pink fist she rubbed at the nub of her nose. Such dark, lovely eyes. No thought crossed this pure little mind to trouble it. She lifted her arms to be picked up.

"Come, come," Mufeeda said, near tears, drawing the child close to her breast.

Saleh had heard the murmurings too, and slightly more: that they had originated with a young Kuwaiti prisoner-of-war who had escaped from Iraq on foot and yet remained unidentified. For Saleh, this vagueness alone warranted a dismissal of the rumor. "How likely is that, Mufeeda?" he said, tossing his briefcase into its accustomed place on the floor of his study. "If Jassim came home would we be silent? No, we'd trumpet his survival to give others hope."

She tried to agree—there was no place like a tea party to stir up a rumor—but she couldn't shake the image of machines converging on an open pit.

192

"If possible, we must keep this from my mother, of course," he said, "but you mustn't worry. Whatever has happened, whether Jassim is alive . . ." he faltered only slightly, ". . . or he is not, it's God's will."

If he'd said no more, she would have felt some comfort from his words—he meant to comfort her—but he added, and with such kindness, "I know you believe this deeply."

She believed. A clearer statement could hardly be imagined. He did not believe.

Observing her shock, he grew harsh with impatience, "And I too, of course. Don't read things into my words."

How quickly he'd become defensive. "I needn't read them," she said. "They speak out to me."

"Then your imagination is colorful." He turned from her. "This isn't worth our time. Now what about Mariam?"

He often used his irritation to intimidate her into silence, she realized. Not now. "Your soul isn't worth our time?"

He regarded her with a surprised distaste she'd never seen before. "We weren't talking about belief or apostasy. We were talking about a rumor designed to make us unhappy. We can't allow it to work."

He had such ease, stepping around the issue while managing to make her seem unreasonable and so weak-minded that she was unable even to follow a line of thinking, ruining his few moments of peace at home. She'd never quite understood this before.

"Mufeeda, what's the matter with us lately?"

He made her sit, and he sat opposite in the other large chair. Leaning forward he took her hand, and her stubbornness left her as if his touch drew it from her body; she had no gift for anger. Nor had she a gift for telling him the contents of her heart if he chose not to read them. Hanaan's words that night had burned him too. *If only He would save us, we'd remake our ways. Oh, fine words! But what has become of our promises to God?*

"It's the stress of Ramadan," Saleh said, and Mufeeda nodded, willing to let this easy target do. "We have to reclaim our peace somehow. Whatever Mariam's provocations, whatever my mother's tantrums, whatever housemaids don't return from abroad." He pressed her hand gently, willing her to look into his face, pulled tenderly at the soft tips of her fingers. "Whatever dark thoughts arise, Mufeeda."

Had he always worked so hard to change her moods? Perhaps it was her imagination. Whatever the truth, she responded. A kiss, chaste, and then his tongue, lingering, tasted hers. Was it a weakness that made her want him so quickly? If so, he knew this weakness intimately.

A knock on the door, impertinent. The spell between them shattered. It could only be Succoreen.

"Sir? Ma'am? There's a letter for Sir!"

Mufeeda answered with undisguised irritation. "Put it in the hall, as usual, Succoreen."

They listened as she tramped away.

"I almost forgot to tell you," Saleh said. "Theo's coming over tonight." He spoke in the bluff and cheerful tone Mufeeda imagined he used for new patients at the hospital. "I told him I needed some company. You're off to the old souks, I think?"

RUNNING A forefinger under the leading edge of her scarf to check its snugness, she rapped softly on the door of Saleh's study and turned the handle.

Theo leapt to his feet when he saw her, smiling, as he always did. "Mufeeda!"

"Theo, I want to say hello to you. I'm going shopping."

The reek of cheese and tomato sauce filled the room. Saleh had ordered a pizza for Theo. Americans, it seemed, could only take so much real cooking. Theo had admitted to her that he often ate microwave pizza in his flat, despite all the excellent restaurants nearby. That he was a physician never failed to amaze her, this young boy on stilts. He hadn't yet found his full physical grace.

"Theo, I wish I could stay tonight to visit with you and Saleh."

"Then stay! Please."

She studied his face quickly, intently. A little hollow-eyed behind the smile. She knew the subtle signs of love and melancholy all too well; and Theo's tender face was without defense anyway. This Hanaan was the cause.

"No, I'm going shopping. You'll enjoy yourself with Saleh."

Theo narrowed an eye. "You're headed to a party, aren't you?"

It had become a joke between them that some day he'd sneak into a ladies' party with her, disguised in an *abaya*. She was half-afraid he didn't consider it a joke.

He tucked in his shirt, making it neat. "You're not getting away without me this time."

"Theo, I'm going shopping, truly. You cannot go to a party with ladies only!" She shooed him back to his chair. "You're too tall. No *abaya* is so long."

"I'll sit the whole time. No one will notice me."

She left them reluctantly, wishing to stay, even if only to go back up to the bedroom to read. From there she could hear their laughter, and Saleh's laughter especially, which had a depth and richness with Theo that she hadn't heard since Jassim's disappearance. How strange that God would send Saleh another brother so unlike the real one, and yet their laughter together would sound so much the same.

She had enforced the ban on Rafiq immediately. Brazio would drive tonight, though she distrusted his skill at the wheel and found his frequent chatter annoying, all of it bent fruitlessly on inspiring her favor.

He scuttled to open the car door for her. "To the old souks, madam? A good, good place, madam. It is a beautiful country to have the old souks. The car, it had so much of cold before, but I have opened the heater and it is warm. . . ."

Mufeeda settled into the deep back seat. The shining top of Brazio's head was just visible in the front. Frederick cut a much more dignified figure behind the wheel, but if Mufeeda asked to borrow him for a single errand, Umm Saleh would surely twist the request into another indictment of Mufeeda's household management.

Her mind's eye returned to Saleh's study. Oh, to be there now, invisible, listening to the men talk. Did Theo speak of Hanaan? The possibility intrigued her. But probably not; he was a man, and for men, affairs of the heart remained sealed there. More likely he and Saleh talked tediously of the hospital and politics, and of the war. Theo was always interested in the war. His questions at their family dinner had shocked her. How could he have disregarded the tenderness of the children who were present? His fine character had this one deep flaw: a lack of tact verging on coarseness. A fault Hanaan shared. But even Hanaan wouldn't have stumbled as Theo had. *You must have been really worried about leaving Saleh behind.*

She'd given him the rebuke he deserved. *But it was in God's hands.*

How certain she felt of that truth, then and now. Yet her thoughts about bulldozers proved well enough that her submission to God's will sometimes faltered. At least those thoughts had been private. Theo had expected her to relay her wartime experiences aloud at the family dinner table, retailing her fear and weakness as entertainment, even to her children.

Still, one could almost excuse Theo. He'd been here only months and was as ignorant of the culture as of God. But this woman Hanaan had been born here. That she was a *bidoon* explained much of her irreverence. And more: she was part Palestinian—those lovers of Arafat who had betrayed Kuwait during the war. She'd even dared to criticize the behavior of the Amir. *He escaped the country at the first gunshot, racing away in a car, and stayed away until the Americans won the war for us.*

Across the table, the younger children, absorbed in their dinners, remained oblivious; but Mariam had followed every word.

No one wanted him back because he stayed away so long, so what did he say? That he will give women the vote. And a wonderful thing it is, the vote!—so that all the women wished him to come home. But he knows he can

196

later say, But ladies, of course you know it's impossible right now. And what
can women say then? Nothing. Without the vote, how can they complain?

How many outrages that woman could pack into a few
words. Mufeeda ticked them off: She had criticized everyone
who left during the war—such as Mufeeda herself; she had con-
demned the Amir and his entire government for its decision
to safeguard his life during the invasion; implied that he was a
coward for going and a coward for asking the Allies for help,
even though many Kuwaitis had died defending their country,
including Saleh's own brother. On the topic of the vote for
women, it was too much to bear. Hanaan apparently wanted
an edict, but the Amir wasn't a king; this was a constitutional
democracy. Duly elected members of Parliament voted in good
time on all important measures. It was women like Hanaan who
had caused the delay these last six years. Who would blame the
Parliament and the Amir for wondering if women were ready for
the vote? Hanaan seemed to expect a decree granting women's
suffrage, which proved that she was manifestly unready for the
responsibility of the vote.

Oh, how articulate one could be long after the fact!

BRAZIO DROPPED her off at a main entrance to the old souks. He
was to park and find her in her procession through the stalls. She
strolled with a sense of relaxation she hadn't felt all day, breathing
in the cool salt air of the harbor mixed with the rich scents of
the stalls. She didn't need to buy much, a few spices, another few
pounds of dates.

She wandered, choosing her dates carefully and bargaining hard. The prices had gone up as they always did during
Ramadan. Many people broke their fast with dates and so the
merchants took advantage, caring little for the simplicity of mind
that the holy month asked of them.

Brazio came puffing up from behind, calling her needlessly,
"Madam! Madam!" his shirt tail loose, his sandals flapping. How

like a gardener he looked. He smiled around eagerly into the stalls. "What you will purchase, madam?"

She handed him the dates.

The old *Beduin* woman still sat at her stall, a black and silent mountainous form among the hubbub of the market. Surely she was ancient by this time, years older than Mufeeda's mother would have been had she lived.

"*Salam al leikum.* How good it is to see you again, Umm Jumma."

The old woman nodded deeply, smiling and murmuring through her *burqa*, though Mufeeda knew she had little hearing and less vision. She saw with her fingertips, feeling her way among her gatherings from the desert, items few women bought any more. Mufeeda's mother had been a sometime customer, buying for old time's sake the herbs and barks and oils in use when she was a child. They'd had no soap. *But mother, how could you get clean with oil?* Just before her wedding, Mufeeda's mother had been anointed with a special mix of perfumed unguents, a disgusting idea to Mufeeda as a girl. But far worse was the news of what Mufeeda's father had done that night to her mother, though they'd been strangers in the morning. *That won't happen to me, Mother. I'll never get married!*

At least her mother had educated her. In her mother's own youth it had still been common to send a young girl off to her husband with no concept of sex. *When he touched me, I hit your father hard, right across the face.* Mufeeda felt sure it was the only time; she couldn't imagine anyone hitting her father in the normal course of events, certainly not a woman. Her own fear of marriage had probably arisen from imagining a man like her father as a husband: devout and formal and rigorously correct. Uneasily, she thought of Saleh. Her father's traits didn't seem quite so forbidding in that light. His faith, at least, was deep and true.

She put a pinch of *dairum* to her nose, a bark used for dyeing lips and gums in the old days, relishing the rough texture and its slight smell of spice and earth, a potent memory of her mother.

Did they ask you if you wanted to marry him? Her mother gave this a moment of reflection. *My heart said no, but they told me to say yes.*

"Mufeeda?"

She turned toward this accented pronunciation of her name. Kit stood before her, smiling happily as she'd never seen Kit smile before.

"I thought it was you. I'm with a bunch of women from the company. Our Bargain Club. What a wonderful place. I bought dates. Look!" She hoisted a fat bag. "We have something like four hundred pounds in the freezer. I ask you, what is wrong with me? These are a kind we don't have, though. That's my excuse."

Mufeeda saw the other women twenty paces behind at a spice stall, dressed in colorful clothing, in open jackets and light sweaters and slacks, with scarves draped around their necks rather than over their heads, all talking and laughing at once. What a flock of parrots American women were. She hoped they wouldn't come this way.

"Hi," Kit said, staring brightly at Brazio. "I'm Kit. Are you with Mufeeda?"

Brazio, struck dumb with amazement at being addressed, stared back openmouthed.

"He is my driver," Mufeeda said hurriedly. "How lovely to see you, Kit."

"Happy Ramadan!" Kit said, tooting the words as if it were New Year's. Mufeeda smiled through it all. "Thank you."

"No, thank *you* again for inviting us all over to dinner last week. That was really wonderful. I've never seen such food. And everyone was so interesting."

"Was it? Not too . . . loud?" What had been Kit's impression of Hanaan, she wondered?

"Oh, no, not at all. I liked it. My family always sat around silent at the table like so many cave men. Well, you know," she seemed embarrassed, "I have two brothers, and my mom told us never to talk with our mouths full. So since their mouths were always full at the table, they never said a word."

The American women had spotted Kit and came on like a herd of trumpeting elephants. Brazio fled to a narrow space between two stalls.

Kit introduced Mufeeda all around, spinning off impossible names at tremendous speed. The women engulfed her, buoying her along in a wave of giddy noise and enthusiasm as they bowled from stall to stall, gleeful at every discovery, bargaining whether or not they desired to buy, all a-glitter with highlighted hair and flashing eyes. *Should I get this?* The local customers sped out of the way as if the women were an oncoming storm. Mufeeda hoped earnestly that the dim light made her look like someone else. *What do you think, should I get it?* Fatma, for instance, came here frequently, and she did not want to see Fatma in any circumstances, let alone these. *That is sooo cute!* She'd seen plenty of garrulous American women in groups on her trips to the U.S., but never before had she viewed the cyclone as one of its vacuumed particles of debris. *You've got to smell this perfume!* Didn't they know what a spectacle they made? Even Kit, shy little Kit, was talking at a near-shout, as if under a spell cast by these women. Had no one told them that in this culture, at least, a woman's voice should be heard in public only when absolutely necessary? *God, I've got to lose some weight.* Too late now to impress any modesty upon them. They seemed incapable of thinking without speaking, and incapable of speaking without broadcasting.

The merchants eyed Mufeeda as a wholly unwelcome part of this group, preferring their American prey without translation abilities. Swept into their midst she could do nothing but come to their aid, babes that they were, embarrassed though she was to be among them; and their senses turned icily keen once they saw the masterful effect of her Arabic. Glances of delight flashed between them, and they leaned over the counters eagerly, their elegant eyebrows cocked in challenge at the suddenly servile merchants, as if Mufeeda were their unbeaten gladiator; and she found herself caught up in their heedless bonhomie. *We're taking her shopping everywhere!* Like children they had no sense of propriety, talking to Brazio as if he were one of the girls. *And so where are you from? India? Really? I've been to India! What carpets!* They allowed him to carry their packages only when he looked as if he might cry if they did not. *Madam, you must!*

"What will you do with these many things?" Mufeeda asked them. Every woman was laden with tea and dates and brilliant spices, shawls, perfume, incense burners, scarves, and dangling bracelets. "It's a hunt," a tall woman with blond, curling hair told her, her eyes bright with what looked to Mufeeda like pure mischief. They rushed along like a single, rollicking creature toward a car somewhere. Mufeeda turned to see Brazio in their wake, his chin tilted high on a pile of packages in his arms.

Kit made her way to Mufeeda's side. "Where are you parked?" The ladies, unburdening a smiling Brazio, sorted their goods with as much noise and laughter as when they bought them.

"I don't know. Brazio must bring the car to me."

"Oh," Kit said, blinking. "Right. Of course. I knew you didn't drive but—not at all?"

"No," Mufeeda said, embarrassed again. Many Kuwaiti women of her generation did drive, and Kit had to know this. "Perhaps one day, *inshallah.*"

"At least it's not illegal here, like in Saudi," Kit said with mild disgust. "You'd have a lot of crazy American women in Kuwait if they couldn't get behind the wheel."

While Mufeeda pondered how this behavior might manifest itself, Kit pulled a small fabric bag from a larger paper one. "Look what else I found. I'd have paid less for it if I'd bought it after we ran into you." She struggled with a string pull and poured into her palm a fragrant avalanche of what was surely *luban.* She tilted it toward the nearby streetlight. "Frankincense! From Oman. I'd never actually seen it before."

Brazio had joined them and nosed in to take a look for himself. "Oh, madam, it's beautiful!"

"Here," Kit said to him, "have some," and promptly dumped out a large share of the incense, expecting him to be ready with cupped hands. He scrambled, catching most of it. He regarded the milky brown chunks as if they were gold, breathing deeply of their perfume. "For carrying all our stuff," Kit said.

Brazio glanced warily at Mufeeda and received her steeliest stare, "Madam, I cannot," but Kit charged on. "Sure you can. Look," and she dangled the fabric bag, heavy with more. "I have lots. I just wish I'd found it before Christmas. I'll have to store it. I don't think this is the sort of thing that goes bad. It's dried sap, isn't it?"

"Brazio," Mufeeda said, icing her voice to zero, "you will bring the car now," and turned back to Kit with a smile. "This is for Christmas in America?"

"Yes," Kit said, a troubled eye shifting to Brazio as he disappeared into the darkness. "There's a Christmas carol," she said. "Three kings bearing gifts." She hesitated. "Mufeeda, I shouldn't have done that, should I?—giving him the frankincense. He loved it so much, and I have more than I need."

"No, no, no! Please, it's okay."

The ladies were piling into their car. *Kit! Hey, come on!*

A timely distraction. Given the blindness of all the American ladies to the difference between her and her servant, Mufeeda didn't know what she could do gracefully but issue denials to Kit of any impropriety. Were these women stupid, or did they set out intentionally to offend common sensibility? She doubted the last, for they all seemed good-hearted. They were not uneducated; she knew this from Kit. But perhaps this was the essence of Americans. They could be fine people: sincere, well-educated, and yet very raw. The thought jarred her. They reminded her of Hanaan.

Kit, laughing, flapped an arm at her friends, asking for a little more time, her face alight with enjoyment. With confusion chastening every thought, Mufeeda imagined herself climbing into the car with Kit and all these women, inundated by their hilarity and nonsense, adding to it herself with jokes and jibes.

"May I drive any of you?" she said to Kit. "The car looks very small."

A blare of a horn. *Hey, Ferguson!*

"Thanks," Kit said, stuffing her little bag of frankincense into a larger sack. "But I think I'm the only one who lives near you."

Mufeeda could see the women in the car craning their necks to understand the delay. Of course Kit didn't want to leave them. Why would she? The backup lights came on. Kit hadn't budged. Heedless of her friends' impatience, she was studying Mufeeda's face.

"Well, but would you take me?" she said. "It's really nice of you to ask." Without waiting for an answer she yelled to the others, "I'm going with Mufeeda! Go on!"

The ladies' sedan, driven by the tall woman with the springy hair, finished an intricate U-turn in the street and came rolling past, a moving chorus of voices singing out their thanks and goodbyes. *You were great, Mufeeda! Hey, Kit, we're going to tell Jack you just spent his whole Christmas bonus! Bye, Mufeeda! Happy Ramadan!* White hands waved from every window. *See ya, girlfriends!*

Mufeeda found herself smiling and waving back. "Goodbye!" She spotted her own car at the corner with toad-like Brazio behind the wheel also waving frantically to the women.

"Your friends, they are so—"

"Noisy?" Kit laughed. "Oh my God are we noisy!"

Peering over the steering wheel, Brazio rolled up ponderously to the curb and double-parked with every light on and blinker flashing, powering down every window but the one he wished to shout through.

"Madam! I am here!"

Mufeeda and Kit got in, and Brazio, scowling in fierce concentration, eased the car into gear.

"You know," Kit said tentatively. "I can imagine how all these women look to you. They look that way to me, too. They're so loud and . . . well, kind of rude sometimes. This is the first time I've ever relaxed around them and not worried about that. They always made me self-conscious before. But tonight, I don't know why, they inspired me somehow. We probably made complete fools of ourselves."

"Not at all."

"Oh, you're always so nice, Mufeeda," Kit said with faint exasperation. "You manage to say that like you really mean it. But women out shopping—help! My mother would turn in her grave. We get so silly." She sank lower in the seat. "But I had fun tonight."

"They're all the time this way—?"

"You mean completely wild? Like little kids?"

Mufeeda bowed her head, disconcerted. She'd never get used to such bluntness.

"No," Kit said with an air of discovery. "But that's what I thought about them too when I first came here. I was such a snob. Don't they ever say anything interesting, or half-way intelligent? Nope. Not when you have six of them together shopping, no ma'am, not a word. And me neither. That's the shock. I have to try to remember this at other times too—that I don't have to be serious all the time, or even grown-up."

Mufeeda caught herself staring Kit straight in the face and grabbed up her hand to break the moment of awkwardness. Kit closed her eyes tight, as a child would. "I did something wrong again, didn't I?"

"No, no! It's that you speak as if . . . as if these ladies are strangers—and they're from your own country."

"Oh no they aren't. Cathy grew up in Manhattan; Maddie's from Los Angeles; Tessa has lived all over the world. I grew up on what used to be a farm. I've never traveled anywhere except here. Everything's alien to me, even other Americans."

Between the packed lanes of the ring road, two motorcycles zoomed up on Kit's side each with a teenaged boy in tight jeans. Spotting Kit they rode parallel with the car. *Pretty lady! Hello, lady!*

Mufeeda bristled. They wouldn't do this to a Kuwaiti woman of Kit's age. Outraged, for Kit really was an innocent, Mufeeda leaned forward to send the boys the scathing motherly look they deserved, and they roared away with worried faces. Everybody knew everybody in Kuwait, and she had a good idea what family these boys belonged to. One whole clan had noses like that.

Kit ignored them, her mind still on their conversation. "It's something I have to work against. You know? Staying small when the world is so big. I get all . . . walled in at home with the kids. The world shrinks down around me—wherever I am, here or back in the States, and I lose my sense of perspective. I see myself and then I see Jack and the kids." Laughing, she snapped her teeth, "And it's me against *them.*"

SEA CREATURE

THE SUSPICION had hit Mufeeda abruptly, as she pulled a pan of *machbous* from the refrigerator and set it on the counter. Emmanuella had covered it with a thin film of plastic wrap after dinner, and only a third was left, though Mufeeda remembered distinctly that the family had eaten less than half. *Machbous* was one of her own favorites, a mild curry of chicken baked with rice and nuts, and perfumed delicately with saffron. She'd meant to sneak a bite or two before bedtime. The servants wouldn't have taken it for their own meals. Emmanuella cooked separately for them, as none would touch anything so bland as Mufeeda's version of *machbous*. They preferred a lip-blistering curry to the exclusion of all else and moped around glumly if they didn't get it.

Too many times now Mufeeda had found leftovers running short. Several incidents during Ramadan rushed to her mind; and more recently there were other disappearances: a flap of bread, the remains of a fat German sausage of the type Saleh had come to love on his travels, a dish of pakoras, and even the remains of the honeyed *Umm Ali* Emmanuella had made for Sara's birthday.

Who was taking this food when none of the staff would eat it? That earlier incident also sprang to mind again: Emmanuella on the staircase the evening of Fatma's party, months ago. Of all the servants it would be easiest for her to take food from the kitchen, of course.

It seemed incredible that Emmanuella would steal food. If anything, the girl looked thinner than ever, drawn and narrow in the face. If she was guilty of the pilfering, though, it would

206

be simple to prove or disprove it. Mufeeda would merely remove her from her kitchen duties for a time. Now that Ramadan was over and the *Eid* past, another housemaid could take over for a while, though this switch would have been far easier if Gloria had returned. A little cross-training was always good for the staff. Surely another explanation for the disappearance of the food would surface and she could soon return Emmanuella to the kitchen as she had returned Rafiq to driving after a proper penance of weeding the garden. She wanted to find one. If Emmanuella were guilty, it would seal her fate in Umm Saleh's eyes, and how could Mufeeda argue on Emmanuella's behalf?

She told Emmanuella of her new assignment as the girl skinned and deboned a chicken for a recipe Mufeeda had brought home from a trip to Tuscany last year: tender fillets of chicken breast sautéed in butter and olive oil; then a simple butter sauce with fresh lemon juice and capers.

Emmanuella worked with a slight, fumbling hesitation Mufeeda had not seen before.

"Emmanuella, I have taken a decision."

The flashing of the knife ceased.

"I will make a change. Carmen comes into the kitchen for a time now, and you will do Carmen's work."

Silence.

"New work is restful," Mufeeda said, irritated with herself for offering any justification. It was a rule to keep things short and clear with servants. Never allow appeals nor even the time for them to develop.

Emmanuella glanced at her desperately, one eye half-mooned with tears. "But ma'am, I'm not tired. I don't need rest."

"Do not cry at me. You've smashed many things. This is because you're tired."

The knife clattered to the granite countertop. "No!"

"Emmanuella!" How did she dare such insolence?

The girl sank at the shoulders, weeping, her hands laid on the counter before her. They looked rough and tight, swollen—wholly uncared-for.

"And look at your hands."

Emmanuella dashed them beneath her apron.

What a fool of a girl she was, whatever her talents as a cook. She didn't know enough to use lotions after her work to soothe her skin and keep it well. She'd have to be instructed like a child, like Sara and Fauzia.

"Let me see."

The girl didn't move. What impertinence. Surely this was the first evidence of her guilt. What else might she do with such a will?

"Give me your hands."

Eyes closed, Emmanuella brought them forth like dead things. Tears flickered on the long lashes.

Mufeeda took them in her own. Hot, and there was a rash, or eczema, areas of dry, reddened skin on her arms; and beneath the skin, a vivid network of purple veins, as if her skin were transparent. Mufeeda eased the girl's curled fingers open and saw her fight a spasm of pain. How hard had she worked this child? Six meals a day, cooking for the family and the staff, and as many snacks in between for anyone who demanded one. And filling in elsewhere when necessary due to Gloria's absence.

"Emmanuella," she said, caught between anger and distress, "I don't want you in the kitchen after tonight. Your hands are very tired."

The girl wept. She needed a break from her work—but the minute Umm Saleh discovered that Emmanuella wasn't carrying her weight she'd descend in triumph from the upper floor demanding that the girl be sent away. Mufeeda's pride railed at the thought. She wouldn't lose the best cook she'd ever had because of Umm Saleh's tyranny.

How pale and useless her own hand looked curled around this sea-creature hand of Emmanuella's, the nails in mother-of-pearl perfection, the smooth, slender knuckles, the gems and golden bands.

A thought rose and quickened in Mufeeda's mind. *I get all walled in at home with the kids.* Kit had no housemaid, and she had told Mufeeda that the family had little furniture and few belongings; her husband's company had allowed them to bring only a small shipment to Kuwait. She could help her kind American friend, and by helping Kit she could solve the immediate dilemma.

"Do you see this American woman who comes to me?"

"No, ma'am," Emmanuella whispered. "Carmen tells me."

"Her villa is across the street. There's no housemaid. Every morning you'll go to her. Begin tomorrow. I will telephone her. You'll come back to me at midday. In the afternoon and evening you'll do a little of Carmen's work."

Silence. Misery and silence. Mufeeda knew her worries: How long could it be before the truth would reach Umm Saleh? A few days? A week?

"Succoreen helps you without one word," she told the girl, leaving her mother-in-law's name unsaid. Emmanuella heard it all the same and looked up hopefully through her tears. "When she says one word, I'll know. I'll tell her she must not speak."

They could only hope for a delay. Succoreen was capable of communicating the essence of the news to Umm Saleh without breaking the official silence Mufeeda would demand. However deaf Umm Saleh could be when addressed by her daughter-in-law, she'd hear every subtle implication from Succoreen that something was amiss in Mufeeda's household.

"The American woman has no heavy work, Emmanuella. Your hands will be well again soon, *inshallah*."

A Small Blue Cross

The buzzer at the gate sounded at eight o'clock, just minutes after Jack had left for work. Kit glanced through the upstairs window. The girl stood outside the gate. Dark hair pulled back into a tight bun, shoulders in housecoat-white. Filipina or Indian, most likely. Well, she'd speak English at least.

Kit took off, pausing at the upstairs intercom to holler, "One moment!" and to firmly nix Carla's traipsing along behind. "Stay here. Take care of Kevin. I'll be right back."

The call had come from Mufeeda last night, the gift of a human being and her labor. Acutely uncomfortable with such an offer, Kit had tried to refuse it, "Mufeeda, you're so generous, but I can't take your housemaid," which had seemed only to wound Mufeeda's feelings. "But Ramadan is over, Kit. I have no need for her. Emmanuella will come every day in the morning. She will help you very much."

And here she was. Kit threw the gate open to find the young woman quailing on the steps below as though Kit might greet her with a blow. Kit whooshed the gate open fully and brought her inside. This wasn't a maid she'd seen before. How many did Mufeeda have? She was pitifully thin, like one of the stray cats in the neighborhood.

The girl recovered some of her dignity but wouldn't look Kit in the eye. "Ma'am has sent me, ma'am." The voice was thin too.

"Yes, I know." She indicated one of the two chairs in the living room. Otherwise the place was barren—if you didn't count the kids' toys everywhere. "Please sit down, Emmanuella."

The idea horrified the girl. "Oh no, ma'am!"

210

"But . . . so we can talk. About your duties."

The girl looked stricken. She held her arms tight-in as if she were cold.

Kit was at a loss. She stuck out a hand. "I'm Kit. I'm happy to meet you."

The girl eyed Kit's hand, then offered her own tentatively, fingertips only. Kit saw a small blue cross on the skin at her wrist. It looked deep, like a tattoo.

"Emmanuella's such a pretty name. Mufeeda told me you're a cook."

Mournfully. "Yes, ma'am."

"But you can do housework too."

"Yes, ma'am."

A bellow from upstairs. "Mommmmeee!" Kevin.

Emmanuella's head came up. "Your baby, ma'am."

Then a bloodcurdling scream. Kit started moving. The scream was Carla's. Kit could guess the circumstances, repeated in the past: hearing Kit's voice downstairs, Kevin had tried to climb the baby gate and had bitten Carla when she tried to keep him from succeeding.

Emmanuella was behind her as they got to the staircase. They heard a whack, total silence, then a startled cry—Kevin's—winding up toward lift-off, and pounding footsteps, all of which Kit could interpret without seeing a thing: Carla's quick slap of retribution for the bite, and her rapid, yellow-bellied retreat.

Kit took the steps two at a time and found Emmanuella right on her heels at the landing where they got their first look at Kevin, bright red, buck naked, and bawling openmouthed at the baby gate. Carla had pulled his diapers off in her effort to keep him corralled.

Emmanuella was smiling. "A boy! He's like my brother!" She swept forward and took him in her arms.

211

What a Family Is For

"Why will you persist in taking blood pressure?" Dr. Chowdhury's scalding glare focused again on Theo. "How many times must I say that it's a waste of time? They're all terrified to death when they come here. How do you expect anything but the appearance of hypertension? We cannot diagnose anything securely on this basis."

Undeterred, Theo continued with his task, taking the reading of a hefty, middle-aged Sri Lankan woman. Two-twenty over one hundred and five. In Dr. Chowdhury's mind there could be no relationship between the tension among the patients in the clinic and the fact that he had made this pronouncement red-faced and at megaphone volume. Theo couldn't argue that the patients' temporal anxieties didn't distort their readings, only that the major cause of the distortion might be Dr. Chowdhury himself. But he didn't make the case, having gradually realized that Dr. Chowdhury believed with conviction only a small percentage of what he adamantly proclaimed. What was normal under the prevailing circumstances for each regular patient would become evident over time, Theo thought.

Dr. Chowdhury regarded him dismally for a long moment. "When you have finally completed that needless bother, you will listen to this lady's heart."

Dr. Chowdhury sat back, arms crossed, gazing upon the scene as though from a throne, ready to lop off Theo's head if he failed in this task. But Theo had divined the truth of these episodes, too: this was, as humbly as Dr. Chowdhury would ever deliver it, a request for Theo's opinion.

Nodding an apology to the haggard woman—was she forty or sixty?—he adjusted his stethoscope and listened for the identifying whispers of a troubled heart. The woman seemed fatigued almost past caring and stared out over Theo's shoulder, her breathing too rapid and shallow for mere nervousness. An odd, lopsided rhythm. He studied its subtle acoustics, shifting the bell of his stethoscope. Possibly a very late-peaking murmur. The voice of the aortic valve was almost completely silent. Or was it closing after the pulmonary? He closed his eyes in concentration. The distinction came to him faintly, uncertainly, difficult to separate from another abnormal sound, the crackling of fluid in her lungs.

Dr. Chowdhury stirred restlessly in his squeaking chair, brimming with exasperation. "She has long-standing angina and now she reports fainting upon exertion."

Theo pocketed his stethoscope, understanding now why Dr. Chowdhury had shunted this particular patient to him: his growing deafness made him cautious of relying upon audio clues for diagnosis.

"I think there may be some stenosis of the aortic valve and possibly CHF," he said. He did not want to say 'congestive heart failure' in front of the patient. "I'd send her to Cardiology."

Dr. Chowdhury threw both arms in the air. "Exactly! She's been to Cardiology in the past. What is she doing here, in internal medicine?" He appealed to the whole room. "She comes to the hospital with persistent chest pain and the screeners in the entry hall of this great institution send her to internal medicine, despite her record." He gave the thin skin of his own arm a vigorous, twisting pinch. "If you do not see suppurating skin lesions, send the patient to internal medicine. I'm the catch-all expert!"

Dr. Chowdhury slumped as if exhausted, glaring balefully at Theo. "Well, we always are forced to adapt in this so-called nation. It is a city-state and nothing more, you know. You don't change the nature of a thing by giving it a grander name. To call it a country is to elevate every miserable village in the world to the status of a nation, and what do we have then? Italy at

213

the time of Petrarch and Boccaccio. Warring cities, incessant bluff and bluster, murder and instability, and tribes like the murderous Medici—but without the Renaissance, without the art and the science, without the medicine and the learning to civilize the mind."

Seeing Theo's surprise at this sudden impassioned eloquence, Dr. Chowdhury smiled loftily and picked up a heavy patient file. "Sister Wafa!" He slammed the file resoundingly to his desktop. "Where is my next patient?"—and the clinic rocketed back to life.

Dr. Chowdhury then twiddled his pen Theo's way. "Well, we must do what we must do. You will now screen for me as a rule. We'll clear one exam room and you'll sit there tomorrow. Of course you will pass all difficult cases on to me."

SALEH SET a whiskey at Theo's elbow. It was well past midnight; they'd both worked late. Theo sat leafing through one of the Arabic newspapers. The windows of Saleh's study showed only a scattering of lights in the neighborhood, though beyond it Theo could see a segment of mercury-vapor lights glowing yellow along the ring road.

"There was a time, you know," Saleh said, "when the press didn't write about this sort of thing at all."

"That's a consolation?" Theo said. He'd been puzzling with minimal success over an update in Arabic on the 'investigation' into the closely spaced murders of three housemaids. From what he could gather, the article impugned the character of all the slain women.

Saleh's head dropped to his chest. "No, not much of one, of course not."

They had both examined the body and the x-rays of the maid whose corpse had been dumped at Al-Ghais's Casualty; but in the long weeks since, the police had kept the autopsy results, the tissue and organ samples, allowing them to do nothing more. It hardly mattered. The cause of death was clear: multiple,

214

massive crushing injuries of the head resulting in skull fragments penetrating the brain. She'd been pregnant. Saleh had made sure that this fact was well-documented and that the evidence was presented unambiguously to the dizzying array of officials. He'd also forecasted accurately to the officials what the media would imply in their coverage: that the girl's sponsor, a well-known Kuwaiti businessman, had been the girl's lover, and that she'd blackmailed him once she was pregnant.

"They've kept me in their grips, you know," Saleh said.

The Ministry had required a blizzard of further paperwork and testimony from him, as if the case hinged on his expertise. This had seemed a hopeful development to Theo, promising an aggressive conviction of the killer, but Saleh had disabused him of this notion. "Our government is a perpetual-motion machine, Theo. It has no goal other than motion. It just spins."

Saleh strolled to the windows, his hands in his pockets. Theo watched him. In other men with so much energy and purposefulness, he had often seen quick impatience, a pompous determination to take charge, a stubborn insistence on his own way of doing things. Not so with Saleh. Over the months, he'd earned Theo's increasing respect. He could have been anything at all, in any nation: soldier, scientist, professor, diplomat; and he had a talent for friendship. It was as if their own had been a long one, as if they had known one another in school, had passed through the rigors of internship together, the sleeplessness, the fuzzy-headed mistakes in the middle of the night.

"It's not easy for you, I'm sure," Saleh said. The amber lamplight softened the grave planes of his face.

"For me?"

"I can see this through your eyes. You're wondering how could this happen."

Theo found himself feeling, oddly, that he should comfort Saleh. "This isn't unique to Kuwait, you know," he said. "Look at Sudan. It's far worse there. Slave-runners steal little kids and brand them like cattle. Mauritania, West Africa, India, Nepal. Traffickers in the U.S. supply people for farm work and the sex trade."

"No." Saleh sat in the opposite armchair, his upright posture swallowed by the generous upholstery. "It isn't the same in the West. It exists on a small scale in the West, and it causes keen outrage there. If the perpetrators are caught, they're prosecuted and punished."

He took a pensive sip of his whiskey. "We have a saying in Arabic. 'The willing contemplation of vice is vice.' Many people in the Gulf abuse their servants, and the murderers among us are almost always protected by their status. We're clannish, we're tribal, and these people have no standing in our culture. So we ignore them. We all know they're mistreated, and yet that fails to move us because we consider them so far beneath us. They're cheap and expendable."

He sat forward intently in his chair. "Think of it, Theo. Despite the way they are treated here, they wait in line for our employment. This encourages profligacy in us. So when these workers die by our hand, we do nothing. Even photographs in the newspapers of their blinded, bloodied faces cause no outcry." He slumped back in disgust. "It's as if we've killed a rat or a roach."

Theo resettled the newspapers, squaring them on the low table. Saleh and Mufeeda had a houseful of servants who seemed to him as servile as any character in *Gone with the Wind*.

Yes sir. No sir. Thank you, sir.

Saleh swirled his glass in contemplation. After a moment, a look of alarm crossed his face. Rising, he reached out to lock the door of his study. Sinking again into the chair, he cast a sheepish smile at Theo.

"Mufeeda." He rattled the ice in his glass. "She doesn't know about my stash. My courier came just yesterday. The whole place is stocked."

It bemused Theo, this euphemism for the young men who smuggled spirits into the country. Saleh's courier, who now supplied Theo as well, was a young local of a prominent but too-extended family out to improve his prospects; he took regular flights to Dubai and was allowed to bypass Customs on his way home due to his exalted family name and some well-placed sharing of the contraband. When Theo had balked at the idea of using a courier himself—he was, after all, a direct employee of a government that banned alcohol—Saleh laughed. "These young men should be rewarded, Theo. They're enterprising young capitalists. How many twenty-year-old Kuwaiti men do you see performing a job that requires actual labor?"

Theo's eye returned to the locked door of the study.

"Yes?" Saleh said, watching him.

"I was thinking what would happen if I ever tried to lock Hanaan out of a room. Oh, man." He studied the golden depths of his drink. "She's like one of her cats, always on the wrong side of the door. What do you make of her, Saleh?"

Saleh, smiling, raised both hands, begging off.

"Come on. I'm still new here. I need an interpreter."

Saleh put some appropriate sentences in order. "She's a very beautiful woman. Accomplished, articulate, well-educated. I can see why you were attracted to her."

Beginning to feel a buzz, Theo laid his head back on the bolster. "You didn't happen to mention opinionated."

"Who's to call her opinionated if you agree with her?"

Liberalized by the whiskey, Theo's curiosity fastened on Saleh. He would have attracted women easily during his time in the U.S. He was handsome, solidly built, with as expressive a face as Theo had ever seen in a man.

"You must have dated a few American women when you were in school. A similar situation, a stranger in a strange land."

Saleh gazed at him, reflective, amused. "Yes. I did date women there. I slept with them whenever I could. Including one who decided she was going to marry me. She had dreams of large houses and Paris vacations and didn't look clearly at my intentions." He ruminated. "Which . . . were never honorable. My marriage was to be an arranged one, and I had no other plans for myself. I wouldn't allow myself to love an American woman."

He smiled at Theo's mild show of doubting surprise. "Oh, I know, I know. Americans believe in free will except when it comes to love, and then they're helpless victims of fate." He grew more serious. "It's likely Hanaan would face similar prohibitions, you know."

Theo pondered. "You mean her family."

"Have you met them?"

"I've seen her brother from a distance."

"Ah, you're well-integrated into the family, then."

"There's no hurry."

Saleh leaned forward again. "Theo, this isn't America. You're spending a lot of time with this woman."

"She hasn't said much about her family," Theo conceded, wondering why himself. "Her father's conservative. I'm non-Muslim, non-Arab." He mimed brushing a beard with his thumb and forefinger. "Her brother's one of *those*," he said, "A fundamentalist. A new recruit, I think."

Saleh dampened his expression but Theo saw alarm. "Really. What else do you know about him?"

"Not much. Except that Hanaan thinks he's a loser. Why?"

"I wouldn't have expected her family to be conservative. Pardon me for saying this so boldly, but she certainly is not."

"Her family isn't conservative in some ways. All the daughters have a good education. Needless to say, she's the black sheep."

"Theo, brothers like this are sometimes very unreasonable, very protective."

It hit Theo as a wild implication. "Are you talking about honor killings?"

Saleh got to his feet. "God protect us. That's the behavior of a beast." He turned to Theo in utter seriousness. "Has there been any talk of honor killings between you and Hanaan?"

"No. But they're reported in the newspapers. Often."

"You must speak with her about this. The newspapers . . ." Saleh dismissed them with an irritated wave of the hand. "You can't believe them here any more than in the States, on any topic. But talk to her, Theo. You must."

He sat again, his overt alarm replaced with an attempt at warm humor. "But tell me now, how *are* things between you and Hanaan?"

Theo's mind snapped to the vision of her marching down the sidewalk with the half-dead cat. "She's . . . unpredictable."

"This is good or bad?"

Theo settled deeper into his chair. He'd unplugged one foot from a shoe. "It's like walking through land mines. I take a wrong step, ka-boom. But then it's over. She doesn't hold grudges."

Saleh's mouth twitched. "That would be your job, to hold grudges—if only you had the qualifications."

"It gives me a sort of survivor's rush, I think, a sense of euphoria to come through it alive."

A low rumble of a laugh from Saleh. "That's adrenaline in the system, my friend. It goes away."

Theo swallowed the last of his drink. "If that's supposed to be advice, I need a little more."

"Oh, no. I don't give advice, you know. Unless you're pregnant, of course."

"Your phalanx of looks," Hanaan recited quietly in her resonant alto. Head down, she studied the phrase. The chapbook lay in her lap. She looked up at Theo, "What does this mean?" and leaned her head to touch his when he failed to answer. "You are saying hmmm."

He captured one of her fingers, crooking it into his own, and advanced to the hand, aware of the soft pulse at the wrist. How to express in words—other than his father's own—these few, ordered thoughts printed on the page about a man in a marriage he couldn't survive and couldn't escape?

"It implies a battle," he said. "A phalanx is a group of soldiers."

"Ah. So Bellona looks at him . . . like a group of soldiers. Enemies." Her eyes widened. "He means that your mother is as powerful as many enemies."

They sat in her dim living room on her lumpy, threadbare couch, fending off cats. The rescued Persian, fully recovered, had already gone to a new home with a couple who worked at the British embassy.

"This is her real name—Bellona?"

"No, it's Katherine." He had slumped down gradually on his spine until his big bare feet stretched halfway across the small room. "Bellona was a goddess of war. Roman, I believe. His poetry was a way to talk to my mother, I think, to understand her. They didn't talk much in real life."

"And he talks to her of soldiers?" Solomon jumped into Hanaan's lap but she pushed him firmly down, her eyes on Theo. "Such harsh words."

He stared up at the low ceiling, pockmarked and scarred by decades of tenants. "Harsh? Maybe. She was the warrior, not him. Sorrowful, yes. He must have felt that his life was mostly out of his control. But at least he could control the words in a poem."

Discontent clouded her face. "Then poetry is his vengeance. No word he says tells the truth. You say he wants to understand your mother, but he doesn't try to describe her. Not inside, not her soul. Bellona, phalanx. These are words of war. He's the same as everyone, Theo. We all throw words in anger, as with stones. Your father uses just a few little stones, beautiful stones, but still they are stones."

He couldn't contest it. He'd gone to the poems seeking a route into his father's mind, hoping to find it generous, wishing for a tender glance somewhere, perhaps, of himself as a child. But the voice of the poems, though silken sometimes, nowhere mentioned the children of the house.

Hanaan was murmuring the lines, making them beautiful. "'To each his own redoubt.' This is to doubt a second time, I suppose. In French there is *redouter* and this means something like to fear, to feel dread. *His* redoubt. He doesn't say *hers*."

She turned her deep eyes on Theo again. "He doesn't trust your mother. Nor anything. I wonder what you have learned from this man?"

Theo felt he knew quite well. Caution. Distance. Chronic loneliness. He kissed her lightly.

"Would I be here if I distrusted you?"

"This is a very smooth answer."

He slipped the chapbook from her hands and closed it with a snap. "My father has said enough for one day."

She allowed Solomon into her lap, finally. The cat curled up neatly to stake the claim.

"I've been wondering about *your* father," he said. The discussion with Saleh he would keep to himself. "Does he know about you and me?"

Hanaan's hands on the cat grew still. "Yes."

He waited but she said no more. "Hanaan, has he said something to you about us? I think I need to know this."

She spoke against her will, as if the topic could remain closed forever if he didn't force it.

"Of course. A thousand words. Your father chooses one or two, and my father says them all. But the message is the same. Everything is the woman's fault."

"'Everything'?"

"You and I. To him, this is everything."

"But why haven't you mentioned this to me?"

"This is his favorite stone, 'blame.' He throws it again and again."

Theo worked against his alarm. "And me?"

"You're worthy only of scorn, you know, to a man like my father."

"Has he threatened you?"

"Yes, of course." He was foolish to wonder. "It is what a family is for. It's an instrument of threat. Do what your family asks or face its punishment."

He took her hand, held it tight to focus her attention. "What does he threaten to do?"

She wanted to be finished with the topic. "He sends my brother to spy on me. My stupid brother who is no better than a dog."

"Hanaan." He struggled to sit up in the sunken couch. "Would he hurt you, allow your brother to hurt you?"

She got to her feet, the startled cat in her arms. "He *has* hurt me. He hurt me with my education. Why not leave me in my ignorance? He wanted to put me in torture, grant me knowledge and watch me suffer with it. So he can punish me." She put the cat down abruptly on the floor.

Theo spoke the words with care. "I mean physically."

Fear or pain or anger—what was it?—arced through her face. "I will not believe it."

IN HIS apartment Theo lay awake, intensely sleepless, as if his eyes had no lids to close. She had admitted to no explicit fear or concern of physical violence and would not allow him to question her further. She charged him with paranoia and said that he judged her father as harshly as her father judged him. He eked out some consolation from this, a tenuous belief in his overreaction; but it evaporated repeatedly in the heat of his memory. *I will not believe it.*

It took an act of will, then.

Sometime after one, he hauled himself out of bed and made his way to the kitchen. Leaving the refrigerator door ajar, he opened a bottle of water and drank it, thinking of Julia, the other child absent from their father's verse. The bluish light cast a glacial spell over the kitchen. What had he written to her about Hanaan? He went looking for his laptop, flipped it open on the counter as he knocked the refrigerator door shut with a foot. The light altered, blue-cold to snow-white, brilliant on his tee-shirt and the long, lean moon of his face.

He glanced back at their last interchange. Julia had fretted about Saddam, pleaded with him to leave. He hadn't given her much in return, obligatory phrases of comfort that were no longer true. *I'm fine. I'm safe.* Not even Hanaan's name. He'd correct that.

I'm in love with her, Julia. Her name is Hanaan.

He stood typing until his feet froze on the unforgiving tile, then piled himself onto the couch in the pitch-black chill of the living room and continued. A long email, unlike any he'd written since leaving home. He told her of Saleh's concern, Hanaan's few but loaded words about her family, the dog of a brother, the threatening father. *And there's my own role as the worthless American unbeliever whose presence might justify violence.* He wrote about honor killings. Saleh had spoken the ugly phrase; Hanaan had not. Nor had Theo been able to pronounce it in front of Hanaan. *Something like a superstition held me back. To say it made it real, possible.* Even likely, though he didn't write this to Julia.

The dead maid's blinded, ruined face came into his mind as he wrote, the impact of her body on the cement at Casualty, the low thud, the jolt of the skull on the curb, the splay of the pale, bruised legs. An honor killing too, preserving the noble reputation of the lover. He tapped feverishly on the keyboard. *A humiliation so deep that murder is the only cure. This is honor. He murdered two, mother and child.* The heart twisted into an acrid thing at the thought of it, an 'honor' that turned rationality and human tenderness upside-down and inside-out, raping it maniacally from behind.

Two-thirty. The hum of traffic on the ring road had died away. He heard only the low throb of music somewhere in the depths of the building, the heartbeat of a radio.

You asked about Saddam, what he might do. I don't know. To understand his brand of honor, see above. His word can't be trusted. But I won't leave, Julia. Can't. Don't ask it.

THE COLOR OF A FACE

THE LETTERS came every few days, regularly, as if John had set a task for himself and determined to accomplish it. *Dear Emmanuella,* written with great care in a large, sloping hand. He'd practiced his handwriting, and perhaps his every word as well. *You will remember that I mentioned my great interest in learning.* He read, he studied, he had plans beyond today and tomorrow *in time to come*—farther than she'd allowed herself to think for two years. He planned to work hard and save money. He named figures that set her laughing in her room, a hand clapped over her mouth, unsure if she thought him remarkable or absurd. They would buy land near their mothers in India and in time build a house *bit by bit over two-three years.* Some of their relatives could live there until they came home permanently. He expected to go home! The house would have more than one big room—*FOUR rooms, I believe*—with a certain kind of tile everywhere, and certain colors, and Emmanuella would make curtains, *blue curtains.* Did men really think about such things? *He* did. She could see him saying these words, his straight, formal stance, those big black shoes, his serious, slow manner of speaking. He creased the pages of his letters just so with hard pressure from a clean and trim fingernail; taken from their envelopes they sprang open like machines; and each followed the same deliberate pattern: an elaboration on the future, a setting forth of the way he'd make the world for them *keeping in mind for when we are old* and how they'd work together. This repetition would carve an easy path. He'd nearly swayed her with these assertions, his belief in his control over events, his ability to influence them; and she grew more confident herself.

So much so that she endured without resentment the barrage of teasing from the other housemaids.

It was Rafiq's job to fetch the mail from the post office every day. Today he had handed it to Carmen at the door, who sorted out the staff's portion. She flirted John's letter at Emmanuella, keeping it just out of her reach. *What will this be?* Emmanuella grabbed, fruitlessly. Carmen pretended to read through the envelope. *Ohhh! I want to kiss-kiss my little Manwella.* Emmanuella snapped it away and thrust it into her pocket and turned to go, leaving the taunting voices to sing behind her. *Such a lover-boy! Every day a letter!* They couldn't see her growing smile.

A WARM noon. Rain threatened. Emmanuella walked slowly from Kit's house back to Mufeeda's, her eyes on the villa where Santana lived. It was the ugliest villa in the neighborhood: peeling paint, a rusting metal carport, tall weeds along the walls. She allowed herself the luxury of walking very slowly. Her exhaustion hadn't eased as Ma'am Mufeeda had suggested it would, and by day's end it tapped into her bones. With half a day of work still ahead, she must portion out her energy.

She hadn't foreseen this advantage in the new job: spying on Santana's sir and ma'am, monitoring their comings and goings. When both cars were gone—bright, new cars, despite the unpainted house—she could walk directly up to the villa's kitchen door and leave Santana's food and letters behind a flowerpot on the step, knocking softly as she left. Completely out of Frederick's realm. Santana's employers always locked her in when they left, but sometimes she came to the window and smiled.

Not today. The woman's car was there. Emmanuella would hope for tomorrow, then. Santana's sir was gone almost every day, from late morning on. He slept late, Santana had told her, after long evenings out with his friends. He often returned drunk and blew on the horn until Santana got up and threw open the big car gates for him so that he could drive inside the enclosure;

and he slapped her when she didn't come quickly. He wouldn't park his precious machine on the street. She didn't want to think about what happened once he went indoors, though she had little doubt. He raped her, as Frederick had tried to rape Emmanuella. For Santana there was no escape.

Emmanuella had seen the husband well now a number of times, a very young man with a hard face. He wore a *dishdasha* and head cloth sometimes, and often Western-style clothes: sleek black pants and an expensive shirt. The wife always wore Western clothes, a short skirt with high heels and hair worn long and swinging to her shoulders. Emmanuella had been crossing the street one day when the woman left. She had a small red car. Slipping on sunglasses, she drove away from the curb fast, flashing her headlights at Emmanuella to get out of the way.

Why was Santana the only servant in the villa when every other household had a multitude? It puzzled Emmanuella. Stories of repeated rapes were common among maids, even on large staffs. In big houses, it was always possible to find a safe place to take a maid. Safe for the man. But as she noticed the peeling paint once again, another thought struck her. What if this couple had money troubles? The young man owned the villa, Santana had told her; his parents were dead. Santana knew little about the wife. That meant the villa was inherited, not purchased by the man. Cars could be gotten easily with loans in this country, Emmanuella knew, and clothes bought on credit. To friends and neighbors the couple would appear wealthy. They weren't so desperate that they had no food for themselves—and yet they starved Santana, beat her, burned her, and forbade her contact with anyone. The rape was easily understood, these other behaviors less so. But Emmanuella now thought she saw the method behind them: This couple needed to keep Santana silent about their humiliating poverty, to convince her that they were capable of much worse than beating and starving her. There was no other way to comprehend their actions. This brutality, they hoped, would keep their secret safe.

Back in the dim seclusion of her room, Emmanuella retrieved the day's takings from the large pockets of her housedress: two bananas, an apple, two dinner rolls, and a can of sweetened, condensed milk. She hurried, pushing the items under the narrow metal bed into the darkness against the wall; Succoreen would be waiting to put her to work somewhere in the villa—Succoreen, who had patience for delays only if they were her own.

Such a small amount of food, but it was all Emmanuella had judged both edible and available in large enough supply at Kit's to risk taking. It had alarmed her at first to see that both refrigerators in the house had locks. She'd heard of such things from both Rosaline and Gloria, who had worked in other households than Mufeeda's—but fortunately Kit didn't use them. To her the locks could mean only one thing: Kit had been warned about the chance that servants might steal. Emmanuella couldn't let this stop her. The lack of real food might, though. This American lady had almost none in the villa, only neat boxes side by side on the shelves, many tins in little towers, including tins of herbs and spices dried to dust, and bags and bags of crisps; and in the freezer, a mound of plastic bags and boxes of frozen food—even potatoes, frozen potatoes!—vanilla and chocolate ice cream, and patties of minced beef. The children ate sandwiches of pale bread smeared with sweetened peanut butter and a gummy red jam; and one time Kit had opened a box with little pastas and a bright orange powder. This she mixed with hot milk and butter and the children ate it—happily! Kit always offered lunch to Emmanuella but she wouldn't accept. Yet poor Santana had to eat whatever Emmanuella could scrounge from there. How the little baby boy could be so fat and bright she couldn't guess, unless Kit kept better food somewhere else, out of sight.

This ma'am had other oddities too. She talked and talked, so cheerily and so loudly, like a little child who spent too much time alone and now had a friend. *How are you? I'd really like to go to India someday. I must have Mufeeda over for tea!* To which Emmanuella could answer nothing. Ma'am Kit would like to go to India?

How this would astonish Emmanuella's people at home. For what reason would she go? To stare at the mutilated beggar children and feel happy she wasn't Indian? Have Ma'am Mufeeda over for tea? What concern was that of Emmanuella's?

Ma'am Kit talked the same way to her gardener—who was not only a man but a Pakistani. Emmanuella saw him crouched beneath the palms sometimes, digging, his back to her. He glanced at her, keeping his head low, but said nothing, and she never met his eye. A foolish woman, this American. She would talk, talk, talk, to anyone at all.

Ma'am Mufeeda had been right that the work was lighter. There was the usual dusting and vacuuming, but there was no silver to polish, no fine crystal to wipe, no display shelves to dust, no *dishdashas* to wash and starch and iron. Just a few pieces of furniture and too many toys. And so Emmanuella's exhaustion mystified her. It gripped her even after a good night's sleep. She worried too much. This was the cause. About Saddam, Santana, her family, and Frederick.

She forced herself to think of something happy. John. Kevin's pink cherub's face came to mind. She loved the little boy, so like her brother Samuel a few years ago, all eager motion and noise—and perhaps, someday, she'd have a son of her own. She played with Kevin often at Ma'am Kit's, sometimes for an hour or more. The little girl pleased her less. Ma'am Kit said she was shy but Emmanuella found her blue eyes cold. And how white she was. How white they all were. She'd never been so close to white people before. Even Ma'am Mufeeda's family by comparison couldn't be called white, but wheat-colored. As a child she'd felt troubled whenever her mother referred to them all as black, and in a tone that spoke of reconciliation to a difficult fact. They weren't black—they were brown, like fresh cinnamon. She remembered looking at her mother, at her lovely, familiar face, her sad and tired face, and thinking only that hers was the very color a face should be. But she could see now, when she lifted the round little boy into her arms, how no other words would come to mind when describing these two kinds of people. Black and white. Night and day.

A thunderous banging on the door. "Emmanuella! What are you about?"

Emmanuella rushed to her feet, but then composed herself with deliberation before opening the door. Succoreen stood in the small passageway, fuming. "Why do you wait here? I have work for you!"

Emmanuella bowed her head and said nothing. Denied her status as cook, she could no longer claim superiority to anyone. She was just a lowly housemaid, so worthless that she was loaned out to the neighbors.

How to Tell a Rooster from a War

Sleep wouldn't come to Kit, no matter how keenly she lured it. Even her sweetest memories of childhood gave way to worry, and as her eyes popped open once more, she saw the moon go dark. Jack slept soundly curled on his side, facing away.

Clouds, only clouds, Kittie.

She cast all thoughts of omens from her mind. Omens played no part in her belief system, if she could reasonably call it a system. She wanted to deal exclusively in facts, but facts were few; only rumor and fretful speculation prospered, especially around the topic of what Saddam might do next. He'd sent all the weapons inspectors out of the country now, prompting the U.S. to claim that he must let them back in or face a 'serious response'—supposedly a 'delivery of missiles'—which made it sound as if they might go via FedEx. The most talked-about scenario had Saddam marching south any day for his second attempt to claim Kuwait. At the very least he was expected to lob a few Scud missiles this way.

The situation had gathered such intense international focus that Jack's company had felt compelled to issue an official policy: if the U.S. Embassy sent its personnel home, so would the company; which made war seem close.

Kit turned, plumping her pillow again. On top of this, she'd done her nerves no favor by watching a documentary about the Gulf war yesterday. As her laundry churned noisily in the background, she saw Iraqi tanks roll through the now familiar streets of Kuwait. One of the company women had dropped by later with a fresh rumor-roundup and a stack of videos the families were sharing, several easygoing movies like, *Little Mermaid* and *Beverly Hills Ninja*. But what had she chosen to watch with Jack after the kids went to bed? *Twister*, a movie Kit anticipated like a treat from home, a travelogue of Oklahoma, with some fine shots of the green countryside and a few zephyrs descending in scenic formations from the skies. She and Jack sat holding hands, venturing guesses about where some of the scenes were shot. Many looked close to home. But the boiling black skies and fields of wreckage didn't settle well with Kit, and this was the result: total, eye-peeling insomnia.

She was turning onto her back again when the impact of the first Scud rolled across the city like thunder. She lay there motionless.

Or was it thunder? The moon had darkened. Clouds.

Jack slept on. She ran to the windows and saw a series of brilliant flashes on the clouded northern horizon toward Iraq. Explosions—or distant lightning. She waited, breathless, for the rumble of thunder. It came, deadened by the miles.

Or was it the thunder of guns? She should have learned her lesson about jumping to frightening conclusions, she knew.

One time, during the first days of their stay in the company guest house, she'd been awakened late at night by an odd noise, a muted electronic whine that rose and fell, rose and fell. It seemed distant, dreamlike, until she remembered how thick the walls of the guest house were and how heavy the door to their room. She sat up in bed, the sheet clutched in her fists. It had to be an alarm. The sound wheedled, a thin three-note warble reminiscent of European ambulances on TV: wee-oh-wee. The Iraqis were here!

She'd shaken Jack hard. He woke boneless and snorting.

"Jack, there's an alarm. We've got to get up, get the children, go someplace safe, get out of here."

He listened for an instant and dropped his head back to the pillow. "It's the rooster next door. Get used to it. Sometimes he crows all night."

In the morning she'd seen he was right. Outside, pecking its stupid way between the Cadillacs and Mercedes Benzes parked on the street, strutted a pinheaded little Bantam rooster.

A good lesson, a solid lesson, but somehow it had become unclear again how to tell a rooster from a war. She wouldn't wake Jack this time, anyway. If this turned out to be a storm, he'd never let her forget her panic.

She looked up and down the dark street. If this were the beginning of a war, surely she wouldn't be the only one aware of it. The neighbors would be running from their villas; the air-raid sirens would go off. And where were the fighter planes? They'd scream over the city if Saddam attacked. Wouldn't they?

A spike of lightning then, clearly lightning, and she sat with a whump in the bedroom armchair, breathing more easily, although a stray thought came eddying up: it could be a war *during* a thunderstorm.

But it was a storm all by its blessed self, earning from Kit a gold star for its imitation of an Oklahoma blaster by producing fabulous forks of lightning and bone-breaking thunder that set the house to shaking and the kids to screaming. Jack even woke up, though not for long. The storm's one omission: no tornadoes. Thank God.

Nerves jangled at that level stayed lively for hours. When the alarm clock went off she hadn't slept more than an hour or two. She swung into auto-mom mode. Clothes on, she joggled Jack awake—he never heeded the alarm—and headed for the kitchen to make coffee. She'd need lots of it this morning. That done, she lumbered downstairs and out the front door to retrieve the morning paper.

The gate swung open with a squawk, and she stepped through. The air was almost crisp, a gift of the storm, and she could taste the herby perfume of dry soil moistened by a heavy rain. Delicious. She swept the paper from the soggy gutter and paused on the steps, reveling in the peace of the early morning. The neighborhood looked almost beautiful in this cool, pearly light under its dome of palms and *sidr* trees. War seemed an impossibility, as far-fetched as time-travel or Aladdin's lamp. She took a deep breath, noticing that one of Mufeeda's servants, the young man who drove the old lady around, was out washing her chariot with what looked like chamois. No one would do that if a war were starting. Restraining her impulse to shout out a good morning—for it was a good morning—she smiled and nodded. He bowed slightly, with impeccable grace.

Flapping the paper open she walked up the steps to the gate. Panic came in a single heartbeat. Three-inch black headlines leapt from the page: 'Iraqi Troops Only Hours Away.' A funereal black banner spanned the page.

Slamming the gate and the front door behind her, she ran into the house to find Jack eating his breakfast, chewing placidly on a piece of toast despite her obvious terror. She threw the newspaper down over his cereal bowl. "Look!"

"What?" he said, as if he were blind. "Oh," taking another bite of toast, extending a buttered forefinger to a subhead. "You didn't bother to read very far, Kit. It's the usual stupid-idiot press. Iraq's only fifty kilometers north, so Iraqi troops are *always* only hours away. That's all this means. Hell, even if they hitchhike, they're only hours away."

She snatched the paper back. The subhead, in an insignificant font, read, 'No troop movement reported; talks continue.'

"God damn it," Kit said. "How could they?"

Her language shocked Jack more than the headline. "For pete's sake, Kit."

"You know, Jack, I think the situation just might deserve something more than 'for pete's sake,' God damn it." It was maddening that he could continue eating when she was so unnerved. "Some of the company women and kids are gone already."

"Kit," he said, in that sudden, hyper-calm way he had, his voice going all downscale as if he were talking to a child, "This country is very well-defended. You shouldn't worry. And you shouldn't exaggerate. Only a couple of the women have left."

If Mr. Perfectly Rational wasn't worried, why should anyone else be?

Their parting for the day had been on poor terms. Sitting at the table with a cup of coffee, she tried to be sorry but wasn't. An accumulation of events had set the stage for her overreaction, and no wonder, although naturally Jack wasn't affected.

The kids were stirring, Emmanuella had arrived, and the offending newspaper still lay on the table. Kit gave it a shove, sending it over the edge and onto the seat of Jack's empty chair.

At least she felt calmer now. Or was this mood called cynicism? She wasn't sure. From one of the spare bedrooms came the comforting sound of ironing. She concentrated on it: the sharp hiss of the iron as Emmanuella ran it across the fabric, the gentle complaints of the old ironing board brought from home, the flap of the cord against its rusty metal crucifix of legs. It could be her mother in there, touching up a shirt.

Kit stood up. She had to do something—now—to drive away that ghostly thought. Shoving her cold coffee in the microwave, she caught sight of a sheet of paper on the counter. Something Jack had culled from his briefcase and left for her. He knew she wouldn't overlook it for long in the kitchen: a memo from the company's liaison with the embassy:

In the event of an attack on Kuwait, the steps below should occur:
1) *A siren will sound city-wide to indicate incoming ordnance;*
2) *You will have approximately three minutes to locate shelter;*
3) *If at home, retreat to your safe-room. The main danger from SCUDs is shrapnel, so choose a room with thick walls;*
4) *If the use of chemical weapons is suspected, seal your safe-room;*
5) *When the danger has passed, a siren will sound an all-clear;*
6) *Return to your previous activities.*

Return to your previous activities?

There was a second page. It listed the pros and cons of gas masks and instructions on how to make your safe-room airtight.

She hit 'clear' on the microwave—no more coffee necessary this morning—and called Tessa, always a good move.

"Calm thyself, Kittie," Tessa said in that mother-goddess voice she could conjure at will. Kit relaxed by a degree. "Let me go over the checklist with you. You have of course renewed the batteries in your shortwave radio along with all the flashlights?"

"Check."

"I wish we called them torches like the British do. It's so quaint and comforting. You've got your torches, do you, dearie?"

Tessa could always make her laugh. "Check."

"And no doubt you have brigades of extra bottled water standing at attention along with every variety of canned food known indigestible to man?"

"I do."

"Gas tank gassed, all important papers in an easily grabbable bag, *abaya* at the ready, kids greased for action, and Jack's mouth firmly sealed with tape?"

"I'll see to that last thing."

"Do, do. Let me tell you, Kit. Blake and I have a friend who's a geologist here with one of the oil companies. He grew up in California and spent half his childhood steadying glasses and bookcases as the ground shook. You know what he says? He says that Saddam is this region's version of the San Andreas fault. He's certainly the biggest fault I can think of. But you know what else he says? You can't stop the San Andreas with a cruise missile. Keep that in mind, girlfriend."

From the doorway came Emmanuella's soft voice. "Ma'am? Please give me things for mending." She had a pair of Kevin's trousers in her hands.

Kit inspected the damage while Emmanuella scurried to pick up the newspaper from the chair and reassemble it on the table for Kit, squarely in front of her like a placemat. 'Iraqi Troops Only Hours Away.'

"Pretty scary, huh?" Kit said, nodding toward the paper.

The topic might as well have been waxing the floors for all the expression in the girl's face. "Yes, ma'am,

A two-inch split had opened along the seam in the seat of the pants. Kit folded the trousers into a rough bundle in her lap. "Don't worry about these. He's grown too big for his britches is all. He has a dozen pairs."

"I will not sew?"

"No, no. Don't waste your time."

Emmanuella seemed to have frozen stiff.

"They're too small for him," Kit said lightly, trying to take the edge off. Still Emmanuella stared. What could it mean? Fear? Shyness? Or did she understand English less well than she seemed to? Kit took a wild stab, worried that she might offend the girl.

"Do you . . . would you know someone who might be able to use them? Someone with a small child like Kevin?"

Presto—she came alive again. "Oh, yes, ma'am!" No problem with English here.

"Then take them," Kit said, laughing too loud in her relief. She handed the trousers over and Emmanuella clutched them to her breast as if Kit might try to grab them back.

"Thank you, ma'am."

She could not understand this girl. "You don't have a son, do you, Emmanuella?"

For the first time ever in Kit's presence, Emmanuella laughed. "No, ma'am! I'll give them to the church."

"Maybe I'm remembering—didn't you say you had a brother?"

"Yes, ma'am."

"Really! How old is he?"

"Seven, ma'am."

"Really?" Kit launched with an escapist's delight into the topic. "Do you have any pictures?"

Emmanuella's uncertainty returned. "Yes, ma'am."

"Will you show me? Please."

"It's . . ." She was all confusion. "It's at Ma'am Mufeeda's."

It? Only one? "I see. Then bring it with you sometime. I'd love to see it. What's his name?"

"Samuel, ma'am."

"Samuel?" Kit gave a clap. "I have a brother named Sam too."

Emmanuella's face closed completely. What was wrong with this girl? Kit forged on. "Do you have other brothers or sisters?"

"We are seven, and my mother."

"Wow, a big family."

"Yes, ma'am."

Kit paused, hearing herself as a bubble-headed television interviewer struggling desperately to fill the airtime until the commercial break. Emmanuella wanted to escape, she knew, but she felt such curiosity about her, this small and silent young woman who was apparently supporting her whole family with a measly little job as a housemaid thousands of miles from home. Sarah, the southern belle of the company women, had told her that some of the locals paid as little as forty *dinar* a month for a housemaid, less than a hundred and fifty dollars.

"And . . . your father?"

"He died long ago, ma'am."

"I'm so sorry."

Emmanuella backed away.

"My mother died," Kit blurted out, her voice catching. "Not even a year ago."

Emmanuella's face filled with a sadness so keen it was as if Kit had told her of her own mother's death. "Oh, ma'am! I will pray for her."

The girl took the children downstairs. Kit retrieved her coffee cup, mopping her tears away, tapping her foot against a flood of others. So weak, that muscle inside that worked to hold her grief at bay.

Aware of the stupid paper again, she flopped it to her horoscope, as amusing as ever: *Expecting to be the centre of attraction, you find that socially speaking you simply cannot keep up with everything that*

237

is expected of you. . . . And the long columns of personal ads from people like Emmanuella who had left their families far behind at home. *Birthday Greetings! Many happy returns of the day to our darling daughter Priyanka Grace, who is celebrating her second birthday in Kerala, India, with her grandparents, relatives, and friends.* While her parents worked in the Gulf a million light-years away.

She turned another page. An ad she'd seen before caught her eye, the schedule for Sunday services at the city's Holy Family Cathedral. Masses were said every hour from seven in the morning until eight at night. The services were in English, French and Arabic, as well as languages Kit had never heard of: Maronite, Sinhalese, Konkani, and Malayalam.

This was the kind of clipping she should send to her father and take to heart herself as well. Here was a strict Muslim country and yet it allowed not just a small church but a number of churches, a cathedral even, and services in several languages. The diversity was amazing. A couple of the company families attended the evangelical church every week. She and the family had been invited but they hadn't gone. Perhaps they would.

She stood up, the newspaper in her hand, remembering the cross tattooed on Emmanuella's wrist, and paused in the middle of the upstairs living room to listen. The kids were outside. Through the windows she had opened for the first time ever that morning, she could hear Carla's shrill and piping voice ordering Kevin around. "Not there! Here! Kevvie, over here!"

She padded down the stairs. The front door far to her left stood wide open, throwing a long rectangle of light across the carpet in the living room. Before her was the door to the down-stairs kitchen. A flash of white there caught her eye. She stuck her head in. Emmanuella stood to the right, in front of the cup-boards with the doors open. As Kit watched she dropped some-thing into the pocket of her dress.

Kit pulled back, flushing with embarrassment.

"Hello?" she called brightly from the hall. She heard the cab-inet doors slam, waited, and stepped slowly across the threshold, turning on a smile.

Emmanuella shrank away, her mouth dropped open in dread.

"It's so nice that the kids can play outside . . ."

Emmanuella wouldn't look at her. Frozen solid again. Didn't Mufeeda give her staff enough to eat?

Kit fumbled with the newspaper, at a loss. Her cowardice appalled her. She should be angry and demand the item back from Emmanuella, whatever it was. The girl had stolen from her, for God's sake.

"I wanted to ask you . . ." She laid the paper flat on the counter. Emmanuella hadn't moved. ". . . about going to church here. You're Catholic, I think, aren't you?"

The girl's glance was terrified. "Yes, ma'am."

"I'm not Catholic, but I wonder if there are non-Catholic . . . but still Christian . . . services here. A cathedral. I'd like to see that."

Kit put a finger on the schedule, willing Emmanuella to look at it with her so they could get beyond this awful moment, but the girl hadn't so much as turned her way. She realized Emmanuella was crying, her cheeks shining, drops at her chin, though she'd made not a sound.

"Emmanuella!" Kit went to her, reached out to touch her shoulder, hesitated, touched. "Please. It's okay."

Emmanuella's head fell forward as she heaved a ragged breath. Kit's arm went around her. She pulled the girl close, touching her cheek to Emmanuella's temple. Her skin was too warm, feverish, with a hint of sweat at the hairline. She brushed it away with her own cool fingers, smoothed the heavy hair back over Emmanuella's ears, took one of the girl's hands in her own. The skin felt hot, too hot. Kit threw all pretense aside.

"You can have anything, Emmanuella. It doesn't matter. I don't care about any of it. And I'm not angry. Please don't cry."

She sat the girl down at the open bar of the kitchen, gave her a paper towel to dry her tears, a glass of cold water. But her ministrations only provoked a total breakdown. Emmanuella wailed like a child. "Oh, ma'am!"

Kit sat with her, shocked by the violence of the girl's deep sobs. Such a frail thing; her bones shook.

"I'm so sorry, ma'am."

"There's nothing to be sorry for. Honestly."

"Yes. I've sinned. Many times."

Emmanuella reached into her pocket to bring out the contraband, but Kit restrained her gently with a touch at the wrist. "No." Such drama, to talk about sins.

"I must, ma'am." Emmanuella dried her eyes, and placed a one-ounce bag of potato chips on the counter before them. "How else can I be forgiven?"

"Easily," Kit said, appalled by the triviality of the item. Then, realizing that the girl meant forgiveness from God, she babbled on. "I know there's a good reason. And if I know it, so does God. Right?"

The girl gave her a drowning look. This wasn't all she'd pilfered. Was Mufeeda some kind of monster? Kit couldn't believe a girl as devout as Emmanuella would steal for the sake of it.

"Emmanuella," she said. "Is it something with Mufeeda? She and I are friends, I think. If you want me to, I could talk to——"

"No!" It was a screech of sheer terror. Another fit of weeping gripped the girl. "She'll send me away!"

"Because you're hungry?" Kit said, aghast.

"Not I!" Emmanuella said, then clapped a hand over her mouth, closing her eyes.

"But," Kit said as gently as she could, "someone is. You're taking food to someone, Emmanuella. Is that what's going on?"

The girl's pained expression told her yes.

"Of course I won't say anything to Mufeeda. I promise. But maybe I can help."

Hope and fear dawned equally in Emmanuella's face. With a sudden intake of breath she whispered the words. "There's a girl. Just there." She motioned toward the front of the house.

"Across the street?"

"Yes, ma'am. She's from my country. But her sir and ma'am, they——" She gathered her courage, fighting tears. "Ma'am. They beat her. The man, he does things." Her anguish left no doubt in Kit's mind what they were. "She is even wanting for food."

"And you've been taking it to her."

"Yes, ma'am." Agonized, Emmanuella said, "I take food to her from Ma'am Mufeeda's kitchen."

"But if she knew why, Emmanuella . . . this girl's being raped."

"No, it's the Grandmother! She'll send me to India!"

All became clear to Kit. Even if Mufeeda forgave Emmanuella, her ponderous mother-in-law would not, and Emmanuella would lose her livelihood.

The faces of the murdered maids published in the paper took gruesome shape in Kit's mind. Would the girl across the street join that tragic company? What could she possibly do to prevent it?

"Well," she said, measuring herself against Jack. He'd forbid her involvement vehemently—if he knew of it. "Then I'll help you help this girl."

BIG TALK

Embassy of the United States of America

MEMORANDUM

To: *All American Wardens*
Subject: Wardens' Notice

> *The U.S. Department of State is permitting the spouses and children of American official personnel to depart the country temporarily, in view of the situation in the region. This permission, known as an "authorized departure," does not mean that these dependents must leave, only that they can leave, at U.S. government expense, if they wish to do so.*

A STIFLING euphemism, 'authorized departure.' It meant evacuation. Theo folded the notice carefully and put it in his shirt pocket. The American administration, headed by a policy wonk elected to a four-year term, had issued an ultimatum to Saddam, who believed himself to be the new Saladin. As absurdities went, this was a pretty good one.

He stepped through the double doors of his apartment building into the ivory-dust early morning air of the street. Starting his car, he flipped on the wipers to clear the lines of grit that lay in rippled streaks across the glass. The rain of the recent storm had fallen so fast and furiously that little had been absorbed by the thin and crusted soil. The gutters lay thick with sand left by the runoff, dry now and patterned by the flow, a fossil of the storm.

He wished he hadn't checked his mail. The flat, desiccated words of lawyerly caution fed his unease, despite a sense that Saddam would ultimately do nothing. It had been his modus operandi since the war to swagger and threaten without follow-through; it proved his power, which he measured by his ability to generate news coverage around the world. The sycophantic American media obliged, increasing his wattage with every report from Baghdad. Few Westerners in Kuwait heard the broadcasts as anything other than Saddam's own propaganda via his American mouthpieces; but by their sheer number and repetition the reports gained credence with the imagination. Added to this was the perennial suspicion among Arabs of America's motivations: How better to deepen American influence in the Gulf than to keep the cauldron bubbling? America didn't want peace—it wanted more McDonald's franchises. Yet clearly it would also be a mistake not to bomb Saddam; the local papers encouraged America to move swiftly ahead—as long as it killed no innocents. Even Hanaan shared this impossible standard. To discuss politics with her lately was to risk a quick descent into silence.

"They can hit a tin of beans with a bomb, Theo. Why should they have to kill babies?"

"Right. I'm saying they should kill babies."

"But they will. If they bomb they will kill women and children."

"You're contradicting yourself," he said. "How can you have it both ways? You want Saddam dead—so do you want them to bomb or not?"

"We wanted him dead during the last war, but they turned at the border. Why? Because we won't need Americans if there's peace. They know where he is. They could go and bomb him at any moment if they wished. Boom!—like a tin of beans. They don't want to kill him."

"I see," he said. "Saddam, the human bean."

Her face went pale, the first stage of deep offense. But it passed slowly over her instead, leaving her exultant in a wave of laughter. "And this is all he is—a human bean!"

Theo made his way through the traffic circle, deserted at this hour. The longhand draft of his report on the radiology department was waiting for him on his desk, still unfinished. Due dates meant almost nothing in the world of the hospital, perhaps at most a deadline for the setting of a new due date; but he intended to finish it anyway.

He needed to shoot off a few emails today too. Friends at home, swallowing the news whole, were writing with urgent requests that he get the hell out of the Middle East. Among them, only Rajesh had remained more philosophical, conditioned by his father's long stay in Kuwait, but his concern had sharpened. *Do you think he's paying any attention, Theo?* 'No' would have to be the answer to that. Theo had seen nothing to indicate that Dr. Chowdhury paid the least mind to politics inside or outside the hospital.

And there was Julia. Her emails had become distinctly muted. She was trying, he knew, to restrain an outright scream of worry.

He turned onto Al-Ghais Street. The hospital, bulky, ochre in the haze of early day, stood above the ragged mass of rooftops to the east. There was little traffic yet, but the Third World workers were out in force: street cleaners in their baggy dungarees, poking with slow, mechanical inattention at the blown drifts of garbage along the curbs; watering crews dragging thick, drooling pythons of hose to skeletal palms along the new roadway; and crews of highway workers crammed into the metal beds of trucks, each armed with a shovel and wearing a grime-darkened turban over a sunburned brow, headed out for another day of back-breaking toil.

Theo pulled up behind a truckload of men at a stoplight, forcing himself to acknowledge their stares instead of gazing past them as if they didn't exist. He nodded slightly and observed them in brief glances. Many watched him intently, as if he were an image on television, taking in the pale face and blond hair, the gleaming car where he sat in clean, expensive clothes and regulated air. But among the young faces Theo saw one man who wouldn't deign to stare. He looked at Theo levelly, as an equal, and then away—boldly—rendering Theo the invisible one.

It was an off-day at the clinic: no outpatients on the docket and Dr. Chowdhury was on his way to give a lecture to medical students at the university: 'Developing the Diagnostic Mind.' Armed with a half-dozen case reports illustrating the brilliance of his own, he gave his staff a preview of the lecture. "It is of course largely a psychological question."

Pacing the clinic floor he donned his winter gear as he spoke: a trim leather jacket and a bright yellow woolen muffler. Despite years spent abroad he still gauged the weather by the standards of his Calcutta youth and considered a day in the mid-seventies as distinctly cool. His captive audience listened in low-profile silence, wishing for no delay in his departure, Dr. Asrar at her tiny desk, Sister Wafa sitting in a patient's chair, Theo slouched against a wall.

"Young doctors must learn confidence," he said, shaking a bony finger at Theo and Dr. Asrar. "Confidence that is well-earned rather than merely foolish is underlain by faultless observation, intelligence and—." He tossed a tail end of the muffler over his shoulder, "—a talent for reading one's own instincts. We underrate our instincts, believing them to be somewhat primitive aspects of intelligence, when in many instances they represent deep knowledge coded into our very genes. We have not fully realized this. You, Dr. Asrar," he said, rounding on her, "should be among the students today."

Acutely embarrassed, she looked into her lap. "Shall I go with you then, Professor?"

"No, of course not. Your duties are here. But I shall give you a copy of the text of my lecture." And he was out the door.

The women, Theo saw, exchanged a painful glance, and Wafa touched Dr. Asrar's shoulder softly as she passed to the door. "I must go to the laboratory," Wafa explained to them both.

Theo let a moment pass, wondering if Dr. Asrar could welcome a comment, however friendly. She had busied herself with a pile of reports.

"Asrar," he said finally. "Don't let him rattle you. You're a fine doctor."

"No." She didn't look up. "He's correct. I have little confidence. And no dedication." Now a glance came. She looked exhausted. Her daughter's illness exacted a great toll, Theo knew. Though she spoke of it only obliquely, Theo understood its nature: severe, chronic asthma. Her husband, upset that the girl was sickly, had divorced her and remarried to start a new family. She'd mentioned this fact only once, and with no self-pity. *A father wants a healthy son.*

"How's your daughter?"

Her pause told him the news wasn't good. "Again she's home from school today. This is my problem: I would wish always to be home with her. Perhaps with more rain the dust will go, and she'll improve, *inshallah.*"

"Asrar," he said. "Go home."

Hope flared and died in her face. "No. Her illness isn't acceptable to the professor. For two years I've come late."

"Listen, you know he'll have a long lunch with that crew out there. If he comes back at all today he'll do rounds. Get out of here."

"Shall I?" She clutched at her purse, tempted.

"Go."

"Yes. Thank you. I will go," and bowing her head she cast him a grateful smile. "You're very bold, Dr. Theo."

"No. I'm learning from Dr. Chowdhury to listen to my instincts."

"And I too," she said, smiling.

STRUGGLING WITH his report in the relative quiet of his office, Theo tried to imagine himself a sculptor chipping away at a huge block of stone. But by afternoon his writing seemed only to have enlarged it, and it stood before him, tilting dangerously in his direction.

Saleh poked his head in. "Have you heard anything from your embassy?"

Theo pushed away the mass of scrawled yellow legal sheets. "It issued an 'authorized departure.'"

Saleh let this register. "I don't think my English is up to that. You're not leaving?"

"No. My sister wants me to. She thinks Oakland is safer." He tapped a forefinger on his report. "After hours, I'd like to have a Scud land just here."

Saleh faced a similar deadline. "You're handwriting it?"

Theo regarded his pencil. "I like the drag of the lead or something, I don't know. Seems more restful somehow."

Saleh came to take a look at the report. "That's in English, is it?"

"It was this morning."

"You should get out of here—that's what your handwriting tells me," Saleh said, returning to the doorway. "And I too. Both of us to our sweet beloveds."

He closed the door, leaving Theo to play over in his mind the slighting, sarcastic tilt of those last words.

STOPPING AT the co-op to buy a few fresh vegetables for dinner, Theo headed to Hanaan's place. She had refused to change their routine, earnestly dismissing his every urge toward caution—*Do not worry, dear Theo!*—and he'd seen no evidence of heightened concern in her, though he didn't trust his skill at divining her emotional state. He wasn't all that skilled at divining his own. His earlier anxiety had lessened, but he felt himself watched when he went to her apartment—and paranoid for feeling watched.

Abdullah rushed out of his room, as usual, the moment Theo pulled into the parking lot, and waited impatiently for him to park. Though the guard had long since given up trying to

247

replace Hanaan as Theo's tutor he'd developed a certain genius for pressing other services on him: cold drinks showed up in Theo's hand; cigarettes, though Theo didn't smoke; a wilted rose "for girlfriend," said with a wry sneer toward Hanaan's window. Errands, certainly—he'd run them at any time day or night. Theo had hired him once to wash the car and Abdullah took this as an unshakable order to wash it every time, orders to the contrary notwithstanding. Theo's car stood, at Hanaan's, in a perpetual field of fresh mud.

The gray day had turned cold, with a keen bite in the air. Abdullah hurried to open Theo's car door and insisted on closing it behind him. "Sir!" A brown finger up in the air. This signaled important information. Abdullah gathered neighborhood news and gossip in the everlasting hope that it could prove remunerative. But today as they shook hands, Theo saw thunderous worry in his creased brow.

He spoke in a turbulent whisper, "Sir," glancing up furtively at Hanaan's window. "Today. Hanaan brother come. Big talk. Angry. He make big noise with Hanaan."

Fear stroked through Theo. "Did he hurt her?"

Abdullah shook a meaty fist at Hanaan's window. "He angry, go see Hanaan. I not see her. He see her, make noise, then he go." Abdullah mimed a ferocious brother behind the wheel, accelerating away, then pointed again to Hanaan's window. "She give him big talk there."

She'd yelled to him from the window as he left. Whatever her brother had done, Hanaan was alive and conscious. Theo took the steps by twos to the scarred vestibule at the top.

Knocking urgently, he spoke her name, "Hanaan?"

Silence, not even a rustle of movement from within. He waited, biting down his fear, his head close to the chill and battered metal, listening as if to hear her breathe.

"Hanaan. Open the door."

Again he listened intently but heard only Abdullah climbing the stairs. The guard paused on the gritty landing, watching

Theo with naked curiosity. Switching into Arabic, Theo raged at him in a whisper, "For god's sake, Abdullah, go away!"

Surprise—then animosity, harsh and elemental—flashed in the guard's face. He had the right to witness this drama, had earned it with his labor and perseverance on behalf of this stupid American, and he wouldn't be denied. He braced himself stubbornly where he stood but gave way under Theo's stare. He would listen from below, Theo knew.

Hanaan might answer the phone. Theo pulled his cell phone from his pocket. He counted the rings—four—and heard the shift to her answering machine.

"Hanaan," he said, hearing his own voice dimly through the gray door. He calmed it to a murmur. "Please let me in. I know about your brother. If you don't let me see you, I'll know he's hurt you."

A door creaked open but it wasn't Hanaan's. On the opposite side of the vestibule, Theo saw the wan face of an older woman peering at him, the neighbor who'd yelled at Hanaan from the window on the first day of his Arabic lessons. Hanaan had told Theo later that the old woman's theme was always the same: the deep shame of Hanaan's existence as an unmarried woman living alone. Framed tight in a black *hijab* the woman's grim face yielded little, but busybody that she was, she had to know that Hanaan's brother had been here and that he'd fought with Hanaan. Did she mean to help? Surely her appearance implied concern. As a woman caught in this brutal place, she would sympathize, whatever her differences with Hanaan.

As Theo took a step toward her, she gave a cry of terror and slammed the door, only to open it again as soon as he backed away. She launched into a tirade, her dark words coming in a torrent, echoing in the close quarters with a hatred so keen that Theo wondered how he'd ever mistaken everyday Arabic for the abuse he was hearing now. She banished him with a violent wave of her black-cloaked arm, "Go away!"—words Theo comprehended readily, having just spat them at Abdullah.

The door slammed again, leaving him in a thrumming silence, alone.

He stood motionless at Hanaan's door. She wouldn't have missed that show. She was within inches of him, he knew, standing breathlessly on the other side of the threshold. Two inches of ugly metal—and a universe—lay between them.

"Hanaan," he said, as if she were at his shoulder. "Call me. I'll go, but please call me." He took a step away.

Then a click, like a trigger. Hanaan's lock had slipped. The moment stretched. Her doorknob turned and she stood before him, calm. A welt on her right cheekbone seeped blood from a tear in the delicate skin.

INSIDE HER apartment, he crashed the door shut and bolted it. She would admit to no other injury. She shook her head again and again as he asked. Her tears came silently, streaming fast. He took her in his arms to check for himself, caressed her shoulders, her arms, cradled her damaged face in his hands.

The antiseptic he used to bathe the wound was the same she'd given him the day they'd met, a brown plastic bottle of drugstore peroxide. She said nothing while he bandaged it, while he prepared a compress of crushed ice to keep the swelling down. He said only what he must, words of simple explanation and instruction. *Let me see it in the light. Lift your chin up a little. You need to sit down now, Hanaan.*

She obeyed him like a docile child, which frightened him as much as the injury: it revealed a deeper wound. He brought her Tylenol, a glass of water. The cats began to meow from the tiny, second bedroom in the flat, where she penned them when she didn't want them underfoot. They grew quickly demanding. Paws came thrusting under the door.

"Let them come to me," she murmured.

They rushed out in a stream, eyes wide, Solomon at their head. Skittish, they splayed out across the small room, scaring one another with their nervousness. A spat broke out in a corner with hissing and a pair of stovepiped tails. Only Solomon came straight to Hanaan, but he came cautiously.

"They heard all the noise but couldn't see me, and they were frightened," she said, reaching out to Solomon. He sniffed with grave suspicion at her fingers. Hanaan laid the ice pack aside and for the first time looked up into Theo's face. The skin below the eye was growing purplish. She swept the cat into her arms. "He's sick, Theo."

"Sick?" The gentle agony in her voice shocked him. "He's a murderous idiot. How could he hit you? How could he *hit* you?"

Her head dropped so that her lips grazed the cat's head. "Solomon. Solomon is sick."

At a loss, Theo sat down beside her. He put the compress to her cheek again and she took it. As their fingers brushed, her eyes took him in with hungry sadness.

"A virus. I don't know," she said. The cat curled and settled in her lap, purring. "Will you listen to his lungs?"

Not knowing what else to do, Theo pressed an ear just behind the cat's narrow shoulder. He steeled himself with patience; she needed time before she'd talk.

An occasional soft pop supported her fears about the cat, though he could see no fluid in or around the nose. He pulled the eyes open slightly. Clear. It proved nothing. A chronic respiratory virus ran rampant among the city's many street cats, a condition that often turned fatally to pneumonia, and it could begin this way. She'd lost cats to it in the past.

"It's not bad, whatever it is."

"Not yet."

"He's strong. Nine lives."

Her eyes met his again. "But how many has he already lived?"

"This isn't number nine."

The hint of a smile, though it ended in a wince of pain. "You can't know this, Theo." She put the compress aside again. "It is too cold."

He took the hand that had been holding it, threaded their fingers together to warm her. She stroked the cat. "His name means sun. And peace."

The skin at her wrist was silken. "I thought you named him the solemn one."

"At first. But to me he became the sunny one. In our history it is Suleyman. God made him able to understand the languages of all the animals."

"Then maybe he understands your brother."

She rubbed Solomon's ears, her face hidden by the fall of her hair.

Gently, he tightened his grip on her hand. "Hanaan—"

She cut him off, her voice rising. "Abdullah has told you. The whole world knows Samir was here. I yelled from the window to him."

"Your face tells me everything I need to know."

"Theo, I must say something to you." She pulled her hand from his slowly. "My father sends me a message through my brother. He says, stay away from the evil and sing to it."

He was supposed to understand but failed to, utterly.

"It's about you," she said. "It's like a lullaby. You keep away the evil spirits with a lullaby. You sing to them."

This sank in slowly. "I'm evil?"

She brooded, prohibiting any drama. "No. My temptation is evil. He asks me to stop seeing you. He will not agree to anything else."

He wanted to have misunderstood her. "This isn't a request. Your brother's giving orders. With his goddamn fists, Hanaan."

"My brother gives me my father's intentions. And how gladly he delivers them! But my brother has no power over me, whatever he thinks."

Theo moved forward to the edge of the couch, his long legs angled awkwardly before him. He gave himself instructions to stay calm. "He hit you. That's his power. He could do it again. Worse."

"A hit is nothing. It's his cowardice. I pity him. He doesn't know how to say anything else." She glanced at him. "My father would not hit me."

"Your father didn't come here."

Restlessly, she lifted the cat in her arms and stood up, then laid Solomon back on the couch in the warm spot where she had been sitting. Her silence struck Theo with grievous weight.

"My father will never agree to you, Theo."

"It's not the time to talk about this. When you're better, in a few days——"

"You don't understand. I told my brother I must see you once more. This . . . now . . . is that once more."

For the first time ever in her apartment, Theo became aware of the roar from the Gulf Road nearby. The reality of the room before him—Hanaan, the cats, the domestic clutter of this familiar space—receded as if he were floating slowly away from it.

"You will think it's because Samir hit me, but this isn't true. It's because of my father. He wishes it."

She swiped a tear away and sat in the chair opposite. "For you, your family is apart from you. You keep them thousands of miles away, on the other side of the world. But we're different here. I'm not separate from my family. We're like this," she said, holding out her hand, palm up, as she cupped her fingers, a flower folding into a bud.

To him, it looked little different from a fist.

"You agreed," he said. "A closeness your family enforces with violence."

Her shoulders sank with the burden of impossible translations. "I have no choice."

He stood up, unable to make himself believe her. "You gave your word to him? It's settled?"

"Yes!" She wept angrily. "I can't break my father's wish. Why must you take every word and pin it to my heart? I choose to see my family, Theo. If I'm with you, I can't go back. They won't see me. My father says he can't make this sacrifice. It would kill him."

"It's our sacrifice, not his."

She couldn't comprehend it. "Oh, Theo. What would I be without my family?"

BEYOND REASON

In Brazio's garden the hollyhocks stood taller than Mufeeda. Strolling along the flagstone path she stopped to gaze into a lemon bloom that looked back at her, eye to eye. It often helped to come here. The delicate lime depths of the foliage against the brilliant yellow comforted her deeply, beyond what seemed the ordinary reach of beauty, and a peace came to her of the sort prayer sometimes inspired. The Prophet, praise be upon Him, had once said that prayer was the comfort of the eye. And so, taken literally, it could also be the other way around: the comfort of the eye was also prayer. She touched a fragile, curling edge of the bloom as she might the soft skin of a newborn child. "Hello, little lovely one."

She had yet to learn this lesson fully: to look at her surroundings simply, with an open heart, and simply look.

Yards away under the date palms, Brazio stood shifting from foot to foot, in no better control of his limbs than of his chattering mouth. She'd exiled him there after almost tripping on him twice as he explained to her the layout of the garden she herself had planned. *Here, madam, I grow for you marigolds!* She walked on, going where he wouldn't dare follow, into a small walled courtyard with raised stone planters, which Saleh had ordered built for her early in their marriage. The privacy here delighted her. The planters, after these many years, were studded with cactus and vigorous philodendron, and draped at this season with bougainvillea in voluptuous bloom. She sat on one of the broad cedar benches under the shade of a pair of olive trees, facing out to more palms at the back of the garden.

But it was the date palms that made the garden into a sanctuary, their branches at the trunk like graceful bones of pale-green and polished ivory, and the speared leaves bisecting the bright sky. Another few weeks and the female trees would put forth their arcs of long-stemmed pale-white blooms, a beautiful sight, like a fountain in slow motion. She had loved the annual ritual of their pollination since she was a girl and her father allowed her to watch as he oversaw the process on his most important trees. Standing tall and commanding as a general under their canopy, he boomed out instructions to the gardener crouched high in the branches of his single, precious male *khalasah* tree, directing him to a particular anther, the one heaviest with pollen at its broad and flattened tip. With a curved knife the gardener sliced off the anther, a stalk as long as his arm, and passed it carefully to an assistant on the ground. It had been Rafiq back then, a skinny young man, terrified of her father, and for good reason: his orders could never be followed precisely enough. *Why do you tarry? Go, go!*

Instructed both to hurry and to guard against the loss of even one grain of precious pollen, Rafiq walked heel-toe, heel-toe, the anther held aloft, a torchbearer on parade, to the base of a female *khalasah*. Up the anther went *Slowly!* into the hands of a third man in the branches, who shook it solemnly over the crown of flowers at his feet.

"Madam?"

Brazio intended a polite whisper but the result was only harsher than his usual, galloping voice. She could see a portion of his tufted head beyond a ropy tangle of vines and glossy leaves.

"Madam, please I must ask one question."

"Brazio, I'm sitting quietly now."

"Yes, madam." He didn't budge. "Madam?"

She closed her eyes.

"The people are saying Saddam will come. What we will do, madam?"

She'd managed not to worry about Saddam in these few minutes. "We're in God's hands, Brazio. *Inshallah* he will not come."

255

The tufted head bowed. "Yes, madam. The Americans are going, madam. My friend, he is a gardener with the American Embassy. Also another friend. Many, many people, they're going."

"My husband and I are not going, *inshallah*," she said. "My children are not going. Kuwaitis are not going. This is also a lot of people."

"Yes, madam." Still he didn't move.

She knew the staff was nervous. During the occupation, Rafiq and Brazio had stayed with Saleh in the house after she escaped south to Saudi Arabia with the children and the rest of the staff; and though no physical harm had come to those who stayed behind, the house had been searched twice by men of the Iraqi *Mukhabarat* looking for Jassim. The stories of their brutality were legion.

"Madam, I must say one thing to you."

"Yes, Brazio." She'd never be rid of him. "Say this thing."

"Madam." He coughed, fell silent, began again. "Madam, it is Frederick." His anxiety almost throttled him. "Madam, he is not good. Madam, he's troubling the women . . . as a man."

The shock bled her voice of volume too. "Come here."

"Please madam, no." He didn't wish to be seen from the house.

"How do you know this?"

"He talks, madam. One day I hear a commotion and he has blood coming at his hand. And he's angry."

"You've seen a housemaid with him?"

"No, madam."

She didn't believe him.

"No women come to him, madam. These women, they are good. For you Frederick smiles and smiles but he—" He paused, in anguish, gathering his nerve. "He has . . . offended one lady, madam."

She spoke with iron deliberation. "You must tell me who."

Agony creased his face. "Madam, my eyes are not good."

"Brazio. Tell me. Now."

256

A car turned into the drive. Umm Saleh's. Brazio began to back away. "Emmanuella," he whispered.

"It's ONE report, and from a buffoon of a gardener who saw nothing." Saleh swatted his jacket on the chair by the bed. "We've seen nothing. Emmanuella has not complained, nor have any of the housemaids. Frederick has served my mother honestly and faithfully for several years. She likes him. Surely he deserves our trust."

"Brazio wouldn't have spoken to me unless he was certain," Mufeeda said. "It goes against his grain completely to tell me anything unpleasant. He spends every moment with me trying to ingratiate himself."

"How is this different? He ingratiates himself by giving you a ripe piece of gossip."

"He's never incriminated another servant before, Saleh. He risks their contempt if he comes tattling to us, you know this, and perhaps vengeance from Frederick."

"They live in close quarters. Frederick's young and handsome and certain of himself. There's some jealousy here, that's all."

She couldn't contain her frustration with him. He sat on the bed, watching her with unsuppressed impatience. She paced the room from end to end to calm herself and turned to him again.

"You fail to take anything seriously, Saleh."

He hunched forward as if these words made him weary to the bone. She couldn't let it matter.

"Mariam is rebellious and you say it's nothing. She's rude, thoughtless, disrespectful. It's nothing, you say. She encourages the attentions of a boy. A kiss! Even this is nothing. One of our housemaids may have been molested. But this is to be completely ignored. When will something matter, Saleh?"

"I know you have a lot on your mind—"

She could stand no more. "Not even God matters to you, so why should I be surprised that nothing else does? What can be of any concern to you if your faith doesn't concern you?"

He didn't raise his voice. "That's a ridiculous charge."

"Is it ridiculous for me to worry that you promised your soul to God and then turned your back on Him? What will happen to you, Saleh, and to your children, who grow up with a godless father?"

The impact of these words left them both silent. Mufeeda stood at the window, trembling with fear and strain.

"I can't talk about this any more," he said. "You're beyond reason, Mufeeda."

She whirled to face him. "Yes, I'm beyond reason. My faith doesn't need a reason as yours apparently does, Saleh. You made a vow and did nothing to fill it. Nothing. In six years. If you're still waiting for a word from God, I must tell you that He's already spoken."

"I don't understand you," Saleh said. "Nor do I wish to understand you when you speak like this."

"'Fear the fire,'" she said, "'whose fuel is men and stones.'"

His reaction at first made her think he'd been humbled by these terrifying words from the Quran. But no. He was only gathering up his tired cynicism to mock them.

"So I will burn in hell. It doesn't matter how well I conduct my life, no matter how honestly and kindly, how earnestly I live, or how much I love you and my children and my mother. Unless I make a gesture to God that you can see and believe in, you'll believe only the worst of me, and I'll burn in hell."

"I'm not talking about me."

"I think you are," he said.

Agonized, she turned again to the window. He was right that nothing could be gained by further conversation.

No realm of her life now remained untouched by anxiety— from her heart, where Saleh had long been the dearest resident, to the world beyond, where big ships and thousands of men waited for war.

DISAPPEARED

THEO HAD finished the draft of his report with the focus of a man escaping something worse than report-writing. The effort had succeeded in keeping his deeper thoughts at bay. But as he drank a long shot of whiskey in Saleh's study and watched his work pass through Saleh's hands page by page, his mind gradually unlocked its defenses, allowing loops of vivid recall. The blood on Hanaan's cheek. Her wrist beneath his fingertips. Her luminous eyes as she told him to leave.

I choose to see my family, Theo.

He would never conceive of striking his sister, could only dimly imagine feeling 'dishonored' by Julia's conduct, whatever the hell that meant. She had never embarrassed him, not since childhood, and not since childhood had he felt an impulse to hit her. The concept of family honor, enforced by brutality, seemed an oxymoron. How could they claim to love her after sending Samir to beat her into submission?

He heard a grunt from Saleh and looked up to see him shunt the manuscript to a side table with a flick of the wrist. Saleh knew that something had happened with Hanaan but hadn't asked for any details. Nothing outside the report seemed to concern him at the moment—not Saddam, not the cruise missiles nosed-up for Baghdad or the troops standing ready, somewhere well out of sight of the city. Saleh was like many other Muslims, perhaps, leaving everything in God's hands, though he never talked about that either.

Lifting a glass of wine, his second, Saleh took a big swallow. "It won't do, Theo. There is no prosecution here, only little slaps of a feather. You must rewrite it."

Saleh would never be pleased with the report. If Theo had said that the hospital should be dynamited tomorrow, Saleh would insist on nuking it today. "I took the tact and diplomacy route," Theo said.

"But what's the point of your report? You don't cut deeply enough."

"The point . . ." Theo said, as if the words were familiar but unknown. "The point was to get the damn thing done."

Saleh watched him with amusement. "You know, when the heavens burst asunder we Arabs will still be spinning words. We speak in fabulous calligraphy, with never a straight line between two points. This is why I wanted you on the committee, Theo, so that something, finally, would be said bluntly. But you've already been in Kuwait too long. You've contracted our fatal disease of compressing the most possible words into the smallest possible idea."

"A compliment at last."

Saleh rose to refill their glasses. He poured Theo's whiskey generously, his apology for his criticism.

"If it were only problems with the hospital, the task of reorganization would seem easier," he said. "But our patients, by and large, know almost nothing about their bodies." He added a crescent of ice to Theo's glass.

"I haven't told you this, Theo. On Sunday, a man brought his young wife to my clinic for the first time. She's pregnant, he says. Her blood has stopped for two months. This is pre-natal care to many people here—it's given in an emergency only—and not just the *Beduin*. But this man is a *Bedu*, forty-two, forty-three; she's eighteen. She can walk only by leaning on his arm. An ectopic pregnancy, but of course I don't know this yet. When I set eyes on her for the first time, her blood pressure is low, she's faint, short of breath, and in pain. He asks me what's wrong, can the baby come so early? He doesn't tell me that she's bleeding. Her *abaya* hides all. I try to examine her. She's terrified of me. She won't disrobe. She won't speak. She won't even lie down—until she faints, and it's only then that we can put her on the table."

Images flared in Theo's head of the husband beating the young wife for losing the child; another bloodied corpse at the hospital curbside; long, dark hair; the blinding flashes of the cameras. The distorted face became Hanaan's in a horrifying portrait printed in the newspaper. *Who can name this woman?*

He got to his feet, paced away across the room. "What is it with this damn country? Women kept in ignorance and fear, denied knowledge of their own bodies, for god's sake, denied life if they step over the lines the men have drawn."

Saleh set his glass down slowly on the tabletop. "Theo, tell me what's happened with Hanaan."

Theo took a moment to calm himself.

"Her brother brought her a message from their father—in the form of a fist. He hit her, raised a bloody welt on her face. Told her to stay away from me."

"How badly is she hurt?"

Theo ran his hand through his hair, exhaustion eating at his voice. "Physically, a blow hard enough to split the skin. She'll have a black eye. Mentally . . . she's given up. She's caving to this animal brother of hers. You warned me about this. I didn't believe it."

"Nor did I," Saleh said. "Not in a family like hers. I thought it was liberal-minded. You said her father gave her a fine education."

"And forgot about the son."

"Sit down, Theo," Saleh said quietly. "Say more."

Theo didn't sit. "You asked me if I'd met her family, remember? I never did. I think she knew but wouldn't tell me. We only had so much time."

"She would not have toyed with you, if that's what you mean."

Theo waved a hand, disgusted. "No. I mean that she knew it couldn't last. She wouldn't tell me that she was endangering herself. I'd have gone away sooner."

"You must not go back."

"I know." Theo sat again, but on the edge of the chair, his shoulders slumped. "How can I stay away?"

Saleh allowed him a moment of silence. "You think you know her, Theo, but you don't. You can't. Let me tell you. A woman like Hanaan will go through a certain evolution in our culture. At first, perhaps, her religion will become a little more abstract, and she'll begin to interpret God's word with greater latitude. She'll dress less conservatively, act and think with more independence. Hanaan has done these things. But that's the easy part, even when it isn't safe, because the deepest religion in our culture is the family itself. She can interpret God's word in new ways, but her father's law is not flexible. She can't soften it with a fresh interpretation."

"But she must have known this would happen. And yet she let things go on. She—"

"—she knew she would be beaten? Don't be absurd. She fell in love with you. This gave her strength. She felt she could defy her family."

Theo wanted to find hope in this—perhaps she still might—and they'd go away together.

Saleh went steadily on. "But her father can destroy her with rejection. Even worse than a beating, he can keep her from her family forever. I will not say what the brother might do. You can't risk finding out."

"What kind of father would beat his daughter? A grown daughter?"

"Many, many fathers all over this world. You idealize, Theo. Even beloved fathers, maybe even fathers in your wonderful America, though of course they're not beloved there."

A tone of irony slipped into Saleh's voice. "Mufeeda's father still looms large in our lives too, though he's been dead for years. Now *there* was a master of intimidation. He scared the shit out of me."

Brooding for a moment, he glanced up to catch Theo watching him. "These two women of ours, they're not so different as they seem, you know."

"I've never known two women more different." Theo smiled grimly. "I thought they'd all be alike here. Religious and cloaked in black."

"Well, you must know the context. Mufeeda and I have had a *discussion*." Saleh sat for a while, saying no more. "In her eyes I've failed to keep a bargain, you see, a bargain she says I shouldn't have made and that can't even exist. Nevertheless, I'm bound to keep it."

"A bargain?"

"The worst kind of bargain." Saleh sighed. "With God."

Theo sat back in his chair.

"I've done many stupid things. A bargain with God was one. Telling Mufeeda of it was another. She's the exacter, not God." He turned in his chair toward the windows, gazing out.

"It was in the time after Jassim disappeared. I was over-wrought. Everyone was. We were all praying, begging God to protect us and restore those who were taken from us. Even I, though I hadn't prayed in many years, not with my heart. Mufeeda and the girls were in Riyadh—little Fauzia wasn't born yet. I was alone, working long hours under too much pressure." He shook his head. "We had so few supplies at the hospital, Iraqi soldiers everywhere, and many pregnant women, many early deliveries. It was as if the terror in the country, the fear of the mothers, their desire to escape, went through the bloodstream to their babies. Everyone wanted out."

Saleh fell silent again, staring at the mirrored surface of the glass. Unasked, he'd never mentioned the war before, referring to it only obliquely in other contexts: his mother's declining health, Mufeeda's increasing devotion to religion, what he saw as the unnatural stillness of his house, "since my brother is gone."

"That first morning of the war," he said. "I didn't believe it was happening. One hot morning in August there was war, heli-copters and fighter planes over our heads, and we were captive in our own country. The Iraqis, whom we thought of as brothers, who are truly family to many of us, to whom we had loaned mil-lions of *dinar* to fight the Iranians, turned on us overnight and murdered us in order to call our land their own. Many of their leaders thought we'd welcome 'liberation' or would at least resign ourselves to becoming part of Iraq, and at first they treated us well, not as their enemies. They thought we'd prefer their dictator to our Amir.

"But the Resistance quickly formed. My brother was with it from the first, and the Iraqis realized soon enough that we were their enemies. That's when the killing and torture began. I remember going up onto the roof of the villa with my brother—because we could see one of the Iraqi checkpoints on the ring road from there. In our own district, foreign soldiers, it couldn't be real—and all across the neighborhood, all across the city, men were on their roofs, watching too; and a cry went up, 'Long live the Amir! Long live the Amir!' To my brother it was a passionate call to action. It wasn't enough for him to stand on the roof and yell. He climbed up our old TV antenna, the big one, twenty feet high, as far up as he could go, and yelled out over the city, 'God is great! *Allah u Akbar!*' I said, 'Come down, Jassim, you donkey. It's dangerous, you'll break a leg and how will a broken leg help the cause?'"

Saleh closed his eyes. "I was worried about a broken leg."

Beyond the solid door of the study, a phone rang in the hall, a distant sound from another world.

"He went underground, was gone all the time, came home exhausted, filthy, covered with scratches and scrapes, full of secrets and enormous, silent pride. He wouldn't speak of it to any of us. Occupied villas exploded, tanks were sabotaged, Iraqi soldiers were poisoned or shot, and a few important Iraqis were actually killed. But it made little difference in the end. Many of the Resistance were only boys out for a thrill, boys with knives or their father's hunting rifles, adolescents with nothing better to do. A few were young men in their twenties struck with an almost desperate love of country. This was Jassim. He'd never felt passionate about anything in his life before and he lost all rationality, as if he were crazy in love with a woman. All his young man's cynicism about his homeland was swept away overnight and he loved this place, he wanted to die for it. This was my brother, and he disappeared."

Saleh lapsed into silence.

"And your vow?" Theo said.

For a moment, Saleh seemed perplexed, as if he didn't know, after all, how to account for it.

"There's a contagious insanity in war. Saddam was the vector, and we all caught this terrible scourge. It took him six hours to overrun our country, Theo. This humiliation added a terrible fever in our minds. Were we so weak or was Saddam so strong? We'd always believed we were strong, but now it seemed we were only arrogant. We began to see the war as a divine measure, God's way of making us humble again, calling us back to him. Even I felt this, and I repented that I'd fallen away from my beliefs and practices. I told God that if he would give Jassim back to me unharmed, I'd dedicate my life to him and never doubt again."

Saleh sagged in his chair. "It seemed to me, Theo, at the time, that he heard me, and even approved. I don't believe this now. But I believed it then, and when Mufeeda came home, I told her of this vow, certain that Jassim would come back. It frightened her from that moment. There I was, believing myself punished for arrogance, and yet offering up my soul to God as payment for his cooperation. God wanted nothing from me but my submission, and I'd asked him to submit to *my* will."

Saleh shook his head in astonishment. "You can imagine what Mufeeda made of this, very quietly, in all her innocence. She came to believe that because I'd made this vow, I must give my soul in advance, to prove my sincerity to God, or he wouldn't bring Jassim home to us. But of course I had no sincerity. The war ended, the fever dissipated. What could I prove to an all-knowing God—to myself—but my insincerity? And Jassim failed to return."

"There's no hope? No word at all?"

"No, of course not. Don't ask. He's dust."

Saleh sat, eyes closed. "This has just come before us clearly, before Mufeeda and me. I can't say how we'll get around it, but we must. And you, Theo, there's no easy path for you, either."

"I love her," Theo said.

"I know. But you must let her go."

DESPERATE CASES

Emmanuella fingered the ten *dinar* note Kit had given her, folded neatly in half in her pocket, an amount equal to nearly a week's salary. In the offertory plate she put a one *dinar* note of her own. John, at her side, did the same, his grave eyes meeting hers briefly.

As they passed into the winter sunlight from the cavernous gloom of the mud-colored cathedral, he said, "Is it necessary to keep Santana secret from the other housemaids?"

"It would make trouble for me. Ma'am doesn't allow us to speak to anyone outside our villa." This wasn't strictly true, but it was a common prohibition by employers in Kuwait and he wouldn't doubt it. She hadn't told him the deeper reason for her secrecy, that she'd stolen food for Santana.

"And your ma'am wouldn't understand even in these circumstances?"

"Her mother-in-law dislikes me."

This was, at least, the undivided truth, one she prayed wouldn't destroy his good opinion of her. "She's always angry with me. She says she'll send me back to Goa."

"There's no understanding these people," he said, requiring no further explanation. "Now: tell me what you wish me to do."

It surprised her to realize that what she most wished him to do was remain sitting quietly by her side, and that she had to check her pride at finding him there. She could no longer imagine that she'd ever thought him homely. He looked upon his surroundings with interest and intelligence, his head held high, and had none of the airs of other young men, none of their flippant humors and teasing ways. But for him, Rosaline and Carmen would be at her elbow as usual after mass, witnesses to her every move. Now they saw themselves as guardians of her romance, the very cupids responsible for her happiness, and gave her as much time alone with him as possible, seeking her out only when it was time to walk to the bus stop.

Going from souk to souk, they filled a small bag of goods meant for Emmanuella, to justify the shopping; and into Emmanuella's pockets they put their careful choices for Santana, items that required no refrigeration: candy bars, bags of pistachios, mixed nuts, dried fruit, packets of dried fish, crackers layered with cheese.

When Emmanuella's pockets could hold no more, John bought her a cup of tea and a pastry. They sat on a brick planter in the plaza area outside the souks, barren of all but a desiccated palm. John told her of his mother's latest letter, and her many expectations of the wedding. His mother would have complained about the dowry, of course, though John didn't mention this. How kind he was, for it wasn't a large dowry and yet her family couldn't afford it. Her own mother's anxiety on the topic was clear: the family had few savings; and yet family pride, compelled by tyrannical tradition, required any daughter to have the equal of her mother's dowry. *I had six silk saris along with under things, and a fine gold necklace and bangles. You must have the same.* That would require at least seven hundred *dinar.* Emmanuella despaired at the thought of it. Fifteen months' salary if she didn't spend a *fil.*

"Your tea isn't hot enough?"

Suddenly, she felt exhausted, unable to muster even the effort to take a sip. She looked up to find his deep eyes upon her.

"You worry about my mother," he said. "Don't. I'm a grown man, with modern ways."

She tried to smile at his sleek tone of self-sufficiency.

He touched the skin of her forearm lightly. "I won't allow pressure on the topic of the dowry. You have nothing to fear."

No, nothing but the loss of her job and deportation to Goa. Still, she was touched by his determination. He didn't realize that what he said would have confirmed any girl's fears: his mother wasn't satisfied and had told him so. Few sons could defy their mother's wishes, and he was a dutiful son.

Ahead, they saw Rosaline standing next to a pillar of the colonnade, looking their way with exaggerated nonchalance.

John inclined his head toward Emmanuella. "How long have you been helping Santana?"

She hadn't marked the time exactly. "Since the weather was hot, too hot to give her chocolate."

This worried him. "It's a long while. You can't go on and on giving and giving, when you're at risk yourself. And her employers, if they're really trying to starve her, will surely begin to wonder at her survival." He gave her a smile at this but Emmanuella became indignant. "She survives because God watches over her. Our God, not theirs."

"One of his angels watches over her."

A foolish compliment. It pleased her against her will. "Ma'am Kit also says that we must do something else. But what can be done?"

His eyes tracked back to Rosaline, who was gauging the moment to come bustling up. "Her employers have her passport?"

"Yes, yes, of course." All employers confiscated the passports of their household staffs.

"What about the embassy?"

A stupid question. Everyone knew that the embassy acted only in the most desperate cases as a sanctuary for Indian citizens, and it dealt daily with housemaids in danger as great as Santana's. "They'll send her back," she said, "and instruct her to do her best. And how would she get to the embassy? Do you have a car?" She regretted this last question. She knew he didn't have a car and had never learned to drive. His family was as poor as hers.

"There is the bus."

Perhaps he wasn't so intelligent after all. "She's to take a suitcase and wait at the bus stop? The police will see her and demand her papers. Then God knows what will happen to her."

"No . . . " He put a finger to his chin. "She doesn't take a suitcase. She leaves with nothing."

The obvious. To have considered luggage, as if Santana were a tourist. It was she who was stupid. "Of course."

Rosaline set forth from the colonnade. She crossed the plaza, elbows pumping, making a show of looking at her watch.

"Emmanuella," John said, as if she might consider it none of his concern. "Are you well?"

She couldn't look him in the eye, though she knew he wished for it. "Yes, yes. I'm tired. This girl, and now Saddam. I can't sleep."

"You must be careful. Please. For me."

DESPITE HER fatigue, she woke at dawn, her imagination crowded with the dangers and possibilities that lay ahead. Giving up on more rest, she crouched next to her bed—how bruised her body felt—and brought forth the stash hidden beneath. It made a satisfying landscape spread upon the floor, a great cache that she herself had gathered, though perhaps Santana wouldn't need it now, not if she made the run to the embassy. The thought of the waste troubled Emmanuella. She hadn't kept track of her purchases and couldn't return them, and much of the ten *dinar* note had been spent. If only she'd talked to John about the embassy before they'd made their purchases. Then Ma'am Kit's money could have gone directly to Santana, a much better use for it.

She forced her mind back to practicalities. She could still give Santana a small amount of money to take with her, and could bring her some food and clothing later—if the embassy accepted her.

And if it didn't?

Then Santana would be forced to go back to the villa, and there could be little doubt that her employers would devise some terrible punishment for her. The food might then be more important than ever, especially if Saddam came. Emmanuella pushed all but a small portion of the bounty back under the bed.

Passing through the front door on her way to Kit's, she saw Santana in the street beyond washing the little red car. This was an early morning chore, a chore done at dawn, yet it was nine o'clock. The girl was waiting for her, disguising her intent with this out-of-synch chore. Emmanuella slowed her pace, alarmed, appraising the risk. The man's car was in the enclosure—both husband and wife were home and yet Santana meant to speak with her. Santana slowed in her scrubbing too, her rag drooping across the soapy windshield of the red car, her wide, dark eyes on Emmanuella. She began to talk too soon, too loudly.

"He's putting clothes in a bag! They're leaving soon! Tomorrow night, he says."

Emmanuella walked slowly toward the dumpster at the curb.

"They're frightened of a war! They're leaving! He says he'll lock me inside!"

Emmanuella shot her a warning glance but she wouldn't be hushed.

"Help me!"

"Shh! Stupid girl."

"What do you care? You have no troubles!"

"No troubles?" Emmanuella's temper flashed. "I have many troubles, and I take trouble for you. I've brought you food." She swatted her pocket. "I've brought you money. Do you see?"

When had she stopped walking? She bolted forward, dropped the bag in the shadow of the dumpster and took refuge there herself. It offered some protection from the windows of Santana's villa. Santana joined her.

"You must go to the embassy. Now. Today. I'm giving money with the food. Take nothing, only this. I have more in my room. I'll bring it to you at the embassy."

"How? The police will see me. I have no papers, no passport."

"You'll take the bus."

"I don't know the bus! I never go from this house. Which bus? They'll send me away from the embassy—and what will these people do to me then?"

270

"The embassy will take you. God will tell them to take you."

"God, God, God." The girl began to back away, into clear sight of her villa. "This is all you ever say."

"You can't stay here. If Saddam comes . . ." Emmanuella forced herself to say the ugly words, though Santana knew the facts as well as she. "In the war the soldiers raped housemaids."

For an instant, terror flooded Santana's face—and something else—an agonizing hopelessness. Emmanuella darted into the sun and grabbed the girl's hand. "You must pray. Pray and go."

But the girl twisted violently away. She wept, mouth agape. Anyone could hear. Anyone could be watching from behind the tinted eyes of glass up and down the street. She glared at Emmanuella like a foe.

"If there is a God why do I earn my living like this, with this . . ." she spat out the words, ". . . stupid boy? You and your God." She sneered at Emmanuella's shock. "He keeps my salary. Why else would he give me *any* money?"

Emmanuella backed away, fleeing across the street to Kit's.

Santana called after her, heedless. "I should depend on you? For a few *fils* in a bag?"

SOMEHOW SHE'D hurt herself in these moments with Santana, she didn't know how. Pain radiated through her body as though she'd taken a heavy blow. Perspiring with her effort to appear normal, Emmanuella sat with Kit's children on the carpet, trying to attend to a puzzle for the boy, a silly board game for the girl. Doing the family's morning dishes had been a misery, every plate a brick in her hands; and how could she do the ironing Kit had laid out for her? Her body sagged with weariness. The children wavered before her eyes.

Kit came and stood beside her, chatting. The words came at Emmanuella as if from a radio far away. She didn't think of responding. *Isn't this wonderful weather? How can it be so beautiful when everyone's talking about war?*

And on and on and on, a flood of words, almost soothing, if only they would go on forever so that she didn't have to respond. But her name came swimming up through the stream. Once, twice. Then Kit was on the carpet with her, face to face.

"Emmanuella? Are you all right? You don't look . . . you look . . ." A cool hand on her forehead. "You're running a fever again." The hand went to her forearm, the soft skin at the elbow underlain with purple veins.

She made herself smile, though her vision spun sickeningly when she looked up into Kit's face. "Oh, no, ma'am. I'm fine. It's my . . ." She didn't know how to say it to a Western woman, and a lie never came easily. "It's a woman's time in the month."

Kit's eyes stayed on her, studying her face as if she were one of the children. She stood up again but didn't go.

"Emmanuella, your period shouldn't cause a fever. You have to lie down. I insist."

"No, ma'am. Thank you, ma'am."

Emmanuella moved a piece of Kevin's puzzle at random, one eye on Kit's shoes at the edge of her vision, praying to God she would please just walk away. After a long while, she did, and silently. Angry, no doubt. She had made another employer angry.

She didn't do the ironing, couldn't attempt it. Kit wouldn't notice until after she'd gone, and she'd say tomorrow that she'd forgotten. *I'm so sorry, ma'am!* Tomorrow she'd be better. If only she could get some sleep.

At noon she closed the door behind her and walked slowly across the enclosure, head down. She could see the Pakistani gardener to the side, watering the palm trees, saw his quick glance, though she didn't meet it, and his flashing intention to speak to her. But he only nodded gravely, looking away as a Muslim man should: the sin was in the second glance.

The street was empty. Longing for her bed, she crossed in silence, watching her feet for fear they wouldn't support her, though even from the corner of her eye she saw that the car of Santana's ma'am was gone and some of the metal blinds of the villa had been rolled down tight. Even the first-floor windows, which were barred, had metal blinds. These, thank God, were open still.

Her own gates lay before her, locked as usual. She caught her breath to steady it before she rang the bell. Rosaline would come.

Frederick appeared instead, stepping out from the kitchen door of the *mulhaq* into the sunshine, a cigarette in his fingers.

She wouldn't look at him. She rang the bell. Rosaline would come.

"You have some big trouble now," he said. He took another drag on his cigarette. "What will Madam say this time?"

He made no sense; she understood nothing. She rang the bell again, pressing down long on the button. Where was Rosaline? She waited, staring at the gate, willing it to open as Frederick came nearer, too close. She stepped back from the gate. If he touched her, even through the bars, she'd scream. Where was Rosaline?

"Na'am?" The fiery voice of the Grandmother roared through the intercom.

Frederick began to laugh. "Big trouble."

A buzz from the gate. Rosaline flung open the front door, her face pale with distress. "Emmanuella, why are you ringing and ringing? The Grandmother is so angry!"

Emmanuella stepped unsteadily through the gate. Frederick slouched alongside, drawing on his cigarette, his voice low. "She'll eat you alive."

In the shining dimness of the foyer, Rosaline waited. "You must go to the Grandmother. Because of you, she'll make it hard for us all."

"Where is Ma'am?"

"Away! She's not here to take care of you now!"

Emmanuella walked on. Rosaline whispered in her wake. "What have you done *now*, Emmanuella?"

SEATED ON a large divan the Grandmother waited for her, alone in her enormous bedroom. Before her, the stash from beneath

Emmanuella's bed, an impressive array, lay on the marble-topped table usually reserved for tea. Only Succoreen would have had the nerve to enter Emmanuella's room in her absence and search for something to bring to the Grandmother.

The old woman let Emmanuella stand in silence before her like a criminal. She motioned toward the tabletop dismissively. "What is this? This candy, biscuits. Say why is this."

It was a shock to hear so many English sounds from her lips. How much less terrifying she was—pitiful, even. Indians with a mere sprinkling of education spoke better English than this.

"This is my property, ma'am." Anger crept into Emmanuella's voice. "Someone takes this from my room."

"Who takes?" The Grandmother rubbed her thumb and forefinger together. "You take. So many things. How? What money?"

Emmanuella kept her voice low in order to control it. "My own money, ma'am. Mine."

The Grandmother let her eyes drift with slow and skeptical derision across the expanse of food. "Your money? No, you take money. Who gives you money? You tell me. Now."

Emmanuella's daily work for Kit was still officially a secret from the Grandmother, although Emmanuella felt certain she knew of it. She considered the risk. *It is a tip from Ma'am Kit.* But she couldn't bring herself to betray Kit's name to this old woman.

She folded her hands before her. "I take what is mine only."

The Grandmother allowed herself some amusement. "Yes, you say this. Your money. My son, what he says? How girl buy so many things?"

Her grammar could not convey whether she'd already told Sir or had yet to do so. Had she telephoned him with the news during the day?

The Grandmother grew sly with implication. "This boy, he give you money. For love."

For a moment, Emmanuella failed to understand. Her courtship was no secret to anyone on the female staff, thanks to Carmen, and so naturally the news would have passed to the Grandmother from Succoreen. Then she realized: The old woman was calling her a whore. A whisper of astonishment escaped her. "You say this of *John*?"

The Grandmother's wide, florid face grew darker.

Emmanuella stepped to the table. "This isn't true. You will not say this to me."

Eyeing the Grandmother in disgust, she reclaimed what she could of her trove, stuffing candy bars and crackers into her pockets as the Grandmother screeched at her in Arabic. Succoreen and Rosaline appeared at the door, their curiosity overcoming their fear. They hadn't been far away.

Emmanuella addressed them all. "You know nothing. None of you. God knows. Your Allah too. *They* know she speaks a lie."

STAGED DEPARTURE

THE WINTER days had brought air so cool that even a light breeze sent a chill through Kit. How thin-blooded she'd become. She pulled a couple of the molded plastic patio chairs from the storage closet under the stairs and put them out in the afternoon sun. Sitting on one with her feet propped on the other, she sipped her tea and watched the children play, a book lying unopened in her lap. It would be cold in London and she wanted to soak up some fortifying sun. Then perhaps she could face going indoors to pack.

The kids' absorption in their separate entertainments amused her. Carlie could pedal her tricycle all the way around the house within the marble enclosure, and did, in endless circles; and Kevin never wearied of tossing old tennis balls into random trajectories. He waddled along the walls, retrieving them one by one to start again. Jack must have been this way when he was a kid: unshakably patient as long as the game and the rules were his own.

She closed her eyes and let her head drop back. How peaceful it was: the middle of the afternoon, a quiet suburb in a modern city. Sun, tee-shirts, shorts. Kids playing. A housewife sitting with a book in her lap. With Saddam poised to strike from fifty kilometers away.

The thought couldn't horrify any longer. It had gone through her brain so many times in these last days that it made no impression any more. She'd grown calloused and tough. She smiled, amazed by this evidence of her adaptability, which she'd couldn't have imagined at her peak of anxiety the other day. Her ravings had tempered her, apparently. She'd looked at events much more philosophically since, as a detached observer, even though the level of crisis had ground inexorably upward. Jack, on the other hand, had slowly, finally, decided that there might be some danger after all. His style remained all-Jack, with an emphasis on maintaining the illusion of control. He'd made his announcement at breakfast, speaking with careful enunciation and gestures, reminding Kit of the way drunks were portrayed in old comedies: the intense concentration required to place the chin in the cup of the hand, or to cross the legs at the knee, as if the messages from brain to body went out in frozen Morse code. Even a change in facial expression went through several frames.

"I'm making it official today, Kit. A mandatory staged departure for nonessential personnel has become necessary. The employees will stay behind at this point."

Staged departure. Christ. "Well, I'm certainly unnecessary."

He came to the surface slowly, from far below. "Hm?"

"You mean you're sending us out. Me and the kids."

The burden of responsibility weighed in Jack's face. "Yes. You're the wife of the manager. With two small children. I'm the one who has to set the example, Kit."

Several of the company women and their kids had already left, waiting for no signs from Jack. But he knew this. His bass voice had dug out a new register. "I've made your reservations for tomorrow night, the midnight flight to London on British Air."

How few concepts Jack could imagine in the form of words. If it was measurable and quantifiable, something he could see and judge and control, he could speak of it. But he had almost no language for the territory of the heart. She knew he worried about the safety of his family. She'd seen him giving the children a goodnight hug as though they might evaporate in his arms; and he'd held her in an uneasy, brooding embrace too. But he could say nothing about it.

The sun brightened, escaping from a thin scarf of cloud. She leafed listlessly through her book, a mystery circulating among the company women. A departure tomorrow night, then. Such

277

a short time. Her father would be glad of the news. She felt no relief herself, which puzzled her. Where were her motherly instincts?

She closed the book. She'd never liked mysteries much. Nothing significant in her own life had ever been left inadvertently in a desk drawer, or thrown in the river, or written in code. It seemed fundamentally dishonest to portray supposedly ordinary people whose lives were so rich in daily consequence, and yet it was all so easily comprehended and corrected once the clues were linked.

If clues really added up to action, wouldn't the more obvious of the world's problems be relatively fixable, such as Saddam? Everyone agreed he was a mass-murderer. No mystery there: he'd left plenty of corpses around to prove it. Nevertheless he was in command of a rich country, a big army, and a solemn corps of diplomats that trudged from continent to continent offering up compromises. If real life were easily comprehended would a teenaged girl be held captive across the street, suffering rape and starvation, eating food smuggled to her by another teenaged girl?

She'd stopped reading the newspaper altogether, wanting to know nothing more of tortured, pregnant, starving, murdered maids. No more television either, except videos that involved no disasters, natural or man-made. She wanted to prevent the kids from hearing the constant talk of war, and felt too much irritation watching it herself, with noble CNN doing its best at that dangerous front between commercials.

Some of the company women, a couple of flighty ones and one or two princesses, had grown panicky in the last couple of days. It pleased Kit to realize that she wasn't among them as they flapped on and on about how many outfits they should pack for winter in London, where they'd be lodged in a fine hotel. They whined and fretted. How long would the crisis last? Would they need their spring clothes?

She imagined herself back in Oklahoma, watching a news story about herself, a young mother with two little kids stuck here while Saddam rattled his sword. The camera would show her sitting in her chair, reading peacefully in the mild sunshine—sitting up straight, shoulders back, with her hair twisted up in a scrunchie in an interesting way, and wearing a little lipstick. Azhar's garden would show in the background—the lush basil and sprouting cauliflower, the row of spindly, baby tomato plants, the marigolds and cosmos—along with the kids, also cleaned up for the camera. Kevin would of course be completely, miraculously toilet-trained: no bulky diaper. As a viewer back home Kit would observe all these details, confounded by such peacefulness and unconcern and seeming normality; and feel a disapproving amazement at the nerve it would take to come to the Middle East—to one of those wild, Arab countries with hundreds of black-eyed terrorists running around and that monster with the Stalin mustache just up the road.

But being on the spot long enough for the initial panic to subside had taken the sensationalism out of it. Politics was mostly hoopla, world-wide. All that hyperventilating coverage on television, and yet here she sat outside her house in a neighborhood made up of other houses and a few little stores with clothing and groceries, coffee, tea, spices, toilet tissue, ketchup, mustard, hamburger buns, Cheerios, electronic cash registers, efficient cashiers, moms wheeling their kids around in grocery carts, cars parked side by side in the lots, bicycles at the curbside, a butcher who waved and smiled, sidewalks and schools, swings and slides and monkey bars. And prayers sent up to the heavens five times a day.

She'd just begun to feel at home here—and now she had to leave. She'd even gotten pretty good at dealing with the street peddlers, and had decoded what they were really saying when they yelled, "Bebseesefenab!" through the intercom, which she'd long assumed meant, "Sodas! Get your sodas!" in Arabic. The truth dawned when she offered Azhar a cold drink one day, "Pepsi or root beer, Azhar?" and he said, "Bebsee, mom." Pepsi. In Arabic there was no P or V. It must be the same in Urdu, Azhar's native tongue. Bebsee was Pepsi. *Pepsi, Seven Up!* Now she couldn't believe she'd missed it. If you expected something to be alien, it would meet your expectations.

THE BUZZER at the gate sounded, startling her. Too late for vendors. "Mom?" came a voice over the wall.

Azhar. As if she'd conjured him with a thought. The children ran to the gate to greet him. Kit swung it open. He'd come by in the morning to water and weed. She teased him. "You can't stay away from your garden, can you?"

He held a child by each hand, smiling down at them, but his eyes came back to Kit, troubled. "Mom. I speak to you."

She detached the children, bribing them with cookies stashed in her jacket pocket. "You go eat these now. Mommy and Azhar have to talk."

Kit expected him to express his worries about her departure, fears that she wouldn't return, concerns for his own safety. But his mind was elsewhere. They walked beneath the palms.

"Mom, this lady, this housemaid for you."

"Emmanuella."

"Yes, mom. Today she talk with girl there." He motioned toward Santana's villa.

Working in the garden earlier, he'd heard every word between them, and on some other days as well. He told Kit all he knew.

"This girl, mom," he said of Santana, "you will help her?"

The desperate earnestness in his face frightened Kit.

"Mom?"

AN ESSENTIAL PRIVACY

MUFEEDA KNEW exactly what would happen next. She had shooed Carmen from the kitchen and directed her to her room upstairs. But the girl would have hovered outside the closed door, listening with increasing alarm to the novel sounds of her mistress alone in the kitchen, preparing food just two hours after Carmen had served dinner. *Yes!—that's the sound of the cutting board. And the clang of the knives. Oh my God, she wasn't satisfied with my cooking!*

Mufeeda opened the swinging door a couple of inches. Crouching in sudden terror before her, Carmen gave a throttled squeak. The girl expected and deserved punishment but Mufeeda had no energy for it. She put on an expression she hoped looked genuinely threatening, and pointed a finger at the ceiling. Carmen dashed toward the stairway, glancing back in amazement as Mufeeda let the door swing shut again.

The digital clock on an oven blinked: 9:07. Saleh had called to say he would be home soon.

The kitchen, quiet and gleaming with cleanliness, eased Mufeeda's anxiety. She forced her thoughts to the household and set to work at slicing smoked salmon onto a plate. Perhaps a small portion of chopped salad too. He wouldn't want much.

Nothing more had disappeared from the kitchen since Emmanuella's removal. Which proved nothing. Any dishonest servant would grow cautious after an unaccountable change in staff. Still, the evidence pointed toward Emmanuella's guilt; and given the circumstances, the mass of packaged food beneath her bed, though none of it was from this kitchen, seemed a very odd coincidence. Why a girl like Emmanuella, modest, unassuming,

281

dedicated, and with a family to support at home, would plot to acquire so much food was baffling. Bad food at that. Crisps and sweets, horrible processed cheese. Mufeeda had always made certain that her staff was well-fed. Emmanuella had done the cooking herself. Why she might then steal from the kitchen was a mystery.

Saleh, your mother wishes to speak with you. There's been an upset.

Silence—he'd fallen so silent—as if he'd rather stay at the hospital than come home to her.

All right.

You'll be home early then, inshallah.

Yes.

She'd rarely seen his mother in such a temper.

You give this insolent girl leave to go to church but she meets a boy instead. What can you expect when you give the staff such freedom? Is she already pregnant? Is this why you've sent her to the Americans? What will my son say?

Mufeeda no longer knew for certain what Saleh might say, bitter proof of the damage done. The bounds of their long-held expectations of one another had shifted. In her memory the words of that night followed one another like fire upon fire.

Not even God matters to you.

You're beyond reason, Mufeeda.

What had she expected from him? A sudden, emotional proclamation of deeply held beliefs? By the understanding that had grown between them in these last years he'd made no concrete statements and she'd required none, preferring to believe in his belief. But she'd known the truth—of course she'd known, for years. So which of them was the hypocrite, Saleh to leave her in doubt of his commitment, or she who had pretended to believe in it?

She set the plate on the wide kitchen bar and wiped the cutting board, washed and dried the knife and put it in its proper slot in the block. There was no more to do. She sat on one of the bar stools, heavy with apprehension.

What had her parents believed? It shocked her that this question could occur to her, when it had surely never occurred to them. Belief was taken for granted then, as easily as air and sun and their devotion to their children. To question it would have been like questioning consciousness itself: Do you believe that you're alive and sentient? But now belief was food for analysis, another aspect of personality, infinitely variable and wholly individual, a matter for each person to choose for himself. As if there were a choice beyond God's.

Yet, His omnipotence had guided this too—there could be no other conclusion. What lay in doubt was her adjustment to it.

A disturbing thought came to her. Was it only pride now that made her put so much at stake? By declaring to Saleh that she doubted him, had she committed herself to following through with rejection? Merely because she'd said the truth aloud?

The clarity she'd felt that night eluded her now entirely. How fatuous she was. How dishonest—knowingly, consciously dishonest. Saleh was unchanged; his doubts were not new, and whatever his sins, her own had been as great. How could she know his inmost beliefs? *Verily Allah is well-acquainted with all that ye do.* Yet she'd claimed the same power over Saleh—claimed to perceive his most private thoughts and then chose to reveal them to Saleh himself—at a time convenient to her argument.

Headlights flashed along the side of the house. Mufeeda stood and sat again. It had been a long time since she'd met Saleh in the kitchen.

A sense of terrible loneliness raked through her. There was, she thought, even in the most intimate marriage, an essential privacy, a place only God could enter, which she'd tried to violate. There were words that shouldn't be spoken, stones that shouldn't be turned—nor thrown, ever. Her own restlessness had driven her to invade that inner space, not a righteous search for truth; she'd already known the truth. Instead, she'd been seeking a target for her own faults, someone to blame for the uneasiness of her own soul, and it wasn't Saleh.

His face, as he opened the door, was painful to see. He didn't know what to make of her presence. Weariness and surprise, hope and dread, all mixed there, ephemeral.

"I've made you a little snack."

"So I see."

"You must be hungry."

"Yes." He took off his jacket and laid it on the end of the counter. Taking a seat beside her, he pulled the plate closer but didn't eat.

"You'll want something to drink," she said, but he put a hand softly on her arm. "No, it's all right. Just sit. Tell me. It must be very bad."

And so it had seemed to her before. But as she told him of the day, of her interviews with Umm Saleh and the housemaids, the problem seemed reduced to just one: her own failure to deal with this problem—or any problem on her own. Even Emmanuella's outburst in front of Umm Saleh could be traced back to Mufeeda's weakness, her acceptance of Umm Saleh's interference in matters for which Mufeeda bore responsibility. Indeed, Umm Saleh was always quick to blame her. In her passivity she'd always pushed her husband into the role of intercessor.

Saleh hadn't touched his plate. He sat hunched over the counter staring across the empty kitchen as if completely alone. She'd long believed herself to be his companion. But she was only a grown-up child who depended on him for love and protection, and she'd chosen this shallow, infantile role for herself. It would be no wonder if he were attracted to another woman, an educated, interesting woman who sought out difficult challenges—such as his assistant. He hadn't taken her as a lover, she felt certain. Those suspicions now seemed the result of a passing sickness, a fevered nightmare. But what might happen in the future?

"Well," Saleh said. "I must go and speak with her."

Simple words, the same words he'd spoken a hundred times before, words of patience and honor, forbearance, love, and humility.

Mufeeda took a breath. "I'll go with you." And when he looked at her in surprise, she said, "Then you won't have to repeat to me what she tells you."

Amusement flickered in his tired eyes. "No, you'll hear it clearly enough through the walls."

"But this time I'll face her myself."

EXILE

The evening crawled by. Emmanuella had kept to the top floor where she could be alone with the day's laundry, her sense of dread magnifying the ordinary sounds of the house below: Mariam's music thudding in the stairway, the piercing commercials on the Grandmother's television.

Her boldness of the afternoon had long since drained away; she felt only exhaustion now. Her body aching, she ironed shirt after shirt for Sir, and a blouse and a skirt for Ma'am Mufeeda, expecting every moment to hear Sir come home and to be called into his presence. But he had failed to come home for dinner and Ma'am didn't call either, though she summoned the other maids. Perhaps it was part of the plan, to make Emmanuella suffer in the waiting. If she were sent home to Goa, at least she'd be able to take all the snacks she'd bought for Santana. They'd be useful as gifts; and though the sweets and crisps wouldn't please her mother, the younger children would be delighted, particularly Samuel. He was tall by now, not a baby any longer but a young boy—who would have forgotten her entirely. As John would do when she was gone.

Santana's fate worried her more than her own, though, for she was still comparatively fortunate. Ma'am and Sir would make her reservations for her, buy her an airline ticket, return her passport to her, and tell Rafiq to drive her to the airport at the appropriate time. And if Saddam attacked Kuwait after she was in India, she wouldn't regret losing her job so much; and no one at home would dare say anything except that by the grace of God she was safe among them.

The clothes dryer sounded, its harsh buzz echoing off the bare walls of the small room. Emmanuella pulled a fragrant armful of bed linen from the drum and folded it carefully according to her training, each piece to a certain size and shape, though she fumbled every crease. She imagined spreading the linen on the small table and lying down until the last washer load was finished. She eyed a tower of soft towels she'd washed earlier; they'd make a fine pillow. Leaning into the table, its metal edge at her thighs, she let her eyes close. It seemed impossible to think she might work for even one more minute. Every muscle in her body longed to stop. Even the floor would feel welcoming, spread with those clean sheets, the coolness of the cement seeping up into her body.

The door swung open the width of a hand. "Emmanuella!" Rosaline at a panicked whisper. "Sir and Ma'am are with the Grandmother!"

The noise of the television had stopped. Emmanuella hadn't heard Sir come home. She gripped a pillowcase to her breast.

"Emmanuella, why? Why did you speak so to the Grandmother? This Succoreen! She smiles everywhere in the house now and we must say nothing."

Rosaline crept away, as if Emmanuella were a leper and the disease of her coming exile were contagious.

The washing machine beeped. Emmanuella transferred its heavy contents into the dryer, and sank onto the cement despite her house dress. What could anything matter now?

But no one came. No summons arrived. The house fell silent below her, and when she ventured into the hallway the landing beyond looked dim. Below, the lights had been turned out and the family had gone to their rooms.

She'd been granted another day.

.

JUST BEYOND THE HEART

TESSA AND her children were leaving on the same flight for London. Even so, she said yes to Kit's request and came to pick up Carla and Kevin at eight in the morning, as early as Kit had ever managed to have them awake, dressed, and fed. Dropping straight to the carpet Tessa sat cross-legged before them. "I get to take you home with me today!" she said, as if the prospect of evacuation could be made more fun only by having two extra kids in the house for a couple of hours.

With three of her own, all older, she bundled and bustled children with the tactical wiles of a general, moving them from point to point before they could conceive of independent action. She had Carlie and Kevin out the door and strapped into car seats in moments. To seal the deal and keep them quiet, they each got a granola bar, the wrappers pre-torn.

"Now." She closed the doors and turned to Kit with a motherly eye. "What's going on? You said you're going to the embassy. Don't tell me your passports aren't in order."

"No, we're pretty much ready to go," Kit said, wondering how she could explain her errand to Tessa when she didn't know herself what she expected to accomplish. "Actually I'm going to the Indian Embassy."

"The Indian Embassy?"

Kit opted for a white lie. "It's for my housemaid. There might be some problems with her documents and I can't abandon her here without checking on them."

"But you and Jack aren't her sponsors. Isn't she part-time with you?"

"Well, yes, but a sort of complication has come up about that," she floundered, "and Mufeeda asked me to try to deal with it."

Tessa, an intelligent, experienced mother and therefore a living lie-detector, gave Kit a solemn nod. "Right." She opened the driver's side door. "You know what I'm discovering, Kittie? You've got a stubborn streak in you. You don't look stubborn but you are."

It was news to Kit too.

"Tess, did you know that the Kuwaitis take their passports from them? From their housemaids, their chauffeurs and gardeners and all."

Tessa eyed her grimly. "Very sensible if they'd bolt otherwise."

Hopping into her car, she glanced skyward through the branches of the palms. "Man oh man, London in the winter! That's what we get for using Saddam as a travel agent. I hope you packed your long johns."

ONE LOOK at Emmanuella dashed Kit's plans, however vague. The girl stumbled in, breathless and pale. Without preface or permission, Kit laid a palm on her forehead. The girl relaxed under her touch, closing her eyes. A slight fever—but the girl's hands were freezing. She tilted Emmanuella's face up to look into her eyes. Something was seriously amiss. Why hadn't Mufeeda seen it? There was no way Emmanuella could go to the Indian Embassy with Kit now. Something else would have to be done, though what exactly she couldn't imagine. Take her to a doctor? Send her back to Mufeeda? Kit wasn't good at thinking fast. Her old plans had been perfectly formless: go to the Indian Embassy; find out how to release Santana from her employers. Get lucky. Save the day.

"You're thinking of your children, ma'am," Emmanuella whispered. "I'm sorry. You think they will catch my illness."

"I doubt you're contagious, Emmanuella," Kit said, hoping it was true as she caught sight of some dry, red patches of skin on

Emmanuella's arms. "My friend took the children for a while. For a treat. But you *are* sick, that's for sure. You need to see a doctor."

Emmanuella's eyes widened but she didn't object to this suggestion, confirming to Kit that more than a menstrual cycle was to blame.

"In fact," Kit said, an idea taking murky shape in her mind. "Emmanuella." She guided the girl to a chair and made her sit. "Do you know that American doctor who comes to Mufeeda's— a friend of Saleh's? His name's Theo Girard."

"I see him sometimes, ma'am. He comes late and I'm upstairs."

Gently Kit took the girl's hand. "I'm going to take you to see him."

K IT HAD seen Al-Ghais and its graveled precincts many times from the freeway so she knew how to find the place. Once inside its doors, though, she lost all bearings. Wall-to-wall humanity lay beyond the threshold, conducting its business at a steady roar. The lobby was almost impassable, clogged with people standing, sitting, walking, talking, even arguing and gesticulating at the tops of their lungs. Wheelchairs, carts, and gurneys, burdened and empty, rolled slowly through the masses, pushed by small, dark-skinned men in what looked like blue pajamas. Emmanuella's icy hand slipped into Kit's. Kit squeezed it gently, wishing for reassurance herself.

Across the sea of the lobby Kit spotted what might be a line of cashiers or information booths—or a big concession stand. It looked most like the latter: flat-roofed and built of corrugated metal without the slightest gesture toward beauty. Pitching her voice to penetrate the clamor, she said "Over there," with much more certainty than she felt.

They plunged in, making their way slowly through the crowd to find a restive mob of forty or fifty people there before them, all juggling for positions closer to the booths. They were manned, she could see now, by a line of plump young women in *abayas*, each of whom sat at a counter facing a pane of thick glass. The glass was perforated by a tiny span of prison bars at counter level, and through this the patients hollered out their demands, hunching down in order to be heard.

Emmanuella shrank against Kit. Kit gave her hand another squeeze and saw, beneath a sign engraved in Arabic, a hand-lettered piece of cardboard at one of the windows: 'Patients Sign In' in English. So they were in the right place—but there were no lines, not a shred of order or priority to the crowd, only a mass of people striving with elbows angled out for a closer berth.

What remained of Kit's nerve deserted her and into the vacuum came low-level panic, flowing fast. Oh, to be in London instead of here, in a fine hotel where everything would be done for her instantly at her request: breakfast, lunch, dinner, room service. The feel of heavy silverware in her hand, linen napkins starched and folded, a polished bathroom with untouched soap, a smooth, controlled seclusion at a price she'd happily pay. Resentment of Mufeeda boiled up in her, and at this sickly girl beside her, at Santana for needing rescue; and especially at Jack, whom she couldn't trust with the knowledge of what she was doing today.

One of the women in the booths seemed to be motioning to her, ordering her with a circular roll of her hand to come closer and not to waste any time about it. Kit hesitated, glancing around at all the other likelier candidates for the woman's notice, including a couple of tottering old ladies. But no, she was looking directly at Kit, and when several people turned to glower at her too, Emmanuella said, "Ma'am, it is for you."

"But why would they let me ahead of everyone else?"

Emmanuella gave her a look of shy disbelief. "Because ma'am," and she touched the white skin of Kit's forearm.

The receptionist stood up ponderously and, fixing a dead gaze on Kit's face, motioned again with both hands as if to an idiot. The crowd parted before them. Flushing hot, Kit walked forward with Emmanuella at her side.

"Hello," she said, leaning into the bars, feeling that her voice fell unheard from her lips. "This is . . . I don't . . ."

The woman regarded Emmanuella with distaste. "She's the patient? She cannot go before. I thought you are the patient." She gave them both a dismissive wave.

"Before?" Kit said.

"She must wait."

"Ah." The people who had been displaced by Kit's paleness pressed in, jostling, from behind. "Oh. I see." Short on practice, she struggled to sound sure of herself. "But I'm the patient, you see. She's just here with me. I'm sick." Someone elbowed Kit painfully in the back, awakening in her something akin to anger. "And I need to see Dr. Theo Girard. He's an internist here. Can you please tell me how to find him?"

"You have a file?"

"No, I don't. This is my first time here."

The woman's apathy deepened. Kit forced herself to the edge of rudeness. "You could start a file for me, couldn't you?" Not adding 'please' nearly choked her.

The woman only shrugged. "The general doctor will attend you. Here is a slip. Go to Room Seven."

"Thank you." Kit turned away before this registered. Already a grizzled man in a dirty headdress had rowed his way forward, shoving Kit aside. She leaned in, not daring to look at him.

"Excuse me. The general doctor? I want to see Dr. Girard. He's a friend. He told me to come directly to him, that no other doctor would do. I already talked to him about my . . . illness, and he said just come."

The woman gave her a slow, arrogant stare up and down. "It's not his clinic day. Come tomorrow."

"I can't. The American Embassy is sending a bunch of us Americans to London. Because of Saddam. We go tonight."

Again she shrugged. "You will see a doctor in London!"

Kit felt low on air. "Dr. Girard said to come today. I know he's here." Was he? She had no idea. The boldness of her lying amazed her. "He's expecting me."

The woman's massive boredom gave way to a smirk. She wrote a brief note in Arabic on another slip of paper. This she shoved at Kit through the bars. She indicated a long wing of the hospital to her right.

"Thank you," Kit said as the crowd surged around them. She gave Emmanuella a wan smile. "Well, we made it this far."

"By the grace of God, ma'am," Emmanuella said, smiling too. A rare thing, a smile from this girl.

"Can you read Arabic, Emmanuella?"

The smile died. "No, ma'am."

"Oh, it doesn't matter. Neither can I. But I wonder what she wrote?" Kit traced the illegible scrawl with a finger, right to left, pretending to read. "Take these horrible ladies straight outside and make them go home."

Emmanuella plastered a hand over her mouth to force back another smile. "Oh, ma'am!"

They couldn't make up for lost time. The place might have been a military encampment. Guards, all men, stood languidly at every doorway—until they tried to pass. Coming awake as if certain of a malicious intent, the men stepped directly in their path, scowling at Kit. "*La*, madam!"

Kit produced the paper. It was read laboriously and with some amusement, but she and Emmanuella were allowed to pass.

"Dr. Theo Girard?" Kit asked the third guard, thinking they must be close.

The man cast a gloomy eye down yet another long hallway. But at its end, at least, there lay no other corridors and no other guard.

A little bird of a nurse let them into an anteroom after reading the note. Kit wondered if she imagined a pulse of surprise in her face, and the appraisal in the quick head-to-toe glance. What did that note say?

"You will seat, please. I will say to Dr. Theo that you're here."

She and Emmanuella sat alone in a dim room. It was fitted out for a small crowd, with chairs lining two walls, and a small desk crouched under the windows. Here, at least, it was quiet, and the place looked orderly, if unloved. Crooked venetian blinds blocked the light. On the sill high above the desk sat a withered houseplant Kit recognized as the dusty remains of a philodendron. It seemed a poor message to send to your patients: I can't even keep a plant alive. It wasn't necessarily Theo's plant, of course, but hadn't he noticed it needed water?

"Ma'am," Emmanuella said quietly into the silence. "They are going also. Santana's sir and ma'am."

"I know," Kit admitted. "Azhar was in the garden yesterday when you met Santana in the street." Knowing this news would horrify Emmanuella, she put a hand on her arm. "He told me about it very kindly, because he thought I could help. But I'm not sure I can, Emmanuella."

Emmanuella bowed her head as if she had failed somehow. "What she will do, ma'am?"

Kit saw in her mind's eye the gray metal shutters rolling down into place, imprisoning the girl. Santana's employers were abandoning her to a danger they wouldn't face themselves. The occupation had lasted seven months.

"Can she make a call out? If they're not guarding the phone any more?"

"They have only the little phone——"

"——a cell phone."

"Yes, ma'am. And they're having this always with them."

"Well, and who would she call? The police? They'll only come if she's dead!"

Too much: she was scaring them both, and Emmanuella was sick. She tamed her voice down a notch.

"Does she know what time they planned to leave?"

Emmanuella shook her head. "By God's grace they have not gone yet, ma'am."

But for Emmanuella's thievery, Kit would go directly to Mufeeda with this problem, where it surely belonged. She was tempted to do so anyway, but it would be at the risk of Emmanuella's job. Kit couldn't forecast how Mufeeda would view a servant's consistent pilfering. Kit's father would never have stood for it from an employee, regardless of the circumstances. *You need something, you ask.*

The only other possibility she could think of depended on Theo Girard. He could help Emmanuella and he could tell Kit how to find Hanaan. Kit knew no other Kuwaiti intimately enough to ask for help, a humbling proof of her isolation from the society she lived in. Hanaan would be a better source of information anyway, bold and irreverent as she was. Mufeeda lived almost as cloistered a life as Kit's. If there were anyone who could help Santana directly, Hanaan was likely to know who and how to reach them. The question was, could anything be done quickly enough?

The door burst open and Theo came through, startling Kit and Emmanuella both. The shock appeared mutual: his face fell as soon as he laid eyes on them. He stared blankly at them for a moment, then without a word turned and went out again, letting the door slam shut behind him.

Kit sat blinking. Had she just been insulted? She could hear people talking in the next room. One of them was Theo, she felt sure, and some other man with a reedy voice. Kit strained to decipher their words but nothing distinguishable came through.

"Ma'am," Emmanuella said with the mildest hint of surprise. "This doctor is your friend?"

The door swung open again, admitting the nurse, hands folded tidily at her waist. Nothing could be gathered from the sweet perfection of her smile. "I must take your letter again," she said to Kit. "The little paper."

Kit pulled the note from the pocket of her jacket and handed it over. The nurse studied it more carefully this time and, folding it, nodded again with the same gentleness. "One minute," she said, and left again.

"What in heaven does that note say?" Kit muttered.

"These people, ma'am," Emmanuella said, "they will say anything."

Perhaps, but just what could have justified such a reaction from Theo went beyond the imagination. Theo had looked far too happy when he opened the door—expectant, even joyful—and far too crushed when he closed it. They'd met once, for God's sake, and at a crowded dinner table. The mere sight of her had never produced such dramatic behavior in a man before, positive or negative.

Again the door opened and Theo reappeared, grimacing toward a smile.

"I'm afraid there's been a mistake." It was clear he had no recollection of Kit. "There was a little confusion about your note," he said to her. "My fault. I misunderstood the translation. I'm sorry, but you'll have to come back tomorrow. We only see inpatients today."

Kit saw that she'd reached a point in her life where politeness would no longer serve her. "Look," she said, forcing her volume past any threat of shakiness. "All I want in this crazy place is Hanaan's address or phone number. That's all I came for."

These words altered him yet again. "What?"

Kit glanced uneasily at Emmanuella. She had to make the personal connection with Theo first. Then she'd introduce Emmanuella.

"I need to contact Hanaan. I need to talk to her about a personal matter. Can you at least give me her phone number before you disappear again?"

With his eyes on her face, he reached with a long arm and drew a chair from the wall. He straddled it. "You're Saleh's neighbor." He snapped a finger, trying to recall her name.

"Kit Ferguson—"

"Kit!" he said, as though it had been on the tip of his tongue.

Kit gazed at him with a growing wonderment that she'd ever found him attractive. That philodendron was probably his after all. "I live across the street from Mufeeda and her husband."

"Saleh. Yes. He's on staff here, too. Go on."

"It's just what I said. I want Hanaan's phone number. And her address."

He capitulated, all the hope going out of him again, "All right. Okay," and pulled a prescription pad from his pocket. He scrawled a few lines and pushed the sheet at her blindly, as if he couldn't bear to look at it himself. "I'd just go straight there if I were you. She's not good about answering the phone. You'll get her machine. Her flat is just off the main street in old Salmiya. It's easy to find, as things go here."

"Thank you," Kit said. She steeled herself for what must come next. "And I want something else too. I want you to examine my friend Emmanuella. Now."

Surely the world would end as a result of this surly demand. Emmanuella seemed to think so too. She gazed up at Kit wonderingly, then shrank away as Theo shifted his meager attention to her.

"She's sick. She's been sick for quite a while."

Theo snuck a glance at his watch. Kit saw the wheedling half-smile he planned to offer up as part of his escape. No reason to tell him now that Emmanuella was Mufeeda's maid. Like Tessa he'd wonder why she was interfering. And unlike Tessa, he'd probably demand to know why.

"It can't wait," she said. "Not even for tomorrow. I have to leave the country late tonight because of this stupid idiot Saddam, and there's no one else who gives a damn about her."

At last, some respect. He nodded, as if to himself. "Of course. I'm sorry." He turned to Emmanuella. "To both of you, I'm sorry. I know it couldn't have been easy to get in here today. A ruse was probably your only hope. It was creative. And it worked."

"Ruse?" Kit felt uncertain of the exact meaning of the word but she liked this turn less than the last.

Theo gauged her, his puzzlement returning. "May I ask . . .? Who gave you that note?"

Kit's last restraints flew from her. "One of those stupid receptionists out in that madhouse of a lobby, that's who. I told her your name. I lied and said you'd told me to come. I said I knew you."

Theo pursed his lips against a smile. "I see. She wrote that my girlfriend was here to see me."

"Your girl—? Then—"

Theo attempted a lighthearted shrug. "I thought—"

He'd thought she was Hanaan. Something had obviously gone very wrong between them. Kit stared at her lap, remembering why she'd liked Theo from the first. His tenderness registered deeply on his face. He made no attempt at the muscular neutrality that blanked out most men's faces to the world. Like Jack's. She took the half-dead plant away from Theo again.

"She and I haven't been in very close touch," he said. "I'm sorry I was rude."

"No, no. That's . . . I'm really sorry."

"Me too."

In the next moment his eyes found Emmanuella's curled, cold hands and shifted to search her quiet mask of a face.

"Emmanuella," he said. "I'm Theo Girard. I'm very glad you came here today."

IN THE parking lot Kit phoned Tessa and told her the truth in telegraphic summary. Tessa, God bless her, didn't press for more.

"There's nothing else I can do here at the hospital," Kit said. "She's going to be in a ward with a bunch of other women. He needs to do tests."

"God—a ward—it sounds so Victorian," Tessa said. "Can anyone actually get better in a ward?"

298

Something Kit wondered too. Only Theo's insistence had prevented her from taking Emmanuella home again. He wouldn't make any definitive statements, only that she needed hospitalization and a series of exams.

"He says any number of things could cause her symptoms."

"Do doctors ever say anything else?"

"Look, Tess, I need some more time, maybe another hour. I've got one more stop. Are you okay with the kids?"

"Of course I'm okay with your kids. They're wonderful. In fact, I'm going to switch them with a couple of mine."

She tried Hanaan's number, but got her answering machine and hung up. No surprise according to Theo, and it fit well with her impression of Hanaan. No doubt she used her phone mostly to make demands of others, not to be summoned herself.

Salmiya was familiar to her from a couple of trips there with the Bargain Club women. She'd never come here alone, and the prospect of wandering around in the tumbledown neighborhoods adjacent to it worried her, a place where hers was the only Caucasian face. She didn't want to get lost in its maze of streets and have to ask directions. She didn't want to call Jack either. *I'm lost!* Bleating like a little lamb. He'd ask why in the world she was in Salmiya. No, she'd cope without calling on Jack. She was a grown woman. It was her own fault that she felt ill at ease here. For all her self-congratulations at coping better than she'd expected in this country and being less prejudiced than some of the other company people, she'd still held herself apart, surrounded herself with Americans, holed up inside her giant house where she could live in her own small world, pretending that all was well. She heard Jack's insistently cheerful voice. *Everything's fine, Kit!*

She oriented herself by driving down the main street. The shops lining both sides had none of the sleek, gaudy splendor of the new malls springing up all over the city thanks to companies like Jack's. They reminded her of Stillwater's stores when she was a kid: squat and ugly, cement-gray and adorned with only the practical necessities of the store's name and its hours of operation.

At the end of the block she turned left. Expecting a continuation of the street, she found herself in a parking lot filled with vehicles in the way a pickle jar is stuffed with whole pickles, a signature of Kuwait. She maneuvered her way out slowly, backing onto the deserted residential street.

Already her sense of direction faltered. She pulled to the curb and took Theo's prescription slip from her purse. Just off the main street, he had said; and on the slip he'd written what passed for an address in Kuwait: three consecutive numbers, one for the area, one for the street, one for the building. But area numbers didn't faithfully follow a consecutive design, and both street and building numbers were hard to locate if they existed at all.

A sharp rap on the window. A figure in black stood stooped at her passenger-side window. A grim face peered at Kit from inside the hood of an *abaya*. The woman jabbered something in Arabic and made as if to roll the window down. A beggar? A thief—or worse? Kit had heard that male criminals sometimes masqueraded as women, and this was not a womanly face. She put the car back in gear, preparing to floor the accelerator if need be.

But she hesitated—those were distinctly English sounds now, the familiar music of plain syllables with no gargling in between. And a smile, the woman was smiling. Clearly a woman. And offering help. Kit powered the window down.

"Hello! I think you may be lost," said the woman in an accent softened by a faint French lilt. "May I be of any assistance?"

She pointed out Hanaan's building exactly. Built of cement painted yellow, it stood just across a barren square, one block away, pale in the late winter sun.

"Thank you so much," Kit said. "You've saved me a lot of time. I might never have found it."

300

"Not at all, not at all. I will give you my number," she said, printing it on a piece of paper she pulled from a deep pocket along with a silvery cell phone. "You may call me at any time. Salmiya is a little difficult. If you are lost once again, you will call me. I am Kholoud. I walk for exercise, every day when it's cool. I know these streets as I know the face of my little son."

She strode away as if on a mission, giving Kit a wave, a pair of brilliant white athletic shoes shooting out from the hem of her billowing *abaya*.

HANAAN THREW the door open to Kit as if she were an old friend. "I know you. You're Kit. Come in, come in. How nice that you have come to see me."

Swept into the tiny flat, Kit found herself knee-deep in cats.

"We'll have tea," Hanaan said, and Kit knew it was no use begging off—it would only delay the ceremony. No force on earth kept Arabs from bringing forth their tea.

"Thank you," she said, squatting to lure the cats. Three came, tail-up, to test her sincerity, just as her cell phone rang.

She stood again, scattering the cats. It was Jack. She couldn't risk talking to him. Anxiously, she let it ring. "I don't answer my phone, either," she said in answer to Hanaan's questioning glance. At four rings the phone fell silent, and she turned the thing off.

Hanaan's pleasure at seeing her was surprising. She'd shown no special interest in Kit when they'd met, and Kit felt herself a paltry nominee as a friend to such an accomplished woman, a woman whom a man like Theo could love and continue to love in the face of what Kit now guessed had to be rejection. Otherwise, how could Hanaan seem so happy? She was almost aggressively happy, rattling on at warp speed about a busy early morning with her students, and how she had just let all her cats out into the living room when Kit came to the door.

"For you, I will not put them away again. Look," she said, opening her arms to frame the whole room, scattered with cats in all arrays of mischievousness and ease. "See how comfortable they are with you so quickly. It's your name. Kit. You're one of them."

"I grew up with cats."

"Did you? Like Romulus and Remus with the she-wolf. Or Tarzan. It's no wonder they like you."

Hanaan set a cracked English teapot on a tiny table stacked with texts, and spiral notebooks, and layers of paper. She delivered sugar, milk, and a plate of shortbread, and pulled Kit's chair out for her.

She sat opposite. "Now. We'll visit. You've come to me with something bothering your mind."

"How did you know that?" Kit had lifted the tiny spoon to stir her tea. She wondered if she imagined the purplish bruise under Hanaan's eye. A trick of the light.

"It's in your eyes, a little move to the side. It's a certain sign with cats. I see it in Solomon. He's been sick for some time and he's worse today. He looks at me but through me, just beyond my heart. He's thinking of something else."

"Solomon?"

"I'm sorry you won't see him. He's in my bedroom, sleeping. Even Theo likes him and Theo doesn't like my cats very much." Hanaan drank her tea black. "And you. You don't come for lessons. American ladies don't come for lessons. They won't learn Arabic."

"No, we're all a bunch of airheads, I have to say."

Hanaan exploded in laughter. "No! How can you say this of your own sisters? I know many intelligent American women."

"But not one of them speaks Arabic."

"Even this isn't true. Don't listen to me when I talk so. I know many American women married to Kuwaitis, and they've learned to speak the language beautifully."

"So divorce is my only hope?"

302

Hanaan gaped. "What a surprise you are! You didn't speak like this when I met you. I thought you were one of those squeaky American women who come here with nothing else to talk about but their husbands and children."

"I am," Kit said. "That's me exactly."

She had confounded Hanaan.

"I need your advice," Kit said. "Your help. That's why I came." She calculated her next words but said them lightly. "Theo told me how to find you."

Kit saw a cat's shift of focus in Hanaan's eyes. Her musical voice fell low. "You've seen Theo?"

Kit pulled his prescription slip from her purse and laid it on the table. She would leave it there. "He gave me directions. It was my idea. He said not to bother to call. You won't answer the phone."

"Ah."

For a moment, distracted, Hanaan said no more and Kit studied her incandescent face, a sadness weighing in her own heart. Aware suddenly of Kit's scrutiny, Hanaan struck out with fiery impatience.

"Why don't you speak? I can't sit here until night."

Kit glanced at her watch. The extra hour she'd asked of Tessa was gone; she hadn't answered Jack's call; and Mufeeda—Kit hadn't thought of this before—Mufeeda would have expected Emmanuella back long before now.

"I don't know who else to ask for help," Kit said. "There's a young Indian woman across the street from me, a housemaid, who's about to be locked into the villa where she works. Her sponsors are starving her, beating her, the woman burned her, the man's raping her. Now they're getting ready to leave the country because of Saddam. They're leaving her in the house, locked in, with the doors and windows bolted. The first-story windows are barred. She doesn't even have a phone."

A stillness had come over Hanaan. "How do you come to know this?"

303

"Through another housemaid, who works for me part-time. I've been helping where I can, sending food, but I need to find a way to get her out of there, her sponsors may leave tonight, and I thought you'd know what to do, who I should call, if there's a social service ministry or rescue society or something like that I can set in motion."

Hanaan was on her feet. "How can you sit drinking tea if this is so?" She peered out the window. "You've brought your car?"

Kit was drinking tea no longer. "Yes."

Cats fled as Hanaan swept toward the door. "Then we must go."

MOSTLY ALONE

Dr. CHOWDHURY prepared to go home for lunch as usual, where his full-time housekeeper would have a curry ready for him. He never touched the boxed lunch made available to all hospital employees and let no opportunity pass without bringing this to Theo's attention.

"This will ruin your constitution, this poor excuse for nour-ishment," he said, zipping his leather jacket up to his throat. He peered over Theo's shoulder as Theo unwrapped the meal's main offering, a pancaked sandwich of white bread with a dark and indefinable smear of filling.

"How can a physician allow such things to pass his lips? It calls your credibility into question, I really must say."

"It's not so bad," Theo said. "You'd eat it too if they'd only curry it."

Dr. Asrar bent smiling over a report at her desk.

Dr. Chowdhury's indignation flared up with happy energy. "Nonsense! That filling is pure fat, nothing else. It's to be avoided, and I'm the one to say so. My blood pressure went up recently, you know."

Theo did know. Everyone knew. Now that Theo's blood-pressure readings had become an accepted part of procedure, Dr. Chowdhury used every patient's minimally high result to recount a cautionary tale in which he was featured in an exem-plary role. Upon discovering that his own blood pressure was slightly elevated, he'd driven the reading back down within a month by eating like a monk and swimming obsessively twice a day. The staff had grown accustomed to his morning aura of self-satisfaction perfumed with chlorine.

Dr. Chowdhury raised a bony forefinger. "Excellent food in small quantities and two swims per day. This is the ticket." He took a couple of swaggering steps toward the door. "I was quite a well-known swimmer in my youth, you know." He turned to gauge Theo's response to this news.

"I didn't know that," Theo said.

"Yes, ask anyone who knew me in those days. They'll confirm for you that I was the only boy in Mumbai who didn't sink straight to the bottom of the pool."

Enjoying his joke, he made a final adjustment to his yellow muffler, tucking it elegantly inside the open collar of his jacket. "You must always live in the same fashion you recommend to your patients," he said to Theo. "I cannot tell my patients to eat less and exercise more to lower their blood pressure if I fail to do so myself. This is why I say to you that this sandwich undermines your credibility."

Theo wiped his hands on his napkin. "May I speak with you a moment?"

"Yes, of course," said Dr. Chowdhury, stepping into the hall. "You must accompany me, however. I don't wish to be late."

Dr. Chowdhury's normal pace was a near-sprint. "Yes? What is it you wish to say?"

Theo slipped his hands in his pockets, refusing to keep up. They'd be in the lobby in no time, and the old man wouldn't be able to hear him.

"I've been getting emails from Rajesh," he said as Dr. Chowdhury accelerated away from him.

"What?" The old man pivoted.

Theo strolled to his side. "He's worried about you, Dr. Chowdhury."

"Who? What *are* you speaking about?"

Theo didn't believe he hadn't been heard. "We exchange email. Not frequently, but often enough. More lately, given the situation."

"Ah yes, of course. This mysterious email." Dr. Chowdhury unzipped his jacket by several inches and stared up at the low ceiling of stained acoustic tiles.

"Tell me, what is the attraction of words that have no presence in the corporeal world? No envelope to slit open, no rich paper to unfold and hold under a lamp, nothing to tuck into a drawer for safekeeping?"

"He says that he can't get you to talk to him on the phone. He asked me to check up on you. He's worried about Saddam."

Dr. Chowdhury peered at him, full of sudden dismal speculation. "Do you get on with your father?—the man who brought you into this world and gave you food and shelter and an expensive education? Please tell me."

Rajesh hadn't thought Theo would get far with this inquiry. "My father died a few years ago."

The news struck Dr. Chowdhury a blow. "But how old a man was he?"

"Not quite seventy. He married late."

"And of what cause did he die?"

"Ventricular fibrillation. He was at his desk, working on his poetry."

Dr. Chowdhury's voice dropped to a whisper. "Dead, over his fine verses. It's terrible." But outrage stirred again. "Surely he had excellent medical care."

"He wouldn't go to doctors. I don't think he knew he was ill."

Theo hesitated to say more, but Dr. Chowdhury's stare compelled him.

"But no, we weren't very close. He was a quiet man. I've been reading his poetry lately, trying to—"

"Reading his poetry! Did you never go home to take care of him in his old age, then?"

"I—"

A sound of deep offense escaped Dr. Chowdhury.

"—I was in school in Los Angeles. No one knew about his heart."

307

This had no weight with Dr. Chowdhury. "What is the matter with you young men nowadays? To disrespect your fathers even as they reach the end of their lives. And you—not even properly married. We must take care of one another, you know."

Turning on his heel, he eyed Theo with scathing disapproval, "You may tell my son that I am of no concern to him. This much is obvious." He strode away.

DR. ASRAR seemed not to have moved when Theo stepped back into the clinic. She couldn't have avoided overhearing some of what had been said: the door stood open to the hall.

Theo slumped into his chair. The thin bread of his sandwich had begun to curl at the edges. Did Dr. Chowdhury really expect Rajesh and his wife to give up their positions in the U.S. to come to Kuwait? Even absent the threat of war this seemed absurdly demanding. And 'properly married'? What in the hell did that mean?

Asrar was tidying her desk with unusual energy as she prepared to leave for lunch. How much she and Wafa and Dr. Chowdhury knew about his private affairs he couldn't guess, but he'd given them something of a spectacle with his behavior in the morning, he knew. Grabbing Kit's note from Wafa's hand, challenging her translation, scolding her for 'misleading' him, apologizing awkwardly. He considered asking Asrar to decode 'properly married,' but it wouldn't be decorous; she embarrassed too easily.

Glancing up, she caught his pensive stare and looked quickly away.

"How's your daughter, Asrar?" he said into the silence. "You haven't mentioned her lately."

"Better, I think." A grateful smile. "She's wheezing not so much now. I'll tell her you asked for her, Doctor."

Left alone, Theo shoved the remains of his lunch to the side, wishing the events of the whole morning could go with them. By late afternoon, some of the lab results for the young Indian woman would come in. They could lead the diagnosis in any of a half-dozen directions and would indicate what other tests he should order. In the meantime, Emmanuella could rest, which was what she needed first and foremost. He suspected that some of her symptoms, the nausea, the cardiac arrhythmia, the breathlessness, were stress-induced. It had taken only a couple of questions along the normal line of queries to any patient to bring forth the story of the maid she and Kit Ferguson were trying to rescue. Kit's 'personal matter' with Hanaan was this raped and stranded housemaid, then. He could guess well enough what Hanaan would say to Kit: *Why have you waited so long?*

He smiled, rueful at the thought of Hanaan in high gear. What energy she had, and how few doubts or inhibitions to action. What in this society had given birth to her? Asrar too was well-educated and traveled, yet despite becoming a doctor she'd never assumed the authority she had earned. She always deferred to Dr. Chowdhury; she refused to speak ill of her coward of a husband; and, influenced by a Quranic warning that the sound of a woman's voice inspired the illicit desires of men, she spoke rarely and never laughed aloud. Hanaan had told him about this preposterous prohibition: *These women will not say a word!*

He hadn't stopped imagining where Hanaan might be at any given moment, or what she was doing. The hardest thing to bear was that it wasn't automatic anymore to know where she was: at her apartment or her parents' house or the university. He could guess, but his heart still wanted to know for sure.

He pulled a yellow legal pad from his desk, meaning to piece together a draft of a letter to Julia. She'd written at some length again, asking him to flee the country. *Please don't take a chance with Saddam Hussein.* He hadn't told her yet about Samir or the break with Hanaan. Again, it had felt like a superstition holding him back: If he told his sister, it was all real—and final. She was still

309

reacting cautiously to the news of his love for Hanaan. *I wonder if this can ever be a peaceful relationship. Can you live in Kuwait together? I'm guessing that might be difficult. Would she come here?* She'd seen much cause for second thoughts. *Please take this as I mean it, Theo— lovingly. Could you respect a religious woman in the long run? Even as a kid you were skeptical of religion.*

Hanaan's comments about their differences had run through his mind endlessly these last weeks. She'd never mentioned religion as one of them. It was his separation from his family that had troubled her. *You keep them thousands of miles away!* In his memory her words now sounded like an accusation, and they struck him with particular pain. Her family was bound together by culture and tradition—and desperate fear. His family's fate too had been sealed by culture and tradition, and by an independent habit of mind that required emotional self-sufficiency at an early age. The atmosphere of Hanaan's family life struck him as threatening and claustrophobic, but the atmosphere of his own seemed hardly less malignant, a solitary indifference in his parents that had forced him and Julia to grow up as well as they could, mostly alone.

Someone Else's Doorstep

Jack Ferguson's deep voice sounded again in Mufeeda's ear. She hadn't liked Kit's husband much when she met him, and she liked this fatuous recorded version less, demanding that she leave a message. She wouldn't do it. For the second time she put the phone down. Where was Kit? And why hadn't she sent Emmanuella home on time? Things were bad enough for the girl without this.

A door banged. Mufeeda kept her face carefully blank as Succoreen came parading by, drawing a vacuum cleaner like a queenly train behind her. Afraid of losing her temper, Mufeeda said nothing. It was clear to her that Succoreen had betrayed Emmanuella to Umm Saleh; but until she could find out why Emmanuella was late, she'd hold her tongue.

Only last night she had felt clear about the course she must take today. Emmanuella would be told that insubordination could not be tolerated; she'd be required to apologize to Umm Saleh and explain the hoard beneath her bed. If her explanation proved sufficient, she'd return to her duties. Last night, all this had seemed easy. *Outside of Frederick, Umm Saleh, I will handle all questioning of the household staff, which is my responsibility.* Saleh, looking both pleased and aghast, had said not a word. What had his silence cost him when his mother began to roar? It might cost him more yet: Mufeeda intended to speak with Frederick after all, for it was certain Umm Saleh wouldn't. *Where did you get such information about him?—from this insolent Emmanuella?* Frederick was a smart one, able to gauge Umm Saleh's vanities exactly, responding with a fine-tuned servility, faultless attire, a little flourish as he opened the car door.

She went to the hall window to look out into the street. Still gone. Kit normally parked her blue car at the curb in front of her gate. If she'd left Emmanuella alone in the house with the children for some reason, surely she'd have instructed Emmanuella to answer the phone. But would Emmanuella do so? Timid and retiring, she was likely to shy away from a ringing phone. Her duties had never included the telephone in Mufeeda's house, and it was certain her family in India had never owned one.

The simplest thing to do was to go to Kit's herself and ring the bell, yet she hesitated. If Umm Saleh found out that she had gone rushing around the neighborhood looking for a servant, particularly this one, she'd be up in arms. *You dare to protect this untrustworthy girl!* But Mufeeda could hardly ask a servant to go. What could she give as the purpose of the errand? *Determine if Emmanuella is there and tell her to come home.* Never. How the gossip would fly. *Ma'am doesn't even know where Emmanuella is!* Mufeeda might as well go straight to Saleh and his mother in abject surrender. *Despite all my bold words last night, I've lost control of the household.*

She made her way downstairs. Had she ever simply walked out the front door and strolled to a neighbor's for an impromptu visit? She detoured to the kitchen, thinking of her store of chocolates in the pantry, a supply she kept on hand for last-minute gifts. She slid a gaudy box from the shelf. Perhaps Kit's birthday was coming up.

But in the hallway she slowed and sat in one of the stiff-backed armchairs posed against the wall, her own absurdity revealed to her. How uncomfortable the chair was in its opulence: her feet barely touched the floor. She might have been a child confined there by a disapproving parent. *And stay put until you have thought the better of your sins.*

A marble-topped table stood at her side. She laid the box of candy on it. A sinful child indeed. Here she sat, plotting an escape from her own house, worrying about what the servants and her mother-in-law might think of her only hours after she'd declared herself mistress of every situation. She didn't run the household; it ran her, and the staff and Umm Saleh would be right to say so. She regarded the box of chocolates in its wrapping of engraved gold foil. How transparent, how ridiculous a lie it would be to take candy to Kit.

At the edge of her vision she caught movement in the living room, a small flash at face-level. Whose face she couldn't tell. Of course they were spying on her. All of them. She looked toward the dining room and made a guess. "Rosaline," she said, matter-of-factly.

The house was so still that she could hear the monotonous chirping of the bulbuls in the palms. Rosaline crept forward in fear-struck surprise from the dining room.

"Yes, madam."

Mufeeda wouldn't look at her. "I'm going to the Americans' house. Emmanuella has not returned."

Rosaline flew to open the heavy double doors to the street. At the threshold, Mufeeda turned to her and said in a voice pitched to carry down the echoing hall to Succoreen, who would also be within earshot. "While I'm gone, Rosaline, you are in charge. I want no difficulty. Say to the others, 'Go about your work.'"

Mufeeda walked directly to the metal gate of Kit's house and pushed the buzzer. Above the enclosure wall she could see the second floor of the villa, where she knew Kit and her family spent most of their time. Blank. No childish faces peeped at her from just over the sills, and no Emmanuella came to the door.

Turning to the empty street, unsure what to do next, she gazed at the dull stone exteriors of her neighbors' houses. She knew few of these people well. Each enormous building, like her own, was a universe unto itself, with its own prisoners and set of laws, its own intricate hierarchy and culture, even its own unique subtleties of language. How carefully chosen her own language had always been, presenting to the world a surface no more revealing than the marble fronts of these featureless villas—except in those most intimate moments of her life. With Saleh. Her breath caught at the thought of his touch.

A car engine in the near distance. She rang Kit's bell again busily, endeavoring to appear properly occupied. How odd she'd look, the matron of a distinguished family, forlorn on someone else's doorstep like one of the abandoned cats of the city. The car came around the corner and shot down the street. Kit's car—with Kit at the wheel, a hand over her mouth and her eyes on Mufeeda. Someone else sat beside her. A woman, though not Emmanuella, and she could see no children in the car. Kit was talking and gesturing at Mufeeda as if in desperation even before she pulled to the curb. My God, what had happened?

Kit burst through the driver's side door. "Mufeeda, I'm so sorry! I should have called you a couple of hours ago."

"What's happened?" Mufeeda ran down the steps to the sidewalk. "Is it the children? Where are your children?"

"No, no, I'm so sorry. Time got away—no, the children are fine, really—it's Emmanuella, I took her to see Dr. Girard—your friend Theo."

Mufeeda had gripped Kit's hands with both of her own. "Theo?" Only then did the other woman's presence register again. She blinked at Hanaan, unable to place her.

"You know Hanaan . . ." Kit said, dissolving into confusion herself.

"Welcome," Mufeeda blurted in Arabic. "How are you?" What was she doing here?

Hanaan's dark eyes regarded Mufeeda with deep suspicion. "I'm fine, but I don't think you can care much about whether people are well or not. You've left it to this American woman to see to the health of your employee. She's in the hospital now, this girl. And there's another here that may follow."

Offended, bewildered, Mufeeda looked to Kit for an explanation. But Kit spoke no Arabic. Mufeeda said evenly to Hanaan. "Surely we should speak English so Kit can join us."

314

"Very well," Hanaan said. "We'll speak English. But the words sound no happier in English."

"What words?" Kit said. "We can't have words." She appealed to Hanaan. "Please, wait a minute."

"We have no minutes to wait!"

Kit turned to Mufeeda. "Emmanuella's sick. We don't know yet what's wrong. Dr. Girard said she had to be in the hospital."

Mufeeda laid a hand on her heart. "I knew she was ill!"

"You knew!" Hanaan said. "And your husband is a doctor. Yet it's this woman who takes your employee to the hospital."

"She couldn't have known," Kit said. "I found out by accident. Emmanuella hid everything from everyone. That's why we're standing here arguing with each other." She tried to calm herself. "Mufeeda, there's something else Emmanuella didn't tell you. She was taking food to a housemaid one of your neighbors is . . . mistreating."

Hanaan gave a wild cry of exasperation. "Mistreating? You mean raping. Beating and starving and raping. Now they lock her in and leave her to be taken care of by Kit. This is what you've ignored," she said to Mufeeda. "And to think we're worried about *Saddam*."

"For God's sake, Hanaan," Kit said. "We have to figure out what to do."

But Hanaan was beyond any figuring. "This is the correct villa?"

"Yes," Kit said. "The woman's car is gone, but that's the husband's car, so——"

Hanaan was already half-way across the street.

"Kit," said Mufeeda, "what's she doing?"

"I think," said Kit, "I think she's going to storm the house."

All Mufeeda's energy dissipated. She wanted only to rush to the sanctuary of her own villa and hide deep inside her quiet room. She wanted no part of this violence, no role in this confrontation. She was made for softer things, for peace, safety,

315

invisibility. For ignorance. She had not sought out this hateful knowledge.

But Kit had moved forward, her eyes on Hanaan, and was waggling a hand at Mufeeda. "Come on, comrade."

Hanaan was banging through the unlocked gate. She pressed the buzzer hard as she passed. Advancing up the stairs to the front door, she pounded furiously on the wood with the heel of her hand.

Mufeeda dragged behind Kit. She had no purpose here. She needed time to think, to digest, to consider and weigh. Things were moving too fast.

"I feel like a soldier marching into the trenches," she heard Kit say.

Fierce and jubilant, Hanaan gave a laugh from the top step. She banged on the door again. "You look scared to your deaths. Like prisoners going to their execution." As they reached the top, she slipped her arms around them, drawing them close.

"This isn't difficult. It's choosing to do nothing that is difficult."

The door swung open, revealing a young Kuwaiti man not far from his teens. Lean and sharp-faced, he had dressed so carefully in jeans and a crisp white tee-shirt that they looked alien on him, imposed.

He took a step back. *"Na'am?"*

Mufeeda had seen him before a few times, briefly, and a young woman too, as they came and went. It occurred to her now that she'd never seen older people here, no one who looked like a parent, and little activity at all but for a lone housemaid washing the cars.

Hanaan spoke in Arabic. "Allow me to speak with your father."

The boy answered with cold offense. "This is my house."

"Then I'll speak with you," she said, standing calmly before him. "Here is our business. We've come to purchase the visa of your housemaid and remove her from your villa. Today. Her name is Santana. The return of the visa is non-negotiable, but we will negotiate the price as long as it's reasonable. You must return her passport intact. In order to decide what you think is reasonable, you should know that your neighbors have been sending food to her so that she won't starve. They know you've beaten her, raped her, and locked her in the house, kept her from associating with her normal society, from going to church, and even from receiving mail from her family. This we know. Decide on your price."

With each phrase Mufeeda expected the boy to slam the door in their faces. But he stood rapt with a sneering astonishment that only gradually gave way to disgust. "How dare you come to my door."

Hanaan spoke with an unnerving calm. "How dare you rape and imprison this woman."

Mufeeda caught something else in the boy's eyes now. Not shock, nor fear, but a cunning glint. Could it be mercenary? She glanced at the weed-choked enclosure, which she'd noted only peripherally before, and the peeling paint of the villa. The hall behind the boy looked barren; and he had opened his own front door, a duty left to staff members in most villas. Yet he wore an expensive watch on his slender wrist, and his sports car—parked only yards away—was a low and gleaming panther of a thing.

Hanaan argued steadily with the boy, her voice gradually rising up in anger. He all but yawned. She pressed forward. "You'll release this woman at once!"

Mufeeda cringed at the resounding volume. How audacious this woman was, and what melodrama all this seemed, three women charging a fortress to save a damsel in distress: Hanaan the wrathful *djin* with her two puny sidekicks. Pounding on the door, raging and howling. Ready to do—what? They had trespassed on this boy's property, interfered in his personal business, ordered him to follow their instructions. On what authority? Mufeeda could already feel the searing heat of the coming gossip. *Have you heard what Mufeeda did?* A genuine scandal. Mockery.

317

Malicious, venomous delight. *Told him to turn over his maid!* She was invading the most private of realms, as far off-limits as Saleh's innermost thoughts, in league with this vulgar, noisy, shameless woman. How absurd Hanaan was. Who did she think would pay the money this boy would extort? And what could they do with the girl besides take her to her embassy?

The boy gave the door a lazy push, smiling with contempt. Hanaan stepped across the threshold to knock it back in his face. "No! You can't do this!"

It seemed then that the boy tripped. He lurched forward with a guttural cough, his body loose as a rag doll's. Mufeeda saw blood on the back of his head. Scrabbling too late for a hold, he clutched at Hanaan, scoring a shoulder, and rapped his forehead hard on the door as they went down on their knees together.

"Go in! In!" Hanaan yelled to Mufeeda and Kit. The boy sprawled, moaning, half-conscious, his hand at the base of his skull. It came away bloody.

Confusion roiled in Mufeeda's mind. Had Hanaan attacked him, kneed him, knifed him? Was he having a seizure? Her body felt heavy, a lead weight dragged agonizingly uphill, but somehow she was moving forward.

"Shut up," she heard Hanaan say to the boy, "You'll live, unfortunately," and glimpsed her leaning over his prostrate form, not to nurse him but to bend his limp arm behind his back. She meant to keep him there.

"Go!" she raged to Mufeeda and Kit, and Mufeeda stepped over the threshold into the villa, over the boy as if he were a pile of refuse. Kit came too, a hand at Mufeeda's back.

In the faint light of the empty hallway the housemaid stood before them weeping, a cricket bat cocked in her hands. She had hit the boy from behind as he stood guarding the threshold, and stood ready to take another desperate swing.

Mufeeda took in Santana's bruised and sunken face, the red and freshly scabbed wrists, the sack of a dress that hung from her narrow shoulders. The girl was quaking with fear. Or was it hunger? Would she be alive at all if Emmanuella hadn't stolen food for her? Emmanuella had taken enormous risks to get that food. She hadn't trusted Mufeeda, who had always been kind to her. Hadn't she? A wrack of pain and horror hit Mufeeda, and she realized she was crying. No booming reproach from God's own throat could have struck her with more force. Emmanuella had been right.

She held out a hand, beckoning gently to the girl. "Come," she said. "Please come to me now."

Empty Rooms

Kɪᴛ ʀᴀɴ on adrenaline now. The answering machine was her first chore. She fast-forwarded her way through a dozen record-ings, impatient with the overwrought messages from aunts and cousins and even her father, all imploring her to leave the country. She listened fully only to Jack's voice, riveted by the progression of his panic as he'd failed to reach her through the day. He didn't say so, but she knew what he'd been thinking: that she and the children were dead on a ring road somewhere or lay mortally wounded in one of the grimy public hospitals. He'd left five mes-sages, each more agitated than the last, ending with a plea that verged on tears. "Kit, where are you?"

His desolation hit her like a blow to the diaphragm, and tears came, a sudden release of the dreadful anxiety she had borne all day. He did love her. His anguish revealed it as nothing else had ever done.

She grabbed the telephone. He answered on the first ring.

"Kit?"

"I'm okay, Jack, the kids are okay—"

"Where are you? Where the hell are you?"

Desperate longing. She soaked it in, eyes closed.

"I'm home. We're all okay. I love you. Can you come home?"

She wanted to make love to him, here and now, before Tessa brought the children back, to give up all the resentment and anger she'd weighed against him for months—for years.

"What?" Suspicion hit him. "Why didn't you answer the phone?

"Emmanuella showed up sick—"

"Who?"

"The maid. Mufeeda's maid." Though he'd welcomed the news that Kit finally had a maid, he'd never met her. "She showed up sick—"

"I thought you were dead! You didn't answer the phone!"

Her lie came as easily as any comfortable truth. "My cell phone wouldn't work at the hospital. She was so sick, Jack. I had no choice."

"It took all day?" A blast of silence while his anger ballooned. "You couldn't walk out to the parking lot?"

"I know. I'm sorry. I didn't realize how much time went by."

"You dragged the kids all over one of those damn hospitals with a sick maid?"

"No." She saw the trap but couldn't avoid it. "Tessa took them. She came and picked them up."

"But you didn't call *me?* Good God, Kit. There could be a war tomorrow and you took a maid to the hospital? What's wrong with you? She's not our responsibility!"

The flight was to leave at midnight like most of the flights to Europe from this barren place. The brutal hour ensured early morning connections in London and Paris and Frankfurt for those traveling on across the Atlantic.

She managed to shove some dinner down the kids, but her own consisted of the scrapings from the saucepan: two table-spoons of gloppy mac and cheese. She couldn't take time for more. Jack didn't come home for dinner at all. She was supposed to have everything packed and ready by nine o'clock, when he'd pick them up to go straight to the airport.

At some moments she felt as if she were floating. A woozy sense of slow motion took over as she watched herself from across the room, this new Kit who managed things so coolly—disciplining the children while keeping them calm, filling four suitcases with neatly folded clothing. The old Kit stood in a corner like a ghost, with the sound of Jack's blistering vituperation in her ears.

What's wrong with you?

She had sundered all the trust between them. But how much had there ever been?

She admitted poor judgment. *Yes, Jack.* She should have told him long ago of her involvement with the maids, and she would have—if only he were . . . someone else.

She rinsed the few dishes in the sink and hustled the kids downstairs, turning off lights as she went. Opening the door to the chill desert air of evening, she glanced back, already recognizing the dark and empty rooms as part of the past.

STRAYS

THE TESTS so far had proved troubling but inconclusive. At the nurses' station Theo looked through Emmanuella's chart again, his thoughts tending toward an immune system disorder, one of fairly long duration that the girl had attempted to overcome in the only way someone of her status could, through prayer and self-denial; but he couldn't yet rule out an insidious infection somewhere, and both things could be at work. Her breathlessness had quickly abated and the medication had curtailed the nausea. But the odd heart sounds had not disappeared; her hands and feet showed inflammation, and she continued to ache all over as if she had the flu. She'd slept almost straight through since last night without sedation. This was easy to understand, at least: exhaustion, both mental and physical. From the moment of Mufeeda's telephone call, letting her know that Santana was safe and staying in Emmanuella's own room at Mufeeda's house, she'd relaxed—after some tears—and fallen asleep.

A Filipina nurse descended on him, plucking at his sleeve. "Dr. Theo, excuse me, sir. Umm Mahmoud's husband comes. You must speak with him, please, sir. He says he will not wait."

A man watched him stonily from the threshold of the ward. Theo gave the nurse a nod, "Okay," and refiled Emmanuella's chart. He didn't pull Umm Mahmoud's, knowing its contents well. Though she'd been hospitalized with dangerously advanced Type II diabetes for more than a week and was under the care of an endocrinologist, she invariably asked for Theo, who'd seen her initially and made the diagnosis, years overdue.

323

The husband, a well-fed man in late middle age, dressed in an elegant black winter *dishdasha*, didn't introduce himself or offer to shake hands with Theo. This was the first Theo had seen of him or any male visitor. Umm Mahmoud's female relatives had come in great number. Laughing at the doctors' orders that she could eat no sweets, they gathered around her pyramidal form in their tent-like *abayas*, drawing forth from the ample folds of black cloth an endless store of candy, cookies, dates, and cakes.

"What's her condition?" A crisp London accent.

The man listened as Theo briefed him on the diagnosis, his face stern in its emptiness. "Then she won't survive."

"No, she'll recover, of course, but . . ."

In the long corridor behind the man, Theo saw Mufeeda emerge from the stairwell and glance around, getting her bearings. He gave her a brief wave, prompting the man to glance over his shoulder. How beautiful she looked, Theo thought, as she came toward them. It was a shock to see her here, in this public place with its stained walls and dismal underwater greens, like spotting a brilliant flower in a waste land. He'd never seen her outside her own house before, he realized.

The man's eyes were on him, dim with disapproval.

"But she has to make some changes," Theo continued. "Significant changes." Mufeeda waited at a discreet distance, reading the yellowing notices on a forgotten bulletin board. "This disease can be controlled, but she has to follow her doctor's instructions. She has to lose weight and change her diet. And her family must refrain from giving her sweets."

"Her family must refrain!" The man spurted a bitter laugh and continued with a growl in Arabic, "They refrain only from refraining."

Theo switched into Arabic as well. "Your wife needs your help. She needs to make many changes in her life."

The man controlled his surprise. His English grew more taut. "She needs many things. There is no end to women's needs."

"I'm speaking of what her health requires," Theo said. "Please excuse me." He turned toward Mufeeda.

She smiled, complicit, having overheard, and Theo bent his head toward Emmanuella's ward. "She's this way."

"Theo," Mufeeda said when they had passed a distance down the hall. "You're speaking Arabic with this man!"

"Not much. He wasn't about to let me mangle your language."

She laid a hand on her heart. "But you sound so charming. Why have you never spoken Arabic with me?"

"Charming!" Theo laughed. "That means I have a really thick accent."

"It's a lovely accent, a very sweet accent. Now—say more to me in Arabic."

"Uh-uh."

"Where is your courage?" She said it the French way. Coor-aj.

"Mufeeda, I know how to say hello and goodbye, how to ask for directions, order food, and how to say a bunch of stock hospital things. I'm fair at disease and poor in polite society. You're polite society."

"Ah, you don't know. I'm not polite at all," she said. At his doubting smile, she grew stern with him. "One can't always be polite, Theo."

They crossed into the ward and Mufeeda halted at the sight of Emmanuella asleep, the covers tucked at her chin. Again her hand went to her heart. "How small she looks." She glanced at Theo, fearful. "Can she live?"

"Yes, of course she'll live."

"—*inshallah*," she said decisively. "Did Hanaan not teach you this word?"

"*Inshallah*. Yes. She did."

Mufeeda stepped closer to Emmanuella's bedside and Theo told her of what he knew and what he suspected. "The heart's a concern. I'm working with a cardiologist. I'm going to consult with Dr. Chowdhury about her too. She's Indian. He may have a hunch."

"Theo, the wife of that man back there, she has diabetes?"

He was impressed. "How did you know?"

"Oh, I know about candies and too much food," she said. "My mother died of this disease, a horrible disease, and my mother-in-law has it too. Many of us here, the rich ones, we suffer this disease. It's a disease of having too much, and here is this girl, all these girls living with us in our same house, with the disease of too little."

She wouldn't consent to waking Emmanuella. "She must sleep. I'll come again, *inshallah*."

"I'm ashamed that Kit must bring her to you," she said as he walked with her down the staircase. "This is my job." She sighed, and Theo saw the light leave her face. "I have not done my job well."

"I don't believe it," he said. He thought of Kit's visit to Hanaan. "Do you know if Kit will come by?"

"She's gone for London. Last night. If there's war, I don't think she'll come to us again. I will miss her."

Another round of intense negotiations with Saddam had begun, headed by the U.N.'s top official.

"Maybe they'll come up with some sort of pretend solution this time," Theo said. "A band-aid."

"You'll not leave us?"

"Nope. I'm staying put."

She hesitated, mid-step. "I almost forgot. Kit said I should tell you something."

He nodded, only mildly interested, guessing it was a thank you for his help with Emmanuella.

"She said, 'Tell him that Solomon is very sick.'"

"Solomon?"

"Yes, Solomon is very sick."

"Hanaan told her that?"

This perplexed Mufeeda. "I don't know. Is this her father's name?"

"Was there anything else?"

"No, nothing."

They'd reached the clinic corridor. Mufeeda regarded Theo with an intermittent but generous eye. He shook off his inwardness only with difficulty.

"So where to now?" he asked her.

"Now you must direct me to Saleh. He'll give me my lunch, he says."

"I hope he doesn't mean lunch here. It comes in a box."

"No. He takes me to the French restaurant on the Gulf Road." She glanced up at him. "Unless a baby comes. Then I must go home."

She was silent for a moment. "I want to ask a favor, Theo."

"Of course. Anything. Name it."

"When Emmanuella wakens—if she's well enough to hear you—tell her that I have bought Santana's passport and visa from this stupid boy. She is with us in our home. Saleh is caring for her. He says she will recover well. He has also gone to this boy in his villa. He has a big headache and some bruises, this is all. I would like to give him more." She looked at Theo now, directly. "Also, I have taken a decision. When Santana is quite well, I will ask her to stay with me. I need another housemaid."

"Mufeeda, that's wonderful."

She raised a hand to silence him. "Another thing more. It's as Hanaan has done. I also send Emmanuella a message she only will understand." She tucked her head again. "Tell her that she makes no trip to India until she earns her holiday. But Frederick goes today."

"I'd rather not give her any bad news at this point."

"But it's good news. She'll understand me."

At his desk again, Theo stared at the telephone. Had Hanaan asked Kit to tell him about the cat? If so, he would call Hanaan this minute. But Kit was gone. He couldn't know. He toyed with

327

the questions he might pose to her if she were here. Just how exactly had Hanaan communicated this information? Did she say something unambiguous like, *Tell Theo Solomon's sick?* Or something more explosive: *That idiot Theo told me Solomon would be fine!* Or—also a possibility—she may have mentioned the cat to Kit with no thought of Theo at all. Whatever the truth, a sentimental and idealistic woman like Kit, a woman roused to rescue a house-maid like a stray cat from the street—two housemaids—might find another mission in a lovesick man, and try to make amends.

He checked his watch—Dr. Chowdhury and the staff wouldn't return for a while yet. He had nothing to lose. He picked up the phone.

Hanaan's machine answered. Despite the perfunctory recording, the music of her voice moved him with its resonant beauty. A devout student of the Quran would agree with her father that she shouldn't speak to him at all.

"Hello, Hanaan. I heard through Kit that Solomon's really sick."

How many sentences might flow from that beginning. His love: unwelcome. Sorrow: punitive. Self-pity: despicable.

"I want him to get better. I hope it's soon. He's as fine a fellow as they come."

THE AFTERNOON clinic dissolved into chaos with the first patient, a burly girl in her late teens who arrived with her parents, one on either arm. All were dressed in modest Western style and neither mother nor daughter wore a scarf. Egyptians, Theo surmised, glimpsing them as he headed toward his own post in the ancillary clinic. In their dark business clothes the parents looked like middle-class professionals, professors or engineers. Their English would be excellent. They advanced three abreast toward Dr. Chowdhury, who sat imperiously at his desk ignoring them in stony silence.

Glancing at Wafa, Theo caught a flicker of wariness in her eyes, confirming his own sense that Dr. Chowdhury's mood was more volatile than usual today, which didn't bode well for his victims. But it was too late for Wafa to divert this trio to Theo's room: Dr. Chowdhury had locked the family in his gaze. With a kingly twist of the wrist he summoned them into his presence.

"Yes, yes. Be seated."

Seeing that Theo was glancing around the clinic, Wafa motioned to a sheaf of papers on the counter, well within his reach. She always knew what everyone needed, often without a word. Theo scooped up the papers, a set of case notes he'd made for consultation with Dr. Chowdhury, among them Emmanuella's.

"Yes, and so what is the matter with you?" Dr. Chowdhury said, flinty with impatience.

The mother answered, setting off alarm bells in Theo's head.

"My daughter is very ill. She sees doctor after doctor, and yet she's no better." The tone was declarative, aggressive. Bodily ills plagued the daughter, the mother said: soreness in every limb, palpitations of the heart, sweats, headaches, nausea—"

Dr. Chowdhury let a long silence accumulate. "And she's mute as well?"

"Oh, no, thanks be to God!"

"No?" Dr. Chowdhury turned a stinging gaze on the girl. "What is your age?"

"Seventeen," the girl whispered, terrified, as her mother put an arm around the wide slope of her shoulders.

"Speak up!"

Her rosy hue drained away. "Seventeen."

"You're crippled?"

"No."

"Do not look to your mother for help. Why are you not at school?"

The mother answered anyway, testily. "She's very ill, Doctor."

"How are you very ill? What's the matter with you that diet and exercise will not remedy?"

The father spoke up, mincing and conciliatory. "My daughter suffers fatigue and spells of dizziness, Doctor. She must remain home often—"

Dr. Chowdhury rounded on the man. "Of course she's fatigued! Of course she's dizzy! You don't allow her even to walk on her own power, and so she has no power. She doesn't stay home because she's ill. She thinks she's ill because you keep her at home. Is there fever? Rashes? Swelling? Vomiting? Congestion?"

"No," said the father, "but she—"

"No. Do her symptoms occur in the morning before she's to be at school, often upon rising? And yet she seems well on the weekends?"

Evasion flooded the father's face.

"She sleeps peacefully on the weekends, does she not?" Dr. Chowdhury said. "She's not ill."

He hadn't touched the patient.

"I see instantly that by your design she has become a hypochondriac. She has no disease. You've been to other doctors at the private clinics and they've told you this already." He whirled in his chair, scanning the room like a raptor for Theo.

"Take them away from me," he said. "It's every inch somatization, but they will never believe it. You may arrange the appropriate lab work to assuage them, but she is not ill. Make this clear to them. I refuse to offer treatment when there is not one sign of disease."

In the late afternoon Emmanuella's condition worsened. A nurse on the floor phoned Theo in the clinic as Wafa closed it down for the day. She'd found Emmanuella distressed and sitting up in bed, unable to breathe normally.

"What did she say, Sister," Theo asked the nurse. "That it hurts to breathe or it's difficult to breathe?"

"It's difficult."

Concerned, he ordered another chest x-ray and asked Wafa to divert his one remaining patient to Dr. Chowdhury. She looked troubled by the prospect.

"It's only a follow-up," Theo said. "It'll take him thirty seconds. Do you know what's up with him today?" His own guess was that yet another contact with Rajesh had gone awry. "He was okay before lunch."

"It's this curry every, every day," Wafa said. "One day, in the brain there's a big fire."

Theo laughed. "I'm wondering about that famous blood pressure of his. You think he'd let me check it?"

"I don't know," Wafa said with a dry little smile. "Maybe you will check every one of us."

He found Emmanuella sitting upright in bed, her breathing labored. Checking her pulse he found it rapid. Her blood pressure was slightly elevated too. When he suggested she lie down she panicked.

"No, sir! I can't get breath at all."

"You can't breathe lying down?"

"No!"

"Is it better when you sit up?"

"A little."

"How about when you lie on your side? Or is it the same as when you lie on your back?"

"The same, sir."

The symptoms suggested congestive heart failure, but at eighteen that seemed unlikely; and her chest x-ray and electrocardiogram had offered no firm evidence of it. A virus could act that rapidly. He drew his stethoscope from his pocket, warming it in the palm of his hand.

"I'll need to take another look at you."

A Filipina nurse appeared at the bedside. "Excuse me, Dr. Theo. A phone call for you."

"Get some more pillows," he told her. "We need an echo-cardiogram."

"Yes, sir. The telephone, sir."

"Yes, Sister, I heard you. Emmanuella, she'll prop you up so you can be more comfortable. Try to relax a little. We're going to figure out what's going on."

When he picked up the phone amid the din in the hall he expected the usual: a call from another physician or a summons to the office of an administrator.

"Theo?"

"Hanaan!"

"Theo, I'm sorry to call you at your work. I know you're busy, but I must speak with you. Solomon is very sick. It's the lungs. I must take him to the vet. Can you drive me?"

He nearly smiled. How rapidly, given the merest encourage-ment, his mind was capable of casting events far into some other, happier future—and she wanted him as a chauffeur for her cat.

"I'm desperate, Theo. His lungs are congested, he can't rest."

Theo's irritation reared up. "Ask your brother. Where's your brother?"

"He's not here. He's gone from the country."

He didn't believe her. "Why would he go out of the country when he's your father's own personal hit man?"

"To become something worse. He's in Afghanistan. Where else do such fools go?"

"Afghanistan?"

There was a pause as she digested his ignorance. Pleading for his help, she could still decide to insult him. "You're so naïve, Theo. They're training men there, to be Muslim soldiers. Warriors."

"I'm with patients now, Hanaan. Sick *people*. Emmanuella's one of them."

"I know this. But please help me, Theo. Whenever you can come, we'll be here."

He spied Dr. Chowdhury striding furiously down the corridor, a chart in hand. "It'd be seven or even later before I could get there. The vet would be closed."

"No, there are hours from half-five until late."

"All right," Theo said. Dr. Chowdhury came to a halt before him, hands planted on his bony hips, heedless of any concept of privacy. "I'll come when I can."

"Thank you, Theo. You're a good man."

Hanging up, Theo faced Dr. Chowdhury's unblinking scrutiny. Though the top of his shining head peaked at something under five-foot-six he gave the impression of looking down on Theo from a towering height.

"It's lupus," he said.

"Lupus? The girl with the parents?"

Dr. Chowdhury scowled. "What girl doesn't have parents? This young Indian girl, of course. Wafa told me of this case, so I came to you immediately. You'll conclude it's viral myocarditis, but this is completely wrong. Diuretics will not do. Nor ACE inhibitors, nor digitalis. She must be given intravenous methyl prednisolone immediately. There will be significant improvement within twenty-four hours."

And what treatment was there for runaway hubris? "Would you care to set eyes on the patient?"

Dr. Chowdhury shook a bony finger under Theo's nose. "You're arrogant with me. No wonder you're a friend of my son—you have much in common with him. But I will tell you: you cannot have seen the many guises of this disease before. It can be, I grant you, an extraordinarily difficult disease to diagnose. Nevertheless it's quite clear to me."

Dr. Chowdhury strode away. When Theo didn't follow, he stopped abruptly. "You'll show me this patient!"

Theo stayed where he was. "Lupus doesn't present with myocarditis. If it's there, it's almost always silent."

Dr. Chowdhury came marching back, and for a moment Theo thought himself in danger of being slapped across the face.

"You're rash," Dr. Chowdhury told him, eyeball to eyeball. "You may never say this about lupus. Lupus may present as anything it pleases. It's a disease of many faces."

"And you've seen them all."

"I have seen this—"

"—You haven't seen 'this.' You haven't seen the patient or heard about the developments this afternoon."

Complacency welled from the man. "I've scanned her chart. I've seen this presentation once before and know of a handful of other such cases. Her sed rate is very high—"

"—non-specific to lupus."

"She has chronic inflammation in hands and feet, recurrent fever, digestive difficulties, fatigue, *livedo reticularis*, all common to lupus. The chest film revealed slight pulmonary venous hypertension and mild pleural effusion on the left. The ECG showed sinus tachycardia, some diffuse ST-T changes—"

"Non-specific—"

"The echocardiogram which you have ordered is likely to show hypokinesia and pericardial effusion. She may soon be in danger of fibrillation. You will call in Rheumatology and you will order further tests, which will prove my diagnosis. I've written the orders." He flopped Emmanuella's chart into Theo's hands.

It all made sense. Theo spoke with more restraint. "She may well have a heart condition, but it isn't necessarily caused by lupus."

Dr. Chowdhury fell silent for a moment, gazing with sudden interest into Theo's eyes. "No, of course not. You're absolutely correct. But this is what we shall discover. In the meantime we must go forth with our best guess. She's eighteen years old. A group of symptoms appearing in close proximity in a patient of such tender years is likely to emanate from a single cause."

Theo nodded. It was an elegant précis.

Dr. Chowdhury waited for more debate. When it didn't come he smiled, genuinely, and with some surprise.

"Well, I'm happy to see that you fail to persist with your disdain."

A tiny twitch had started up in Theo's left eyelid. He pressed a fingertip to it.

"You have something in your eye. Please let me assist you."

"No, a twitch. It'll pass."

"Ah," Dr. Chowdhury said. His mood had shifted once again, this time to unbearable benevolence. "We have a saying in India, you know. If a man has a twitch in his right eye, it means something very good will soon happen to him. But this is your left eye. So I must warn you: you will have a bad day today."

"Thank you, Dr. Chowdhury."

Dr. Chowdhury turned to resume his walk down the hall, peaceably now, his hands clasped behind his back.

"Now come, Doctor," he said. It was the first time he'd ever addressed Theo as such without mockery. "Let us go together and take a look at this poor girl."

As THEO crossed the landing outside Hanaan's apartment, his ear caught the warm vibrancy of her voice on the other side of the door. She was on the phone, speaking Arabic.

He hesitated, knowing he shouldn't: the old goat across the vestibule would see him lurking there and fire off a second round of hysterical rebuke. Worse, she might be a spy for Hanaan's father, ready to report any sightings of Theo.

"Not now," he heard Hanaan say. The words jumped from a mass of others he couldn't comprehend. "I don't know. He's very sick."

He stepped closer to the door. She'd turned, or walked down the hall, and he could no longer make out anything but her tone. Soft, caressing. He gave her doorbell a long ring so he wouldn't overhear more. Of the final lines he caught only the last two words as she came to answer the door: *"Ma'salaama, habibi,"* and the clunk of the phone.

Habibi. My love, my dear one. The male form of the word. An endearment used with close friends, family, spouses, children.

335

Her father, possibly—or her brother. How thoughtful of Samir to check in from boot camp.

The door opened an inch. At shin-level he saw a pink nose and one glaring eye, a spray of whiskers. "Back, you cats!" Hanaan said, rattling the doorknob. "It's your old friend, Theodore. Pasha, away!"

The door closed again soundly. Hanaan spoke through the metal. "Theo, I'll put them away. They're all crowding the door. They want to see you first, and that's my right."

He waited, impatient, hearing footsteps, her contralto voice in melodious persuasion, yowls and mutterings of sour complaint. Then she let him in. Her smile was all he saw.

"Theo. *Ahlan.* Welcome." She offered her hand and he took it, breathing her in as secretly as he could, reluctant to let go.

"Come sit. I'll give you tea."

"No," he said, knowing that she couldn't want to take time for tea, however ironclad the tradition. His voice sounded hoarse to him, as if creaky with disuse. "We should go. The sooner the better. Let me help you with Solomon."

"No-no. I'll be one minute." She turned down the hall, her dark hair gleaming across her shoulders. "He'll stay calm if I'm alone to put him inside his box. If you come, he'll suspect me."

He sat waiting at the tiny table near the windows. It had been only weeks since the night she told him, touching her temple with the tip of a finger, "You're here," and then the swell of her breast near her heart, "and here."

But love did not conquer all, not in her family. Fear held that power. Even rebellious Hanaan had bowed to it—as had he, by necessity. Yet she had called him—as soon as Samir was offstage, it seemed. Had she wanted to see him so badly that she'd used Solomon as an excuse? Or was Solomon her true and only motivation? His devout wish for the former unnerved him. It endangered them both.

The room darkened as he gazed out the window. A rainstorm had finally formed in the river valleys of the north, and swept south from Iraq late in the day, purpling the horizon.

Stolen of its light, the room closed in on him, and he saw the hard cement walls, and the tile floor beneath the tired carpet. The little table where he'd taken so many lessons lay deep in books and papers, the debris of a recent meal, the usual basket of dates. A slip of notepaper protruding from under the base of the basket caught his eye—covered with his own handwriting. He pulled it loose. The prescription sheet he'd grabbed as notepaper when Kit came to see him. On it, directions to Hanaan's flat.

Why not leave Kuwait together? Would she even consider going? A constellation of outcomes sparked in his mind, from black tragedies to Hollywood bliss. He steadied himself on the darker thoughts, doses of reality, the bloodied face of the dead maid in Casualty. The bottom line: Hanaan's father had prohibited everything, and Hanaan said that her family came first. End of story.

And yet, here he stood.

She brought Solomon out in a crate. Moving to take it from her, Theo heard the cat's labored breathing. No doubt now about Hanaan's motivation. This was pneumonia. She saw him note it.

"They'll give him antibiotics," she said. Her black eyes searched his.

"It's viral, Hanaan—"

"—and an antihistamine will help, so he can breathe, and vitamins. They'll give him an infusion—"

"Right, to hydrate him, but—"

"We must go."

Of the two veterinary clinics in the city, Hanaan said the one in the industrial area on the western edge was the superior. It was a low, gray cinderblock hut stuck behind the stinking pens of the main sheep market of the city. Theo didn't want to make a guess as to what the other one looked like.

"We will have a long wait," Hanaan sighed, looking at the crush of parked cars.

Inside was bedlam. Two large, leashed dogs snarled at one another like prizefighters in the middle of the small waiting room, surrounded by people and pets. Arabs, Indians, pale-faced Westerners sat side by side with their scrawny kittens and wormy pups. One Arab man had brought a pair of native bulbuls so frantic in their tiny cage that they could only have been wild-caught. A young Arab boy sat with a bedraggled and miserable cockatoo hunched on his shoulder. A matchstick South Asian boy sat quietly with something gray-green and heavy sunk in his lap. Theo studied the rounded, inert shape. A turtle.

In light of Emmanuella's case this was an especially humbling sight, the idea of caring for so many animals when his own skills seemed too paltry for even one disease in a single species. What common ground could there be between a cockatoo and a turtle?

Their entrance had brought about a stillness and the unblinking stares of curiosity and suspicion, the reason they'd avoided appearing much in public together in the past. Hanaan fixed her attention on a young Pakistani man shuffling toward them down the hall.

"What number is next?" she demanded.

He was dressed in a baggy gray uniform and cap. He ignored her, thrusting into Theo's palm a crumpled slip of paper printed by hand with the number ten. "The doctor is not here," he said. "Wait."

The few chairs were taken; they took a place against a wall. Theo held Solomon's crate in his arms, knowing that Hanaan would not want the cat on the floor with the dogs, which had begun to spar and bark, teeth flashing. Hanaan withdrew, stepping closer to Theo as the barks rang like bullets in the drum of cement. She scolded the owners. "Control your dogs! There are sick animals here."

One, an American contract worker by looks, sallow, crewcut and paunchy, squared his jaw at this rebuke and hauled on the leash, but only until the dog gagged. The other, a young native dressed in the usual linen gown, played deaf, giving his Rottweiler the full length of the leash as he talked in undertones to a friend at his side.

"Idiots," Hanaan said with perfect clarity, and Theo caught an acid look aimed directly at him from a putty-faced blonde he took to be the American's wife. Hanaan turned to croon softly to the cat, her head so near Theo's chin that he could feel her warmth.

A falcon screamed in the back, arresting the dogs for a moment, as a group dressed in silks and heavy linens walked in: a man with another falcon on his fist, followed by two women in embroidered *abayas*; and a second man carrying a rock hen by the neck, gripped as though it were a bottle of pop. All ignored the doorman's offer of a numbered slip, and swept through the lobby en masse into one of the examining rooms at the back.

Hanaan's face hardened. "Rich *Beduin*," she whispered.

Theo gave her a broad wink of false confidence. "Oh, they'll kick them out. It's only fair."

This brought a smile. "Fair. Yes, when cows grow wings." Her eyes flickered from his eyes to his lips and back again. "Isn't that what you say in America?"

"Always."

More interlopers expanded the wait to ninety minutes. Eventually, Theo and Hanaan inherited chairs and sat gratefully, Theo with the crate on his lap. Even in the constant clamor of the little room he could hear the cat's every breath.

"Ten!"

The vet was a kind and portly Filipino with dark rings of exhaustion under his eyes. He gave Theo a quick and piercing once-over, his anxious look sliding then to Hanaan, whom he obviously knew well from other visits. She faced him with challenging solemnity.

"You have brought a cat, Ma'am Hanaan."

"Yes, Dr. Boyet."

The examination room didn't look bad to Theo after the waiting room. The vet had at least washed his hands between patients, careful to avoid the grimy surface of the tiny basin. Several posters and signs had been taped haphazardly to the peeling paint of the cement walls: advertisements for sheep feed, an illustration of pigeon breeds, and a diagram sketched quickly by hand in Magic Marker of what looked like a dog with horns and long toenails. It was inscribed in Arabic and English: 'The 7 Faults of an Unproductive Goat.'

Dr. Boyet handled Solomon with respectful caution and listened to his lungs with his stethoscope. It was hardly necessary: a lobe of blood and pus exuded from the cat's nose.

"It's pneumonia, ma'am," he said softly. He wiped Solomon's face delicately with a paper towel. "Ma'am, you must let me put him down."

Hanaan's expression didn't change. "If you cannot cure him, Dr. Boyet, I can. Give me medications."

"The antibiotics are finish, ma'am." The vet sighed with weariness. "Next week, *inshallah*, they will come."

"Do not say to me 'they will come.' You don't believe it. And antibiotics won't help him. You know this. You will give me something for his breathing and I'll do the rest."

"Hanaan—" said Theo.

"No!"

With a glance of resignation at Theo, the vet gave the cat a shot, then scraped together for Hanaan a scanty offering from a nearly barren cabinet. None of it would help, but it was all he had.

"You are very strong, Ma'am Hanaan."

"This is why my cat will live," she told him.

A STIFF rain-scented wind swept the dust in sheets outside, and yet no rain came. Theo drove across town to Hanaan's flat through the cold, sandblasted gloom, the silence between them filled by the roar of the heater. Solomon had to be kept warm.

Theo braked at a corner to let a bareheaded Egyptian laborer cross the street to a bus stop opposite. The man stepped off the curb cautiously, surprised at even this minor accommodation from a motorist, and staggered forward, his long *gellibiya* beating against his legs like a flag of desperate surrender. He had no protection against the oncoming weather. His unmatched plastic sandals, one pink, one green, glowed in the halogen beam of Theo's headlights.

Like another stray cat, Theo thought, left to fend for himself on the streets, wretched, fearful, desperate, dying.

Hanaan's eyes too were on the Egyptian. "I know what you think of my cats, Theo," she said softly. "You think of people who need help, here and all over the world, and you think I waste my time. But you help me anyway. This is kind."

He didn't feel kind. He bit back a swarm of words, self-pitying to the last, as the Egyptian raised a hand in thanks for this twenty-foot passage across the barren asphalt. Theo pressed the accelerator and lifted his hand in return.

"Solomon's dying, Hanaan. Even if you had all the medications you need, it'd take incredible luck to pull him through. Is it kind to prolong his suffering?"

"He loves me," she said, "and so he trusts me. If he didn't he would have died already. I can't turn my heart from him, Theo, whatever others think. If he's willing to struggle, then I'll struggle too."

At the door to her flat, she took Solomon's crate from Theo's arms and dropped her head against his gaze.

"Hanaan—"

"Go," she told him, closing her eyes. "Oh, please go now, Theo."

HE DROVE, paying little attention to where, making his way between big sedans careering along, between overburdened trucks swaying from lane to lane and sports cars blurring by. It was true that Hanaan's deep involvement with her strays had sometimes struck him as trivial, even self-indulgent. Perhaps it was. Or perhaps it had been his jealousy speaking when he felt less important to her than her cats—and you couldn't get more self-indulgent than that.

Sometimes, when he'd tried to imagine Hanaan meeting his mother, meeting Julia, or living with him in the glowing loveliness of California, her face became hazy and the vision failed, making him feel it as a confirmation of Julia's worries: this partnership couldn't work. But now, remembering Hanaan's profile in the darkness of the car set against the scouring night, he felt that she was inscribed in his mind whole and he would never forget a line.

Dr. Chowdhury's words came back to him. He began to make sense of them now. *And you—not even properly married. We must take care of one another, you know.*

He remembered telling his mother of his decision to come to Kuwait. Typically, she'd reacted with impatience. *You won't change the world, you know, Theo, taking off like this.*

No, the world hadn't changed, except for his own.

He turned toward the hospital as it began to rain, bringing mud down from the dust-thick sky and smearing the glass. He jogged toward the Casualty entrance from across the graveled lot, the gritty rain in his face. Seeing him, the guard threw open the doors with the flip of a switch.

"Good evening, Dr. Theo."

"Thanks, Rajiv."

Rajiv eyed the muddy splotches on Theo's pale shirt with grave misgivings. "Oh, sir, look: the rain has brought the earth to you."

How his father would have liked that phrase, Theo thought.

He stopped on the floor first and spoke with the head nurse as he reviewed Emmanuella's chart. Vital signs, stabilized: she hadn't grown worse. Echocardiogram: it showed diffuse hypokinesia of the left ventricle with an ejection fraction of thirty-five percent and mild pericardial effusion. But for the percentage, exactly what Dr. Chowdhury had predicted.

In the ward he found Emmanuella smiling, surrounded by three visitors: two of Mufeeda's other housemaids, Carmen and Rosaline, whom he knew by sight, and a tall and ugly young man of striking dignity, whom he didn't.

"You look better, Emmanuella," Theo said. "Your friends are good medicine."

Carmen introduced the boy as John. He stepped forward like a soldier to offer his hand. "Good evening, sir."

"We brought him, sir!" Carmen said. "We said to him, 'Stand in the corridor,' and we came to Emmanuella very quietly and said, 'We bring a gift for you in the corridor,' and she is thinking, What can it be? What can it be?"

John's earnest eyes shifted to Theo. "The doctor will like to see Emmanuella."

"No, please. Stay. I'll be back in the morning. I can see she's in good hands tonight."

IN THE clinic, Theo raided the supply closet, coming up short; but Saleh might well have what he lacked. He headed out, crossing the deserted lobby and found Saleh fresh from the delivery room, stripping off his gloves. To Theo's request he said, "What do you mean, decongestants for a three-kilo child? What secret life is this, my brother?"

But he gave Theo the drugs: "You owe me," eyeing him with the mixture of fond regard and kind restraint that Theo loved in him.

"I'll give you a call," Theo said at the door, dropping the drugs into the sack with the glucose solution. It would have to do.

"Not tonight," Saleh said, "unless you're giving birth. Mufeeda waits. I'm going home."

THE RAIN swept across the city, casting in a custard haze the chain of lights on the freeway. Beneath the *sidr* tree, Theo switched off the ignition and sat looking up at Hanaan's window, the yellow light of her living room glowing in the rain, illuminating her useless balcony, a ten-inch ledge with bars. Abdullah had retired for the night; the pale, stuttering light of a television filled his ground floor window, and Theo heard a laugh track sandwiched with American voices as he passed the door, heedless of the rain.

Quiet at Hanaan's threshold. He rang the bell. Her voice came through the scarred metal: *"Na'am?"*

"It's me. I brought more drugs."

Again she swept the cats into another room. The bolt scraped, the door opened. Her ardent look flashed through him. "Theo."

"This should get him through, if anything can."

She took the sack, taking his hand as well, tightly, as if fighting against a sudden slope. He could feel her heartbeat, too fast, in the ends of his fingers, at her wrist. His eyes wandered to her forehead, to the soft dark brow and down her cheeks to the line of her neck as it swept below her collar.

"I'll go now, don't worry."

Her voice rose faintly from her lips. "Thank you, Theo. And she released him.

But she didn't close the door and he didn't leave. Across the gulf of the threshold they looked at one another in silence, until she reached out and took him in.